SOUTH

A NEAR-FUTURE THRILLER

BY LANCE CHARNES

WOMBAT GROUP MEDIA — ORANGE, CALIFORNIA

Wombat Group Media
Post Office Box 4908
Orange, CA 92863
https://www.wombatgroup.com/

First Printing November 2013
Second Printing October 2016
Third Printing November 2017
Fourth Printing December 2019
Fifth Printing December 2020
Sixth Printing September 2021
Seventh Printing October 2022

ISBN 978-0-9886903-3-2

For Betty

who put up with this again

Glossary

ACU	Army Combat Uniform, the successor to "fatigues"
AFV	Armored Fighting Vehicle
autodrive	Generic term for the autonomous-navigation mode in late-model cars
babu	(*Hindi*) official, authority
black site	Covert facility, usually for holding captives
bruja	(*Spanish*) witch
BRV-O	Humvee replacement for American military and law enforcement forces
burner	Cheap, disposable phone, untraceable to its user
cabrón	(*Sp*) bastard
capo	Chief of a cartel
cariña	(*Sp*) darling
CBP	U.S. Customs and Border Protection
chaat	(*Hindi*) Appetizers or snacks; Indian *tapas*
chhaavi	(*Hindi*) girlfriend
chica	(*Sp*) babe, chick (*derog.*)
chipku	(*Hindi*) irritating person
choli	Midriff-baring, tightly-fitted Indian blouse shell; sleeveless to long-sleeved
churidar	Type of Indian trousers; loose to the knees, tight through calves, worn long
claro	(*Sp*) Of course, certainly
CI	Confidential informant

compa	(*Sp*) contraction of *compadre*; comrade
compartment	Collection of related intelligence classified above Top Secret
dataspecs	Eyeglasses fitted with data displays fed by earpiece-mounted phone pods
EAD	Executive Assistant Director; high-level manager within the FBI or ICE
El Norte	(*Sp*) United States
el otro lado	(*Sp*) the other side [of the border]
ERO	Enforcement and Removal Operations, a branch of ICE
Feeb	Derogatory name for an FBI agent
feng	(*Chinese*) crazy
FLETC	Federal Law Enforcement Training Center, Glynco, GA
gabacho	(*Sp*) white guy, Anglo
HemaSafe	2032 synthetic blood substitute used in first aid
hermano	(*Sp*) brother
hijo de perra	(*Sp*) son of a bitch
hijo/hija	(*Sp*) son/daughter
HSI	Homeland Security Investigations, a branch of ICE
ICE	U.S. Immigration and Customs Enforcement
jamaica	Mexican hibiscus tea, served iced
Krinkov	AKS-74U, cut-down variant of AK-74 with folding stock; used by Russian special forces
kronk	Synthetic opioid; derivative of Vicodin
maha	(*Hindi*) Great, excellent

mango lassi	Yogurt-based, mango-flavored smoothie popular in India
maquiladora	(*Sp*) Factory set up near the US/Mexico border to take advantage of low wages and easy shipping
México Unido	2032 political front for Zeta *narcocartel*
mierda	(*Sp*) shit
mijo/mija	(*Sp*) endearment for son/daughter
mojado	(*Sp*) wet; (*applied to a person*) wetback
la mordida	(*Sp*) "little bite"; bribe
MRE	Meal, Ready-to-Eat; US military field rations
NANU	North American Nurses Union; Canada-based successor to the banned American Nurses Assn.
narcomanta	(*Sp*) Banner used by *narcocartels* to mark turf or threaten enemies
NVG	Night-vision glasses or goggles
oye	(*Sp*) hey
patrón	(*Sp*) boss, master
pendejo	(*Sp*) prick
qin	(*Chinese*) dear; used in place of "girlfriend" in greeting ("Hey, qin!")
rubio/rubia	(*Sp*) blond man/woman
Ryantown	Homeless encampment, usually located on abandoned parkland
SAC	Special Agent in Charge; chief of an FBI or ICE field office
Sharpoo	Shar-pei/poodle mix; 2030s trendy celebrity pet

sicario	(*Sp*) gunman
telenovela	(*Sp*) short-run Latin American televised soap opera, often known for convoluted plots
tonto	(*Sp*) fool, idiot, dumbass
vidboard	Billboard-sized video screen; used to show full-motion-video ads in public
vidframe	Picture frame that shows video graphics instead of photos
yaar	(*Hindi*) dude, bro, "mon"
zakat	(*Arabic*) donations to charity; one of five "pillars of Islam"
zip	Fifth-generation synthetic evolution of methamphetamine

For bonus chapters from ***South***, a downloadable glossary and character list, and an interview with the author, check out https://www.wombatgroup.com/south/south-bonus-material/

Cast

Luis (Lucho) Ojeda (aka Juan): *auto shop manager/*coyote *for the Pacifico Norte cartel*
- Mirabel (Bel) Ojeda: *ER nurse; his wife*
- Ignacio (Nacho) Ojeda: *deployed U.S. Marine; their son*
- Christiana (Christa) Ojeda: *their deceased daughter*
- Alvaro Ojeda: *Luis' father*
- Graciela Ojeda: *Luis' mother*

Ramiro (Ray) Esquivel: *Southern California "area manager" for the Pacifico Norte cartel*
- Salma Morales: *schoolteacher/makeup artist; Ray's long-term girlfriend*

Octavio (Tavo) Villalobos (aka *La Almádena*): *Southwestern "regional manager" for Pacifico Norte; Ray's boss*
Nestor Villalobos (aka *El Tiburón*): *Tavo's brother and Pacifico Norte capo*

Nura (Nora) Khaled: *FBI agent; Luis' client*
- Boulus (Paul) Khaled: *chief counsel for the Arab-American Institute; her husband*
- Butrus (Peter) Khaled: *their son*
- Raja (Hope) Khaled: *their daughter*

Jack McGinley: *Special Agent, U.S. Immigration and Customs Enforcement, Homeland Security Investigations*
- Carla Jean McGinley: *his kidnapped wife*
- Joella Murchison: *Carla's kidnapped friend*

Carl Jorgensen: *FBI Special Agent; McGinley's FBI counterpart in JTF-30*
Calvin Gennaro: *ICE Special Agent, El Paso field office, Enforcement & Removal Operations*

Friday Tranh: *ICE Special Agent, Phoenix field office, Homeland Security Investigations*

For bonus chapters from ***South***, a downloadable glossary and character list, and an interview with the author, check out https://www.wombatgroup.com/south/south-bonus-material/

SOUTH

1

Luis Ojeda scanned his binoculars along the rusty sixteen-foot fence to the dirt road's visible ends. Nothing. A dead floodlight at the curve over the arroyo left a patch of twilight in the line of artificial day. The lights on either side leached all color from the night.

The patrol was late. He'd been out here face-down in the dirt for over an hour, waiting for the right time. These desert mountains turned cold after sunset, even this late in a nasty-hot May. He was prepared for it. Army field jackets and winter-weight ACU trousers like he wore now got him through January in the 'Stan all those years ago. He could wait all night. Usually, the travelers couldn't.

He glanced downslope over his shoulder. Five brown faces stared back at him, their eyes glowing orange in the floodlights' glare. This run's travelers. Each wore a backpack holding everything they could bring with them from their old life to their new one.

The young mother lay at the group's left edge. Her dark anime eyes stared at him from under a road-weary hoodie. Her little girl—four, maybe five tops—pressed her face into her mom's shoulder, the woman's hand winding through her tangled black hair. Luis usually tried not to bring kids this young, but they had nobody else anymore. When Luis looked into the girl's eyes, he saw his daughter at that age: scared, sad, and trusting. So here they were.

Back to the binoculars. Dust shimmered in the floods to the west, then a whip antenna, then a tan cinder block on wheels crawled up the rise. The BRV-O's six-cylinder diesel clattered off the rocks around them. It swung around the dogleg over the arroyo, chunked along at around fifteen, then trundled east.

It stopped.

Two men heaved out. Tan utilities, helmets with no covers, desert boots: contractors. *Mierda.* They strolled back the way they'd come, M4s slung across their chests, hands resting on the grips. One lit a cigarette. They stopped at the edge of the pool of dark to look up the pole.

The one not smoking leaned into the radio handset on his shoulder. Then he turned to look straight at Luis.

Luis became a rock. The guard was probably half-blind from the light; Luis doubted the guy could see him in the semi-dark, even if he knew someone was out here. Chances were the *gringo* was going to take a leak. Then the guard's hand went for the tactical goggles hanging around his neck.

¡Chingado!

As the guard seated the goggles over his face, Luis went flat. As long as he didn't move, his infrared-suppressing long johns and balaclava would defeat the goggles' thermal vision and make him fade into the petrified sand dune under him.

The travelers didn't have that gear. Luis peered back into the dark. All five travelers should be shielded by the ridge, but "should" didn't mean shit if the guard caught the bright-green return of a warm human body on his scope. If he did, they'd all find out at 2900 feet per second.

The area around them hushed, letting the little sounds fade forward. The breeze rattled the creosote and pushed pebbles around. Luis could hear the contractors' voices—an off note in the wind—the shush of rubber boot soles on gravel, his heart going crazy, his sweat plopping on the sand.

Fucking contractors. Border Patrol agents had a code; they were civilized, they had to be nice and usually were. These contractor assholes shot people for fun, the way he had in the 'Stan before Bel reformed his sorry, angry ass. A month ago, these *idiotas* were probably losing hearts and minds in the Sudan with every full magazine. Now they were doing the same thing here.

A whimper. Luis cranked his head back to check the kid. She squirmed, a little dark bundle rocking against a dark background. The mom forced her daughter's face tighter against her shoulder. Her big, terrified eyes found Luis.

Chill, he told himself. *Be the rock.* The travelers could smell fear. If he was calm, they'd be calm; if he stressed, they'd scatter like sheep. He tried to smile back at the mom, hard as it was to do with crosshairs on them all.

Boots scuffed gravel at his ten o'clock, then at nine. Voices mumbled a few yards off. Somewhere out there, the sound of a huge mosquito buzzed the border. Had they called in a drone? If they had, game over. Dirt lodged in Luis' nose and mouth; ants crawled on his right hand; something sharp dug into his hip. Twenty-plus years after Afghanistan and here he was in the same shit, just with different players. *Be the rock.*

A laugh. Then the night exploded.

The first bursts were recon-by-fire, looking for what came bouncing out of the dark. Disciplined soldiers know to hunker down and wait it out, but the travelers weren't soldiers and they weren't disciplined. Two of the men broke and ran the instant bullets sprayed off the ridge top. Luis yelled "Get down!" but it was too late. He jerked his face back into the sand at the next burst, but not before he saw a runner throw up his hands and fall face-first.

The little girl started screaming. Her mother's eyes went all white and she tried to stuff her sleeve into the kid's mouth, but the girl wouldn't stop shrieking. Bullets churned the dirt in front of them.

¡Mierda! ¡Chingado! "Don't do it!" Luis hissed to her. "Stay there!" His voice sounded like he'd huffed helium. He didn't care if he drew fire as long as that pretty young mom with that sweet little girl kept her head down—

The woman bolted.

He screamed "No!" and before he could think, he was charging toward her. More shots. Dirt kicked up around his feet. A line of bullets tore across the woman's back, each one marked by a splat of blood. She let out a little "Ah!" and went down hard.

A burning-hot something slammed into his back, knocked him ass-over-heels down the slope. *Hijo de perra*, it hurt. He spit out the sand he'd eaten and rolled onto his back. A bloody hole in his chest on his right side, a weird noise when he breathed, pain when he did anything.

Luis tried to catch the breath running away from him, but it was hard and it hurt and he wanted to just lie there. Little sharp spikes of fear stabbed at him. The gunshot echoes faded away into the breeze. Those animals up there would come out to see what they'd shot. If they found him, they'd arrest him, or maybe just shoot him again. Or they'd call in a gunship drone and kill anything bright green. Any way this went down, he'd never see his wife or son or home again. That thought hurt worse than being shot.

He wrenched his head to his right. The mother and her child lay roughly twenty feet away, two dark, still shapes against the sand. *You* cabrones, he fumed. *You killed a baby.*

Or had he killed her by bringing her here? *Get away. Think later.*

The oldest traveler—slight, late fifties, his hair mostly gone to silver—took Luis' hand in both of his. He had dark smears on his face and upper arm. "Mister? We go."

Go? Luis could hardly breathe. He waved toward the lights and fence. "You go. Keep heading south. Mexico's that way, you can still make it. Go down the arroyo, through the culvert. Understand?"

The old man nodded. The floodlights glimmered in his eyes as he looked toward the two dark shapes just upslope. He'd protected and comforted them even though they weren't blood.

"I'm sorry," Luis said.

The old man nodded again, then shook Luis' hand hard. "*As-salaam alaykum.*"

"*Alaykumu as-salaam.*"

Then he was gone.

Luis managed to get two magnesium flares out of his pack. They might blind the guards long enough for him to get over the next rise and for the old Arab to make it down the arroyo to safety. Just before he popped the first flare, his eyes snagged on the mom and her daughter. So small, so dark, so still. Another bad picture to add to his collection.

This used to make sense. This used to feel worthwhile. He used to be able to tell himself it was worth the risk to stand up to the *locos* who'd wrecked his country and caused all this—risk to himself, to his family, to the travelers. But the camps filled and spread. It was all so futile, not worth that little girl's death or his own.

If you let me live, he told the sky, *I'll stop. I'm done.*

2

The U.S. ranks 103rd in the 2032 Corruption Perception Index, one below Madagascar and far below all its OECD peers. Gross underfunding of government at all levels, elimination of public-sector pensions, and widespread contracting of public services to unscrupulous private firms, has led to an epidemic of corruption reminiscent of Russia under the late Vladimir Putin.
  -- "Release of the 2032 CPI," Transparency International

FRIDAY, 30 APRIL
TWO YEARS LATER

Luis opened Coast Conversions' front office at six-thirty to give the techs time to set up for the day's work. One of them— Tyler— already waited outside, as usual. He was one of two who lived in a former self-storage place three blocks away. "Where's Earnes?" Luis asked.

"Angels Stadium. The free clinic." Tyler limped through the door, stowed his pistol behind the counter, then passed into the shop and started turning on lights and compressors. Fluorescents glinted off the shiny SUVs and luxury sedans waiting at each station for their armor and ballistic glass.

Luis began to ready the front office for what he hoped would be the morning rush. A full shop and one man down. *Great.* Earnes could be waiting in line all day to get into that Doctors Without Borders clinic. Luis would have to ding him a day's pay, too, something he hated to do.

That was the downside of managing this place: having to knock heads without being able to hand out rewards. The upside? Routine. Safety. Some thought "same shit, different day" was a curse. For Luis, it meant not having to cross deserts or climb mountains. Not being chased or shot at. Not having people's lives in his hands—and fumbling them.

He leaned against the doorway, watching Tyler make his rounds through the workstations. "How're you doing? Leg okay?"

"Okay, sir."

Tyler left half a leg in Yemen. All five of Luis' techs were vets; they had good work habits, and it was the only way to get guys with mechanical and metalworking skills now that most community colleges were closed and the unions were long gone. Luis made it a point to hire guys out of flops or Ryantowns. A down payment on karma? He hoped he'd never find out.

The strip lights cast shadows on Tyler's hollow eyes and cheeks. He worked full-time and still didn't eat enough. Like everywhere else, the pay here was shit even for Luis, and he was the manager. Xiao, the owner, wouldn't cough up a cent more.

The door chime's synthetic *bing-bong* broke Luis out of his thoughts. He called out "Not open yet" before he looked back over his shoulder. A cop swaggered to the counter. *Mierda.*

The cop—Schertzer, unfortunately a monthly regular—leaned an elbow on the blue laminate countertop, chewing his gum. "How's it hanging, Ojeda?"

"You're two days early," Luis growled as he stalked to the counter.

Schertzer shrugged. "So call a fucking cop. You got it?"

It wasn't like this steroid-square *cucaracha* was a real policeman. He was just one of the contractors the city pretended was a police force. Dark-blue utilities, black tac vest, jump boots: all Luis saw was a school-crossing guard with a gun.

"Yeah." Luis opened the lockbox with his key, pulled out a white envelope, and slapped it into Schertzer's outstretched hand. *La mordida, El Norte* style. "Now get out."

The cop waggled the envelope to get the feel of it. Apparently satisfied, he shoved it into the patch pocket on his right thigh. "The widows and orphans appreciate your money, Ojeda." He smirked, then turned toward the doors and waved over his shoulder. "*A-dios.*" He stopped with his hand on the push bar, looked back. "By the way, a road crew's coming through in a couple days. They'll want their cut, too."

"They're finally going to pave the street?"

The cop shook his head, bottling up a laugh. "Shit, no. They'll get their taste; you know how it goes. That's why I'm early—make sure we get what's coming to us. See you soon."

Luis watched Schertzer ooze off to the right, no doubt to collect his bite from the other garages and workshops along this light-industrial strip off Newport Boulevard. He'd bled money into these *pendejos* for years. He'd run across people like Schertzer in Mexico and the 'Stan, but it burned his gut to see them in this county. It was easier for the kids; they weren't old enough to remember when cops and fire marshals and road crews weren't all on the take.

He sighed. That was old-timer talk. "There goes the lowest bidder," he said to himself.

Luis glanced up from taking a customer's payment to catch Ray's face outside the window. Ray raised his hand; Luis nodded to him.

The customer—a big-busted Newport Beach trophy blonde in tiny clothes—paid up and wiggled off with her bodyguard to claim her husband's newly up-armored Range Rover.

Ray turned to watch her go, then let out a long breath through pursed lips as he ambled through the front doors. He was a big, square outline against the morning sun. His thumbs hooked in the pockets of fashionably tight, white *churidar* slacks, their calves stacked just so over expensive new designer boots. Just like he'd stepped out of a vidboard ad, if those models had faces that looked more Aztec than conquistador. A long way from his old *caballero* style.

Ray gave Luis his crooked smile. "Hey, *hermano*. All your customers look like that?"

"Enough do." He shook Ray's hand, which felt like a brake drum. "*Oye, compa.* Long time. How's it going?"

Ray rocked his hand side-to-side. "About normal. How's Bel?"

Luis shrugged. "Fine. The usual."

"Nacho hanging in?"

Nacho—Luis' son Ignacio—was a Marine on his first deployment to Sudan. "Yeah, he's okay. The stories he tells me, it's like what we did in the 'Stan."

"Never ends, does it?" Ray's dark dataspecs scanned the office's lights and corners. The gray that used to be in his hair was gone. "Have any bug problems in here lately?"

"Stopped getting it swept two years ago." They weren't talking about the six- or eight-legged kind. Luis used to have to worry about those things; no more, thank God. He peered closer at the corners of Ray's nose and mouth. "Are you taking tighteners?"

"A couple months now, yeah. Like it?" Ray turned his face to let the strip lights flash off his shiny, smoother skin. "You could do with some too, *hermano*."

First he'd lost his tattoos, now this. "Can't afford them. Besides, I like looking like a grownup."

Ray shrugged. "Look, the boss wanted me to talk to you. He's got a job for you."

Luis put up his hands. "Save it. I'm out, remember?"

"I know, I know. He told me to ask, so I'm asking." Ray leaned in to lay a hand on Luis' shoulder. "This job, it's a special one, you know? Some good coin. Check it out." He tapped the phone pod on his left ear.

A few moments later, the store slate peeped. Luis brought up the email, then the attached picture. A studio portrait: a dark-haired man and woman, two cute kids, nice clothes, healthy-looking. The guy could almost pass for Latino, but the woman had the sharp features of a high-caste Arab. After fifteen seconds, the picture dissolved into empty black, literally blown to bits.

"Which one?" Luis asked. "The guy or gal?"

"All four. Told you it was special."

That was strange. Back when he was in that business, Luis moved a lot of older people and young women. The young men were usually dead or in a camp. Still, not even the money got his interest. "No way. Besides, I thought you guys had some new kid doing that."

"Federico? Yeah." Ray planted his hands on the counter. "We did until he got dead a couple nights ago." He leaned forward and dropped his volume. "The boss is pretty hot to move these people.

He'll make it worth your—"

"I said no." Luis heard the heat in his own voice, backed off. "Even if I survive it, Bel will kill me."

Ray smiled and straightened up. "Yeah, and probably me too right after." He scratched the back of his neck. "Look, this puts me in a bind, you know? He asked for you specifically. Tavo trusts you. You maybe have some bargaining room here. At least say you'll think about it."

"Bargain? With a cartel sub-boss? Are you crazy?"

Luis noticed a gray Ford Santana parked across the street, screaming "surveillance." Cops following Ray? Or were they after Luis because of Ray? Either way, he wasn't going through all that again. He needed to care for his parents and help provide for his family. He'd already sacrificed enough for a lost cause.

"I'm not thinking about this. No. Do I need to spell that?"

Ray sighed, shook his head. "Tavo's gonna be pissed." He stuck out his hand. "Come down to the bar sometime. I never see you anymore. Salma misses you, too."

And Luis missed them. But every time he went to visit Ray and his long-time girlfriend, Bel's temperature dropped thirty degrees and Luis got frostbite. "Sure, *compa*." He shook Ray's hand. "Soon."

3

Since the 10/19/19 terrorist attack, approximately 430,000 people have been imprisoned in over 220 known facilities associated with the Terrorist Detention Program (TDP)... an estimated 90% identify with one of the Islamic sects and approximately 75% are U.S. citizens... Only 27 are known to have faced charges in a court of law, and three have been convicted of any crime.
  -- Introduction, Held Without Hope, *Human Rights Watch*

FRIDAY, 30 APRIL

McGinley lounged in his rain cloud-gray government sedan across the street from Coast Conversions, a gray, flat-roofed, cinderblock of a building with a faded green awning and half-dead flowers in a planter out front. Two Mercedes SUVs and a big Merc sedan sat outside with grease pencil on the windshields, next to a Maserati SUV, a Range Rover, and one of those new Cadillac Olympias, big as a tank. All of them waiting to get armored up. Must be a lot of scared rich folk in these parts.

Two weeks away from his home turf and McGinley was still doing basic legwork for the local law, the useless sacks of shit. This Luis Ojeda character would be the sixth ex-coyote he'd corralled in the past four days. The other five were tired old duffers who hadn't crossed the border since gas was only five bucks a gallon.

But this Ojeda was in his forties; not much older than McGinley according to his file, though McGinley couldn't say he was real impressed with that file. And that big Mex who'd come out twenty minutes back was Ramiro Esquivel, what they used to call a plaza boss back in the day before the cartels got all corporate and started using titles like "area manager." Maybe Ojeda was still in the game. Worth a look-see, at least.

How to play this? McGinley didn't expect much this first

meeting; this was rattling the cage to see what the animal would do. A badge most likely wouldn't ruffle Ojeda's feathers. He was probably used to the local ICE crew, and McGinley reckoned most of them went native a long time back. Hell, if they'd been doing their jobs, the Joint Task Force boys wouldn't have dragged him all the way out here to look into why they couldn't keep their rags in the camps where they belonged.

Something alien to Ojeda might rile him up. Back home in Texas, McGinley could dress up nice and lose most of his accent and go talk sense into some peckerhead CEO who's busing in illegals instead of just paying good Americans the same shit wages. But here, in California? The big asshole redneck seemed to shake up everyone. That was easy; all McGinley had to do was be like his dad.

McGinley ambled across the cracked asphalt and through the shop's glass doors. Streaming news about the Presidential primaries scratched away in the empty front office. He skirted the counter, peered through the window set in the back wall, then pushed past the half-opened door into the workshop. Five service bays full of expensive cars being taken apart or put back together, loud music, louder tools. He felt eyes on him, none of them friendly, not that he gave a shit. McGinley strolled toward a familiar face next to a bronze Lincoln Discovery SUV in the second bay, its glass and doors all gone.

He flashed his badge once he'd closed in. "Luis Ojeda? Jack McGinley, ICE."

"Yeah?" Ojeda looked up from the slate perched on his forearm. He'd aged since the file photo; his short, wiry black hair had a fair sprinkling of gray around the ears now. Five-ten or so, fit, decent-looking enough squarish face, respectable blue button-down shirt and chinos. The pistol on his belt hinted at something harder under the surface. He said, "I was born here," then waved toward the young bucks working on the cars. "So were they."

McGinley shrugged like it didn't matter, which it didn't anymore. "Why, congratulations, *amigo.*"

Ojeda frowned. *The accent? Good.*

"What I'm looking for here is five rags. In your 'hood four-five days ago, now they're gone." The runners hadn't been seen anywhere since they broke out. "Y'all know anything about this?"

Ojeda glared at him, working his jaw. "Why would I?"

"Because you're a coyote, Ojeda." McGinley swayed in another pace, trying to crowd Ojeda, push him out of his comfort zone. No reaction. Harder with the Latins than with whites; they didn't have the same personal-space issues. "Just like your daddy was. If anyone 'round here knows how to get them rags over the border, it's you."

Dark spots began to bloom under Ojeda's armpits. Just what McGinley wanted to see. "Your intel's shit if that's what you're hearing. I'm just a guy trying to make a living. Besides, it's illegal to leave the country now? I thought you people wanted them out."

The air wrench behind McGinley had stopped screaming. He glanced back to catch a shaggy-headed wrench monkey staring at him over the hood of some fancy-ass four-door McGinley didn't recognize. McGinley showed him how a stare was really done. After a minute, the kid stalked to the workbench behind him.

"It's illegal to skip on a camp," McGinley told Ojeda. "These five came out of Barstow, two weeks or so ago? Got told these boys were headed this way. Sound familiar?"

"Heard about it on the news. More people must've got out than they said."

"Well, don't believe anything you hear on the news." The engine was ticking over behind Ojeda's eyes, but he was still way too cool; time to rile him up. McGinley half-turned and waved across the cars. "I reckon it's way too loud in here for you to think right. How 'bout I just shut this place down a spell, so me and you can talk private-like."

Ojeda's neck flushed red. "That's money out of my pocket, *cabrón*. This a shakedown?"

Score. "Should it be?" McGinley read the sudden heat coming off Ojeda and dropped back a couple steps, resting his right wrist on the pistol butt in his belt holster. Casual; just a reminder. The file said Ojeda had been Army in Afghanistan back in the day. He'd probably been carrying as long as McGinley and knew how to use that weapon of his—what was it, a Sig Sauer? Serious piece, nothing cheap. Ojeda looped a thumb over the belt in front of his holster. Casual; just a reminder.

For a few long seconds, McGinley stared at Ojeda, waiting for a twitch. Well, the man had some balls. Would he really draw down on a Fed? Hard telling. These days, people did what they had to to protect their turf or their lives, and a badge didn't carry the same weight it used to.

Finally, McGinley smirked and dropped his hand. He'd rattled the cage enough. "Well, then, Ojeda. Y'all keep your eyes and ears open. If you hear anything about these Muslim former Americans, you let me know right quick." He stepped forward and flipped a business card out of his shirt pocket up into Ojeda's face. "Meantime, I reckon I'll find out where you've been the past few nights. Just curious, you know. Your daddy smuggled a lot of people into this country back in the day, and, well, like father, like son, right?"

The red crept into Ojeda's hairline. He might look respectable, but hit the secret button and he spun up right nice. "That business is *over*. Nobody wants to come to this country anymore. People like you saw to that."

"That so? Say, your son's a Marine, ain't he? Damn good training for the family business. All them long marches—"

"Leave my son out of this," Ojeda snapped. "Yeah, Dad was a coyote. That's long done. Nacho's got nothing to do with this, and he never will." He snatched the card out of McGinley's fingers. "Watch the door on your way out."

McGinley snorted, shook his head, looked around. "Some place you got here. It yours?"

"No. I'm the manager. A Chinese guy up in Sierra Madre owns the chain."

"You don't say." He had to poke one last time. "Just wondering. If we ran an ID check on your boys yonder, how many do y'all think you'd lose?"

Ojeda's eyes had turned black and ice-cold. "Have a shitty day, McGinley."

"I often do, *amigo*." He slapped Ojeda's shoulder, turned and strolled outside.

This one might be worth watching.

4

United States: Citizens traveling to or in the United States should be aware that U.S. security forces and many citizens are suspicious of anyone they believe to be of the Islamic faith... Boarding trains, undergrounds or commercial aircraft may be a lengthy, difficult, or possibly unpleasant experience and should be avoided whenever possible.

-- "Traveler's Advisory," Republic of Turkey Ministry of Foreign Affairs

FRIDAY, 30 APRIL

"All right, now, get your clothes off," the TSA agent drawled. A black woman: hard-faced, mouth downturned, "Lebow" according to her ID. "All of 'em. Put 'em on the table."

Nora Khaled's sense of humiliation scorched her cheeks. She'd been furious when she and her husband Paul and the kids got pulled out of the Dulles Airport security line and dragged back here. Now her brainspace filled with embarrassment that was only going to get worse.

"Look," she said as calmly as she could, "I know you have procedures; I get that. But I'm an FBI agent." She held up her ID folder for the zillionth time this morning, hoping the badge would finally do some good. "A Federal officer, like you. Can't we   "

"Don't care who you are, lady." Lebow folded her wiry arms across her chest. "System says you're a threat, so we gonna check you out. Now get your clothes off. The girl, too."

Nora glanced at Hope. Her daughter clung to her jeans pocket, staring wide-eyed at the woman. "You're going to strip-search a four-year-old? Is that really necessary?" She nearly choked on her tongue, trying to fight down her rising anger.

"Gotta see what's under her clothes, so there's no bomb or

nothing."

"She's just a baby!" Nora stopped, gulped down a breath when Lebow slid her hand toward her sidearm. "Do you have kids?"

"Yeah. And they ain't gonna get blown up by no terrorists, not if I can help it." Lebow slipped her telescoping metal baton off her belt and extended it with a flick of her wrist. Hope whimpered. "Now you get yourself naked or I'll get a coupla guys out there to come help, understand?"

If only she could've worked out getting into Canada. They could have driven, avoiding all this. But everyone wanted to go to Canada and the Canucks were really cracking down, so getting a guide across the border would have cost more than her family had. Mexico wasn't so choosy. Unfortunately, driving from D.C. all the way to Paul's parents in Southern California—the cover reason for this trip—wasn't an option.

Nora had expected to be stopped at the airport, questioned, scanned multiple times, maybe frisked. She hadn't counted on ending up in a frigid, overlit, windowless room with the most obnoxious TSA agent ever, on the verge of having the last of her and her daughter's dignity ripped away.

Nora over-carefully set her ID folder on the table—once again, the badge had failed her—and struggled to put her game face on. More than anything, she couldn't let Hope be hurt by this. "Get undressed, Cupcake," she whispered to Hope. "Put your things on the table."

"But why? Are we in trouble?"

"No, no. We haven't done anything wrong. It's just… the rules. Be a good girl, okay?"

Nora stripped quickly, ignoring Lebow, relying on sheer momentum to get her through. Paul and Peter were going through the same thing somewhere beyond that closed door. Paul never got used to institutional dehumanization the way Nora did in the Army; this would be so humiliating for him. She remembered how devastated her father—a born-again American patriot if there ever was one—had been the first time this had happened to him.

At least these idiots were playing it by the book. Some women at the mosque had told her of being searched by male TSA agents.

Laminate-and-metal tables lined three of the room's dingy off-white walls, leaving plenty of space for more victims. Nora shuddered, not just because the scratched linoleum floor was cold under her bare feet. She took off her Panama hat last, set it carefully on her clothes pile behind her. Only her chunky silver pendant was left; they'd need those male guards if they wanted to take it. She didn't bother to cover herself. Even though her face was on fire, she wouldn't give this cockroach the satisfaction of seeing her as weak.

Hope hunched against the cold next to her, arms folded tight across her bare chest, shuffling her feet. She'd removed everything except her tiny white cotton panties. Nora hugged her to her side and hoped almost naked was good enough for this woman.

"Get the girl's drawers off," Lebow ordered. She pointed her baton at Hope, who shrank back against the table's rim.

Nora felt an explosion inside her. *If I had my weapon…* She was about to pin the woman's ears back but saw the void in her eyes and clamped her mouth shut. All this was normal to this pig: just two more half-humans to put in their places. *I have to succeed*, Nora told herself, *so this never happens to us or anybody else ever again.* She knelt before her daughter and kissed her forehead. "I'm sorry, Cupcake." Then she took away Hope's last bit of modesty.

Nora's hands trembled with rage as she dropped the panties on the rest of Hope's clothes. "Satisfied?" She didn't bother to hide the snarl in her voice.

Lebow collapsed her baton, clipped it to her belt, then pulled a pair of latex gloves from her back pocket. She pawed through their clothes, probed every pocket and seam.

"Put your hands on your head, fingers interlaced." Her bored voice recited rather than spoke the instructions. "Open your mouth." A bony, latex-coated finger rummaged through Nora's mouth. "Squat and spread your knees."

Nora followed each command without protest, choking back tears of shame and anger. She coughed on cue, stood, turned, bent over the table.

Lebow shoved her finger inside Nora, poked and prodded. Nora gasped at the pain. She tried to hold back her tears, her curses, her feelings, but couldn't. She'd been born here, just a few miles away. She'd fought for this country, risked her life for it. She was a federal officer. How could this happen? How did she become a criminal?

"Spread your cheeks."

The woman switched orifices.

Nora slammed shut her eyes and clenched her teeth so hard her jaw ached. Her *daughter* was watching this, her four-year-old *daughter*, seeing her mother violated. Nora could hear Hope's soft sobs next to her. She wanted to kill this woman, beat her down with her own baton, then empty her own pistol into her. She could do it; it was there, inside her. They thought she was a terrorist? She'd show them a terrorist.

"Right. Stand up, turn around."

Nora smeared the tear tracks off her face before she turned to glare into Lebow's bulging eyes. She pulled Hope against her again, felt her daughter's tears burn down her bare hip. "It's okay," she murmured to Hope, never taking her eyes off Lebow. "I'm okay. She didn't hurt me. And she's not going to hurt you."

She was giving up everything: her home, her career, her friends, her country, maybe her life if things went wrong. But she was also giving up the slights and insults, the suspicion, the graffiti on the front door, her children beaten up by bullies, her tires slashed. All to bring the truth to vermin like this. To show them what they'd become, what they'd done to the nation they supposedly loved so much. She would *not* let them see her break down.

Lebow broke off the staring contest and shifted her narrowed eyes toward Hope.

No. Way. Nora pushed Hope behind her. "If you touch my daughter…"

The woman switched her attention back to Nora. "You threatening me?"

"What would you do," Nora growled, "if I was about to rape your kids?"

Lebow's eyes settled back into round two of the staring contest. Nora had lots of practice at this from facing down suspects during interrogation. After a few moments, the woman scanned Nora up and down once, then slowly met her eyes again.

Then Nora saw it: fear. Just a flash, but it was there and

unmistakable. Lebow had seen Nora's hard abs, the sinews quivering in her neck and arms and thighs, the furnace burning behind her eyes. Probably nothing like any Muslim woman this dog had ever seen before. One who wasn't afraid. One who'd fight back.

"Get your clothes on," Lebow sputtered. "You're done."

Nora gave her the hardest smile she could manage.

No. You and everybody like you… you're done.

5

This boom in gene-based therapies has caused average life expectancy to surge to above 90 among those Americans earning the top 10% of incomes... However, for those in the bottom 60% who find health insurance entirely unaffordable – and for those with pre-existing conditions, the elderly, and pregnant women, who are considered uninsurable – life expectancy has plunged below 70 for the first time since 1964.
    -- "Study: Longevity Linked to Income," LATimes.com

FRIDAY, 30 APRIL

Mirabel Ojeda stared out at the Pit and felt her heart break for the first time that morning.

A hundred people packed into the Emergency Department waiting room designed for forty-five, piled on the faded plastic chairs, sitting on the floor or each other, leaning, standing, whatever they could do. Another sixty or so clotted outside around the entry door. The racket and stench slammed into Bel as soon as she pushed through the automatic double doors from the treatment area. She could tune out the noise, and after all these years she was used to the funk—she was never away from this place long enough to get the stink out of her sinuses—but she couldn't avoid the faces, the pain and pleading and fear in their eyes. She felt both utterly helpless and so angry she wanted to turn the Taser strapped to her waist on the first hospital administrator stupid enough to wander into this cesspool.

Bel tugged the surgical mask back up her nose, squared her goggles and started her first hunt of the day. Only the bleeding or unconscious would get treatment anytime soon.

Worn-out faces turned up to her as she pushed down each aisle. Fingers plucked at her scrub pants. She had to pretend she

20

couldn't hear the soft calls of "Nurse!" and "Please!" that followed her. In the Army, she'd never pass a patient who asked for help; here, it seemed to be all she did. *Nostalgic for Bagram?* She'd have laughed at that idea twenty years ago.

She found a little boy with a raging case of measles; he'd have to wait. She stepped over the legs of a ragged, dirty guy with sores on his face, asleep against a concrete pillar. Hard telling what he wanted; he was breathing, so he'd get to wait, too. Bel paused briefly in front of a lost-looking white couple in clean clothes, good gym shoes, and nice haircuts trying to hush a red-faced, screaming infant. Poor little thing; probably an infection. *Wait.*

Bel stopped again to squat beside an elderly man at the end of the row. His shoulders huddled under a frayed cardigan (with the room temp at egg-poaching level thanks to the half-broken A/C), his breath whistling in and out. Old folks were over a third of the ED's patients now. Bel pictured Luis' dad Alvaro, how his Medicare had become vouchers that could almost pay for insurance that didn't cover anything, and how his big heart was slowly coming apart like a junker car. He'd respond to proteomic therapy if they had any way to pay for it. She reached out to squeeze the old man's hand; the man peeked up enough to give her back a trembly, bashful smile. There: Bel's heart broke a second time in ten minutes.

Bel turned toward a ruckus at the door. Two dirty men in filthy blue overalls dragged a boy between them, their taped hands under his arms. The scrap-metal plant's daily casualty. She shoved her way through the crowd and reached them just before they got to Reception. "What happened?" she demanded.

"Saw got away from him." The shorter man dug in his breast pocket. "Got the fingers right here."

That's when she noticed the bloody cloth wrapped around the boy's left hand. She tried not to show the catch in her throat. "Hold onto them, give them to the doctor. How old is he?"

"Twelve, thirteen maybe."

Oh, God. "Follow me."

She marched into the ED's treatment area. All the cubicles were full—she'd helped fill them—but maybe she could find someplace to put this boy. She risked a glance back. He was as dirty as the grownups, swimming in his overalls, his head wobbling as if there were no bones in his neck. His hair had been mowed down to an eighth-inch brush. He reminded Bel of Nacho when they'd shaved his head after he'd managed to pour paint over himself and let it dry. He'd been bright blue. She and Lucho took turns with the clippers while the other sneaked off to laugh until their sides burned.

She'd love to laugh like that again. It'd been so long.

Bel grabbed an orderly, growled, "Get me a gurney, stat!" then found a stray chair outside an exam cube. The men dropped the boy into it with a grunt. "We gotta get back," the taller one said. "They clocked us out."

"Wait!" Bel already had the boy's overalls open, exposing a stained undershirt over a shrunken chest. "What's his name?"

"Cullen," the shorter man said. He looked up at the other man. "Know his last name?" The other man shook his head. "Sorry, miss. They took his badge when we was going out. Look, we gotta go."

Bel accepted the wad of bloody paper towels holding the boy's fingers and waved the men away. They'd fired him on his way to the hospital. They wouldn't even spring for an ambulance. *Bastards.* Where were his parents? Did they send him to the plant? Did he have a home, or just some nasty little tent someplace?

She peeled off her left glove, reached out, hesitated, then stroked the fuzz on his scalp. Soft, like a puppy's. Cullen rolled his head back and peered at her through grayish eyes sloshing with tears and pain. *I'm so sorry*, she wanted to say. *About everything. You'll be okay, really. We'll make it better.* But she couldn't shove the words out of her mouth; she couldn't lie to him. So she simply caressed what was left of his hair and tried to not let her tears out.

The orderly—a doctor from Myanmar who couldn't practice here—arrived with the gurney. Bel helped him ease the boy onto it. "Clean him up and re-wrap the hand," she told him. "Take his vitals, type him, and give him a tetanus booster. See if you can find a doctor. Thanks." She took one last look at Cullen, stuffed down a sigh, then trudged back to the Pit. The hospital could help the boy. She'd seen too many patients turned out the moment they could stand, though, to believe this time would be different.

The screaming in the Pit drilled through the double doors into the treatment area.

Bel, scurrying to the lab cart with samples of what she hoped wasn't typhus, stopped and stared toward the doors. It wasn't the normal screaming. Ros—one of the older nurses, Bel's age maybe—caught her eye from the exam cube across from her. Bel passed the samples to an orderly and hit the doors running.

A swarm of Pit inmates heaved in the open area in front of Reception. Next to a nearby concrete pillar, a frail, hairless woman wailed over the still body of a man. Taser leads trailed from his back across the floor. Three Pit creatures pointed guns at the man while a security guard threaded plasticuffs around his wrists.

Bel followed the path Ros cleared into the center of the scrum. There she found Dortmund kneeling next to a bundle of blond hair and blue scrubs curled into a ball on the blood-spattered linoleum. She gasped. "Oh, God."

The bundle was Pippa, a way-too-young nurse's aide from someplace in the Midwest. Blood and snot poured out of her battered nose, one eye was already swelling shut, and she squealed every time either Dortmund or Bel touched her. Pippa whimpered "I'm sorry I'm sorry I'm sorry" between hacking coughs.

"What happened?" Bel demanded of Dortmund. He was about the same size as her husband, but he seemed huge compared to the rest of the nurses.

"I dunno. He was yelling about waiting three days for a doctor before I put him down." He leaned close to Pippa, crooned, "Hey, Pips, it's okay, you're safe."

For once, the ED staff worked like the machine it was supposed to be. A gurney crashed into the Pit, Bel and Ros gently rolled Pippa onto a backboard, and the girl soon disappeared into the treatment area, surrounded by nurses and orderlies.

Bel stood rooted next to Pippa's puddle, waiting for an orderly to come clean up. She sucked air through her cupped hand, trying to calm her stomach. That could've been her. Coming into the Pit unarmed was like wearing a meat dress in a kennel, but the hospital wouldn't buy enough Tasers for all the nurses.

Ros pressed her arm into Bel's. "Does one of us gotta get killed before we do something?"

Not this again. Ros had been carrying water for a union organizer for the past eight months. Every day, Bel expected her to disappear and wind up in a landfill. "You want us all to end up like that?"

Ros crossed her arms hard. "They can't afford to do that. We have skills. It's not like they can just drag random people out of a Ryantown and put 'em to work here."

"You're sure?" She swiveled on Ros, dropped into a whisper. "I was in the union at Regional. I did what you're doing. Remember how they broke our last strike? I lost two friends. So no, I'm not going to help you get the nurses fired or murdered. I know how you feel, Ros, but I just can't fight anymore."

"Bullshit. You're still in this dump. You're fighting every day." Ros' narrow jaw went hard. "We need you, *qin*. The younger nurses, they respect you, they'll follow you."

"They'll have to follow someone else." Bel broke away and stalked toward the doors. A union, these days? That was a fantasy. Bel couldn't see risking her family and life for a fantasy. "I'm sorry."

"Nurse Ojeda to Reception, please."

Oh, hell. Bel shoved her frustration back into its cave and trudged through the double doors into the Pit. To her left, a broad-shouldered man with a red-blond crew cut stood near the bulletproof glass window stretching across the three reception stations. He stood out from the others because he looked healthy and wore a vaguely disgusted expression.

The reception clerk must have pointed in her direction, because the man paced straight for her. He flashed a badge a couple steps away. "Mirabel Ojeda?"

A cop? Was Lucho in trouble again? "Yes?"

"Jack McGinley, ICE." He had some kind of Southern accent. "I just jawed some with your husband a while back."

Not in uniform, she noticed: newish jeans, tan combat boots, a white, short-sleeved snap-front shirt with blue pinstripes. A gun peeked out from behind his right hip. Bel was glad she still wore her surgical mask so this McGinley couldn't see her worry. She fumbled a moment for something to say. "What... what do you want?"

"Well..." McGinley ran his gaze around the Pit. His mouth screwed up into a knot. "Could we step out somewhere that ain't the Black Hole of Calcutta? You reckon that's possible?"

This wasn't the first time she'd faced questions from ICE or the Border Patrol or DEA. They didn't make her nervous anymore, just resentful. At least this time—for the first time in ages—she wouldn't have to lie. As she led the cop outside, though, a single thought stomped up and down her brain: *Lucho, what have you gotten yourself into now?*

6

*The economic activities of Mexico's three corporatized
narco supercartels have completely displaced the rump
federal government in the 28 Mexican states under their
control. Legitimate and illicit business activities in the
United States, Latin America and Asia support the cartels'
generation-long funding of local infrastructure
development and maintenance, law enforcement, and
education, as well as the regional military forces that
prosecute Mexico's ongoing civil war.*
*-- "Unclassified Key Judgments (from October 2030
NIE)," National Intelligence Council*

FRIDAY, 30 APRIL

La Paloma—Ray's biggest bar in Orange County—occupied a hundred-plus-year-old brick building on the southern edge of downtown Santa Ana. Luis figured every cop in Southern California knew that like all the other businesses Ray managed, it was also a Cartel money laundry. As he entered through the brick courtyard, Luis could see his name being typed on some watch list. Not that he had any choice.

When the *patrón* calls for you, you come.

Ray met him at the weapons check. Luis traded his Sig for a claim ticket, then Ray ushered him into the main bar.

Inside he found brick, dark woodwork and the normal early-Friday-night crowd: twenty or so people drinking, a half-dozen couples dancing *bachata*—slower and sexier than salsa—to a DJ. They wore their best shabby clothes and their much-repaired good shoes. The women had done what they could with home perms and cheap makeup or had just hacked their hair short like Bel and half the actresses on the web. The drinkers, the dancers, even the DJ were various kinds of lean, some hard, some sick; low pay and

26

expensive food made for a great weight-loss plan. A couple hookers—not obvious, but dressed better than the normals—worked the room. Luis knew the local zip and kronk dealers were in the second bar across the breezeway. One-stop shopping.

Luis checked the place Tavo used as a meeting room, sticking into the bar floor off to his right. Venetian blinds blocked the big windows. "Is this one of those talks where Tavo brings out the sledgehammer?" He tried not to sound like a school kid waiting to see the principal.

"No, no." Ray waved away the idea. "He just wants to talk face-to-face, you know? Tell you his side of things. Be chill."

"A cartel sub-boss calls me in for a lecture, and you want me to be chill? Seriously?"

"Just…" Ray spread out his hands, palms down. *Even it out.*

They stood off to the side of the room, watching the action swirl around them. Ray paid a lot of attention to the waitresses—tall, dark, full of attitude, short black skirts and blood-red shirts—and they returned it, smiling and flashing eyes his way. Luis would've enjoyed the show more if his attention hadn't been nailed to Tavo's door, imagining what would happen when he went through it. "What kind of mood is Tavo in? Is he pissed?"

"He's… been happier. Things are fucked up down south. You know someone took out *El Tiburón* a couple days ago, right?"

That was Nestor, Tavo's brother and the Pacifico Norte *capo*. For a few moments, Luis forgot about Tavo's dragon's den. "Who did it? Who's running the Cartel?"

"Nobody knows who did it yet," Ray said. An especially pretty waitress sauntered by, lots of hip sway, and winked at Ray. "Who's running the Cartel? Don't know yet, but maybe…" He nodded toward Tavo's door.

Great, Luis thought. *The new* capo *wants to yell at me.*

The door swung open. Ray nudged Luis. "Looks like it's time."

The blond *gabacho* coming out was a hand shorter than Luis, wearing a white polo with the triangle-in-a-triangle logo of the company that owned the contract cops that passed for Santa Ana PD. He nodded to them as he headed for the bar.

"That time of the month," Ray said under his breath.

That morning's McGinley visitation replayed in Luis' head.

Had that cracker been trying to shake him down? The Feds were paid more than the average rent-a-cop—which wasn't saying much—but like everyone else, they got no retirement.

Tavo's office had been a private dining room back when La Paloma was a restaurant. A big wood slab of a table still filled the middle, circled by twelve wooden ladder-back chairs. Tavo sat at the far end with his slate. "Gentlemen," he said in Spanish. "Please come in."

Luis first met Octavio Villalobos almost twelve years before, when Tavo had recruited him to coyote for the Cartel. He'd expected the man who ran the Cartel's business in the Southwest to be a cliché *narco* boss from the music vids—lots of gangsta bling, a shiny suit and $4000 cowboy boots. What he found instead was a guy who looked and dressed like a successful accountant, with conservative hair and quiet office clothes and a high-end Chinese smartwatch.

They stopped two chairs back from the table's end, Luis on one side, Ray on the other. Luis said, "*Hola, patrón.*"

"*Buenas noches*, Luis. You look well. Mirabel is well too, I expect?"

"Her job's hard, but she's okay."

"And Ignacio? Your son is still in your Marine Corps?"

That first time here, Luis had also expected a lot of swearing and macho bullshit. Tavo never swore, and he hated nicknames.

"Yeah. He's deployed, but he's doing good."

Tavo nodded. "Excellent." He motioned toward Ray. "Ramiro tells me you won't escort this *Moro* family to the south. Is that so?"

Just what Luis was afraid of. A bead of sweat trickled down the back of his neck. "Yes, *patrón.*"

Tavo gave him a slow scan. While most of him resembled a bureaucrat, his eyes were hard and always a little distant. "You've recovered from your incident?"

"Mostly. I still feel it sometimes." The dreams were still there, in the shadows.

"Of course." Tavo leaned forward, steepled his fingers and put them to his lips. "I appreciate that your experience has made you… reluctant. But this is a special situation, and I can pay you well for your efforts. Would $50,000 ease your concerns at all?"

Fifty grand? He'd never had that big a payoff before. "What's so special about these people?"

"The woman's an agent in your FBI. She wishes to defect."

That took a moment to sink in. When it did, every alarm in Luis' head started blasting. "What? That's crazy! How do you know this isn't a trap? I—"

"We've verified her story," Tavo said. His voice had turned a few degrees frostier. He leaned back in his chair and folded his hands on the table. "Please give me the courtesy of believing we aren't fools. I respect your experience and discretion, Luis. That's why of all the men I have available, I ask you to do this."

Luis glanced to Ray, who arched an eyebrow as if to say, *well?*

Fifty grand. Not nearly enough to get their heads above water, but damn good. He could pay a couple debts, maybe clean off one of the credit cards. He might even be able to get his parents in to see doctors for the first time in a few years, the way a good son should.

Or he might get himself killed.

Or Bel might kill him for breaking the promise he'd made to her after his last run. He heard her words at his hospital bedside: *I don't want that money. I want you alive, with me.*

"I'm retired," he finally said. "I'm too old and slow to be running around out there anymore. My family depends on me. If anything happens to me, it's over for them, too."

Tavo's eyes became completely opaque, like the black glass on the cars in Luis' shop. "I don't remember giving you permission to retire."

Permission? "I was a contractor." He picked his words carefully. "That was our deal. I take only the work I want."

"That changed when we provided your medical care after your incident, and the support while you recovered." Tavo swept his slate screen with the edge of his hand. "Do you know how much we invested in you?" He poked at the slate. "Three hundred ninety thousand dollars. I have an account here if you'd like to review it. Hospitals are so expensive in this country."

Luis squashed the anger trying to climb up his throat. "I was working for you when I was shot," he said as evenly as his heart would let him. "I thought the deal was, if I was hurt or arrested, the

Cartel would take care of me." He stared into Tavo's stony eyes and remembered the nickname the Nortes had for (but never used around) him: *La Almádena.* Sledgehammer. Ray told him it was Tavo's favorite weapon.

"And so we did." Tavo leaned forward, touching his steepled fingers to his lips. "We made this investment in good faith with the understanding you'd rejoin us once you recovered. You've been on extended leave as far as we're concerned. And now you say you've recovered. It delights me to hear this. So now it's time to come back to work."

Bel would want Luis to tell him to go to hell. She'd tell him herself, damn the blowback. But Bel wasn't here, just the Sledgehammer. "How do I retire?"

"Ah." Tavo nodded sadly. "Luis, if you truly wish to retire, of course you can. All you have to do is repay what you owe to us."

Almost four hundred grand. More money than he'd get for running the shop over the next twelve years. *Dios mío.*

"This debt is now two years old, you understand. We expect all our loans to be repaid promptly. Interest will be involved as well, it always is." Tavo narrowed his eyes a fraction, just enough to squeeze the last warmth out of them. "Do I need to continue?"

Sweat soaked the back of Luis' shirt while Tavo stared at him for what seemed like an hour. Go back to dragging strays over the border or pay off an impossible debt. What kind of choice was this?

Could he escape with Bel? Go over the border, disappear someplace the Cartel would never find them? Was there such a place?

Tavo asked, "Do you remember Hernando Vega? I believe he used to be your logistics contact, yes? Well, he won't be your contact anymore. This is why." He held up his slate.

The screen filled with a picture of a man sprawled on bloody asphalt, naked and riddled with more bullet holes than Luis could ever count. Luis cringed, turned his head away.

"He owed money to us—less than you do—and thought he could run away from his obligation. We found him in Manila. This picture was taken there. Would you like to see what we did to his wife?"

Luis shook his head, nauseated.

Tavo switched off the slate and laid it carefully on the table. "It isn't the money, you understand. It's the principle. A debt is a matter of honor. Everyone must pay their debts. One way or another."

It was like Tavo had read Luis' mind. His life and Bel's life had just become worthless. Ray was no help; he stood staring at the floor, as if he was trying to drill through it and disappear.

"I need to talk to Bel. I can't just ignore her." *Brave man, hiding behind your wife.*

Tavo pursed his lips. "No, that would be wrong." He leaned back. "Talk to your wife. Tonight. Tell Ramiro of your decision tomorrow morning. Make the right decision, Luis."

7

FRIDAY, 30 APRIL

Luis drove north from La Paloma on city streets to avoid the tolls on the 55. He dodged police roadblocks and ID checks, his head crammed with angry, frightened voices, most of them his own.

It was never supposed to come to this.

Ray had hooked him up with Tavo. He'd be a contractor, they'd told him, free to take runs as he chose, stop when he wanted. Luis had been glad for the help after months of guiding escaping Muslims into Mexico on his own: more money, more logistical support. Even Bel had approved back then. "We can't just let those poor people get locked up for nothing," she'd said.

He couldn't afford to turn down anything at first. His Public Works job had vanished when the Orange County government went private. In those first couple of years with the Cartel, he ran hundreds of Muslims over the border, sometimes thirty or more at a time.

The years passed, the groups and fees got smaller, the going harder. Then an old buddy from Public Works told him about the job opening at Coast Conversions, put in a word for him. Luis started turning down runs. The Cartel accepted his refusals without much grace, but accepted them nonetheless.

Then he ended up half-dead in that hospital in Sierra Vista with no way to pay the bill. When Ray arrived to tell him it was handled, Luis had been in no condition to ask about the terms. He thought it was just the Cartel taking care of its people the way it always did. He'd seen them pension off *sicarios* who'd been shot on the job and figured that was their plan for him. The Cartel had made a lot of money off his work, after all.

Now the bill had come due.

Luis' neighborhood in south Orange wasn't a combat zone yet; not all the houses had bars on the windows or reinforced doors. Dusty cars lined the street or squatted on the driveways, most of them small, none less than fifteen years old. There'd be no place for them all if several weren't at the second job or the night shift. Dogs bayed from behind iron gates. No streetlights: like most everywhere else, they'd been gutted by scrappers after their copper wire.

Strips of light glowed along the edges of the garage doors. Most families on the block had someone living in their garages, relatives or friends or strangers who could pay rent. The "garage granny" was so common, she was a stock character on web shows. The Fuentes a couple doors down had a mini-sweatshop going 24/7. Luis' garage was dark. Rilie, Christa's old high-school friend, was already gone to her twelve-hour night shift in a call center, helping rich Indians with their cell phones.

A nearby pair of Neighborhood Watch busybodies with AR-15s slung across their backs gave his truck the evil eye as he pulled into his driveway next to Bel's little blue econobox. When Luis got out, they sniffed and turned back to photographing the license plates of the cars parked along the street.

The lingering aroma of his mother's Mexican stir-fry woke up his stomach when he stepped into his clean-but-not-neat 1970s rancher. Graciela sat straight at the little IKEA table at the living room's far end, nursing her homemade post-dinner *café de olla*. Bel clattered dishes in the kitchen.

His mother squinted at him through glasses that hadn't been

the right prescription for at least two years. "*Hola*, Lucho," she said in Spanish. "I saved dinner for you." Graciela still wore her work clothes. It never stopped pissing him off that at her age, she had to spend twelve hours a day standing at a register for Walmart.

"*Gracias, Mama. ¿Donde Papi?*"

"*En nuestra sala.* He was dizzy, so he went to lie down." That was happening more often. Not something Luis could process even if he wanted to.

Bel's voice chimed out of the kitchen. "Lucho? We need to talk." He could hardly hear her over the clattering vent fan.

Yes, we do. "In a minute."

In the bedroom, he emptied his pockets into his nightstand, took off his gun, washed his face and hands. Supplies Bel had swiped from the hospital for her medical bag splashed across the foot of the bed. Through the open door he could hear the tail end of tonight's round of sniping between the two most important women in his life.

"Shouldn't you put on some clothes?" Graciela, in Spanish.

"Can't you stop burning dinner?" Bel, in English.

He tuned out their snapping and stopped at the dresser. Pictures of the kids dissolved one into another in the black vidframe. He cradled it in his hands, tapped the screen to freeze a shot of Christa in a long dress for the junior prom, the last good picture of her they had. Luis missed her smile. Four years tomorrow. Bel would be a mess tomorrow night; she still blamed herself.

You're stalling.

Bel stood at the kitchen sink, scrubbing the dinner pots and dishes. She'd changed from scrubs into faded denim shorts and a thin tank top that wasn't a color anymore. Luis leaned against the doorjamb and watched. Endless hours a day on her feet—walking, bending, lifting, squatting—worked better than any gym. She still had a great pair of legs. She had a great pair of pretty much everything. Her strong jaw and forehead and proud nose and generous mouth shouldn't add up to pretty, but they did. And how. After twenty-three years, he still loved to just look at her. *How'd I luck out?*

She ignored his inspection, bore down hard on something

stubborn in a big iron frying pan. Luis ambled to her side, put an arm around her waist and kissed her temple. Her brutally short black hair smelled like the hospital. "How was your day?"

"The usual. Long and ugly and I don't want to talk about it."

"Okay." He sighed, hugged her against his side. She kept washing up.

Bel stacked the last glass in the dish drainer, wiped her hands, then steered Luis out the sliding door onto the cracked concrete patio. It was July hot in April and the smoky tang from the fire in the hills half-masked the smog's chemical smell. The evening's gun battles crackled from the other side of the 55. "Is there something you need to tell me?"

"Let me guess. A guy from ICE showed up? McGinley?"

"Uh-huh. Who is he? I haven't seen him before."

"Some turd they brought in from outside. It's about that breakout at the Barstow camp."

She shook her head and paced out onto the lawn. Grass fried beige by nineteen rainless months crunched under her flip-flops. "He asked me where you've been for the past two weeks."

"What did you tell him?"

"The truth. That you've been here with us." She crossed her arms and turned to face him. "What've you done, Lucho? Why is he asking about you?"

"I haven't *done* anything." *Yet.*

Bel raised an eyebrow. "Why weren't you home for dinner?"

Luis avoided her glare. "I gotta tell you something. You won't like it."

⬗

He's been fired. He's having an affair. He has cancer. He's leaving. Nothing like working in an ED to help gin up worst-case scenarios. All of Bel's alarms started screaming. "Lucho…"

"I have to go back to work for the Cartel." It came out all in a rush.

"You *what?*"

He plowed through how he owed those gangsters some ridiculous amount of money for keeping him from dying after he was shot. Her mind went on broil. *Those bastards!* They'd set him up. They'd broken their promise. His so-called friend had screwed them both and—

"I'm sorry," he said.

Sorry? She spun in a little circle, not sure which way to look. Everything on Lucho's face was tight—his eyes, his lips, his jaw— and she figured he was as mad as she was getting. "How much again?"

"Almost four hundred grand."

She gasped. "Four years at UCLA for Nacho when he comes back."

"Almost, yeah."

"Gene therapy for Alvaro."

"Jesus, I get it, all right?" He gulped down his irritation. "This job pays fifty."

"Wonderful." She massaged her eyes with her fingertips for a moment, trying to hold back the jumble of angry words fighting to get out of her mouth. The last thing they needed was for both of them to go kinetic. "How… oh, God… this'll bury us! I'm juggling money all the time just to pay the bills we have now. We can't—"

"I know. I never saw it coming."

"How did this happen? They weren't supposed to own you."

"That changed when they paid my hospital bill."

"Nice of them to tell you. What if something happens to you? Do I owe them the money? Do I have to work for them? Does Nacho?"

He raised his hands to hold her off. "No, nothing like that. Nothing's going to happen to me. And if it does, Ray'll work it out."

"Like he did for you?"

"I don't think he knew this was going to happen."

"Well, now he does. Did he try to help?"

Lucho looked away, his jaw set.

"That's what I thought. So what are you going to do about this? How are you going to fix this?"

"I told you already. I have to do this job for them."

"Again? The last time almost killed you! It almost killed me. And once you start again, how does it stop? I've already lost a daughter, isn't that enough?"

"Look, I'm—"

"You're sorry, I know." She was too tired and angry to keep the frustration out of her voice. "I'm sorry, too. I'm sorry you let those people into your life. *Our* life."

"I remember someone who looked like you agreeing to this way back when," he growled.

"They changed the rules!" She hated how whiny she sounded.

"It's their game."

"It's not a game!" Bel slapped away the hand he'd reached out to her. Her mind screamed through all the alternatives it could find, crashing into walls and falling through holes. "We could leave. Run away. How far can they—"

"Anywhere. They can find us anywhere."

"I don't believe that. There's gotta be someplace they won't go. We'll get your sister to take your parents, we can go right away, tomorrow, we can—"

"Is that what you want? Really?" Lucho's voice had turned hard and angry. "Here's how that works. We'll never be able to stop. Ever. We'll never be able to have a home, we'll have to change our names, work under the table, no friends, no contact with Nacho. We'll be living in shitholes. And that's the *rest of our lives*. However long that is. And that's if they don't decide to go after Nacho or my folks or brother and sister to flush us out. Sound good to you?"

His anger had spun up her own. She slapped both hands into his chest. "Yes! If it means you stay alive and we're not slaves to those people, then yes. They're never gonna let you go, you know that. You *know* that, Lucho! They'll string this out forever. We'll never be out from under this! We're never gonna be done!"

The points of Lucho's jaw turned white. "I'm going to work it off. They agreed. It sucks, I hate it, but all the other options are shit. There's no place we can go to get away from them. I work off the debt or they put *both* of us in the ground." He screwed shut his eyes and took an endless long breath. A bad sign; he was trying to keep from erupting. "Listen to me. I'm not arguing about this anymore. There's no point. It's done, we won't change anything." He opened his eyes, still hot but not as hard. "I need you to back me up here."

Bel took her own deep breath, trying to stay on the right side of the line between screaming and crying. "I've loved you ever since you walked into my hospital that first time. But I can't watch you go out there again and again and wear out your luck and your body and get yourself killed and leave me—" Her voice broke. Bel gulped down enough tears to keep them off her face. She'd cried buckets the last time and it hadn't changed anything; she'd be damned if she did that again. When he leaned toward her, she shoved him back with both hands. "Don't touch me, you stupid *mojado*."

"Fine." He spun and stalked back to the house, his neck and ears bright red.

"Where are you going?"

"I'll sleep in the garage tonight."

"Wait…"

The moment the patio door closed, Bel's insides shattered. She'd driven him away, the one thing she never wanted to do. Bel squatted in the weeds, buried her face in her hands, and sobbed harder than she had since seeing Lucho in that hospital bed two years ago. She prayed she wouldn't see him there again… or in the morgue.

8

The reconstituted Zetas remain the most formidable of the narco supercartels. Their organization and reputation for extreme brutality have enabled them to establish effective control over more than 50% of the country, while their associated political front México Unido (Mexico United) (MU) stands as a serious competitor to the established PRI and PAN political parties.
-- "Unclassified Key Judgments (from October 2030 NIE)," National Intelligence Council

MONDAY, 3 MAY

McGinley spun in his desk chair at the sound of his name. Jorgensen, the FBI agent he dealt with most often, waved at him from the far end of the Joint Task Force's big open-bay office.

Jorgensen's white shirt positively glowed. "Got your runners!"

McGinley thought on this lucky break as he crossed the concrete floor to the databoard, a slate the size of a sheet of plywood hanging on the wall. It had the usual electronic notes and random pictures scattered across it, nothing he gave a damn about. Jorgensen—an Aryan poster boy for the Bureau whose shirts never seemed to get dirty—pushed the digital crap aside, double-tapped the board, then brought up six mug shots. Then he called up a seventh picture.

"Jee-sus," McGinley spat. He'd seen hundreds of these, but he never got used to seeing the heads lined up all neat on a curb, dead eyes staring out, blood dripping down the concrete. "Reckon Zetas did that?"

"So says the *narcomanta*." Jorgensen tapped the bottom edge of a white banner in the background. He then circled the left-most head with his finger, drew a yellow line to the top mug shot. "Poor bastards didn't even make it out of Mexicali."

39

Zetas in Mexicali? That far west? "What about the woman?"

Jorgensen tapped the only female mug shot. "Her? No sign. Keep an eye on your Mexican pornos. She'll probably show up in a few weeks." Once he had four of the heads linked to their camp photos, he thumped the fifth. "The coyote. Federico Salcedo, a freelancer. He's done work for Pacifico Norte over the past couple years." The Feeb thumbed the long scar under his chin. "You wanted a cartel connection? There you go, Mac. All yours."

McGinley nodded, half-listening. Pacifico Norte—put together out of bits and pieces of other cartels that went bust— owned the Baja peninsula and some of Mexico's west coast. They could mainline straight into one of the biggest markets in America.

He let his focus wander over the picture with the heads. The Mex news was full of shots like this. But this one was different in little ways he noticed over time. The blood was still red; the skin was pale, not turning black in the heat as they usually were. These heads were fresh. The web shots from down south almost always had the owners' watermarks; this one didn't.

"Does it strike you," McGinley said after a while, "that this here picture ain't a news shot? Where'd this come from?"

Jorgensen sniffed. "Never mind. It doesn't matter."

Need to know. What a wonderful thing.

McGinley stared at the woman runner's mug shot. Another gal disappeared into that shitstorm down south, one more out of thousands run through the Zeta meat grinder. *Shit.* He left Jorgensen with his expensive toy and headed for the door.

McGinley reckoned Camp Pendleton was like Yuma with a beach. Take the pistol range down the street from JTF headquarters, for instance. Leaning back against the gun bench, he could see a slice of Pacific and the oil rigs off on the horizon, one of them flaring, just like in the Gulf. There was a whole lot of brown between him and the blue, though.

Zetas in Mexicali. Did these boys out here even have a clue what that meant?

He did.

Those evil fuckers owned the Mex Gulf Coast and a big chunk of the interior and the Rio Grande, which meant they owned the Texas border. Had for years. Things stayed quiet in their half of the country, mostly because anyone who made trouble ended up as loose parts in trash bags or with their heads lined up like bowling balls. And that wasn't saved just for Mexes.

Carla Jean's face came back to McGinley.

She was such a pretty thing, smart, too, and why she'd taken up with him, he'd never understood. He hadn't believed she'd marry him until the day she did. She dragged him off to church and told him about all the do-good things she did, like she was trying to make up for all the heads he busted and dirtbags he shot. He loved her for that as much as he'd ever loved anything or anyone.

Then she went to work for a week at an orphanage the church ran in some shithole *barrio* in Matamoros and fucking *disappeared*. A Mex woman at the place had been hooked up with someone who'd pissed off the Zetas, and the Zeta way was to burn the whole family to the ground. Carla Jean and the other five women she'd gone with were just in the way.

McGinley turned, seated his ear protectors and emptied another magazine rapid-fire into the silhouette target twenty-five feet away. The spotting scope showed all fifteen rounds in the black, eleven in the nine or ten rings. Shooting was near the only thing he could focus on when his brain went back to that bloody lobby at the orphanage.

He set his pistol on the bench, braced his palms on the plywood. The ache in his gun hand felt right, like the gunpowder stink burning his nostrils. A little hurt to help him feel Carla Jean's pain.

It'd be one thing if they'd left her dead on the floor. It would've gone down hard, but at least he'd know what happened to her. Not knowing near to drove him crazy. For a time, he was in Mexico dogging those worthless bought-off Matamoros cops almost as much as he was in his own office in San Antonio. He looked at dozens of pictures like that one on Jorgensen's databoard, blowing up the faces, hoping he'd see Carla Jean and praying he wouldn't. He watched God knew how much Mex porn—another Zeta product line—to see if she'd show up. If a dead woman went on a slab in Tamaulipas or Nuevo León, he'd pound the locals until they confirmed it wasn't her. It never was.

Three years, and nothing. Gone like she'd never been.

So he'd made it a personal mission to bust every Zeta shitbag who turned up on the wrong side of the Rio Grande. They weren't hard to find. Once they'd sewed up their side of the river, they'd gone to work on McGinley's side, buying off local law so their shipments to Houston and Dallas and Tulsa and on up went through smooth as lard. Not that it was hard to buy a badge these days, Lord knew. His SAC let him run and didn't look too hard the times McGinley shot one of those fuckers for resisting or escaping.

Once he'd seized a semi northbound out of Nuevo Laredo carrying a load of Mex whores with a Zeta guard. First he broke the asshole's ankles and threw him into the trailer. Then he checked the whores' faces. No Carla Jean. Then he untied them, closed the cargo door, and waited for the guard's screaming to stop. That'd been a good day.

Now the Zetas were out here. And funny enough, so was he.

McGinley reloaded, holstered his weapon, policed up his brass. He had reports to fill out and some research to do. Then he could give some serious thought to Mexicali and the Zetas. Maybe it was time to pay another visit to that Ojeda character. That ol' boy was connected: only three steps from the top of the Nortes. He had all those nice pressure points—family, house, job—McGinley could poke. Maybe Ojeda already knew what the Nortes were doing to defend their turf.

If he didn't, McGinley could give him some real good reasons to find out.

9

*Over-the-air broadcast radio ceased as a mass
communications medium in the United States in 2023,
shortly after the similar end of broadcast television... Clear
Channel Communications and Cumulus Media now control
94% of the market for fee-based satellite and terrestrial
broadband streaming audio service in the U.S.... the U.S.
is now the only developed nation without free over-the-air
radio programming.*

-- *"History of Radio," Wikipedia*

MONDAY, 3 MAY

Luis poked at his new burner phone, trying to ignore the racket hammering out of the car's streamer. Nortec metal, like a microphone tossed in a trash compactor mashed up with accordion samples. Why was Ray listening to this crap?

He stabbed a finger at the streamer. "Turn that shit off, will you? It's giving me a headache."

"Just keeping up with the street, you know?" Ray thumbed a button on the steering wheel. Sensato rapped out "Crazy People" on the Urban Latino Oldies feed. "Man, remember this?"

Luis remembered. Out of the Army. He and Bel were still in San Diego, getting their degrees on the G.I. Bill. A whole different world.

He glanced up at what used to be the Santa Ana main library across the street. The place was a wreck: warped plywood over the windows, marble stained pigeon-shit gray. He used to go there over lunch hour to read when he'd worked for the county. "I hate coming down here," he mumbled.

"You know," Ray said, kicking back in the driver's seat, "they've got drugs for that arthritis in your thumbs. I take 'em, it works great."

Luis had to use his index fingers on the phone. "Can't afford them," he growled.

"Well, then get a new phone. Cavemen used that brick you've got."

"It's a burner. It's supposed to be cheap. Besides, that thing with the glasses? Drives me nuts."

"It does for a week or two, then you can't live without it."

Luis beat on his phone some more. Better it than Ray. "Can't afford anything better. Especially now."

Ray sighed, shook his head. "Look, *hermano…*"

"Save it. And thanks a whole fucking lot for Friday."

"I'm sorry. I didn't know Tavo was gonna unload on you like that."

"Yeah, but you sure spoke up once you found out. Oh, wait, you didn't, did you?"

"You know how Tavo gets. He—"

"No, I don't." Luis punched off his phone and glared at Ray. "You're the one who hangs with him, not me. Tell me how he gets. Then tell me how I get out from under this."

Ray clicked down the music's volume, then let his head fall back against the headrest. "Just do what you're doing. Pay it off with work. I mean, you got a fifty-grand down-payment here, you know? It won't take long—"

"The next one won't pay that, will it? Or the one after that?" Luis slashed at the air with his hands. He'd had way too much time during the weekend to stew over this mess. "What's my fee going to drop to after I pay off the first couple hundred grand? Will I be working for gas money? Tell me how Tavo gets about that."

"You think we'd do that to you?" Ray recoiled at something he saw in Luis' face. Probably the low-level anger that had been burning Luis' gut since Friday night. "Look, I feel you. I've been putting him off calling you back in. I told him you weren't ready yet. But I couldn't keep doing that, not with this."

"You did?" Confusion watered down Luis' anger for a few seconds.

"Yeah. Look, just work it off. Tavo'll play straight with you. If you want it to go faster, I can get you on a few runs moving product. You'll pay it—"

"No. You know better than that."

Ray held up his hands. "Just sayin'. You have options if you want them, you know?"

"Options? How about I just disappear with Bel?"

Ray leaned in, his face suddenly dark. "Don't fucking try it, *hermano*. Tavo told you *personally* not to do that. You run, it's like you spit in his face. He'll get the skip tracers on you, and you saw what they do. I mean, come on, Manila. You're good, but you're not that fucking good."

That picture of Vega still flashed, unwanted, through Luis' brain. It was fading, though, the more he thought about the situation and the risk to Bel. "You don't know how good I am. Me and Bel talked about this over the weekend, in between her yelling at me. She's ready to go. She's ready to pull the pin on this whole—"

"Don't be stupid." Ray stabbed a couple fingers towards Luis' nose. "I'll get you the vid of what the skip tracers did to Vega's wife, *while* they were doing it. Vega got to watch. You can show it to Bel, see if she's so hot to go then." He sat up, slapped his phone pod. "What?" He frowned. "Where?" Ray hit the steering wheel. "That wasn't the plan—"

"What's going on?" Luis asked, his voice anxious. "Did she bail?"

Ray muttered "*chipku*," then growled an address into the car's nav system. While the gunmetal-blue Lexus slid itself out of the parking lot onto westbound Civic Center, Ray pulled the battery from his phone, then turned to Luis. "She's gone squirrelly. Changed the meet."

"Will you drive the fucking car?" It was one thing to use autodrive on the open highway; Luis still didn't trust it on a city street, especially ones as bad as these.

"It's fine, don't stress." Ray clamped a big hand on Luis' shoulder. "Listen. Don't screw me on this. I'll make sure it goes right for you. But you gotta trust me, understand?"

"Sure." Luis turned away to watch the city scroll by. He couldn't afford to lose it, not now. "Know what else I understand? If this goes bad, I'm the one taking the bullet, not you."

10

Monday, 3 May

Nora stewed behind the wheel of her rented Geely sedan. She hated being penned in like this, only one way in and out, but the rotting building hid her from the street and blocked the view of any witnesses. There was no way she'd accept a meet location someone else had set up. Who knows what these *narcos* would have her walking into?

Graffittied plywood masked the old post office's glass. Scrappers had torn most of the aluminum letters from the tan brick out front. The landscaping was long dead, and trash and an old, ugly couch littered the cracked parking lot. A nasty place, but not one anybody would think to look for her. The neighborhood—if you could call it that, all barred windows and hungry-looking dog packs and rusted cars on cinder blocks—felt hostile, almost feral.

She climbed out of the car, drew her Glock, then patrolled the scene one more time. No too-shiny American cars, no men wearing dark windbreakers, no helicopters, no snipers on the rooftops, no obvious drones. The closest natives sat on a yard sofa four doors down. All was quiet except for a big dog barking down the street.

Back in the car, Nora considered how to deal with these cartel people. They weren't service workers like movers or landscapers who deserved at least basic civility. They were criminals. One thing she'd learned in the Military Police and with the Bureau was that it doesn't pay to be nice to criminals. They respect the hard line. Any sign of weakness and like those half-wild dogs down the street, they attack. Time to roll out Kick-Ass Khaled.

Luis pointed out the windshield toward their ten o'clock. "There, by the loading dock."

A silver Chinese Geely four-door—the kind all the rental-car outlets had—sat at the end of the handcart ramp leading to the dead post office's loading dock. As they crept closer, the driver's door swung open. A head in a baseball cap and sunglasses appeared above the roof. Then so did a pistol, aimed at them.

"I think that means 'stop,'" Luis told Ray.

They got out at the same time and stayed behind the Lexus' doors. Luis had his hand around the Sig's grip, ready to go. His scalp tingled. Was this some sort of trap? Their car and hers were at most twenty feet apart; if shooting started, not many rounds would miss.

Ray said, "Nora? I'm Rico, this is…" he checked Luis' face "…Juan."

Her aviator shades shifted between them. "Come out from behind the doors." She had a clear, strong command voice. She'd done this before. Luis didn't feel better for knowing that.

Ray muttered something Luis couldn't catch. "You called us here, remember?"

"Come out in the open. Keep your hands where I can see them."

Luis shot Ray a what-is-this? glance; Ray blew out a breath, then shrugged. They both slid around their doors at the same time, keeping their hands at hip level, palms flat, visible but not out of action. Leaving that door behind made Luis' gut clench.

She aimed between them, leaving her options open. "Put your weapons on the hood."

"Sorry, *chica,* no way." Ray said it with more heat than Luis liked. This woman was worth a lot of money. She could hold a gun on him for a while if she wanted… as long as she didn't shoot him.

"Uh, Rico?" Luis said. "The customer's always right."

"Not always." Ray took a couple strong steps forward. Luis had tried this ploy before; sometimes the most bad-ass dog will slink away from a show of force. Sometimes, though, it'll rip your leg off. "Look, *chica*, secure your weapon and we'll have a nice talk, like people. But if you don't stand down, one of us is going to have to put you down. Got it?"

The woman's Glock stared right at Ray. Sweat rolled down Luis' back. Would she slink or rip?

After a tense moment, she asked, "First Battalion, 26th Infantry, right?"

Luis felt his insides freeze. *How did she know that? What else does she know?*

Ray swallowed. "Say what?"

"You're Ramiro Esquivel, the plaza boss here. Aren't you, *Rico?*"

Ray literally chewed on this for a moment. "Area manager."

"You look younger than your file photo. Good trick." She slowly raised her pistol until it pointed straight up, then holstered it.

The knot in Luis' bowels loosened just a bit. "I hope you're Nora, after all that."

"I am." She edged out from behind her door, slid to her left, and touched her fingertips to the fender. She was smaller than he'd imagined, five-six or so and slender, with a black long-sleeved tee shirt tucked into fresh, dark jeans. A blue Disneyland ball cap threw a shadow over her face.

When Ray and Luis reached the other side of her car's hood, Luis could see the face in the portrait Ray had shown him: high cheekbones, thin, slightly hooked nose and full lips below her sunglasses. Her skin was about the same shade as his: light for a *Mexicano*, dark for an Anglo. Judging from the definition in her neck and hands, she was seriously fit.

Ray said, "Were you followed? Is that why you changed up on us?"

"No, no physical tail. I was just being careful. I have to be."

The aviators gave Ray an up-and-down scan. "I know who you are, but"—she jerked her chin at Luis—"who's he?"

She didn't know him. Luis felt a tingle of relief. "Your tour guide. Where's your family right now?"

"None of your business."

He'd half-expected this need-to-know shit, but she said it as if he'd asked to roast her children on a spit. Luis took a breath before he answered. "I'd hoped to meet all of you so I have some idea what I have to work with. It helps me figure out how to get you across."

She crossed her arms and aimed the mirrored shades at Luis— real sunglasses, no tell-tale data-feed glow on her cheekbone. Her mouth puckered. "Not yet. If you have to know, they're at Disneyland, where I'm supposed to be, and where my Bureau phone is. They track our phones." She looked toward Ray. "If you don't mind, can we get this over with so I can get back there? I'd like to use the ticket we paid for."

No doubt: one day would've cost over a grand for the four of them. The last time he and Bel could afford to go, Luis worked for the county and the kids were in grade school.

"If you've got that kind of money," Luis asked, "what do you need us for? Why don't you just fly out of the country and not come back?"

She gave him a tight, bitter half-smile. "If it was that easy, we would. The Bureau controls all our travel. We have to ask permission to go international, and they don't give permission unless you leave a family member behind for insurance. They'd be all over us the minute we bought tickets. They're really sensitive about losing agents."

"Defectors?" Ray said, a half-laugh in his voice.

"Yes. Defectors." Her voice got even harder. "We've lost a dozen agents to Canada just in the past year. Now they've flagged us in the system so we come up red when we scan out at a border crossing." She turned back to Luis, her mouth even tighter. "We'd *love* to do this ourselves, believe me. I arrest people like you. You're the last ones I want to come to for help, but here I am. Can we get on with this?"

Luis swapped a do-you-believe-this? look with Ray. With her attitude, they'd earn their money. Ray's shrug said Luis could walk out on this job anytime.

If only he could.

He turned back to Nora. It bothered him that he couldn't see her eyes. It was like talking to a robot, which he still wasn't used to. "How old are your kids?"

Her mouth worked while she digested this. "Six and four."

Luis flashed back to the little girl on his last disastrous run, that silent bundle under her dead mom. "Well, that makes things harder. Littles don't understand secrets or using a fake name. They don't have our stamina. You can't tell what they're going to say."

"If you're trying to tell me to go without them, forget it. We leave as a family, end of discussion. All right?"

"Yes, ma'am." He asked Ray, "We working their IDs?"

"The lab's standing by. We still need photos, prints and scans."

Nora asked, "How good are your IDs?"

"Good enough for this," Luis told her. He could usually tap-dance around the subject and normal travelers didn't know the difference. He knew better than to try that now. "They'll get you through a Level 1 scan about 98% of the time. Level 2's maybe fifty percent. It's hard to beat the databases. With any luck, you'll only have to use them once."

Her mouth turned down. "They'd better work. I'm paying enough for them."

Travelers were usually grateful, not bitchy like her. Luis counted to five before he replied. "We're going to need to see all of you very soon. I need ID photos of the kids, and we'll need to change your face and your husband's."

"Change our faces? Why? Aren't we hiking out? I thought that's how it's done."

Ray shook his head. "Are you going to argue with everything, *chica?*"

The glasses stared at Ray for a few long beats. "I may not speak Spanish, but I know what *chica* means." Ice cubes clinked in her voice. "If you call me that again, I'll shoot you. Do you understand?"

50

Chica? Seriously? She'd put up with enough of that crap in the Bureau; she certainly wouldn't take it from this scum. Let him get away with it and he'd grope her next.

This Esquivel meathead must've caught that she was serious. He put up both hands and said, "Five-by-five."

The other one—Juan, not his real name—tapped the Geely's hood to get her attention. "We can't go overland because of the kids, so we'll have to try to take you through a crossing. We'll need to get you past the facial recognition to do that." He gave her a thin smile. "Don't worry, you won't end up looking like some movie monster."

While Juan spoke, the Esquivel jerk had snapped a battery onto his phone pod. He now stepped away from the car, tapped his earpiece, then said "It's me." She couldn't hear the conversation by the time he reached the ramp.

Nora swapped stares with Juan for a moment. "Okay, I get it. You might as well know, the more information you give me, the better I do. How long have you been doing this?"

"Since the beginning."

Twelve years? That would make him one of their senior *coyotes.* Good; they were taking this seriously.

Juan tapped the hood again. "Did the *mapache* back East tell you how this works?"

"You mean the Baja 'trade representative'? Not really."

"Okay, the short version. I get you over the border and hand you off to my guy down there. He takes you to the Tijuana airport and puts you on a plane to Mexico City. Once you're there, you're on your own. We don't care where you go." Juan's face turned sour for a moment. "I guess this is where I remind you I'll be taking your family into the middle of a civil war."

Like she needed the reminder. "I'm aware of that."

"Okay. Since you're FBI, I guess you're a citizen."

"I was *born* here." She used to be proud to say that. Now it made her mad to have to keep repeating it. "So was Paul, so were the kids. How often do *you* get asked that?"

"Pretty often, these days. Why are you doing this?"

"Why do you care?"

"I'm sticking my neck out for you. I need to know what it

means to you."

Nora paused to size him up again. This Juan wasn't anything like she'd expected. He was mature, businesslike, not some swaggering, macho young punk. Even though the flop sweat under his arms showed he was nervous, his eyes were… calm? Was that the word? At least he wasn't looking at her like some bimbo in a bar, the way the other guy had.

"Probably the same reason your other customers do it."

"I don't think so. You've got a secure job, you've got money. Why are you leaving?"

She should just blow him off. It wasn't his business. On the other hand, Juan was going into harm's way for her. She couldn't bring herself to curry favor with him, but she could at least align his interests with hers. Besides, she didn't have to tell him everything— just enough.

"My husband is a lawyer. Paul's chief counsel for the Arab American Institute. It's a K Street lobby back home, the last Islamic one left." She glanced toward Esquivel to confirm he was still out of hearing range. "I found out they're going on the list of groups that support terrorism."

"They don't, do they?"

She kicked out a short, nasty little laugh. "Of course not, not that it matters. Look at what happened to the ACLU and the SPLC."

"SPLC?"

"Southern Poverty Law Center. No, they'll go on the list and Paul will be in a camp in a week. I'll lose my security clearance, and then I'll lose my job and I'll probably end up in a camp, too." She heard the anger in her voice and tried to squash it. He didn't need to know how much this insanity hurt her. "But they won't let me be Paul's cellmate or anything. They'll send me someplace special because of what I know. Pecos, maybe, or Dugway." She licked her lips, turning her gaze toward the dead gas station next door. This part was the hardest. "Then the kids… they'll give our kids to some white couple who'll turn them into good Christians. That's what they do to orphaned Muslim kids, did you know that?"

"I had no idea. I know sometimes they put them in camps, too."

"Yes, the darker ones. The ones they can't foster out." She checked Esquivel—still on the phone—then focused on Juan. "That's why I'm doing this. Is it a good enough reason for you?"

He nodded. "Yeah. If it's true."

Nora geared up to let him have it for questioning her, then stopped. Suspicion cut both ways. Or had he picked up the editing she'd done on her story?

Esquivel jogged to the car, his feet crunching on broken glass and litter. "Sorry, folks. We good here?"

"We're good," Juan said. Nora nodded.

"Okay. Nora, that number you called me from—is it a burner?"

"Yes."

"Good. Hold onto it. We'll call you in a day or two." Esquivel grabbed Juan's elbow and turned to go.

"Wait a minute." Nora put her fists on her hips. Now that Esquivel was back, she could feel her blood pressure rising. "Make it fast. We have eleven days of vacation left. If we're not back home by the end of it, they'll come after us. I don't want to be on this side of the border when that happens."

"We'll go as fast as we can and still be safe," Juan said.

Somehow, she wasn't reassured.

"She's gonna be a pain in the ass," Luis said. But at least now he sort-of understood why. She had a pretty good life, and it was about to get blown up; he'd be bitchy, too. Not that it mattered—it was still worth the fifty-grand down-payment on his debt. That's all she had to be: a walking paycheck.

"No shit," Ray said.

The car drove eastbound on 17th, crashing over potholes and busted pavement, Pitbull rapping on the oldies feed. The pipe-stall-and-tarp jumbles of street markets in the parking lots of failed strip malls added back some of the color lost from the faded signs and bleached paint. Vidboards flashed splashy moving ads for booze and cigarettes and guns. Gray smoke and smog hid the hills in the distance. Luis was glad for the car's A/C so he didn't have to smell the place.

Ray smirked. "Maybe this'll make it hurt a little less. That call? That was Tavo. Looks like he's the new *capo*, at least for now. He's out of this."

"This? You mean Nora?"

"Yeah. He's cleaning house down south; he doesn't have time. So he gave it to me."

"Meaning?"

"Meaning I get Nora sorted out, I get the money." He shrugged. "He's buying loyalty. I get it. He probably needs all he can get. But who cares? It's a wad."

That got Luis' full attention. "How much?"

"Two hundred large." Ray grinned at him. "Want half?"

Half? A hundred grand? That would wipe out a quarter of what he owed the Cartel. But why would Ray just hand him that kind of bonus? Then it hit him: Tavo was moving up. So might Ray. He was buying loyalty, too. And it was a bribe to not run away. "You serious?"

"There's a catch. I can't deal with that *bruja*, I'll strangle her. You do it. Set her up, take her south, get rid of her. Believe me, she stays like that"—he thumbed out the back window—"you'll earn it. Deal?"

Luis tried to trace all the strings wrapped around Ray's gift but got lost in the tangle. It couldn't be worse than a short life on the run, though. They shook hands over the shift knob. "Deal."

11

TUESDAY, 4 MAY

While he waited for a call from his boss back in San Antonio, McGinley sat at his JTF desk going through his Zeta message-traffic draw. He called it his "shitbag file." Every workday for three years, he'd had a bot rake through all the law-enforcement and collateral databases it could get to for anything about Zetas north of the border. It came up empty every once in a while, but not often.

And not today. Feeb reports, Border Patrol logs, an update to the CIA wiki about a Mex politician the Zetas owned. The usual.

Then he read an ICE arrest report filed through the El Paso Enforcement and Removal Operations field office. Some troop tripped over a blacked-out panel van with a flat tire on U.S. 180 northbound out of Deming, New Mexico. When he stopped, the stupid son-of-a-bitch trying to change the tire drew down on him, and the ICE troop put the scumbag away. The knucklehead's Zeta tat wasn't hard to find. Inside the van, the ICE troop found half a dozen whores in what the report called "poor condition"—no doubt drugged up and starving—and the usual guns and drugs. *Good work*, McGinley told the agent.

He skimmed the particulars on the whores—habit by now—and disregarded the obvious Mex ones. But one stopped him cold.

```
U/I NHWF, unresponsive, app. 30-35, app.
5'3", app. 80#, red/blue. DNA/prints
submitted for ID.
```

Unidentified non-Hispanic white female. Sure to catch McGinley's eye whenever and wherever he saw it. Carla Jean might be a *U/I NHWF* if she ever turned up.

Unless Carla Jean had done some serious changing, though, this girl wasn't her: two inches too short, blue eyes instead of green, red hair instead of blond. This one was probably some dumb little twinkie who'd reckoned to make her fortune on her back with some *narco* boss and ended up hooked on kronk, servicing *sicarios* out of a single-wide somewhere. Still, he'd follow up. That, too, was habit by now. He shot an email at the arresting agent asking for the whore's ID when it came back from the lab.

12

*"A: Clearing through an official CBP border crossing or
port station is required before leaving the United States.
This ensures DHS agencies will receive prompt notification
should you fail to return by your intended date and time.
The State Department and CBP can then determine
whether you have been detained or injured during your
stay abroad."*
-- Traveler Safety Initiative FAQ, *U.S. Customs & Border
Protection*

TUESDAY, 4 MAY

The Customs and Border Protection trooper handed the ID back to Luis without comment after a Level 2 scan, then moved on to the old Ford two-door next in line.

The trooper's buddy wasn't done with Luis' Cartel-loaner Hyundai Tucson SUV. He was a Latino kid, head shaved almost bald, probably just over the minimum height requirement of five-six. A surgical mask covered the bottom half of his face to filter out the smog, just like so many other people on the streets now. His tan utilities had turned brown with sweat even though the morning wasn't all that hot yet.

"What're you guys looking for?" Luis asked. "When I worked El Paso, we never searched outbound, just inbound."

The young guard hauled his stick-mounted mirror out from under the Tucson and peered over his sunglasses at Luis. "You was an agent?"

"A few years ago." More than one person had told Luis he looked like a cop when he put on reflector shades and a button-down shirt. He wore both today, along with a battered CBP ball cap. It used to work wonders while he hunted intel. Had that changed too?

"Huh." The kid chewed his gum a few times. "Ragheads. They skip on a camp, we get BOLOs, you know."

"Oh, yeah. I heard about that." Luis glanced back at the Ford. He could just make out the red warning box on the trooper's slate, signaling a busted scan. The driver—a young, dark-haired woman—was about to have a real bad day.

"You're clear, mister." The kid shouldered his mirror and headed for the Ford.

Luis checked his watch: ten to nine. Ninety-plus minutes in line waiting to get to this point. He was committed to crossing now, which meant another hour-plus down the drain waiting to come back in. He still had nearly two hundred miles of shitty roads to cover to hit all the border posts from here to the Colorado. Since he was considering moving Nora during the daytime, he needed to finish recon before sunset. He couldn't afford to miss two days of work for this; the Cartel was going to get all the money, not him.

A few minutes later, he broke free from the traffic on Boulevard Ganta de Otay heading into Nuevatijuana. He cut east on the broad, jumbled De las Bellas Artes until he reached a knot of semi-new clinics and dentists' offices. He stopped outside a *farmacia*, picked up some Piraflox antibiotics for Bel's medical bag—his cover reason for being here—then found a *panadería* and got a *café de olla* and *pan dulce* to help him think.

If a boat was still doable, this would be the perfect job for one. He'd used that option a dozen times or more before the blockade went up. Now the Navy and Coast Guard had a picket line of ships stretching fifteen miles out to sea off the border, and Border Patrol boats infested the water off Imperial Beach south of San Diego. Anything going either direction got boarded and searched with dogs or thermal scanners. Officially it was to catch refugees or drug shipments from down south, even though the drugs moved up in semis or were made in the U.S. and refugees knew better than to come north.

Twelve years ago, armed shakedowns by Mexican border police were the biggest danger at the land crossings. Hardly anyone cared who went south; it would've taken maybe ten minutes to get across the border. Then CBP started scanning IDs, supposedly so it would be easier to tell if tourists fell into the shit down here. Few people noticed that the change happened when hundreds of Muslims were fleeing the camps every day, causing a PR nightmare on YouTube or foreign news shows once across the border. Luis noticed; he'd barely escaped arrest on his third run south because of it.

Two years ago, CBP checked only IDs. Now they were giving southbound traffic the same going-over as northbound. Tijuana and Otay Mesa—the two busiest crossings in California—were both backed up for hours. Busy was okay to a point; people could get lost in it. But every minute spent waiting in line was one less minute before your luck ran out. *Pass.*

Luis threaded through the rocky, drought-baked foothills of the Laguna Mountains eastbound on State 94 to Tecate, eighteen miles from Otay Mesa as the vulture flies but forty by road. The roads hadn't been repaved since he was a kid, so a drive that had once taken an hour now needed twice that. His windows radiated heat that the A/C was just able to beat down.

An oncoming county black-and-white SUV with a low-profile light bar closed slowly enough for its forward-facing camera to suck up his license plate. After re-entering at Otay Mesa, Luis had switched the electronic plates to a number used by another Tucson of the same color but didn't have any control over which one. This cop might run his tags just for fun, see that this car was registered in San Francisco and decide to find out what it was doing down here.

Luis' hands clamped hard on the wheel. He checked his speed, watched the cop's brake lights flare in the mirror. The Cartel's on-board license-plate app didn't check the owner's record. Was the registered owner wanted for something?

The deputy—a contractor, according to the corporate logo decals on the SUV's tailgate—disappeared around a corner. Luis pried his hands from the wheel one at a time and wiped his palm-sweat on his jeans. Welcome back to the family business.

He remembered these mountains well. Years ago, his dad had taken him on long hikes out here, taught him how to read maps and navigate at night. He could still hear the coyotes yip, the moan of a startled cow, scree skittering downslope under his feet. Hiding from the occasional San Diego County sheriff's car or Border Patrol cruiser rolling by, always too close, too slow.

Luis had known Alvaro was training him for something. He didn't know *what* exactly until that first night when he helped his dad herd twenty-some *migrantes* into Imperial County. Luis had been ten years old and nearly as terrified as the people he'd been guiding.

He helped on his father's last half-dozen runs before the cartels moved in on the work and border security became too difficult to avoid. The experience helped him on those long route marches up and down the jagged landscape of Afghanistan. It had also drawn Tavo's attention. Not for the first time, Luis wished Alvaro had pushed him into playing soccer instead.

Luis reached Tecate by 12:30. It was little more than a collection of scrubby lots, a few sagging ranch houses and a diner. Two CBPs in utilities circulated around the half-dozen cars waiting to pass through the sleepy two-lane crossing. *This could work.*

Another hour and thirty-five road miles brought him to Jacumba, a recent ghost town smashed against the border. A swarm of tan Border Patrol BRV-Os and contractors infested the weedy main street. The sun glinted off the standing-seam metal roofs on the guard towers. Luis didn't bother to stop. *Pass.*

Eastbound Interstate 8, Imperial County. Pavement choppy from the triple-bottom semis. Glare from the sinking sun fired the dust on the Tucson's back window. The hacked FasTrak pass beeped every couple miles, spitting out garbage data to the toll sensors. The sprawling, boxy factories and warehouses to the north blushed slightly in the mid-afternoon light. To the south, beyond the worker slums and shanty towns, the dark mountains of Mexico floated above the haze.

Luis switched the car to autodrive, then stretched and twisted to work the kinks out of his back and butt, which had turned to lead. He couldn't afford to stop for a rest.

Cabbage and onion fields used to stretch green to the horizon on both sides before the *maquiladoras* came up here to escape the Mexican civil war. Smog and garbage stink had replaced the old, inescapable smells of fertilizer, dirt, and ripening vegetables. His dad had worked the fields out here the first year after he'd come to *El Norte*. Alvaro still had the wide-brimmed straw hat he'd worn during harvest, just to remind them all how far he'd come.

Calexico West, Calexico East: Otay Mesa all over again, mile-long lines of semis hauling cheap stuff from the *maquiladoras* southbound into Mexicali. CBP contractors hassled drivers, poked through trunks and cargo beds. *Pass.*

Andrade, fifty miles and seventy-five minutes east of Calexico. It was a dusty wide spot on State 186, a casino and two trailer parks, all three full of snowbirds who'd spent their last dime to get this far and couldn't afford to fly back home or keep going. The thermometer on the rear-view mirror said it was 107° outside. Thank God he had this Cartel loaner. His old truck's A/C didn't cool anything anymore.

Luis paid his ten bucks to park in the huge lot the Quechan Indians ran at the border. He found a spot near the CBP booth. From there he could watch from behind the safety of the Hyundai's blacked-out windows as a line of people stuttered through the checkpoint to see a doctor or dentist in Los Algodones on the Mexican side. A much longer line of people across the street waited to come back in.

While he watched—tracking the guards, timing the lines—he took stock.

The big crossings were out. The easy overland routes were walled up tight. In the old days, he'd used a couple of his dad's tracks through the Sierra Juarez east of Jacumba, but those required heavy hiking. Adults could do it, babies could ride, but four-to-six-year-olds were at that awkward age when they're too small to walk far and too heavy to carry. That left Tecate and this place. Not much of a choice.

There was always Arizona.

Luis turned his head toward the black spew from the big, new coal-fired powerplant by Yuma's airport, seven miles away. It was tempting. Once inside, there were plenty of options for crossing. The Arizonans didn't care who left, just who came in.

No, Luis warned himself. *That's like going back to the Wild West.* Hostile natives, brutal cops. He didn't like to take travelers into the state; one wrong word or move and they might get lynched, him along with them. That *gabacho* contractor had shot him over there, just yards from the border.

And crossing from Arizona would put him into Sonora. Zeta country. Enemy territory.

Pass. Big time.

The easy way out was the old-school way: go through a friendly guard at a crossing. The Cartel had compromised all the border stations in California; it was high time he took advantage of it. Nora and Company wouldn't stand out the way a mixed group of women, teens and old people would. They'd need only one or two guards on the Cartel's payroll to pull it off. Someplace small and quiet, like here or Tecate. Maybe Ray could use his juice and be helpful after all. This could be faster and easier than he'd figured.

Luis cranked the Hyundai to life. With any luck, he'd make it back home before Bel went to bed. He left the parking lot and drove into the setting sun.

13

Following its suborning of over half the regular Mexican army, the Zeta cartel's armed wing has returned to its roots as a special operations force. It is also tasked with intelligence, electronic warfare, internal security and targeted assassinations... These forces are assessed to be responsible for most of the atrocities associated with the Zetas.

-- "Unclassified Key Judgments (from October 2030 NIE)," National Intelligence Council

TUESDAY, 4 MAY

Tavo watched the two bloody, naked men twist slowly from the chains linking their wrists to the barn's roof truss. Their blood dripped onto the concrete pad a few inches below their feet, dribbling into the drain in the center. He butchered hogs here for roasting during fiestas. "Anything new?" he asked the thin man standing between his two projects.

Ruelas methodically rubbed a wet towel over his bare chest and fire-scarred left arm. The towel was nearly pink by now. "No, *patrón*. Tenorio and Flores are the only two they named. They know nothing else."

That was bad enough. He'd seen the dark looks and subtle signals those two had been throwing during Nestor's funeral that morning. Now was the time to deal with them, as they slept off the food and drink from the reception. Rebellion was contagious.

"Is there anything left to be got from them?" he asked Ruelas.

"No, *patrón*."

Tavo grabbed the five-pound sledgehammer leaning against the nearby wooden table, circled behind the hanging men and slammed the hammer's head into the backs of their skulls. Just like killing cattle. "Good work. Feed them to the sharks."

He dropped the sledge by the drain, pivoted and marched toward the stripe of night showing between the barn's big doors. His bodyguard slotted into step behind him. Since his lieutenants in Baja Sur and Nayarit refused to accept his succession to Nestor's position, he'd fire them. Permanently. He tapped his phone pod. "Jericó? I have a job for you."

Outside, the loamy smells of earth and grapevines overlaid the smoke drifting from the fire pits of his Ensenada vineyard's fiesta ground. All the lights were off in the house on the rise ahead. That was odd. "Jericó?"

A *splat* sound, then the thud of a body. Tavo spun to find his bodyguard splayed out on the ground, a dark patch covering much of his forehead.

Before Tavo could react, a bullet smashed through his right shin. Instantly he was face-down on the ground screaming from the pain, his lower leg useless and on fire. He managed to roll on his side, grit his teeth. He'd dropped his gun. "Jericó! Where are you?"

His chief of security didn't answer. Instead, a dark human shape grew out of the ground about ten meters to his left. Then another. And another. Small red dots danced over his chest as the men drew near.

Tenorio's and Flores' men? No, too fast. They'd hardly had time to make this move... unless they'd planned to eliminate Nestor themselves, before he did.

Five men converged on him out of the night: tactical gear, balaclavas, night-vision goggles. Their boots rustled against the gravel. Tavo considered pretending to have a gun, making these bastards shoot him instead of letting them capture him. Before he could push that thought through his stuttering brain, he was surrounded.

The man in front of him stepped forward casually. He dangled a bulging plastic Walmart bag from one hand, shone the beam of a Mini Maglite in Tavo's face with the other. Tavo tried to shield his eyes with his hand.

"Octavio," the man said with a smile in his voice, as if greeting an old friend. "We missed you at the house. A very handsome house."

"Just kill me, *cabrón*," Tavo growled through his pain. "I won't tell you anything."

The man laughed. "No, no, no, we won't kill you yet. We need you. And yes, you'll tell us everything eventually. Everyone does, you know."

Tavo struggled to prop himself up on his elbow. "Who sent you? Tenorio? Flores?"

"No, no." The man shook his head. "You had a very beautiful wife, Octavio."

It took a moment for the word "had" to seep into Tavo's head. Anger mixed with horror exploded inside him. Then he knew: these were Zetas. "What have you done to Pilar? Where is she? You—"

The man upended the Walmart bag. Its contents thumped to the gravel half a meter from Tavo's face.

Pilar's dead eyes watched him scream.

14

"The Bureau's ability to track and arrest fugitives has improved by an order of magnitude in the past ten years... We can seize and monitor a person's entire electronic footprint in less than an hour. This capability helps us to apprehend the average fugitive in less than three days."
-- Director of the FBI, in testimony before the House Judiciary Committee, 22 February 2030

WEDNESDAY, 5 MAY

One a.m. Nora was wide awake, staring at the dark ceiling. Paul buzzed softly next to her, on his side facing away. She'd always envied his ability to sleep no matter what. The whispering and giggling out in the suite's living room had died out, meaning the kids had finally gotten over the excitement of going to that live pirate dinner show and now slept on the sofabed.

She was too wound up to even close her eyes. The reality of what she'd done, what she was about to do, crashed in on her after meeting Juan on Monday. She'd hardly slept since. In a few days, they'd be leaving this country forever. Leaping into the unknown.

Nora slid out of bed, padded to the window, and peeked out through the blackout curtains as she had for half the night before.

Their hotel was a few blocks south of Disneyland; their room was on the fifth floor at the front. A long driveway stretched empty to the big street—Harbor Boulevard—and a platoon of palm trees stood in neat lines. The Indian restaurant on the corner was dark, as were the businesses across the street. The orangeish streetlights (they worked here) glared off the occasional passing car. Hardly any windows in the two hotels on either side of theirs had lights on. Even the pools were dark.

Stop making yourself nuts. It's going to work.

Something caught her eye to her left. She moved to the far

right-hand side of the windows and squinted into the floodlit night.

A reflection on a wall. A flashing blue light.

Then she noticed the back end of a black SUV and a man in a dark windbreaker. "FBI" in large, yellow letters on his back.

Her heart plummeted to her knees.

"Paul, get up!" she barked. "They're here. They're coming for us."

"Wha? Honey, how—"

"Get up! Get the kids up! We have to go!"

She jumped into a cleanish pair of jeans, tucked in her sleep shirt—no time for underwear—jammed on her gym shoes and Disneyland ball cap. Paul was already in the suite's living room, rousting the kids. Nora dumped all their toiletries in a plastic hotel laundry bag, stuffed it into her carry-on bag with the slates, her purse, pendant, burner phone, and weapon.

"Mommy, what's happening?" Hope whined when Nora rushed into the living room.

"Just get dressed, Cupcake."

They were in the corridor overlooking the enclosed atrium in less than five minutes. Nora took point, led them into the nearest stairwell. No cameras here. Multiple sets of heavy, echoing feet jogged up the stairs below. She led her family on tiptoes up to the seventh-floor landing. The feet and jingling web gear burst through a door two floors below.

Safe. But only for a moment.

The Bureau, here? Her stomach started the slow process of turning itself inside out.

Assume the worst. She'd done everything she could to not set off the Bureau's alarms, to not leave a trail at headquarters, but even the hardest-packed sand shows footprints. But why would they have looked? It didn't matter; obviously they had. What next? A BOLO to all the field offices. A warrant for—no, forget the warrant, a national security letter, no judges—freeze what's left of the bank accounts, search the house, track the rental car, track Paul's phone, track her work phone.

Her Bureau phone. She'd left it on the dresser. That might buy them a minute or two.

What's their next move? Come up all four stairwells, recall the elevators to the ground floor, post guards on all the exits. They'd have someone at the car. There might be a chopper or a drone overhead to spot anyone leaving the hotel. Any minute now, the entry team would discover she was gone and the beds were still warm. Then they'd search all the common areas. After that, all the guest rooms.

They were out of the room, but she and her family were still in a cage.

The kids hung onto each other, their eyes sleepy but scared. Nora squatted before them. "I need you both to be very, very quiet, okay?" she whispered. "You need to do everything I say and Daddy says and don't ask why."

"Why?" Hope whispered.

"Are we in trouble?" Peter asked.

"Shh. I'll explain later." She tried to smile at them—it felt completely wrong—then stood and stepped close enough to Paul to whisper in his ear. "They're after me, not you, not with all this force. If we get stuck, I'll lead them away. You get the kids out and call Juan, okay?"

"No way," he hissed back. "I'm not letting you—"

"Don't argue." She hated to cut him off, but this wasn't the time. "Take the batteries out of the slates and your phone." Nora kissed Paul, patted down some of his bedhead, then kicked off her shoes. "Watch the kids. I'll be right back."

The gray-painted concrete steps were cool against her bare feet as she tiptoed down to the landing just above the fifth floor. Her brain clicked into combat mode, shoving her emotions into a mental closet and spinning up the part that made plans and decisions. *Complete the mission. Get out, get safe.*

Boots paced on the next landing down. A radio squawked. "Sierra Eight," a voice grumbled. Pause; then, "Negative, Sierra Six, all clear."

Nora filled in the pause: "Did you see them?"

She'd reconned the hotel after they checked in. Each corner of each floor had a camera covering the two intersecting corridors and the stairwell door. The one on the fifth floor would've caught a perfect picture of her whole family charging into the stairwell…

which the command team would be seeing just about now.

Guards in the stairwell. Cameras in the halls. Trapped.

Back on seven, Nora tugged on her shoes while her brain sorted through the possibilities. A search team would be in this stairwell any second. She and her family had to be gone by then.

The only logical move was the most illogical one.

"We're going up." She pointed toward the ceiling. "Quiet."

The little sounds they made climbing the steps—clinks, sniffles, the squeak of a rubber sole on concrete—banged off the cinder-block walls. Every moment, Nora expected SWAT or the Quick Reaction Team to burst through the doors above and below them.

As they passed ten, a metal door squeaked open a few floors below. Nora caught the hush of a whisper, the tinkling of web-gear hardware. The search team, in stealth mode. She glanced behind her. Paul was two steps down, his arms wrapped around Peter, pressing her son's face into Paul's neck. She hefted Hope, patted her back and resumed the climb.

At each landing, she held up a hand and stopped to listen. Rubber soles scraped concrete a few flights below. Radios hissed, then fell silent. They were getting closer.

As she climbed, Nora considered what they might find when they reached the top. If the Bureau had a helicopter, it would be circling at roof level, and the pilot and spotter would be wearing NVGs. There'd be no way out. But choppers were expensive and loud, and she hoped the QRT brought their small drones instead. They'd fly twenty or thirty feet above the ground so their cameras could pick out the faces of anyone exiting the building, leaving the roof open.

Nora scurried up the last two flights of stairs to the roof level. As she set Hope on the floor, her daughter opened her mouth to say something. Nora pressed her fingers across Hope's lips, shook her head. Paul made the landing, deposited Peter next to his sister, and sighed in relief. "Long way up," he gasped.

"Shh." Nora pressed her ear against the metal door leading outside. She heard the hum of machinery, Paul's panting, the kids' squirming next to her, and the relentless scratch of boot soles on concrete drawing closer. No helicopter. She held up a finger to

Paul, took a deep breath, and slipped outside.

She crouched on the steel-lattice deck, watching for moving lights or heat distortion in the city lightscape beyond the roof. No alarms, no camera above the door, no helicopter. Just a flickering florescent bulb in a metal cage. *Praise Allah.*

She pulled open the door and beckoned to her family. Paul herded the kids out. "Now what?" he whispered in her ear.

"Go to the back of the building. Stay low, move fast. Go inside the next stairwell but stay at the top. Wait for me."

"Wait." He grabbed her arm. "Where are you going?"

"I have to do something. I'll just be a minute." She hoped. Nora stepped back into the stairwell and carefully closed the door behind her.

Shuttling between stairwells wasn't going to fool anyone very long. They had to get away, but they couldn't just walk out past the guards and drones watching the exits. They needed a diversion, something to overload the Bureau teams.

Like a fire alarm.

The boot-shuffling sounded very close now. Nora slithered down the steps, her heart thudding at triple time. Every second she expected to see men pointing guns at her. She craned her head to see around the corner at the bottom of the first flight. Nobody on fourteen, the top floor, but she could clearly hear breathing.

Nora scrambled down the last stairs, not caring how much noise she made—they'd know where she was soon enough—and burst out into the atrium. She yanked the plastic fire alarm handle so hard it broke off in her hand. An ear-splitting drone filled the hotel, drilling through her skull. Nora pelted down the corridor toward the opposite stairwell. A glance behind: the first agent had just leaped into the corridor. She crashed through the metal door, dashed up to the roof again, burst out into the warm night.

The alarm wasn't as obnoxious outside. She jogged to the building's opposite corner where her family waited, picturing elevators full of SWAT and QRT heading to the fourteenth floor to flood down all four stairwells. They'd assume she'd try to get down to the ground floor. Going up made no sense—she'd be trapped with no way out except over the side.

They didn't know her family wouldn't be the only ones going

down the stairs.

In the northwest stairwell, both the kids buried their heads in Paul's stomach to escape the noise, while Paul plugged his ears with his index fingers. His grimace told her it wasn't working. His lips said, "Let's go!" but she couldn't tell if he spoke or just mouthed the words.

Nora shook her head at him, held up a hand to signal "stay," then ran down to the landing between the roof and fourteenth floor. As the first confused, sleepy people in bathrobes stumbled out through the door just below, a pair of SWAT agents shoved through them and pounded down the stairs, carbines ready. She signaled to Paul to come down slowly.

By the time they passed the tenth floor, a herd of thirty or more evacuees surrounded them, some fully dressed, some in sweats or shorts, others in less. Nearly half were children; she and Paul blended in perfectly carrying the kids. Nora put her ball cap on Paul. She set Hope down on the landing above eight, rummaged through the carry-on and found her dark-blue FBI fleece. She turned it inside-out to hide the seal, pulled it over her sleepshirt, then flipped up its hood. At least she didn't look so much like what the cameras had seen of her.

An Asian man in an FBI windbreaker stood at the fifth-floor stairwell door, watching the crowd go by. Nora's heart tripped into overdrive. What if he recognized her? Could she attack one of her own? She hefted Hope higher in her arms, looked down at her feet, and tried to avoid the agent's gaze. She saw his eyes flick from face to face, sometimes shifting to get a better angle. Occasionally he'd glance at the slate in his hand. Nora managed to catch a glimpse: a stillframe from the hotel security video, just minutes old.

Nora shuffled past the agent.

Hope blocked her view, and his. She saw his head bob, trying to look at her face. Her flight instinct sparked through all her muscles. She'd run if she had to, put Hope down and bull her way through the crowd. She wouldn't get very far, but it only had to be far enough to let Paul get away with the kids.

No shout, no hand on her shoulder. She turned the corner to go down the next flight of stairs. Nora started to breathe again. She hugged Hope, said a little prayer of thanksgiving. This was going to work. It *had* to work.

On the ground floor, a SWAT guy just outside the alarmed exit door had a finger jammed in one ear and all his attention on his radio. Nora slipped past him, melting through the knot of shuffling evacuees into the parking lot. A drone whined overhead, paused, then its blinking red marker light disappeared around the next corner. So far, so good.

Paul herded the kids around Nora. "Now what?"

She'd walked the grounds when they checked in. A parking lot surrounded the hotel, leaving no cover for fifty yards behind the building. Behind that, a Ryantown in an old park.

Nora pointed toward the tents and draped tarps crowding the long-dead grass. Here and there she could see people moving around or watching the show at the hotel. "We're homeless now," she said. "Let's go meet the neighbors."

15

Ryantown is the popular term used in the United States to describe organized encampments of unhoused people on abandoned or neglected land, especially former public lands such as parks... A 2030 UN-HABITAT study revealed that 81% of Ryantown residents of all ages are employed, but at wage levels that do not support traditional housing arrangements within practical proximity of their workplaces.

-- "Ryantown," Wikipedia

WEDNESDAY, 5 MAY

A distant ringing sound dredged Luis out of a dream that evaporated the moment before he was awake enough to remember it. Why was the bed so hard? Then it came to him: he and Bel were still playing emotional chicken, and he was still sleeping in the garage. Damnit.

He fumbled for the burner phone next to him on Rilie's ratty, fake Turkish rug. "Huh?"

"Mr. Juan? It's Nora."

What the fuck? He pried open his eyes, squinted at the time on the phone's screen. Two-eleven. "What's wrong?"

Her hesitation woke him up. "The Bureau… came for us at the hotel. We got out—"

Luis hijacked the conversation. "Where are you? Are you safe?"

"For now, I think. We're in a Ryantown behind the Embassy Suites on Harbor south of Disneyland. It looks like it's on an old driving range."

"Cops?"

"They're all over the hotel. Locals and Bureau."

After they got done with the hotel guests, they'd widen the search, start busting up the Ryantown. Nora and her people didn't have much time left. Luis woke his personal phone, brought up Google Maps, zoomed in on the area and switched to satellite view. "You need to get out of there ASAP. Did you leave your work phone in the hotel?"

"Yes," she snapped. "We also took the batteries out of Paul's phone and our slates."

"Good move. Are you with someone now, or just hanging out?"

"We're with Jiminy Cricket."

"What?"

"She works at Disneyland. She wears the Jiminy Cricket costume. I guess she can't afford rent. Why?"

"Keep moving. See if she can get you into the neighborhood just west of the park. I'll pick you up at the apartments on Chapman—that's south of you—just east of Debbie Lane. Cricket should know where that is. Hide in the parking stalls until I call you. Got it?"

"Okay. How long will it take? The kids are scared to death."

"I'll be there. Give it an hour."

Or less. He needed the money more than the cops did.

⬤

A police helicopter picked its way across the sleeping neighborhood next to the apartments, its spotlight stabbing into the back yards below it. Its clatter filled Nora's ears and brain. Did the locals have drones out, too? Ones that could pick up their infrared signatures in these carports? Waiting was agony, but she had no choice. It was up to the *narco*.

Nora's hand ached from trying to crush her burner phone. The last time Juan called, he said he'd be here in a couple minutes. So where was he? "Do you see him?" she snapped at Paul.

"I'll tell you if I do, all right?" He was in the next garage over, lost in the darkness.

The kids hid in the shadows behind Paul, eerily silent. She hadn't told them that their lives were about to change forever. Now they'd learned in the worst possible way, and it was all her fault.

Paul announced, "A car's coming."

A sedan's red taillights and white backup lights rushed down the driveway toward them. Nora drew her weapon and slipped into Paul's garage. Another unneeded bucket of adrenaline drenched her system. What would she do if it was a cop? Could she shoot a badge?

The car—a newish Toyota—chirped to a halt under the balcony overhanging the next garage. The locks clunked. Nora slithered toward the opaque driver's window, pistol ready.

The glass whirred down. Juan scowled at her. "Get in. Now."

The car darted out of the driveway before Nora could even grab her seat belt. They jolted onto a broad street flanked by apartments and split by the dead landscaping of a median strip.

Juan demanded, "Were you followed?"

"Not that I saw." Nora buckled up, then stretched to touch Paul's knee in the back seat. He cradled Hope, whispering to her as she blubbed into his chest. Peter clung to two fistfuls of his father's sweatshirt and stared at Nora with eyes the size of poker chips. Twin knives stabbed her heart.

"The Cricket?"

"Um… I gave her some money. I think she thought it was all a big adventure."

"Great. Let's hope she doesn't tell her friends at work about it."

A patrol car blazed by going the other way, its light bar strobing. Nora's overloaded system jammed instead of reacting. She was wide-eyed exhausted, her body trembling, thoughts pinging off her skull like rain, emotions tumbling like a pack of weasels fighting over scraps.

The next coherent thing out of her mouth was, "Where are you taking us?"

"To a safe house. You'll stay there until I can move you."

"How safe is your safe house?" Paul asked. "We don't need to do this twice in one night."

"We change them out pretty regularly. We haven't lost one in ages." They swung right onto a two-lane street that rapidly turned into dark, struggling-to-stay-respectable residential. Juan checked the mirror, then glanced toward Nora. "Why come for you now? Why tonight?"

"I don't know." Nora sort-of knew but needed Juan to focus on his job, not her. "Maybe AAI went on the list today. Maybe they're after Paul."

Juan frowned. "I drove past the hotel. It's a zoo. Too much for one lawyer. What did you do?"

Before Nora could cobble together a convincing lie, Paul said, "It's about me. I have contacts. They probably don't want me using them." He leaned forward. "I'm Paul Khaled, by the way."

"I gathered that." Juan nodded to the mirror, then turned to Nora. "Your FBI buddies. How much of the stuff on the web is true?"

"You don't know?"

"I deal with ICE and CBP and the Border Patrol, not the Bureau. What's their next move?"

Was it that different? A few moments' stuttering thought confirmed it was. "They'll track me. Us. They'll track us."

"No joke. How? What do they track?"

Her flight-combat-mother-wolf reserves of energy were collapsing. Her nerves pulsed from adrenaline withdrawal and lack of sleep. Nora sagged in her seat, buried her jittering hands under her thighs. She whispered, "Everything."

"Define 'everything.'" Juan's voice was growing harder.

"*Everything.*" Nora wrestled the manual into the front of her brain. "The IDs and credit cards, the bank accounts, email, online memberships. Mobile service on the slates. The phones."

"Okay, so you stay offline."

"Black boxes in the cars." Her voice sounded dead to her. "Toll passes. Gas pumps. Private security cams. Traffic cams. ATM cams. Dash cams on PD units." A thought stumbled into focus. "We've got to avoid the cameras."

"That's why we're on a side street. Besides, the windshield and all the windows are blacked out. Keep talking."

She'd seen that and forgot already. She was becoming a hazard. "Oh. Look, I… I haven't slept since Monday. Can you just get us to the safe house? We can go over all this in the morning."

Juan swooped into a fire-hydrant space along the curb, then swung on her. "No. The game just changed. I need to know—*right now*—exactly what to expect. So talk."

She'd take his head off if she wasn't completely wasted, but her body had pulled her emotional drain plug. Focusing hurt like childbirth. "Whatever. Fine. Let's just… go."

The Toyota lurched back on its way. "Right," Juan said. "What if they get a hit on you?"

Nora screwed shut her eyes while she corralled her thoughts. "Okay. We'll get a tower dump, throw blanket wiretaps on—"

"A what?"

"A tap on all the phones using a particular cell tower so we can find the right one. It's how we get around people having burners." She watched suburbia scroll by without seeing it. "That works for a limited area, like a block or two usually and static. We have to get NSA to help for bigger searches. That's a pain. They're slow and hard to work with. If we—"

"What do you mean, 'static'?"

"Just that. Staying in a couple-block area. To beat it, you drive a few blocks away and keep moving while you talk. Anyway, if we narrow it down, we task a drone to stake it out." She flashed back to the hotel. "The QRT was on the raid—"

"QRT?"

"Quick Reaction Team. It's kind of a super-SWAT. We've got six of them now. Heavier weapons, more hard-core training. They do a lot of our terrorist response."

Juan shot her a glance. "You know, I'd feel better if you stop saying 'we.'"

Nora sat up, scrubbed her face with her palms. "Sorry. Habit."

"You do this all the time? Listen to everybody, track us?"

"No, no. Only if you end up on our radar. It's too expensive to do all the time to everyone. Nobody wants to pay for us to be the Stasi, otherwise we probably would be."

"That's comforting. What about warrants? How long do those take?"

"No warrants for terrorism. We get a national security letter from the SAC—sorry, Special Agent in Charge—and we can do pretty much anything."

"That holds up in court?"

"Court?" she snorted. "You're serious?"

They turned onto Garden Grove Boulevard, another broad, divided street lined with a mixed bag of houses, stores, and strip centers. Even though the road was deserted, Juan kept the car below the speed limit. The neighborhood slowly deteriorated around them.

Nora twisted to look back at Paul. He gave her a washed-out smile. Peter and Hope curled against his sides. Hope sucked her thumb, a bad sign. The fear on Peter's face nearly broke her heart. She reached out to stroke his skinny, bare leg. "It's okay," she whispered.

"Once we get to the safe house," Juan said, "you don't go outside for anything. We can't take the chance you'll show up on a face match. There should be food and water to get you through a few days at least. Stay off your phones and slates. Understood?"

Nora swung back to Juan. "We need clothes. We left everything back there."

"Oh, Christ." Juan frowned, massaged his temple. "All right. When we get to the safe house, write down all your sizes, I'll see what I can do."

"But…" She shut up before she could say what screamed through her mind—*that's my job! Nobody else buys clothes for my family!* Instead, she fell back into her seat and screwed her eyes closed. Despair flooded the void inside her. She was supposed to protect her family, take care of them. Tonight, they'd almost ended up in prison because of her. Now she couldn't even give them clothes. Everything was out of control.

"The kids can't even go out to play?" Paul asked.

"No," Nora groaned. "It's like we're in a holding cell."

Juan nodded. "Beats the hell out of a camp."

16

Thanks to the growth in public- and private-sector use of CCTV surveillance, traffic and dashboard cameras, and drones, the average American living in an urban area is now imaged at least 675 times a day...
　　　　　　　　-- Electronic Privacy Information Center

THURSDAY, 6 MAY

McGinley fired off his daily report—a lot of words to make nothing sound like something—caught up with his shitbag file (still no word from El Paso on the whore), then turned to the imagery. Now that Esquivel had moved into that big place in Newport Beach where Villalobos used to live, McGinley was real curious to see who'd come calling.

Wednesday's drop was in its folder under "Bayadere Terrace": thirteen still-frames from the drone video that the Feeb intel weenies marked with names and reference numbers. No on-the-ground surveillance. You don't hassle the campaign contributors that way, and the city cops—real cops, not contractors—wouldn't play ball with the FBI anyway. When the Feebs have to collar a rich guy for show, they go to Malibu, where the locals aren't so friendly with the big bulls in D.C.

He stepped through the pictures, half-hoping to find Ojeda in there. He wasn't. Most of the men getting into or out of vehicles or walking across that big patio were the same folks who'd visited Villalobos in the past three months. Of course they slipped in four hi-res shots of the little blonde swimming naked in the pool out back. McGinley had seen a lot of her so far, so to speak. She was some kind of maid or something, but the show she'd put on with Esquivel in the pool when he moved in on Monday showed the silverware wasn't the only thing she polished. He reckoned that video was already on one of those drone-porn websites.

Then he hit the link for "2032-126-009." Up popped a "Resource restricted" message.

What the hell? Three months of imagery and this was the first time *that* had happened. Damn FBI, playing "I've Got a Secret" again. He pounded out an email to Jorgensen asking for that picture and any other intel about its subject. McGinley was real anxious to meet any visitor that sensitive.

17

*"Who's In Your Store? Making Facial Recognition
Systems Work for You"
-- Breakout Session, National Retail Federation 116th
Annual Convention*

THURSDAY, 6 MAY

Luis started rolling down the loading-dock door before Salma's station wagon had pulled all the way inside. Probably nobody was watching this belly-up cabinet outlet—another of Xiao's properties—but he couldn't be sure. The less visible activity, the better.

Salma burst from her car and spread her arms. "Stranger!" She hauled him into not exactly a hello-friend hug. She felt way, way too good, and Luis couldn't decide whether to pull away or let the embrace go on for another couple days.

Salma's day job was teaching fifth grade, but she made most of her money as a makeup artist and costumer for e-*novelas*, the web version of the old *telenovelas*. There'd been an extra flirty something in her voice when he'd called her on Monday to set this up. Ray had said a couple things that suggested it wasn't all sunshine and unicorns at home. Had Luis ever seen her alone, without Ray? Better to not think about that.

Eventually they both stepped back, grasping each other's arms. She'd swapped her shapeless teacher's clothes for a short, tight aqua skirt and a saffron-yellow *choli* that showed off a strip of flat stomach and a fair amount of cleavage. Luis worked hard not to notice… much. "You look great."

"Don't sound so surprised." She peered into his eyes, gently brushing his cheek with her fingertips. "You look tired. Is everything okay?"

Usually about this time on other visits, Ray would be hovering, his unsubtle way of reminding Luis who held Salma's deed. Maybe a chaperone was a good idea; Luis teetered on the edge of falling into her big, caramel eyes. He squeezed her elbows and broke away. "It's been a weird few days. Let's get you unloaded."

They started emptying the station wagon's back end—garment bags, wig boxes, files of sunglasses and shoes, a mound of tech gear—piling everything next to the door leading into the front showroom. Salma asked, "Where are they?"

Luis thumbed toward the door. "They've been locked in a safe house since yesterday morning, so they're a little wound up. The woman—Nora—she's a lot wound up, but that's kinda how she is. How is it living in Tavo's old place?"

Salma stopped, looked down, pursed her lips. "I didn't go. Ray asked, but I could tell he didn't want me to, so I said no. Now he's in Newport and I'm in Villa Park and I'm waiting for his pit bulls to come throw me out." She gave him a poor attempt at a smile. "That's all I've got to say about that."

"Sorry. Ray's a fucking idiot." Luis sighed. He added the last couple wig heads to the pile. "Nora thinks I'm 'Juan,' by the way. Ray's fault."

"That figures. He never did have any imagination. I'm still Edith." She set down her boxy 3D printer, brushed off her hands. "Introduce me to your new friends?"

As he shuttled Salma's stuff into what used to be the manager's office next to the now-empty showroom, Luis paused occasionally to watch the action in the room's center.

Nora stood in line abreast with Paul and the kids while Salma examined them from hair to heels. It was like an Army open-ranks inspection with the sexiest training officer in the world.

Paul was around five-ten, wavy black hair, moustache, wearing a faded UCLA sweatshirt and board shorts. Not exactly soft, but Luis could tell from the round edges that he spent most of his time behind a desk.

Salma poked and prodded and fiddled with Paul's hair while he joked with her. Then she turned to the coltish boy standing next to him and held out her hand. "Hello, handsome. What's your name?"

"Peter!" He wrapped his dinky hand around Salma's fingers and shook in the same sincere meeting-the-client way his dad did. A future lawyer? Maybe, if Luis didn't screw this up.

Salma pushed her fingers through Peter's curly black hair, measuring its length and body. "Have you been to Disneyland yet?"

"Uh huh. It was great!"

Next time Luis passed through, Salma squatted in front of Nora's daughter, a dark-haired pixie with round cheeks and huge, black eyes. "What's your name, sweetie?"

The girl fidgeted her feet a bit before she said "Hope" to the floor.

"That's a pretty name. Did you like Disneyland too?"

Hope shuffled some more, then nodded.

Salma stood, gave an unreturned smile to Nora, then pulled a slate from the bright-green satchel she'd left to one side. "I need some scans so I can make appliances to get you through face matching. I'll start with you, Nora. Come over here…"

Luis had seen this before, but it still seemed like science fiction. Salma used a laser strobe to get 3D scans of all four sides of Nora's and Paul's heads, then stuck the cable for a probe into the slate and pressed the glowing, pen-like tip against several points on their faces. "So I can get accurate colors," she explained.

"What about the kids?" Nora asked.

"They don't match children. Their faces change too fast." When she finished, Salma said, "Magic takes a while, so get comfy," then disappeared into the office.

"Now what?" Nora asked once Edith left them.

Juan pulled some note cards from his shirt pocket, then doled them out to her and Paul. "You're Patrick and Nicole Ramirez. You'll get the IDs Saturday. You're fourth-generation Americans, so you don't have to speak Spanish. Corona's a suburb east of us. That's a real address—you can look it up tonight. Memorize the stuff on those cards, then burn them."

Nora scanned her card. She hadn't done undercover work since

Quantico, but she'd have to now. "Why are we Mexican?"

"Because you won't pass for Chinese." He waved toward a half-dozen blue vinyl garment bags he'd hung on metal shelf brackets sprouting from the otherwise bare walls. "Those are your new clothes. Might as well take a look while we're waiting."

Nora stepped up to the three bags she'd already spotted—"Woman" or "Girl" written in Sharpie on masking tape on each one—reached for the first one's zipper, hesitated. She'd made a very specific list of what she wanted. All this Edith person had to do was follow the list. How hard is that?

She unzipped the bag. A surprised squawk jumped out of her before she could stop it.

"Is there a problem?" Juan stepped next to her, an eyebrow raised.

Nora pulled the taxicab-yellow sundress from the bag by its hanger, held it against her body. It hit well above her knees and would leave her shoulders and the upper half of her chest completely bare. She shoved it toward Juan. "Is Nicole Ramirez a stripper?"

He pushed the dress back at her. "It's a sundress, not a thong. It's fine."

"But—"

Juan cut her off with a slash of his hand. "Stop. These clothes are for her, not you. You know how CBP knows it's dealing with a Muslim woman?"

Nora sputtered, but couldn't answer.

"Her clothes. Forget the headscarf—ninety degrees outside and she's got on long sleeves and long pants, or a skirt down to her shoes. This isn't optional. We're not giving the cops any help finding you."

She would've stuffed the thing back in the bag in a wad if she hadn't suddenly become very aware she was still braless—after almost two days, the longest she'd ever gone without a bra since she grew breasts—and without her fleece, this… *narco* would know immediately. She hugged the dress tight. "Is it all like this?"

Paul appeared at Juan's shoulder, a garment bag flopped over his arm. Juan glanced at him, sighed, paused a moment. "No. There'll be dark stuff for nighttime and some casual clothes. Don't be surprised if she got you shorts or a tank top, though."

"Honey," Paul said, "it's okay. It's a costume. I've seen your old pictures. You used to wear a lot less."

"*Used to.*" Nora glared at Juan, her embarrassment simmering. "Can I keep my hats?" she finally asked, touching the brim of her Panama hat.

"Why? What's with the hats?"

"The *hadiths* say I should cover my head; they don't say how. This doesn't scare people the way a headscarf does. Please tell me this Nicole Ramirez person wears hats."

"How in hell did you get through the FBI?" Juan considered her fedora for a few moments, then shrugged. "Talk to Edith about it. I'm sure she'll have some ideas. Now go try everything on. If it doesn't fit, Edith can fix it. Stop arguing."

Nora snatched the garment bags off the wall, grabbed Hope and stalked toward the women's restroom. Once there, she worked her way through the rest of the wardrobe Edith had bought. Hope giggled at each costume change. The sundress hung ignored from the stall door.

Most of the clothes were worn and soft from washing. There were lots of lacquer reds and bronzes and jade greens and a dark top with Chinese calligraphy, styles she recognized from three or more years ago. It was mostly cheap—jeans from Myanmar, shirts from Angola, cut-rate, American-made knockoffs of Brazilian or Indian labels, flimsy underwear. Nearly everything was a size too large. It made her feel cheap and a bit sleazy. For the money she'd given these people, they couldn't even get new clothes?

Who was this Nicole? Nora pulled her burner and the index card from her purse, keyed in the address, and brought up a Bing Streetside view. It showed a two-story apartment building: weathered paint, dead landscaping, at least two balconies with laundry hanging from lines.

Then it hit her. Nicole Ramirez wasn't cheap. She was poor.

Nora had never been poor. Her father's business success had bought a nice house in McLean, private school for her, soccer and horseback-riding lessons, and four years at UVA without loans or having to work. Between Paul's income and hers, they'd socked away a nice chunk of money—now all gone to the Cartel. Nicole's life was alien to her.

"What's wrong, mommy?" Hope asked. She sat on the vanity counter in her new clothes—a pink Disney Princess Artemis tank top and pink denim shorts, both a bit too large—with her arms around her knees. "You're making a face."

Nora glanced up from her phone. "Am I?" Hope nodded. "I'm… learning something."

"Like at school?"

"Yes. Like at school."

She switched off her phone, took off the faded black jeans and blousy plum half-button shirt, and reluctantly stepped into the sundress. Thin cotton, elastic bodice, spaghetti straps. Something she'd have worn twenty years ago, not now. She tugged at the skirt—tight, but not as short as she'd feared—and shuffled out to look in the mirror.

"You look pretty," Hope said.

"You *like* this?"

"Uh-huh. It's all sunny and happy."

Nora hadn't worn anything this bright for years. Blues and blacks and greens and grays: that was her palette now. The yellow set off what seemed like acres of exposed skin. She felt half-naked, but only compared to what she normally wore.

Staring in the mirror at this dress from her distant past, she finally understood what Edith had done. She *got* Nicole Ramirez.

Nicole's occupation was "call-center operator." Paul's—um, "Patrick's"—was "building maintenance." They lived in a cheap apartment. She'd lost weight from skipping meals but had kept her old clothes. She bought the kids' things big so they'd last longer. And she had this one "date dress" for special occasions. An entire new person defined by a few rags.

Someone rapped on the restroom door, startling her. "Hey, it's me," Paul's voice said.

Nora let him in. He halted just inside and looked her up and down, his eyes growing wide. "Wow. I like that."

"You would." She checked out Paul's costume: a rough blue cotton work shirt, sleeves rolled up, worn open over a white crewneck tee shirt, rumpled khakis, and brown work shoes. "Where's your tool belt?"

"They forgot it. But I think my evening stuff came with a low rider."

"You get a toy, but my things are three years old? We need to talk."

"You look funny, Daddy," Hope said.

"And you're really pink, Princess Girl." Paul slid next to Nora and wrapped an arm around her waist. "Listen for a minute?"

Nora sighed. "You're going to tell me to behave, aren't you?"

"Uh huh." Paul towed Nora into the stall. He murmured, "This is hard for you, I know. It's hard for me and the kids, too. But it's going to be worse if you keep fighting with Juan."

"It's just—"

"Shh. Juan's the guy who knows how to do this. That's what we paid for. The more you harsh on him, the more you argue, the better the chance he'll just dump us somewhere. Can you chill until this is over? It's hard to keep scraping you off the ceiling."

Nora looked up into her husband's gentle brown eyes. They told her to let go a little bit, to save the fight for when it counted most. She hoped they were right.

She changed into a more sedate outfit and left the restroom, Paul and Hope trailing behind. Peter stood in the middle of the showroom, chattering Juan's ear off. Nora handed Hope a deck of Uno cards from her purse. "Peter, honey, come play with your sister. Sit over here."

"Aw, do I hafta?" Her son trudged to the corner nearest the restrooms to join Hope.

Nora felt Paul's heat on her ear. "Go on," he whispered. "Play nice."

She paced to a spot next to Juan, who nodded to her. He said, "I usually got the same answer when I told my son to play with his sister."

"You have children?"

"Well, only one now and he's not a child anymore, but yeah."

Grown kids? Maybe gone? He was older than she'd thought. She took another good, close look at Juan. She could usually spot criminals in a crowd, but as hard as she tried, she couldn't see the criminal in him. Maybe Paul was right. "Mr. Juan?"

"Yeah?"

Nora hesitated, trying to scrape up the right words. "This is really… hard. For all of us." She stalled, watched the kids bicker over their cards. "It goes against everything I believe in. Everything… all my life."

When she turned to face him again, she found him watching her calmly with a bit of sadness, as if he knew what she was feeling. Their eyes locked for a few moments.

"It'll be okay," he finally said.

The individual changes weren't huge, but Luis barely recognized the version of Nora he guided into position in front of his counterfeit State of California ID photo backdrop. She wore a streaked-blond wig with the hair piled on top of her head, a broader nose and chin, severe dark eyebrows, dramatic eyes turned hazel by contacts, bright red lipstick, and nail polish. The latex pieces had come off Salma's 3D printer and matched Nora's face perfectly. Luis took a photo, right thumb print and right-eye retina scan with his balky old slate.

"You like?" Salma asked.

"Great work," Luis said. "You're the best."

"I know."

Salma had shaved off Paul's moustache, added a broken nose, padded his cheeks to square out his face, and straightened his hair. While Luis got the slate set up again, Paul prodded his new nose. "Is this really enough to fool the cameras?"

"All it has to do is knock the match score down to seventy or so and they don't bother following up." Luis took the mug shot, moved in for the thumb print. "Relax your hand. Any problem putting this stuff on yourselves?"

Paul shrugged. "We'll see. Edith gave us two more sets of everything and drilled us on what to do. I can't say I have a lot of experience with makeup, though."

"It's not that hard. First time's a little rough, then you get the hang of it."

"Hope you're right." Paul shook out his hand while Luis lined up for the retina scan. "You know, running away just feels so wrong. We ought to stay and fight more. I mean, if we don't, who will? What happens to the country if people like us leave?"

"The ones who tried to fight were the first people in the camps. Hold still." Luis snapped the retina scan, then stepped back. "You know, most of my clients are so scared or so beaten down, they can't even think about resisting anymore."

"Well, they should. Somebody has to."

Echoes of Luis' talks with Bel, with Ray, with Salma. "You know, I read a little. We've gotten totally stupid before. We usually get better."

Paul put on a resigned half-smile. "I hope you're right."

As Salma started breaking down her equipment, Luis handed two sturdy, dark-blue backpacks each to Nora and Paul. "Load up your stuff. Make sure you can carry them. I'll take you back to the safe house when you're done."

Nora examined the packs. "Do you have a plan yet?"

"Yes, I have a plan. I'm working on a way we can just drive across. It's easiest, but it may take another couple days."

"Drive?" Nora said, instantly edgy. "With all the guards? In the open?"

"Yeah. This may shock you, but the Cartel owns a lot of Border Patrol and CBP troopers. Once I hook up with the right one, we can pass through a station with your new faces and IDs. I'll drop you in downtown wherever. My guy down there takes you to Tijuana, you fly to Mexico City, then off to wherever you're going. Questions?"

Paul shook his head. Nora scowled. "You've done this before, right?"

"I've taken hundreds of people south. We don't usually do the IDs and the disguises. It's expensive and not everybody can pull it off, but it works. So yeah, I've done this before."

"What if it doesn't work?"

"Then we do something else. I said this is the easiest way, not the only one." He had no idea what Plan B would look like, though. "Got it?"

Paul said, "Got it." For once, Nora stood quietly, eyes closed, and looked nauseated.

18

McGinley was about finished two-fingering yesterday's activity report at his Task Force desk when he heard snuffling behind him. Had to be Tenley, Jorgensen's lapdog, and his damn allergies. "What can I do for you, Tenley?" he said without turning around.

"You were asking about this Jorge Casillas douchebag?"

McGinley swiveled his chair to face the Feeb. Tenley wasn't one of the Master Race like Jorgensen, just a wiry little dark-haired peckerhead with a mouth full of lemons. "I did?"

"The image from Wednesday's drop. You wanted access."

McGinley stepped on his own smile. Little turd just gave away more than he should've. Casillas must be the star of the mystery picture. "Why, yes, I do recall that now."

Tenley shoved his hands in his pants pockets. "Well, you can stop asking."

McGinley leaned back in his chair and stared into the little Feeb's eyes, just to see if he could push the man into talking some more. It didn't work. "Why would I do that?"

"'Cause you don't need to know. Leave it, all right?"

"Is he someone's snitch?" Tenley just raised his shoulders. "Where the hell is Jorgensen?"

"Out. You're not gonna get a better answer running to Daddy. Just drop it." The Feeb skulked off to his side of the room, sniffling.

McGinley watched him go, turning his chair back and forth. This Casillas was sniffing around Esquivel, and it looked like the Feebs wanted to keep it quiet. The Bureau was never much good at sharing, but why this guy? Something in a dark place in McGinley's brain told him this was more than the usual Feeb I've-got-a-secret bullshit.

He wasn't going to drop it. Now that he had a name, he'd use his own sources. McGinley was damn well going to find out what the hell was going on.

91

19

"English is a promiscuous language," says Dr. Walter Keller, professor of linguistics at Harvard. "It will take words from any source and make them its own." These days, that source is increasingly the same as our popular films, fashions and tech gadgets: India and China, the two largest, hippest, richest nations on Earth."
-- "Sallang Slang: How Bollywood and Shanghai Shape English," Slate.com

FRIDAY, 7 MAY

Back before the world changed, Luis had never much liked Horton Plaza. It had been a standard mall stacked up four levels, full of tourists and suits, with no stores he couldn't get at any other decent shopping center. Now that so many suburban malls had closed or turned to shit, Horton Plaza was like a blocky pink-stucco time machine with festive banners, reminding him of how things used to be. Even though the place existed mostly for San Diego's downtown business community, it was still open to anyone. Not like South Coast Plaza back home, where you practically had to go through a credit check to get past the doormen.

Luis lounged on a concrete bench outside the fourth-floor food-court *chaat* shop, nibbling a samosa while trying not to look like he was waiting for someone. The security cameras hung right above his head, pointing each way along the walkway. It was like the mall cops wanted to leave a hole where people could do their shady business unrecorded. He wondered how many crooked city purchasing agents got their payoffs right here.

He hadn't wanted to do this, but Ray forced the issue. "You want this guy, you deal with him," he'd said on the phone. So here he was, a Disney Store bag snugged against his hip. His sign.

A young *gabacho* strutted down the walk from the escalators, hands in his jeans pockets. His shades were just bulky enough to be dataspecs. He bobbed his head in time to something other than the Taylor Swift oldie playing on the mall's overhead speakers. He slowed a step when he saw Luis, glanced sidelong at him and the bag as he passed, then ducked into the *chaat* shop.

Luis sat quietly, finishing his last bite of samosa even as he grew more disgusted with himself. He'd done this before. Every month he paid bribes to cops and all the other bloodsuckers that blew by the shop. Why did it always make him feel so filthy?

The young guy edged out of the store with what looked like a mango *lassi* in a clear plastic cup. He thumped down on the bench a foot or so away from Luis and sucked his highlighter-orange drink through an extra-wide straw. The head-bobbing kept on. He watched a couple good-looking Asian women pass by, their suit skirts short and tight. The kid tilted his head as they walked away, admiring the back view. "Love the mall," he said.

"I feel you." *Get this over with.* "Justin?"

"Yeah. Glad you caught me, *yaar*. I gotta go back tonight."

"When are you on duty next?"

"Sunday. Date with my *chhaavi* tomorrow."

"All right. Sunday before noon, a brown Geely four-door will pull into your crossing. I'll be driving. Wave it into your lane, give everyone a Level 1, move it through. Easy easy. Got it?"

Justin bobbed for a moment. "Whatcha hauling?"

"No dope, no guns, no money. And no questions."

Justin took another hit off his mango *lassi*. "I'm asking 'cause the *babus* are all *feng* about something, see? Like, on our asses."

Had "crazy" changed since Tuesday? Facial recognition for everybody? Spot DNA checks? "Know what that's about?"

"Maybe we didn't make our numbers, I dunno. Some bullshit. You know how the *babus* are, yeah? They don't tell us shit."

"Don't worry about it." Luis stood, leaving the bag.

Justin peeked inside. "Hey, *yaar*. Can I have the mouse? 'Cause my *chhaavi's* kid would really like it."

"It's yours." Luis wanted to go take a long, hot shower without Bel's damn timer shutting off the water after two minutes. That wasn't going to happen tonight, though. He nodded to the kid. "See you Sunday."

20

*Dylan Tunstall has become the first American labour
organizer to be granted political asylum in Canada...
Citizenship and Immigration Canada cited the on-going
violence against persons connected to trade unions,
including the murders of an estimated 300 labour
organizers between 2021 and 2030... At least 105 similar
applications by American trade unionists are still "under
review."*

-- "Ottawa Grants Asylum to U.S. Trade Unionist,"
TheGlobeAndMail.com

FRIDAY, 7 MAY

Bel had driven to and from the hospital along the same route
for nearly five years. Every dead tree, every pothole, every busted
stoplight, every liquor store and 7-Eleven and street market were as
familiar as the hallway from her bedroom to the kitchen. She
mostly didn't notice it anymore unless something stood out.

Like a woman being chased down the sidewalk by four men.

Bel couldn't make out her face or hair color in the near-dark,
but the woman was running for Olympic gold. The men—all in
variations of thugwear, black hoods and dark padded jackets,
gloves, and boots—were only fifty feet or so behind and gaining. In
the couple seconds Bel took to scope out the action, she noticed
aluminum baseball bats and a long riot baton.

She didn't have to think.

Bel swerved her little blue Chevy Breeze into the first driveway
ahead of the woman, then shoved open the door. "Get in! Hurry!"

The woman took two huge strides, then leaped through the
open door and careened into Bel's chest, knocking her back into
the driver's door. "They'll kill me!" she shrieked. "They killed
Zach!"

That voice...

The thugs grew larger by the second in the open doorway. Bel shook her head clear, slammed the car into reverse and stomped the gas. Headlights filled the back window, horns brayed, then a screech. Then a *thud.* Not a collision; she snapped a look over her shoulder.

There in the headlight glare, a male figure lay spread-eagled across her rear window. He raised his right arm in silhouette. It held some kind of club.

Bel yanked the gearshift into drive and squirted forward just as a big sedan swooped by with inches to spare. The clatter of aluminum on asphalt rang through the still-open door, and the man-shape clutched at the car's C-pillar with both hands.

The woman collected herself in the passenger's seat, hauled the door closed and strapped in. Bel called out "Hold on!" as she slalomed the Chevy across both lanes. The little hybrid Breeze's batteries were long dead and gone and the gerbils running the two-cylinder gas engine began to scream as loud as the skinny tires. The cars behind her dropped back.

One of the thug's arms kept popping free as she swerved back and forth, but he was always able to regain his grip. "Get off my car!" she yelled more than once. The next time she saw an arm fly up, she mashed down the brake and sent the car squealing toward the center line. The thug-shape disappeared as something heavy rolled onto her roof. Then she smashed down the gas. The car lurched forward, and in her rear-view mirror she saw the thug's body tumble off the roof into a heap on the street.

"Bel?" her passenger gasped. "Oh my God, I had no idea. I didn't mean to get you in—"

Bel immediately recognized her voice. "Ros? What the hell?"

A block went by before either of them could catch a breath. Bel heard little snuffling noises coming from her right and sneaked a quick peek at Ros. "What was that? Who were those guys? And who's Zach?"

Ros let her head fall back against the headrest. Bel couldn't tell whether her ragged breathing was from running, crying, or both. "He's dead. Those animals, they... they..."

"One thing at a time. Who is he? Was he?"

"The NANU organizer I've been working with since last fall. I was meeting him tonight. Then those assholes showed up. Zach made me hide." Her throat made a tiny cracking noise. "I heard them beat him to death. It was horrible. I couldn't do anything, just listen."

"Where was your gun?"

"I left it at work. I was in a hurry, I forgot it. Can you believe? The one night..." She sniffled, then pushed her hair back from her face. She was trying to put on a brave front, but Bel could see Ros' hands shake even in the dark. "Then one of them heard me or saw me or whatever and they came after me. That's when you showed up."

Bel gulped. A minute one way or another and she'd never have seen Ros again. "Who were they? Do you know?"

"No." Ros hugged herself tight. "Company goons, private security. What difference does it make? Zach's dead. Now... do I even have a job anymore?"

Bel still tasted bile when she remembered being flushed from Regional the day after the strike. "Did they see your face?"

"I don't know. I don't think so. It was dark." Ros choked back a sob. "You warned me. I should've listened, you tried—"

"Never mind that." Bel didn't try to take the snap out of her voice. "I knew management would never let us organize, but I didn't think they'd go this far. I've been worried for you ever since you started this, though."

Ros sniffed. "Really?"

"Yeah. If it helps, you're probably okay at work." Bel confirmed there were no armed mobs following them, then swooped into a curbside parking place. She undid her seat harness, twisted toward Ros, and spread her arms. "Come on."

Ros folded into Bel's embrace. They held each other for a long moment. Then Ros snuffled. "I owe you, *qin*. I owe you big."

"No, you don't." Bel was relieved they were both alive and intact. She didn't want to keep score.

"Yeah, I do." Ros pulled back. "You saved my life, girl. Anything you need, ever, any help, anything, you let me know." She wiped her nose on the back of her wrist. "God, I can't even call the cops."

"Don't even think about it." The glimmer of a tear track traced the edge of Ros' sharp cheekbone. Bel could only imagine what she was going through. "Just come to work like nothing happened. It's all you can do."

Ros finally let Bel go, sniffed loudly, and tried a brave smile that rippled like water. "I need a drink. Drink with me. Please. Come on, I'm buying."

"Okay. I'm taking you home with me. We'll drink there. You don't get to be alone tonight." Lucho had his strays, now Bel had hers. It was fair. And for a few moments, Bel understood how he felt about his travelers.

21

True to form, the United States is the least generous of its OECD peers toward its pensioners… Private pensions are almost unknown, and it abolished its Social Security old-age scheme nearly ten years ago. The entry of that system's vast trust fund into the financial markets helped inflate the equities bubble that burst catastrophically in 2025… Over 50% of America's over-65s live in poverty and subsist entirely on support given by their children and grandchildren, an arrangement more typical of developing nations.

-- "International: Paying for Gram," Economist.com

Friday, 7 May

Luis returned home from San Diego via I-15 through Miramar and Lake Elsinore to avoid the mess around the I-5 CBP checkpoint at Camp Pendleton. By the time he'd left the loaner car at the dropoff and walked the couple blocks to his house, he found all the lights off and everyone in bed. A dark lump took up the sofa; he could see enough face to tag her as Ros, one of Bel's hospital buddies. He'd ask tomorrow.

He retreated to the patio with a beer, pulled up a bleached-gray plastic lawn chair and watched the fire in the hills. The wind had kicked up at sunset; flames fringed the hillcrests. Twin torches marked what used to be a pair of houses at the nearest slope's bottom. They must not have paid their fire insurance.

He hoped Sunday would end this job. He'd driven more in the past week than he had in the previous two months. He hadn't slept more than a couple hours at a time since Tavo extorted him into this a week ago. He missed Bel, not just in bed but everywhere, and he'd come to dread that hurt-sad-angry look in her eyes whenever they passed in the house.

98

The sliding screen door scratched open and closed behind him. He looked back to see his father Alvaro shuffle toward him, the three-quarter moon glowing on his white sleeveless undershirt. He rolled as he walked, and his slippers made a *scritch-scrrraaaatch* sound on the cement. While Alvaro approached, Luis ankled a nearby lawn chair and settled it next to his.

His father's hand clawed his shoulder. "*Oye, hijo.*"

"*Oye, Papi.* Why're you up so late? You okay?"

Alvaro took a minute to carefully lower himself into his chair and hook his cane on the arm. Every move came with a grunt or sigh. Bel had told Luis that soon his father wouldn't be able to walk on his own. He hoped she was wrong but knew she wasn't. "Can't sleep," he wheezed in Spanish. "Your mother snores."

"She says you're the one who snores."

Alvaro waved that thought away. "You on a run now?" Luis nodded. "More *Moros?*"

"Yes, *Papi.*"

"So why aren't you with that pretty wife of yours?"

"She's pissed at me. Did Mom get on your case about doing this?"

Alvaro stared at the fire, nodding and wheezing. "Of course she did. Gracie would get mad, make me sleep in the truck. I go out, she'd cry and cook all night until I called. Your sister told me this. Then I come home, kitchen's full of food and Gracie yells at me some more. Then we make up." He smiled, maybe remembering the making-up.

"I remember now. I'd watch her cook and wonder if it was the onions making her cry." Luis sighed. "I bribed a guy today to let me cross with the travelers."

"Did it work?"

"We'll find out soon. You know, I've been paying bribes to cops for years when they ask for them. But every time I bribe one without them hitting me up, it just feels so slimy."

Alvaro shrugged. "It's part of the job, *hijo.* Back then, I bribed men, leaned on them, you know. They had their hands out then, too."

"I don't remember seeing you do that."

"I didn't do it in front of you. So you wouldn't think I was *malvado*, you know. So when I get old, you think I'm a hero and take care of me."

Exactly the reason Luis had never told Nacho or Christa. Especially Christa. She hadn't needed to know where the money came from for her braces and her *quinceañera*. Now only Nacho remained, and if he stayed in the Marines, who could tell if he'd ever be able to take care of his parents when they couldn't work anymore?

He watched his father slump in the chair, hands trembling, dragging each breath over sandpaper. He'd been so strong; not big but barrel-chested from the warehouse work, hands like Vise-Grips. He'd worked so hard all his life and had nothing much to show for it. He wasn't even seventy yet but looked ninety. *Me in twenty years.*

Luis laid his hand over Alvaro's and squeezed. "I'm sorry, *Papi.*"

"What for?"

"That things didn't work out the way they were supposed to. That you're sick and we can't get you to a doctor. That you had to sell the house. That all your retirement money went down the toilet. That… that all I can give you is a little room in a little house."

Alvaro rocked gently in his chair for a few moments, then snorted. "More than I gave my *padre*. I left him back home, never got back to see him, sent money like that meant something. You're here for me and your mother. Your *mujer preciosa* cares for me like a daughter. So you stay with us until we're gone. That's all we can ask."

Luis nodded, swallowed. He hoped that would be a long time, but he heard reality every time Alvaro coughed. Still, it was his duty, and he'd do it as best he could.

Just one more reason to get Nora to *el otro lado*—the other side.

22

*Dr. Ajayan says the last unmatchable human forensic
sample he recalls coming to the L.A. Crime Lab occurred
in 2025... "Between federal, state, local, and private DNA
databases, our samples can hit [match a database entry]
three or four times." ...Private databases can be
problematic, however. Studies show that like the online
"background check" services of the 2010s, for-profit DNA
databases often misidentify profiles or store corrupted
data.*
    -- "LAPD: No More 'Unknown Subjects'," LATimes.com

SATURDAY, 8 MAY

After a passel of reports and meetings and what-all kept him
from doing any real work, McGinley finally got back to his desk to
find the usual email backup on his slate. The fifth message from
the top was from Special Agent Destry Park out of ICE ERO, El
Paso field office. That name was familiar somehow. It came to him
after a moment: Park was the troop who found that white whore in
the Zeta van in New Mexico.

The email got right to the point:

```
joella marie murchison, 32, 339 tophill
rd san antonio. subj id conf by dna
match via txdps. rptd missing to sapd
6/21/29. call if u need more.
```

McGinley slumped back in his chair, staring at the message.
He knew exactly where 339 Tophill Road was. Northwood, just
under the north edge of the 410 Loop. Three blocks from his
house.

Joella was one of the five women with Carla Jean when the
Zetas got her.

The infirmary at the ICE Otero Processing Center was every bit as depressing as McGinley remembered these kinds of places being, though nowhere near as bad as that sewer where he'd talked to Ojeda's wife a few days back. Lots of chipped not-quite-white and almost-tan paint, linoleum, metal doors, staff that checked out a long time ago, and orderlies who looked like they belonged in orange jumpsuits.

McGinley hunkered down in a plastic chair across from Joella's room, waiting on the locals to let him see her. A nurse had warned him about what he'd find in there: 20% underweight, twice the intox levels of kronk in her system on admit, every STD known to man and a few they weren't so sure about.

There'd been seven of them back in Northwood, a gang of pretty girls, and if you found one you didn't have to look far to find another couple. Joella was the cute redhead, the one Carla Jean called "sorta trashy" on account of the tight tops and short skirts that got her into trouble with the bluenoses now and then. Her husband Kyle sure loved to show her off. McGinley held that picture in his mind: Kyle and Joella in their back yard next to the grill, laughing at what-have-you, her all freckles and pale skin and legs and straight, white teeth.

Kyle. McGinley didn't know whether he ought to envy or pity the poor son-of-a-bitch. He was getting his woman back… broken. Never gonna be the way she was again.

But she was still alive. He'd spent the whole flight from Santa Ana to El Paso trying not to think about what that meant. His brain had almost convinced his heart that Carla Jean was dead, that she went fast, without pain, and he'd been chasing a ghost. Joella could blow that story all to hell, but not in the happy-ending Bollywood way.

"You McGinley?"

He looked up into an ICE polo and an olive face with a salt-and-pepper moustache. "Guilty as charged. I reckon you ain't Park."

"Nope. Cal Gennaro, ERO. I'm the investigator assigned to her." He nodded toward Joella's room.

After they shook hands and played do-you-know and generally sized up each other, McGinley said, "Reckon I can get some time with Joella in there?"

Gennaro scratched the back of his head. "Remind me again how you're involved in this. Park kind of waved his hands around it."

McGinley had been as vague as he could when he explained it to Park. "Joella was one of five women with my wife when they disappeared in Matamoros back in June of '29. She's the first proof we got that any of 'em survived."

Gennaro nodded. "So you're *that* McGinley. Your case popped when we IDed her. And I know you're not assigned to that case. But what the fuck, I'd be here too if it was my wife." He rubbed his hand across his chin. "How much do you know about Zetas and hookers?"

"A fair bit. I learned fast back then."

"I'll bet. So you know the white ones are in demand. Old Paco'll pay extra to fuck a *gringa*. They load them up on kronk to keep them quiet, work them hard, then when the kronk eats too many holes in their brains, they take them out in the desert and put one in the back of their heads."

McGinley glanced away, nodded. That movie had played a few times in his brain.

"Sorry to be harsh. I guess I'm saying… even if the woman's coherent enough to talk, she may not tell you anything you want to hear."

"I know that." McGinley took Gennaro's measure. The man was lean and almost as dark as a Mex, with a drinker's nose and squint lines like gullies. On the job a long time and showing it. "She can't tell me nothing I ain't already told myself. So. Can I talk to her?"

The little room smelled like alcohol wipes and bleach. A skeleton wearing a ratty red mop on its head lay in the middle of a tangle of machines and tubes. McGinley cued up the picture of Joella on his dataspecs and peered at the skull under the frazzled hair. Her eyes and cheeks were sunk deep and her nose had been busted along the way, but McGinley found the mole on her left temple and the little scar under her lower lip. For an instant he saw

Carla Jean there, not for long but long enough to curdle his stomach. He took a deep breath, flipped his dataspecs to "record," then leaned closer. "Joella?" he said as gently as he could. "You awake, darlin'?"

Her half-mast eyes slewed his way. She frowned. "I… know you."

"Yes, you do. I'm Jack. Carla Jean's husband?"

"Jack." Her eyes flickered. Recognition? "Jack. Jack."

He pulled a photo of Carla Jean from his shirt pocket and held it in front of Joella's face, careful to not look at it himself. He didn't dare, not here. "Remember her?"

A scratchy little sound creaked out of her throat. For the first time, her eyes—the white parts mostly red—really focused. "Carla," she whispered.

"That's right, darlin'. Carla. What happened when they took you, down Matamoros way? What'd they do with all y'all?"

Her eyes sloshed around a bit more. "Jasmine. Shot her. Don't… don't know why."

"Jasmine?" Gennaro asked.

"Holtz," McGinley said. "Oldest of them, thirty-five maybe back then." *Damn it.* McGinley knew why they shot her—nobody wanted an old whore. Carla Jean was next oldest. He bent closer to Joella. "What'd they do with you then?"

She breathed through her mouth. He could feel it on his cheek. Her eyes drifted here and there for a spell. "Took us… to a place."

"What place?"

"Some place. Gave us stuff… made me sleepy. Took our clothes. They… they…" Pain bust through the glaze over her eyes. "It hurt."

Gang rape, beatings, and drugs until they stopped fighting. The part he'd hoped Carla Jean had been spared. Those evil fuckers. "You're doing fine, darlin'. Now, think hard. When was the last time you saw Carla Jean? Where were you?"

"Who are you?"

Lord. "Jack. Jack McGinley."

"I know you."

"I know you do, darlin'. Think, now. When was the last time you saw Carla Jean?"

The machines beeped and hummed. She squeezed shut her eyes, then eked them open again. Her left eye fuzzed out with a tear. "A few... few months... maybe."

He'd prepared for anything she might say—anything but that. McGinley stood bolt upright. *Carla Jean could still be...*

No. That wasn't possible. She survived... all *that?* There'd been too many false alarms, too many mystery-blonde sightings, too many bodies with bleached hair. Looking at Joella—a bundle of sticks held together with Kleenex—he couldn't reckon whether he could call this "surviving."

"You okay, McGinley?" Gennaro asked.

"Yeah. Yeah, reckon so." He bent over Joella again, wrapped a hand around her scrawny arm, more to convince himself she was real than to give her any comfort. "Where was she? Where'd you see her?"

More fading in and out, more head-rocking. She squinted through him. The tear trickled down her neck, followed by another. "Beach place," she whispered. "Lotsa soldiers. We... we were in trailers... by a... a big hotel or something." Her eyes landed on him again. "Who are you?"

◆

"The GPS on the driver's phone said he came from Puerto Peñasco," Gennaro told McGinley in a shabby break room down the hall from Joella. "You know that place?"

McGinley shook his head. He hadn't memorized the whole damn country.

"R&R spot for Zetas and their army buddies on the Gulf of California. Closest beach to Arizona. Back before the war, folks from Phoenix and Tucson would go down there for the weekend."

"Zetas got it now?"

"Had it a couple years. They've got the Nortes pushed back almost to the Sonora border. Anyway, big logistics base for them, bivouac, some parts of the Mexican Navy they own. It makes sense they'd keep hookers there for the 'recreation' part of R&R."

Another picture of Carla Jean that McGinley didn't want, and reckoned he'd never be rid of. "If they moved her, where'd they move her to?"

Gennaro shrugged. "Anywhere. Sometimes they put 'em in RVs and work the forward units. But maybe there's another story. That GPS? The dumb fuck had it set for his destination, too. A big open-cut coal mine up on the Mogollon Rim in Arizona east of Payson. The Christopher Creek Mine. It's run by this big Ozzie company. We think they contract with the Zetas for security and probably drugs and hookers."

"So why ain't you busted them?"

"We didn't have anything on them worth a warrant until now. My office's working a warrant for the whorehouse they probably have on their property, based on the van full of hookers headed there."

"Ain't whoring legal in Arizona?"

"It's Federal land. Sitgreaves National Forest." Gennaro set a hand on McGinley's shoulder and leaned in. "If she's there, we'll find her, Jack. I promise."

McGinley's wheels started turning. He slammed a door on the horror movie starring Carla Jean playing in his head and concentrated as hard as he could on what Gennaro was telling him. "I want to be on that raid."

Gennaro pulled back, threw up his hands. "Yeah, I get it. But you're HSI—this isn't your party. You're not even on the investigation. You're outside your lane here. I—"

"I do that a lot." McGinley loomed over the other agent. "Get me on that raid. I know the women, they know me, they'll talk to me. Hell, look what I got from Joella, and that girl's brain is half melted." He bent to stare at Gennaro straight on. "I've had straphangers on raids with way less reason to be there. If my wife is there, I need to be the one who finds her. Got it?"

"I got it." Gennaro sighed. "I'll see what I can do."

A notion came to McGinley: probably nobody knew more about what the Zetas were up to around Baja than the Nortes. And he just happened to have a line on one of them. He'd arrange another talk with Ojeda… this time, a serious one.

23

Despite the war and the hassles in crossing the border, it's not all blood and guts. The border towns totally controlled by one of the cartels—like Tecate, where we were crossing, or Nogales—are pretty chill now. It's the ones where the cartels crash together that get scary. At least, that's what our guide Fidel told us.
-- "Moto in the War Zone," OutsideOnline.com

SUNDAY, 9 MAY

Luis parked the Geely in a dirt lot scattered with sorry-looking trucks a couple hundred yards from the Tecate crossing. He steadied his elbows on the top of the open driver's door so he could watch the action through his Chinese Zen-Ray compact binoculars.

The brown hills of Mexico wavered in the heat haze beyond the checkpoint. Eight cars waited to get through the border station: three in each southbound crossing lane, two waiting in line on the road behind. Justin was in the left lane; a sunburned kid with a sunshade draped over his neck was in the right lane. A third guy in utilities hovered in the middle, dumpy but not fat, pacing between the two. He'd duck his head to peer through a car window, look over a guard's shoulder, circle a vehicle as if on an inspection.

Hijo de perra. Justin hadn't mentioned a shadow. Was the guy in on it? Not too damn likely; if he was, he'd be hiding out in the nice air-conditioned booth in the middle of the road under the overhead. Luis palmed the sweat from his eyes.

"Why are we stopped?" Nora asked. She leaned far over the driver's seat, frowning out. Her huge, round sunglasses made her look like a bug but would help screw up facial recognition.

"There's too many cars waiting. We'll let a few get through before we go down there." Which was true as far as it went. She

107

didn't need to know about the extra trooper yet. "You and Paul should switch places. I want them to have to work at it to see you."

Whispering and door slams went on while he scoped the crossing. Like a lot of the smaller border posts, there wasn't much to it: a chalky tan overhead structure on big, square pillars, and the Mexican eagle-and-snake crest over the southbound lanes. You could pass through the California version of Tecate without noticing it, but the Mexican town beyond was far bigger and busier. A not-bad place for Nora and family to land—easy access to Tijuana, a couple semi-decent hotels, and safely removed from the battle lines between the Nortes and the Zetas.

All they had to do was get there.

The backup bled away. Luis slid behind the wheel and stashed his binoculars in the glove box. He punched off the streamer's news feed when it switched from coverage of Hurricane Bailey in Delaware to the President's noontime sermon and Bible reading.

Paul—Gargoyles, cream-and-olive guayabera and old chinos—tried to sit easy in the passenger's seat, but his drumming fingers gave him away. "How's it look?" he asked.

"Fine so far." Luis glanced in the rear-view mirror. The kids goggled out the back windows at the strange-to-them landscape. Nora's bug lenses stared back at Luis. The fake nose and chin still made him do a double-take. "You guys okay back there?"

"I'll be better when we're through the gate." She tugged down her sundress' skirt hem.

Justin waved them into the left-hand inspection lane behind two other vehicles, an ancient, dusty SUV with Baja plates and a newish Fiat hatchback from San Diego. Luis watched the three CBP troopers work, trying to pick up if anything they did was worth worrying about. The dumpy guy spent more time looking over the other guard's shoulder than he did dogging Justin: good news. Luis had almost convinced himself the guy was a trainer when Officer Dumpy lurched up to the Fiat's passenger window and rapped the glass with his left knuckles.

"Is that normal?" Paul asked.

"Not really. Can you see what he's doing?"

Paul sat straight, pulled on his fingers while his head followed the guard's movements. "Someone rolled down the window. He's leaning over, it looks like to talk to someone." The hatch jumped open. "Here he comes."

Officer Dumpy circled to the Fiat's back end, flung open the hatch and aimed his Mini-Maglite inside, using the tip of his collapsible metal baton to poke around. What would he make of the four backpacks in the Geely's trunk? Nora and Paul had drilled the kids on the cover story for the past hour. Still, they were way too unpredictable. Sometimes CBP would question the kids to get the real story of why mommy or daddy was going south.

The SUV lurched off in a cloud of diesel smoke, hesitated as the steel barrier dropped, then rattled away. Justin motioned the Fiat forward; Officer Dumpy held the hatch open as the car inched ahead. Luis didn't quite close the gap. His paranoia—what he called his survival instinct—told him to not get too boxed in.

"Is he the one?" Nora asked. "The young guard?"

"Don't worry about it. Just chill."

Justin collected IDs from the two people in the Fiat and fed the first one to his field reader. Luis timed it: roughly twenty seconds, a Level 1. *Good boy.* The guard in the next lane let a thrashed old Tata mini-truck full of wooden pallets through the gate. *Just another couple minutes*, Luis told himself. *No problem. Easy easy.*

"Wow!" Peter said. "Look at all those men with guns over there."

Luis turned to his side window. A string of white, one-story cinder-block buildings lined the northbound lanes. Six CBP troopers in tan utilities, black balaclavas, and tac gear clustered under the nearest building's overhanging roof. Four wore full battle-rattle, complete with helmets and rifles.

Luis could swear they were looking straight at him.

"Peter? Sweetie?" Nora's voice rattled with sudden tension. "Come sit next to me."

"But Mommy…"

"Now!"

"What's… happening?" Paul whispered.

Luis tried to watch these new guys and Justin at the same time. This post didn't usually have this much staff. Even if the cameras hanging from the overhead had IDed Paul despite his makeup and the blacked-out windshield, the locals wouldn't have had time to truck in reinforcements. Were those guys looking for Nora?

Nobody knew he'd come here… except Ray and Justin.

Both Luis and Paul jumped at three sharp knocks on Paul's window. Officer Dumpy's upper half filled the view outside. Luis downed a deep breath, lowered the window and leaned past Paul to look up in Dumpy's face. They didn't put nametapes on the uniforms anymore to make it harder for the cartels to figure out who to bribe or kill. "Yes, officer?"

"Sir, could you open the trunk for me, please?"

Luis hesitated, then pushed the trunk-release button on the dash until he heard the *thunk* in back. Once Officer Dumpy reached the car's rear, Luis whispered to Nora, "Where's your weapon?"

Nora twisted to glance out the back, then squeezed the kids a bit closer to her sides. "In my purse."

"Leave it there."

An old Nissan pickup pulled up behind the Geely, closer than Luis liked. Justin handed the IDs back to the Fiat's driver, then talked with him instead of waving the car on its way, pointing and snaking his hand around toward the Mexican side.

Officer Dumpy returned to Paul's window, leaned down far enough to peer into the back seat. "Excuse me, son. Where are all of you going?"

Paul said, "We're going to—"

"Not you, sir. Him." Dumpy pointed to Peter. "Where to, son?"

Luis checked the rear-view in time to see Nora give the man an almost-genuine nervous smile. Peter's eyes had doubled in size.

"Uh…"

Paul glanced at Luis, panic edging into his eyes. He gripped his knees with white-knuckled fingers.

Luis felt sweat soak his shirt's back.

Remember your story…

"To his ranch." Peter pointed at Luis. "We're gonna ride horses."

Dumpy's eyes lingered just a little too long on Nora. Was he looking at her face, or at her boobs in her tight top? Luis hoped the guy was a breast man, for all their sakes.

"It'll be just a few more minutes, sir." Dumpy nodded toward Luis, then straightened.

Luis gulped down a breath and turned back to the action in front of him. Justin stepped back from the Fiat and swept his hand toward the gate. When the Fiat moved forward, the barrier's yellow-painted metal cliff sank into the road. No getting past that when it was up; it would smash the car's bottom half. Luis shifted into drive and waited for Justin to wave him forward. *Almost there, just another minute…*

"Wait here, sir," Dumpy said.

Wait?

Dumpy stepped toward Justin, holding up a "stop" hand. Across the street, the six troopers formed up in line abreast and stepped off, two with rifles on either end.

Three cars filled the right lane; too close to get by. The approaching troopers blocked the left. The Nissan crowded the Geely's bumper. Luis gulped down the baseball in his throat. "Nora," he whispered, not taking his eyes off the oncoming rifles, "put the kids on the floor."

"What's happening? Talk to me."

"Just do it. Now. Paul, roll up your window so they can't see in."

Luis tuned out the kids' complaining, keeping his focus glued to his left. The CBP troopers strode across the farthest northbound lane, heading straight for the Geely. The two men without rifles drew their sidearms.

"Do you have your weapon?" Nora asked.

Luis glanced in the mirror. Nora had her pistol half out of her big black shoulder bag. "Put that thing away. We're not getting in a firefight with nine guys, not with kids in the car."

"Mommy, what's happening?" Hope's voice wavered with fear.

"Shh. Be still, honey. Stay down there."

Luis watched the men close in, his stomach in his throat. This wasn't the way it was supposed to go down—penned in a car, no way to run. He wiped his palms on his jeans, scanning the cars around them. Everyone else was watching the CBP guys, too. He doubted any of them had as much to lose.

Only Justin knew *when* they'd be here. Did that little shit sell them out?

The CBP men were less than twenty feet away when movement ahead caught Luis' eye. Justin slowly backed away from Dumpy, his hands half-raised, his head swiveling from Dumpy to the other guards and back. His mouth moved, but Luis couldn't hear the words.

What the…?

The six guards swarmed past the booth in the middle of the crossing, weapons at ready. Luis could hear the muffled shouts of "Freeze! Show us your hands!"

"Get down!" Luis barked. "Now!" He braced for the first shots.

The guards swept past the Geely and raced toward Justin. Stunned, Luis watched as Justin turned and dashed toward Mexico, losing his ball cap. The other guards, Dumpy included, screamed at him all at once so their words melted into a barrage of noise.

Justin made it over the border's painted line. Two riflemen aimed and fired, echoing firecracker sounds. Justin's arms flew wide before he crashed face-first on the street, then rolled onto his back.

¡Chingado! We almost made it! So close, just another minute, goddamnit…

The Nissan behind them screeched away in reverse. The panel van beside them wallowed through a three-point turn and followed. Luis figured they knew what he did: nobody was going south for hours and CBP was going to be all over everyone here.

Luis cranked the wheel hard to the left, jammed the gearshift into reverse, and stomped the gas. The Geely squealed into the empty northbound lanes. He pounded the brakes, shifted to drive, then floored it. They leaped through a cloud of rubber smoke to race north, away from Tecate, the men with guns, and Justin's dead body.

24

Throughout the Inland Empire, neighborhoods ravaged by home abandonment or bank foreclosures are slowly coming back to life as squatters reclaim vacant houses – sometimes houses they used to own... In one Upland community, over 80% of residents are squatters who have started a Neighborhood Watch program and take turns filling potholes in streets the city has written off.
-- "Banks Demand Crackdown on Squatters," LATimes.com

SUNDAY, 9 MAY

"What was that?" Nora asked.

"Our tame guard got capped." Juan's voice carried a sharp edge she hadn't heard before.

She mentally replayed the scene over and over. The guard was crooked and tried to run; he got what was coming. On the other hand, he was their ticket over the border. How should she feel: good or bad?

"How did they find out?" she finally asked. Juan didn't answer. "I thought this was the easy way."

"If it was easy, you wouldn't need me."

Still, after all the buildup, all the hope…

The kids hadn't seen any of it, praise Allah. She'd told them there'd been an accident and they couldn't go to Mexico today. If they could tell the grown-ups were more quiet and serious than usual, they didn't show it. Hope curled up next to her, drowsing. Nora reached out to stroke Peter's back as he peered out his window, watching this strange world go by.

"When do we get to go to Mexico?" Peter asked over his shoulder.

"I don't know, honey. Mr. Juan's in charge of that."

"

Peter tore himself away from his window and leaned toward Juan as far as his shoulder harness would allow. "Mr. Juan? Are we gonna go to Mexico?"

"Don't bother the man," Paul warned. "He's driving,"

"No, it's okay." Juan tossed a tight smile at Peter. "Pretty soon, don't worry."

"How soon?"

"Not now." Nora gripped her son's shoulder. "Settle down."

Peter crossed his arms and frowned, then turned back to his window.

Nora stared hard at the road unspooling behind them, looking for pursuing cars or helicopters. The black dot of a drone flew its perfect circle over what must have been the crossing. Other than that, all she saw were the rocky brown hills on either side of California 94, strewn with gray-green scrub, set against a flat, chrome-blue sky. After a few silent minutes, she felt Paul's hand squeeze her knee. "Honey, can I borrow your phone?"

"Um, okay." She handed over her bag without breaking lock on the road. At least he was talking again; he'd been the grim kind of quiet he got when he was upset.

A couple more minutes passed before Paul said, "I don't think this is about us."

"Why not?" Juan asked.

"There's a story on the news. CBP announced Operation Hoover. It says they arrested 237 CBP and Border Patrol agents they think are taking bribes."

"Two thirty-seven? That's all?"

"It says it's just in California and western Arizona."

The moment he said that, it struck Nora odd. Why just there? "That's not how we'd do it. We'd take down the whole border at the same time. Otherwise, you're just warning the others."

"You're doing that 'we' thing again."

"Sorry." How long before her brain realized she wasn't an FBI agent any longer? Or would she ever stop being an agent?

"Nora?" Juan said. "You know how these guys work. Think there's an indirect link?"

Nora sat straight in her seat. She unkinked her neck, gave Hope a quick one-armed hug, stroked Peter's hair. Juan's eyes watched her in the rear-view mirror. He listened, asked good questions, was calm under pressure, and she still couldn't smell criminal on him. Sometime soon she might need to rework her Juan estimate.

"Maybe someone decided today was a good day to take down crooked agents," she finally said. "Or maybe they did it to make it harder for us to get out."

"Well, it sure does that. If it's only happening here and western Arizona, it's just the guys on the Norte payroll. How long before the FBI sees the camera vids from back there?"

"If they ask, a few hours. If they don't, then never. Why?"

"I'm wondering whether they'll see our little bug-out act and send someone after us."

It could happen. They must be monitoring the traffic cams in San Diego and Orange counties by now. "We weren't the only ones to run out back there. It's possible, though." She watched the hills roll by for a few moments, then looked behind them again to search for tails.

"Now what happens?" Paul's voice vibrated with tension.

Juan didn't answer right away. Did he have a plan yet? She'd paid for at least two.

Nora kneaded Paul's shoulder, hoping it would be enough comfort for now. Paul was fearless on the Hill, in committee hearings, and handling people who had more money and power than brains. She'd been dazzled the times she'd seen him in action; she'd never be able to do the kind of work he seemed to toss off naturally. But his work didn't involve violent death or dealing with *narcos* or being chased by armed men. This was *her* world; it was as alien to him as his world was to her. She hoped it wouldn't poison the decency and gentleness she counted on so much.

"I'll take you to another safe house," Juan finally said. Nora felt her stomach sink; she'd hoped her family could sleep someplace decent tonight. "Then I need to get rid of this car. It's been seen. I need another loaner."

A Cartel motor pool? She laughed. "Does it come with a kilo of coke in the trunk?"

Juan hiked an eyebrow at her in the mirror. "No, they're just for getting around. They're registered to front companies. They have no GPS and they're scanned every day for trackers and bugs. They get new e-plates every time they're used."

Great intel. Too bad the Bureau didn't want her input now. "Fine. Then what?"

"I need to drop back and work out Plan B. This may be harder than I thought. I've never moved someone with so much heat on them."

She looked away, down to Hope snuggling next to her. Was even the ridiculous amount of money she'd given the Cartel enough to get her and Paul and the kids to safety? She wondered what she'd do if the *narcos* decided she was too much trouble. "Can you… can you still get us to Mexico?"

"I have to." Resignation weighed down Juan's voice. "I got no choice."

The toll pass peeped one last time as the car trundled off I-8 and swung north onto a disintegrating low-rise commercial strip. The city street was more river bottom than roadway. Two gas stations—long-dead brands, signs still showing unleaded at only six dollars a gallon—welcomed them into what once had been a community.

"What's this place called?" Nora asked.

"El Cajon." Juan sounded distracted. "It used to have one of the largest Muslim populations on the West Coast. Forty thousand people, just gone."

They turned right onto a street lined with modest 1960s and 1970s houses fronted by long-dead lawns, brown pines, and neglected palm trees wrapped in sun-broiled fronds. The roads and houses became more ragged the farther they were from the main street, with boarded-up or busted-out windows, robust weeds, and flaking walls. A burned-out shell appeared on the left. Nora's heart stumbled over the faded, hand-painted declaration on its side: *I Am An American.*

Paul asked, "Riots?"

"Yeah." Juan slowed the car to a crawl to pick their way through the potholes. "This used to be an Iraqi neighborhood.

Most of the people who didn't leave during the riots or go south got sent to the camps. Then the banks foreclosed on anyone who was left after the '25 crash. The county's got no money to fix the streets. It sucks for the folks who used to live here, but it's great for hiding safe houses."

The car stopped at a one-story, '60s-vintage rancher, formerly cream, now a peeling, weathered gray. Faded red-asphalt shingles covered the sagging roof; plywood hid the windows. A two-car garage dominated the front, while the main entry sheltered at the end of a walkway lined by a weedbed and a dirt yard. Juan said, "Welcome to your new home."

"Cozy little place," Paul snarked. A good sign; his sense of humor was coming back.

Nora examined the house for a few moments. She sighed. "How long will we be here?"

"Until I can get Plan B nailed down. A couple days, maybe."

Juan disappeared into the back yard while Nora, pistol drawn, edged onto the front step. She scanned all the rooftops and the few open windows for movement or faces. Only the hot breeze disturbed the stillness.

Juan slipped through the side gate, nodding toward Nora. "Let's make sure nobody's home." He unlocked the door, drew his pistol, and slid inside. Nora felt silly working an entry in this dumb dress, but she switched into work mode and followed close on his heels.

The house smelled musty and sour with a topnote of mold and dust. They made it to the living room at the back of the house before Nora's eyes adjusted to the murk. Juan nodded toward the side hallway, then led the way weapon-first. More debris, the stink of an unflushed toilet, a dead rat, and buckling drywall from a roof leak in one of the two bedrooms.

Nora stuffed down her disappointment. At least the other safe house didn't smell this bad, and it had furniture. She could deal with this—she'd lived in worse in Somalia—but sleeping on the floor wouldn't do Paul's fluky back any good, and she could just imagine what the mold and dirt would do to the kids. "Any cleaning stuff here?" she asked on the way back to the front door.

"I'll get you some when I go for food."

Soon they had the Geely in the garage, the garbage in a big green trash bag, and the water turned on with every tap in the house wide open to clear out the rust. The children roamed the house with wrinkled noses while Nora, Paul, and Juan gathered in the kitchen.

"About a quarter of the houses around here have squatters," Juan said. "Like you. Keep out of sight as much as possible. Lock the door. If someone knocks, don't answer." He shook a finger at Nora, who'd peeled off her wig. "Don't go outside. You're the web star; we can't risk someone seeing you."

She'd been afraid he'd say that.

Paul asked, "Can we let the kids out to play in the back yard?"

"Don't risk it. Wild dogs and coyotes live out there. The four-legged kind, not like me."

"Okay, but you may not have a house left after a couple days."

Juan smiled a little. "I'll take that chance. Make a list of things you want. I'll buy you supplies before I go home. Paul, do you have a burner?" Paul shook his head. "Great. I'll get you one. You can use those knocked-down moving boxes in the garage for ground pads. Be careful with your phones and slates. If someone breaks in, Nora, take care of it. Questions?"

Paul exchanged a dubious glance with Nora. "When are you coming back?"

"I have to take care of some business and line up some stuff. It's good to let things cool down a bit, too. It may be a few days."

Locked in this dump? Nora shuddered. They'd all go stir-crazy.

Juan pointed to Nora. "I'll call you if anything comes up." He checked their faces. "Look, I'm sorry this isn't a spa. I've used this neighborhood a few times before and everyone came out okay because they followed the rules. So follow the rules, all right?"

Nora nodded. Paul mumbled, "Okay."

Juan left through the garage door. Nora wrapped her arms around herself and stared through the twilight gloom into Paul's eyes. They betrayed the same doubt and fear she felt. A voice in the back of her brain asked if they'd ever see Juan again—or if the next knock they heard would be the Bureau, come to haul them to a place from which they'd never return.

25

Bel stared at her shadow on the door before her, cast by the weak fluorescent bulb in the hallway. Lucho was on the other side, still sleeping in the garage. The scratched doorknob scraped her fingertips.

Today had been the worst: knowing he was out there on a run, knowing what happened last time, knowing she hadn't told him "I love you" for over a week. It had to stop.

Lucho wasn't the enemy; Tavo and that asshole Ray were. He couldn't have known those Cartel bastards would do this to him (_but he should've!_). Nothing she was doing hurt _them_ one little bit—_she_ was the one sleeping alone, worrying every day that something would happen to Lucho, and she'd never get to tell that big doofus how aggravating he was and how much she loved him.

She pushed open the door.

After a moment, Bel saw light reflecting orange in a pair of eyes. The garage was even warmer and stuffier than the house—no windows, just a ceiling fan—and once her eyes adjusted, she could see Lucho hadn't bothered with a blanket. She shuffled toward the light shape of his underwear and knelt beside him on the old sleeping bag he used as a cushion.

She peered deep into his eyes for a long time. "Hey."

Lucho touched his fingertips to her bare knee. "Hey," he finally said.

His touch shot straight into her brain. Bel kept her arms locked tight around herself so she couldn't reach out to grab him and hold him the way she'd been squashing his pillow for the past few nights. "Did it go okay?"

"No, it didn't work. We'll have to try again."

Damn it. "Who are these people?" she asked after a stretch of silence.

He cocked his head. "You sure? You usually don't want—"

"I'm sure. Who are they?"

"A family. Mom and dad, a little boy and girl. They're wanted. The guy's supposed to go in a camp."

Bel shook her head. "Those poor babies." She looked down at her knee and his hand and hugged her short, ratty robe tighter around herself. "Are they good people?"

His eyes searched the garage ceiling for an answer. "I think so. They're in a bad situation. You know how that goes. The guy's nice enough, kids are cute. The woman… she's a tough one."

"Good. They'll need that. When are you going again?"

"Couple days or so, once things calm down."

They never do. He used to come home from runs all cut up and exhausted and bruised and filthy. She'd keep the kids away, and while she patched him up, he'd do his best to convince her it'd been easy, no problem. But she'd read too much about the things that happened on the border, and what she read between the lines scared her witless.

"You said they're wanted. Does that mean you are, too?"

"No more than usual."

"That bad, huh?" Bel stared at her knees. She heard all kinds of things he wasn't telling her. After all these years, she could tell when he was hiding something. But she wasn't here to start another fight. She took his hand in both of hers and squeezed. "You're going to come back, right? All in one piece?"

"That's the plan." He didn't sound nearly confident enough to make her forget what he looked like in the hospital after he was shot. "I'm sorry, *cariña*. I never meant for this—"

"I know." She freed a hand, laid it on his chest, feeling his heart beneath his undershirt. She tried to memorize each beat. "You're doing what you think you have to, I know. It's just…" She chewed on the insides of her lips for a few moments. "You let the Cartel buy you—*us*—so you could go on saving people you don't know. I don't know if I should be mad at you for being an idiot or at them for changing the rules."

Luis sat up and ran his fingers through her hair. She pressed her head against his palm. "I'll get us out of this. I promise."

Bel closed her eyes so she could concentrate on the warmth of his fingers on her cheek and let her hand trail down his chest. After a few moments, his lips found hers. She leaned into the kiss, giving him back a week's worth of longing and exasperation and fear, and soon she had his face in both her hands and could feel his touch leave burning trails on her skin beneath her robe. Bel pulled back to catch her breath, then glanced down. "These look way tight," she whispered, tugging at the waistband of his shorts. "We better get them off."

They made love in a rush, desperately making up for lost time and borrowing from the future, saying *I love you* and *don't leave me alone* and *I'll always come back* with their bodies and lips and eyes. When they at last chased away each other's dark shadows, Lucho settled onto his back so Bel could lie on top of him. She buried her face in the hollow of his throat, smelling his soap and sweat, riding each *thump* of his heart, each lift of his chest. He stroked her back from her shoulders to the tops of her thighs, up and down, slow and gentle, a sensation almost as erotic as holding him inside her.

After drifting awhile, Bel stretched up to kiss him, then folded her arms across his upper chest and rested her chin on her forearms.

Lucho gave her a lazy smile. "Am I forgiven?"

"Duh." She kissed his chin. "We haven't done it on the floor in ages."

He shifted his hips under her with a little grunt. "For a reason, I think."

"Are you saying I'm fat?"

"No." He cupped his hands around her rear and gave her a squeeze. "You're perfect. But the floor's hard and my knees are old."

Bel laughed, kissed the little notch at the base of his throat. "I can fix that." She sat up so she could gather her robe and his underwear, then stood and reached out her hand. "There's too much bed for just me. I'll share."

26

A USA TODAY *poll shows the average American spends approximately 46 hours a year in identification checks run by Immigration and Customs Enforcement, state and local police, and private security firms.*
        -- "POLL: Two Days in ID Checks," USAToday.com

Monday, 10 May

Luis was in the shop's toilet when he heard, "Immigration and Customs Enforcement! ID check! All y'all put your hands on your heads!"

Goddamn McGinley.

Luis had less than a minute before someone dragged him out front. He yanked his burner phone from his pocket, tapped the shred app, watched the red progress bar as it deleted and overwrote his call history and directory, then itself. He tore out the SIM, flushed the chip, then dropped the phone in the restroom trash.

A Costa Mesa contract cop wrenched open the door. "You! Get out here."

The rent-a-cop shoved Luis onto the shop floor. The five techs stood where they'd been when the raid started, hands on their heads, trading glances. The shop's pulsing thrash-*punta* background music snapped off mid-shriek. A white ICE twenty-passenger bus with wire mesh over the windows blocked the driveway.

McGinley leaned against the white Olympia in the middle bay, arms crossed, looking pleased with himself. "There you are," he boomed. "What was that y'all said couple weeks back? You were born here? Well, guess what, *amigo*. You get to prove it."

Luis stalked toward McGinley. "What the fuck are you doing in my garage?"

McGinley smiled. "Law says I can conduct an ID check in any

public place or place of employment. So here we are."

The contract cops lined up the techs in the parking lot. McGinley pointed to Tyler, the only Anglo, then jerked his thumb toward the street.

"No, sir," Tyler said. "I'll stay."

"Suit yourself." McGinley turned to Luis. "Give me your piece, your phone and your ID."

McGinley ran his ID through a field reader four times; each time it came up green. That didn't stop him from throwing Luis into the bus.

Luis couldn't decide whether to be angry or scared. He settled for both and paced the aisle, praying he'd get to go home again. Was this about yesterday? Did they trace the car to him? No, there was no way. This had to be McGinley being an asshole.

All McGinley had to do was call his ID fake, revoke his citizenship, and this bus would take him into the Sonoran desert. Being a citizen had nothing to do with it. He'd heard ICE liked to leave people in the middle of nowhere with nothing, not even water, sometimes not even clothes, and let the bandits or the Zetas get the ones who didn't die of thirst or exposure. No phone call, no appeal, no due process.

He finally perched on the back seat. Breathing took a continuous act of will and his heart threatened to explode with every beat. The last time he'd been this scared was when that *gabacho* contractor had shot him on the border.

After an hour—long after ICE was done with the techs— McGinley swaggered up the bus' steps with a 7-Eleven coffee cup. He said to the driver, "Why don't y'all take a walk?" Once the man left, McGinley unlocked the steel-mesh cage fencing off the seating area, ambled inside, and sat sideways on a front bench seat. "Here we are again, Ojeda, just me and you." He knocked back some coffee. "Octavio Villalobos. *La Almádena.*"

Luis stuffed down any reactions before they could show up on his face. "He's some cartel heavy, isn't he? In the news?"

"Aw, now, ain't it a little early to be shoveling that kinda shit?" McGinley actually looked disappointed. "Get your sorry ass up here. I ain't gonna yell at you all day."

"This is bullshit, you know." Luis edged into a seat across the aisle and a couple rows back from McGinley. "You want to talk, come in and talk. Don't hassle my guys. It's hard enough to make a buck these days."

"Don't you be telling me how to do my work. Let's try this again. Friday night 'round seven you went to La Paloma. Nice place, pretty waitresses. Y'all remember?"

Mierda. "Are you following me?"

"Why, no. But we do have an interest in that place, you might say. I'll assume you remember being there."

If they were watching the bar, did they have it bugged, too? Someone inside? How much did they know? "Yeah. A friend of mine works there. Sometimes I go by to see him. Have a beer, you know."

McGinley smirked as if Luis had confessed to being a terrorist. "Your 'friend' at La Paloma is Ramiro Esquivel, ain't that so?" He didn't wait for an answer. "I mean, we got enough pictures of the two of you together. Army buddies. Used to work in the local government before it went private. Are y'all gonna waste my time saying you don't know this man?"

Luis stewed a moment. "No."

"Well, that's progress, then. Now, are y'all gonna tell me you don't know he works for Villalobos? I sure hope not, 'cause I'm a betting man and I bet there's more'n bone in that *cabeza* of yours."

Luis tried hard to think of what his reaction ought to be. Surprise? Outrage? Fear? He couldn't come up with anything fast enough to keep it from looking fake. "I don't ask about who owns his bar. He doesn't ask who owns my garage."

McGinley shook his head, then stared out the windshield. He drained his coffee, stuck the cup on the floor, then turned back to Luis with a tired-of-the-world look on his face. "Ojeda, I'm not in a mood to play this bullshit with you. So before you go on insulting my intelligence, let me tell you something about me." He swiveled in his seat so he could stare down Luis more easily. "There are two things I'm real serious about. One of them is catching terrorists. I don't like terrorists, I don't like them coming here, I sure as hell don't like them living here, and I don't like the things they do here. I hope we don't have an argument about that."

Luis stifled his answer. Anything he said right now would

probably be wrong.

McGinley shook his head. "The other thing I'm serious about is Zetas. They are evil sons-of-bitches and you can't believe the things they do 'til you see it with your own eyes. I reckon they're worse than terrorists, 'cause at least terrorists do what they do for their Allah, but the Zetas do it for money and for just plain mean. We got enough problems of our own without them animals bringing their shit over to this side of the line. Is all this clear to you?"

"Yeah." At least he hadn't babbled about it being his Christian duty to run the mud people out of the country. It meant he might not be a complete nutjob. There were a lot of those around and they'd always scared Luis. The more the man talked, though, the more confused Luis got. "I don't have anything to do with terrorists or Zetas. What do you want from me?"

"Hold up, *amigo*, we're getting there. Y'see, we know the cartels have this nice little business going, running rags over the border. The rags pay good money to go. They got skills all y'all can use down south. Some of them even got military training—you can always use that. And every so often, one of them comes back up here, ain't that right?"

"I told you, I'm not—"

"You're not in that business, yeah, I know. But you were. Seems my local *compadres* here know all kinds of interesting about you, but never did anything about it. I ain't had time to find out why just yet, but I do have the notion that maybe you're someone's CI so they just let you be. If that's so, then y'all won't have a problem snitching for me, too, now, will you?"

The locals hadn't done anything about Luis because they had way too much else on their plates. He was small change compared to drugs and gun-running and cross-border hits. But if the file had half of what he'd done, the thought of it getting into McGinley's hands made his insides shrink.

His normal way to respond to fear or uncertainty was to come on hard. He couldn't go that way with McGinley, though, not when he was locked in a bus that could take him straight to Hell. "I... don't know how I can help you," he finally said. "As far as travelers go, I don't know if they're still in that business."

"Oh, they are. They had some ol' boy called Federico Salcedo moving the meat, so to speak. You know him?"

"No." *They knew about Rico?*

"So it won't bother you none to hear the Zetas handed him his head in Mexicali, and that ain't no figure of speech."

Jesus. Ray and Tavo had told him Rico was dead; they hadn't said who'd killed him. Mexicali was supposed to be Norte turf. When did Zetas show up there? "That sucks for him."

"That is a true thing. And let me tell you something else. Remember them runners I asked you about last week? The ones from Barstow? Well, we found 'em. They were with Salcedo. Leastwise, their heads were."

The picture that leaped into Luis' brain came so quickly and was so clear he couldn't mask his disgust fast enough. He turned his face to the window, staring out through the wire mesh while he got control of his gut.

McGinley watched him for a moment, then gave him an empty smile. "Quite a picture, ain't it? Now here's where I tell you what I want. You might want to pay attention. First, I want to know about any runners the Nortes are moving south, and any rags coming north. That's what I came here for, and that's what I need to hand the locals. I don't give a damn about quitters. If they're leaving 'cause they just want to get out, well, more power to 'em. But if they break out of a camp or they're coming up here, their asses belong to us. You got that so far?"

Luis nodded. He couldn't figure how this would get worse, but knew it would.

"Second. I want to know about Zetas, and what you Nortes plan to do about them. Where they are, what they're doing, who they're talking to. *Especially* if they're talking to Nortes. I won't say I came here for this, 'cause I didn't, but I'm here and them fuckers are too and that's one of them things I'm real serious about, remember?"

Luis nodded again. He wanted nothing to do with Zetas or even asking about them. That mental picture still vibrated in the back of his mind. "You want me to snitch."

"Yes, I do."

People who told stories on a cartel—any of them, not just the

Nortes—ended up tortured and dead by the side of the road, usually in pieces. On the other hand, if he didn't play ball with McGinley, what would happen? Would ICE throw him in jail? Dump him in the desert? He turned back to the window, tried to take a deep breath. "I don't have that kind of access."

"Then get it. They got a job opening. I expect you to go for it." McGinley raised his finger as if he was going to shake it again. "You know, something real interesting happened a few days back. Someone put Nestor Villalobos away. You know who he is, don't you?"

"Another cartel guy?"

"You can say that. He was the big chief of the Pacifico Norte cartel, but you know that. Now it looks like his brother Octavio is fixing to replace him. If you're keeping score, that means your best buddy Ray Esquivel now works di-*rectly* for the man who runs one of the last two cartels along the border. That sound like access to you?"

Chingado. "I never asked about Cartel business. On purpose. I can't just start now."

"You'd better." The smile disappeared; the amusement in McGinley's eyes dissolved. For the first time since Luis met him, the man was dead serious. "I can arrange for you to lose that nice job of yours so you'll have some incentive"—*oh, fuck, no no no*—"but I won't just yet, 'cause I want something to keep your attention, you know? I can arrange for that pretty wife of yours to end up in an ID check, and damn if there won't be a problem with her ID—"

"Stay away from my family, goddamnit!"

McGinley shot a finger at Luis. "I'll do what I have to, Ojeda. If that means your pretty *mamacita* winds up in a desert on the other side of the line, well, it'll be real bad for her. And your mama and papa? They're a little old for a camp, but—"

Luis charged out of his seat. "Leave them alone! Your beef is with me, not them. Leave them out of it."

McGinley drew his pistol and aimed at Luis' chest. "That's too close. You set your ass down *now*."

Angry but not suicidal, Luis backed into his bench. It took a few moments for him to put out enough fires inside his head before he could sit. All he could hear was the roaring in his ears.

"It's up to you, *amigo*." McGinley rested his weapon on the forearm he'd draped over his seat back. "Be a good boy, they'll be fine. If you don't, I'll fuck up your life so bad you'll *want* me to deport you. But I won't, 'cause I reckon you'd do just fine down there and I'd rather put you in a camp where I can keep track of you. I'm thinking Elko. How's that sound?"

Jesús Cristo. That was the badass camp, the one where the violent prisoners went. A hundred miles of desert between it and anything else. He'd never survive a place like that.

McGinley would destroy Bel, his parents, maybe Nacho too if his reach went that far. He'd probably leak Luis' name to the Cartel just for spite. And there was nothing—*nothing*—Luis could do to stop him.

McGinley smiled at him. "We understand each other, now don't we, *amigo*."

Yeah, they understood each other.

Luis was trapped.

27

This justifiable fear of eavesdropping has led to some extreme behaviors... Based on sales figures released by the two remaining American wireless carriers, CTIA estimates 37% of Americans carry a second mobile phone, usually a prepaid, non-contract handset not registered in their names...

-- "The Burner-Phone Shuffle," Wired.com

MONDAY, 10 MAY

The last cop car screeched out of the parking lot. The bus had left a few minutes before.

Luis stood on the sidewalk in front of the shop, shaking with rage and humiliation. McGinley had trapped him like a chicken in a pen. He wanted to hit something, kill something, the way he'd felt so often when he was young, before Bel had turned him into a civilized man.

He let the feelings flow for a few minutes to clean them out of his system. When his hands started to ache from clenching his fists, he used the positive visualizations he'd learned in the VA to drain the festering mess inside him. Bel's and Nacho's faces flashed through his mind. He loved them, and they'd suffer if he didn't wise up and think.

Luis needed to warn Ray and Salma. He had to get his burner back online. That meant a trip to Target for new chips and a new identity for his phone. Thank God the cops didn't find it.

Until then... email? No; the cops had been in the office unsupervised. Planted a keylogger? Installed a camera? Bugs?

Paranoid?

He couldn't discount paranoia. Now that McGinley had him by the *huevos*, he'd have to live knowing people really were out to get him again. With any luck, it would keep him alive.

Tell Bel? No, not yet. McGinley wouldn't do anything to her until Luis pissed him off. This would just set her off again. He'd tell her when he had to, which he hoped would be never.

Another complication: they had his truck for over two hours. Had they planted anything? Did he dare go anywhere if there was a tracker on it? He'd need a sweep immediately, this morning. Worry started backing up in his stomach.

Luis borrowed a phone from one of the techs. He called a car service number he had on a sticky note under the counter and told them to come to the corner. No names, no destination on the phone. An unregistered cab, no meter, GPS disabled, drivers with terrible memories for faces and places. The way poor people got around in the 1950s and '60s, still working today.

Pacing usually didn't calm him down, but he tried it anyway. It still didn't work.

He bought a dozen new chips at Target with his Cartel expense card, a Visa drawn on a Gambian bank in the name of a front corporation with two or three cutouts between it and a pot of some exotic online currency. Since it didn't require a signature, there was nothing to tie it to him. A thousand pounds fell off him when his burner phone blinked on with a new number.

The big problem with burners was that if used right, nobody would know the number, and so couldn't call them. He had to register his phone with the Cartel so the people who were supposed to be able to call him could.

Through the phone's browser, he hit a website with a name that was all numbers ending in ".pl"—Poland—and got the expected 404 error. He keyed in a PIN; the site downloaded the shred and 512-bit encryption apps and uploaded his new number. This system worked out all the call-forwarding.

Nathan the Exterminator came by just after lunch and ran a full scan of the shop. No bugs, no keyloggers. He found a tracker puck in the truck's rear bumper, though. "Pull it out? Leave it in?"

Luis tried to read his vee-shaped face for a clue to the right answer. As usual, Nathan's dark eyes revealed nothing. "Can you hack it?"

Nathan turned the puck over in his fingers, said "hm" a few times, then, "Let me see what I can do." Half an hour later, he waved Luis into the shop's racket. "Fixed it. If you're here or at your house, it'll report the right position. Anywhere else, it'll offset two miles west and a random distance north or south. They'll figure it out eventually."

Ray phoned a few minutes later. "You clean?"

"I think so. The bar's under surveillance. McGinley told me this morning."

"Yeah, we've seen them. I think they want us to see them, you know? So, what happened?"

Luis told him about the ID check but didn't mention McGinley's offer-he-couldn't-refuse. There are things that have to be said face-to-face. "We need to talk."

Ray paused long enough for Luis to wonder if the call had dropped. "Yeah, we do. There's shit going down you need to hear about. Not on the phone, you know?"

What now? Ray rarely got too cagy to talk on the phone. "Sure. I can get down there around three. Make sure you call it in. Do I need to be worried?"

"No." Ray didn't sound very convincing. "Maybe. Hell, yes. Just... be careful out there, keep your eyes open. See you at three."

28

MONDAY, 10 MAY

Luis slumped in the driver's seat, the Cartel-loaner Nissan in neutral, on Jamboree half a block north of Highway 73, waiting in line to leave the United States and enter Newport Beach.

The full-motion ads on the vidboard a block back—the last he'd see in Newport—couldn't have been more different from the ones in Orange. High-end products (North Pole cruises, genetic breast augmentation, Bentley, voluptuous models wearing the latest from Mumbai) and political ads ("Re-elect Senator Kardashian"). Back home it was guns and booze, and nobody bothered with political ads. Poor peoples' votes were bought and sold or disappeared in the system. Actual green grass stretched along the parkway next to him. It was hard to believe Newport was still officially part of the U.S.

The "No City Pass" lane inched south while the "Resident" and "Employee" pass lanes to his left flowed freely. Ads crawled across the e-plate on the car ahead of Luis. On the opposite corner, riot cops pounded a clutch of scraggly "Eat the 1%" protesters into the otherwise-pristine sidewalk. Up-armored SUVs and big luxury sedans—probably some of Luis' customers—whooshed north out of the city, the coveted blue "Resident" passes bright on the blacked-out windshields.

Luis eventually reached the entry gate and a starchy NBPD cop in pressed blues. Ray had remembered to call in an appointment, thank God. A Level 1 ID scan, mirrors under the car, a trunk-and-engine-compartment search. The cop slapped a red three-hour visitor pass on the center-top of his windshield and waved him through.

Sunscreen-smooth streets. Working stoplights. New cars. Pretty Anglos and Asians—somehow, they were all pretty—in the latest clothes and most fashionable tropical colors, wearing the latest phones, talking into the latest dataspecs. No surgical masks for the smog (no smog), no empty storefronts. Knots of well-fed teenagers out having fun, not working. No thrift stores, no missions, no street markets. Luis felt like a skunk at a wedding reception.

Tavo's—no, Ray's—neighborhood was all sprawling, low-slung ramblers set just feet apart, with huge banks of glass looking seaward and manicured plantings. Luis doubted anyone lived in these three- and four-car garages, and he bet all the streetlights worked. He parked in front of Ray's white modernist blockhouse, sat back, and stared into space as the engine ticked away its heat.

He'd spent the afternoon thinking hard about what to tell Ray, and how. It ought to be easy: "Ray, McGinley wants me to snitch. What do you want me to do?" But nothing's ever that simple. With *El Tiburón* dead and Tavo jockeying to replace him, everyone was running scared. Luis would take the fall for any leaks even if he didn't have anything to do with them. It's faster and easier to kill the known snitch than find the new one.

But if he didn't tell Ray, he'd be dead the moment someone found out. Well, not "the moment"—they'd draw it out—but close enough.

Which way to go?

Luis heaved out of the car, nodded to the lurking guard, then stepped along the pebbled concrete path into the entry courtyard. No sound from the doorbell. It probably worked anyway.

A moment later, a pretty, tanned young blonde hauled open the front door. She was what they used to call a "surfer girl" back when the ocean was clean enough to surf in. Was she here three years ago, the last time he'd visited this place? She sure hadn't been barefoot, in tight denim cutoffs and a low-cut yellow tank top. That, he'd remember.

"Welcome back, Mr. Ojeda. Follow me. Ray's waiting for you outside."

Ray stood up from behind his glass-topped patio table. His collarless shirt's iridescent blue matched the water in the big infinity pool. Sun glinted off the frames of his dataspecs. He reached to shake Luis' hand. "Ever been here in the daytime?"

"No, just at night. Jesus." Balboa Island and Newport Bay stretched golden in the afternoon sun from the foot of the bluff to the blue curve of the Pacific. Haze fuzzed the dark hump of Catalina and the spiky silhouettes of drilling rigs on the horizon. The coast was far enough out that Luis couldn't see or smell the oil sludge he could picture flopping onto the shrunken beaches, but close enough that the breeze could carry off the smog to Luis' house.

Luis heard a palm slap denim, and a quick giggle. When he turned, he caught Ray watching the blonde's cute little butt wiggle away. "Who's the *rubia?*" he asked in Spanish.

"Keira. She came with the place. She's the maid."

"That all?"

Ray snorted out a laugh. "Don't ask questions you don't want answered, *hermano.*"

Luis gave him a hard look, glanced back to the house, then shook his head sadly. "You didn't just dump Salma, you dumped her for a fucking *maid*. Nice."

Ray's jaw tightened. He stabbed a finger at Luis. "Fuck you. Anyone but you says that to me, I feed them to Pancho. Sit."

They settled into chairs on either side of the table. A six-sided blue umbrella screened them from the sun and any lurking drones. Luis watched the guards melt into the tall hedges on both sides of the yard. A wolfish dog sprawled panting on the pool apron a dozen yards away. Ray hadn't had a dog at his old place. "Pancho?" Luis asked, pointing.

"Yeah. You should be glad we split, you know? Salma's always been sweet on you. Now she's available. Go for it."

Luis crossed his arms and frowned. "I'm married."

Ray shrugged. "Look, I got bad news. The Zetas got Tavo Tuesday night."

"They *what?*" Luis lurched halfway out of his chair. "How did that happen?"

"Sit down. Nobody knows how it happened. They killed the guards, they killed Pilar, the kids, the guests. They shot one of the damn horses; not sure what that's about." Ray paused. "Thing is, they *took* Tavo, they didn't kill him. Nobody knows where he is. I didn't tell you before now because I'm working the problem and I knew you'd freak."

"Goddamnit!" Luis rattled the tabletop with a fist. "You know what this means, right? They're going to find out about all of us. What we're doing, where we live." Disgust turned to panic inside him. "Are we working for them now? For the Zetas? Is that how it is?"

"Not yet." Ray leaned forward, spread his hands. "Look, *hermano*, we need a *capo* before the Zetas give us one. Me and a couple of the other guys, we're working up a three-part *capo*—"

"I think they call that a troika."

"Whatever. If we spread out, it's harder to cut the Cartel's head off."

"Bad choice of words, *compa*."

"Yeah, yeah."

Luis fell back into his chair, wiped his palms down his face. He'd heard about what happened in Sinaloa and the three or four other cartels the Zetas had taken out in the past few years. The people they figured might be useful got a visit and an invitation nobody sane would refuse. The others—and the ones who said "no"—ended up hanging from a freeway overpass or lying in pieces in a parking lot. Now it was happening to the Nortes.

He finally focused on Ray and not Ray's words. Lounging around out here by the pool, grab-assing with his new toy girl… he wasn't acting like someone high on the list of people expecting a Zeta knock on the door.

"All kinds of shit's going down." Ray held out a hand toward Luis. It's like he'd been listening to the static in Luis' brain. "I'm just hanging on. This could get real bad, you know? I need to know you're behind me. I need good people backing me up. If everything goes right, there's room for you to move up, get you out of that sorry-ass garage. I need—"

"When was the last time I said I wanted to get in deeper with the Cartel?"

"Come on, I'm talking the legit businesses here. I know you don't want to do the other. Look, we'll talk about this again when things settle. I need to know you're with me, okay?" His tone said he wasn't asking. "Anyone comes looking around, you let me know."

That was Luis' cue. His eyes aimed at the view, but he didn't see it. "How come you didn't tell me Zetas killed Federico?" It was stalling, but he needed to think some more.

"Does it matter who killed him?"

"*Claro*, it matters. If they're that far west, I'm running out of crossings in Cartel territory. You want me to drop these people into the middle of the war? Where's the front line now?"

Ray leaned back into his chair, the pool reflecting in his lenses. "We're almost out of Sonora. There's fighting around San Luis." The Nortes' last Arizona crossing. He switched his focus to Luis. "McGinley tell you about Federico?"

"Yeah. He's all spun up about the Zetas moving west. He's also hot on the Cartel moving terrorists, which I think he thinks means anybody Muslim."

"Like your client," Ray said. *Your* client, not *our* client. "Why'd he tell you all this?"

"Maybe he likes the sound of his own voice." *Tell him?* Luis flipped a mental coin. "But mostly because he wants me to feed him intel."

Ray took a deep, loud breath, then nodded. He examined the tabletop.

"Look, Ray, if it was just me, I'd tell him to take his best shot. But he threatened Bel and my folks."

That got Ray's attention. When he looked up, Luis could see the anger in his tight mouth. "*Chingado*. Let's just get rid of that *pendejo*. I can do it easy."

He'd said that as casually as he'd say "hello." "That'd just make things worse. Someone else would come after me, and they'd probably figure you or Tavo had something to do with it."

Ray sat there for a long minute, elbows on the table, staring into space. The silence was the worst part. What was he thinking? Who he could get to kill McGinley? Who could kill Luis? Ray had always been able to "make things happen," but Luis had never thought of him being able to make *that* happen. Not until now. Not until it might happen to him.

Ray pushed out of his seat and drifted toward the patio's edge, his hands in the front pockets of his white *churidars*. A stylized black sketch of an eagle took up most of the area between Ray's shirt yoke and belt, perched on an outline branch. Its head swiveled back and forth, then it shook out its wings. Ray's shirt cost more than Luis' house payment. *Nice threads*, compa.

"What have you told him?" Ray finally asked.

Luis reluctantly crossed to his side. "Nothing. I wanted to get with you first, see how you want to play this. I guess we could feed him fake intel if it looks good enough."

"Good. Good call." Luis felt a tiny bit of tension leak away when Ray said "good." He might survive this. "Tell him Tavo's alive and we've got him hid. *El Tiburon* used a double sometimes. Maybe they'll think Tavo did, too. If it gets back to the Zetas, maybe it'll give Tavo a break, who knows. *¿Comprendes?*"

And move the crosshairs off Ray? "*Claro*. I doubt he'll buy it, but whatever."

"He'll buy it if you sell it."

"Sure. Got anything I can give him on the Zetas?"

"I guess. I get intel reports on the fighting every day. I can slip you the ones that are a couple days old. Nobody'd care." They stood quietly for a moment, gazing out at the town and ocean. "What's next with the *bruja*? How you gonna get her out now?"

"I'm working it. Security's tougher since I did this last." Luis looked straight into Ray's dark glasses. "Promise me something, will you? If you think Bel's in danger, don't wait. Let me know. And make sure you take care of Salma. The women don't deserve to get dragged into this."

"I'll take good care of Salma, don't you worry." Ray turned and clapped Luis' shoulder hard. "Be careful, *hermano*. There's sharks in this water. But if you swim right, even with sharks you can come out okay."

"Yeah. Or I can end up as lunch."

Ray shrugged. "That's the thing with sharks, you know? I'll call you. Keira'll show you out." He paced toward Pancho, tapping his ear pod. For the first time Luis could remember, Ray didn't shake his hand before he left.

29

Monday, 10 May

Nora stood in her penlight's faint blue glow, watching through the master bathroom's door as the kids slept in the tub. They curled up together on a couple of the cheap beach towels Juan had bought for them. No rats or rabid dogs would get to them in here. They might escape unnoticed if someone came through the front door.

What was I thinking?

She should've quit the Bureau when they chained her to a desk. Most of the other Muslim agents had. But no; she had to be stubborn. She'd grown up with superpatriots for parents and had "duty" and "honor" and "service" pounded into her skull from the time she could walk. Nobody was going to chase *her* out, not after everything she had to go through to get in.

So she'd dug in, took all the crap the Bureau could pile on her, and powered through the everyday humiliations and frustrations. *Never quit*, Dad had always told her.

Then he quit. The abuse finally got to be too much, even for him and Mom. Nora could still see the heartbreak on their faces as they walked into Dulles that last time on their way to exile in France. Now the bill for her own stubbornness had come due, and the most important people in her life were paying for it.

She glanced over her shoulder at the sound of shuffling feet on carpet. Paul's undershirt reflected the penlight as he neared. He yawned, rubbing his eyes. "Kids okay?"

"They're fine," she murmured. "I guess they really can sleep anywhere."

"Too bad grown-ups can't, huh?" His arms looped around her waist, pulled her back against him. He kissed her ear. "Are you okay?"

Nora nestled against Paul's reassuring warmth, wrapping her hands around his. "I can't sleep."

"What else is new?"

"No, really. It's worse here. I hate not being able to see outside. I can't tell if…"

"If zombies are coming for us?"

"Zombies I can deal with. It's the QRT I worry about." She flung a hand toward the bathroom. "Look. Our kids have to sleep in a bathtub so they don't get shot or eaten. Mom and Dad told me about how they did that in Beirut in the civil war." Nora swallowed a catch in her throat. "We should've left when they did. I was so stupid—"

"Shh. You'll wake the kids." Paul squeezed her hard. "We decided to stay. *We* decided. Both of us. You and me. So don't go putting it all on yourself—I'm in there too."

"It was stupid, and this is even worse." She trapped a sudden sob in her throat before it could escape. *No, not now, not here.* "I'm sorry. I'm so sorry."

"For what?"

"For this." She waved her arm around them. "For putting you and the kids in danger. For handing our lives over to some *narco*. For…"

"Doing the right thing?" Paul's voice was firm but not unkind. He kissed the back of her head. "Don't apologize for that."

"Is it the right thing? Is it going to matter? Will anyone care?" Nora twisted in his arms to face him. He was only a dim shape, even up close, and she wished she could see into his eyes. They could never lie to her. She'd fallen in love with his eyes before she'd come to love the rest of him. "We're fugitives. We have no country anymore. Everything we own is in those backpacks. I've ruined our lives." She squelched another sob before it broke.

He tilted up her chin with a thumb. "Stop. You're not the only one who makes decisions around here. Remember our wedding contract? Decisions we make together belong to us both. We can't renounce them unless we both do, and I'm not changing my mind about this one." He bent his neck until his forehead touched hers. "Yes, it'll matter. Yes, people will care. Besides, if we stop doing the right thing, what are we?"

Nora sniffed and frowned up at him. "Leave it to a lawyer to bring up a contract." She nestled against him, thanking whatever force had brought her this man who was the good part of her, the one who kept her from living alone in a fog of distrust.

Paul held her close, stroked her back and hair, rocked her gently the way she would Hope or Peter. He began to murmur something so low she couldn't catch the words, just the sound. After a few moments, she understood: he was praying.

She tried to pray, but after everything she'd seen and done, it was so hard to believe anyone listened. Allah had abandoned them all: her and her family, all those poor people in the camps, the wretches she'd seen dying by the roads in Somalia. All His children. She kept asking Him questions, but He never answered. Had He given up on this world in disgust?

She couldn't blame Him if He had.

30

I hereby further authorize and direct the Secretary of
Homeland Security and the said Federal agencies to take
such other steps as he or the appropriate agencies may
deem advisable to enforce compliance with the restrictions
applicable to each Homeland Security Area hereinabove
authorized to be designated, including the use of Federal
troops and other Federal Agencies, with authority to
accept assistance of state and local agencies.

-- Homeland Security Presidential Directive 266, 19
December 2019

TUESDAY, 11 MAY

The skanky twenty-something guy chunked cash down on the counter for a film job on his truck's windows. Based on the guy's glazed eyes and runny nose, Luis figured cooking zip had paid for this and the new pickup, too. Luis pulled out his burner when it buzzed in his pocket and held it between his ear and shoulder as he counted the money. "Hello?"

"Lucho?" Salma's voice, urgent. "Did you see it? What have we done?"

"Hold on." He got rid of the ziphead, then opened a browser on the office slate. "What am I looking for?"

"Go to Fox."

Luis brought up the Fox News page and recoiled at the pulsing red "TERROR ALERT" banner at the top of the screen. He tapped it, wondering what sad sack got crossways with Homeland Security today.

The headline said, "Wanted by FBI: Nura Amad Fakhir al-Khaled."

Below it glared Nora's face.

Luis stared through a gap in the back fence at the El Cajon cottage where he'd stashed Nora and her family. It had taken him over two hours to get here from work; a good thing, since he'd had time to cool down and get thinking straight.

The "alert" was typically light on details: Nora was "wanted for questioning in connection to several major anti-American terrorist plots over the past ten years." It said nothing about her being an FBI agent. The picture looked like a mug shot—Nora after a three-day bender, nothing like the buttoned-up woman Luis knew.

His first reaction had been panic. He'd never had a celebrity traveler before, especially not one like this. He could see SWAT busting through the shop's front windows and FBI agents hog-tying Bel at the hospital. A bad few minutes flew by with Luis pacing a circle in the office, his brain spinning at the speed of light.

He'd started to think again in the Cartel-loaner Toyota. Was this true? It was the kind of thing the FBI would do if it wanted to catch someone, terrorist or not. On the other hand, maybe Nora was a good actress. Maybe she was a behind-the-scenes type, moving money or weapons. He remembered her in the showroom last Thursday night: watching over the kids like a mother hawk, the moments of affection between her and Paul. He hadn't seen an ounce of political or religious fanatic in her. Hardass, sure, but no more than some platoon sergeants he'd known.

But even if she wasn't a terrorist, she wasn't innocent. She'd done *something*. That wasn't Paul's picture on the news, and that circus around the hotel last week hadn't been there to lock up some desk jockey. She had a lot of explaining to do.

A mental news flash: he was the only person who knew where Nora was. Who was more of a threat to him—the FBI… or her?

Luis rolled this over in his mind. After a few moments' debate, he stood, drew his pistol, and stepped through the fence gap into the safe house's back yard. He'd go in heavy in case she was bad news and was waiting to jack his car; he could dial down faster than he could dial up.

He quick-stepped through the weeds, unlocked and edged through the side door into the garage, then tested the knob on the kitchen door. It turned. *Here goes.*

He entered, leading with his weapon. Nora's startled eyes locked on him through a doorway into the living room. She knelt on a beach towel, hands on her thighs, a green-and-white patterned scarf tied over her hair. The harsh, bluish-white light of an LED lantern washed the color out of the left side of her face. Her lips formed an "O."

Luis stopped, surprised. The headscarf reminded him why she was supposedly on the run. It was then he noticed her long pants and long-sleeved shirt. It was past one—mid-day prayers?

"Honey, what's wrong?" Paul's voice asked. His upper half appeared beyond the kitchen pass-through when he stood. He saw Luis and froze. "What is this?"

"Where are the kids?" Luis asked.

"Right here."

"Take them to the back." Luis cleared his throat to break up the tension in his voice. "I have some business with your wife."

"What are you—"

Nora held up a hand toward him. "Paul, please do it. It's okay." She glared at Luis. "I'll be fine."

Paul scowled at Luis, then gathered up the kids and herded them down the hall to the bedrooms, leaving behind a trail of "Do we hafta?"

"Can I stand?" Nora asked. Luis glanced at her holstered pistol resting on the kitchen counter, then nodded. She carefully stood, keeping her hands visible at all times. She was barefoot, making her seem more vulnerable than he'd ever seen her. Her angry eyes balanced out that impression. "Are you going to explain this?"

"Since you're the star on Fox, I'll ask you the same thing."

She frowned. "What are you talking about?"

Her reaction might tell him which way to go. He pulled his phone with one hand while the other covered Nora with his pistol. He thumbed on the phone, laid it on the dusty, medium-blue living-room carpet, then stepped back. "This. Nice picture."

Nora plucked the phone off the floor, checked the screen, and winced. Once she scanned the story, she heaved out a huge sigh. "I can't believe they did that," she finally murmured, half to herself. "That's my ID photo. Someone doctored it. Probably Fox."

"You're taking this pretty well. Want to explain what's going on here?"

She looked up, startled. "You don't really believe this, do you?"

"That you're a terrorist? Not sure. That you did *something?* Yeah."

"So you're going to shoot us now?" Paul demanded as he re-entered the living room. His voice and face were equally angry.

"Not unless I have to."

When Paul reached Nora's side, he asked, "What's the problem?" Nora handed him the phone. Luis watched his eyes get big and his anger bleach into shock. "Oh, shit."

Luis took back his phone from Paul—who looked stunned—then aimed his pistol at the floor. "Now talk," he said to Nora. "We'll start with something simple. What's your real name?"

"Real?" She folded her hands around Paul's. "You mean, my official name? The alert got it right for a change. But I've always been just Nora."

"The 'al-Khaled' part's my family name," Paul said. "We all have Arabic names. Mine's 'Boulus,' Peter's 'Butrus,' Hope's 'Raja.' We don't use them, not the way things are now."

"You're not really Juan," Nora said.

"I'm not on Fox, either. What did you do?"

"I told you," she snapped. "We're leaving before Paul can—"

"Stop." The more she danced, the darker the picture Luis' imagination painted. "This isn't about Paul. This isn't about them thinking you're going to defect. It's too big for—"

"They're desperate to find us." Nora's hands held Paul's so tightly, her knuckles shone white. "They're getting their shots in now—"

"*What did you do?*"

Nora glanced up at Paul, then shook her head. "You really don't want to know."

Luis' frustration exploded inside him. "Bullshit! I'm tied to you until you're in Mexico. If they did this to you"—he held up his phone—"what'll they do when they find out about me? The same thing? No thanks."

Nora broke away from Paul, clenched her arms across her chest and started stalking back and forth across the room. "If I tell you—

if they know you know—you'll be a target, too. More than you already are. Just leave it alone and do what you're being paid for."

Murder? Espionage? Treason? Luis had even come back to thinking she might actually be tied up with some terrorists, crazy as it sounded. "Remember what happened to that guard in Tecate? That's what's gonna happen to anybody with you if they catch you. You tell me what this is really about, or I drive away and you guys find your own way south."

She stopped pacing and glared at him. "Your boss won't like losing our money."

"Less than an hour's take in L.A. If it keeps us away from a terrorism beef, they'll figure it's money they can do without." He closed in on her, grabbed her arm. The surprise jolted her features. "Last chance. I have a family, too. I almost got killed last time I did this. Something you're hiding just made you famous. That flashes all kinds of red lights for me. Talk or I'm gone."

"Honey?" Paul took a step toward her, then stopped when Luis twitched his gun hand. "Tell him. He'll find out eventually. He should know."

Nora met her husband's eyes. "That's our insurance! What'll stop him from—"

"Tell him, or I will. We need him."

Nora and Luis both gaped at Paul, who glowered back at them, fists on his hips. Luis hadn't thought the man had those kind of *cojones. Good for him.*

Nora deflated. After a moment, she closed her eyes and sighed. "Okay. Can you get my slate?"

Paul threw a half-angry look at Luis, then hurried down the hall to their bedroom.

While they waited, Nora untied her scarf, rolled up her sleeves, and slipped on her shoes. She stood at the pass-through, gripping the faux-marble counter's edge so hard that all the veins and sinews in her hands popped. "Thank you for not scaring my children."

Luis holstered his pistol. His shirt was drenched with sweat. "Whatever you did, I figure it didn't involve them."

"In a way, it does. It involves everybody. You just don't know it yet."

31

TUESDAY, 11 MAY

Nora took the slate from Paul, then signaled to Juan to join her at the pass-through counter. Paul slipped away to watch from the kitchen. "Remember 10/19?"

"Oh, God, yes," Juan groaned.

Nora wondered if anyone alive then *didn't* have those numbers stamped into the front of their brains, like 9/11 before it. She detached the little data-chip module from the base of her chunky silver pendant, plugged it into the slate's side, then poked at the screen to bring up the folders. "The 2019 National League playoffs, game five, at Wrigley Field. The Cubs and the Phillies." She swept the slate's screen with her fingertip a couple times. "The game was sold out, 42,719 in attendance." She handed the slate to Juan.

He grimaced at the video frame she'd cued up. "Do I have to?"

"Yes. Twice."

She didn't have to look at the screen. How many hundreds of times had this played on the news? How many dozens more times had she examined it frame-by-frame at headquarters?

The security-cam view of traffic flowing by on West Addison Street. A stream of people stroll the brick sidewalk; a line of out-of-service buses waits along the curb for the game's end. A few seconds later the truck arrives, a semi with a Budweiser box trailer and North Dakota plates. It curves into the curb ahead of the lead bus, just a few feet away from the no-parking sign outside the stadium's Gate F. Then a black four-door sedan pulls past, full of dark faces, its nose disappearing into the camera's blind spot. Just as before, a dark-skinned guy in gray work clothes scrambles out of

147

the truck cab, then jogs to the sedan's open back door. The car squirts away before he can even close the door behind him. Then those three security guards and the Chicago cop close in to check out the truck. Ninety seconds of head-scratching. A few frames of pure white. Then static.

Juan sighed, handed the slate back to Nora. The "what happened next" images were still vivid: the fires, rubble, bodies, gray dust coating the outfield wall's ivy, bleeding people staggering past crumpled cars in the street. That iconic shot of the Cubs flag burning over the stadium.

"Two thousand eighty-one dead." There was no emotion in her voice or head. "Including the mayor and six Phillies starters. Over four thousand injured." She held up the slate to show him pictures of four all-too-familiar dark-brown faces. "Twenty-three blocks north in Lakewood, CPD pulled over a black 2009 Chevy Impala for speeding. These four Yemenis were in it—two of them born here, one green card, one on a busted visa. They said they were late for work. ICE locked them up. You know the rest.

"I joined the Bureau in '20, the last class that let in Muslims. I'd've been happy to stay in the Army, but it was going private and the contractors didn't have any use for women, especially not Muslim women."

"Infantry?"

"Military police. Anyway, a few months after Quantico I went to Counterterrorism Division at headquarters. That's what happens to agents like me who speak Arabic and Farsi. It was a huge career boost—that's where all the action was back then."

She'd been so excited at first. Then they started yanking female agents off the streets because the Attorney General and the President didn't think it was "appropriate" to have wives and mothers in "those kinds of roles." She was doubly cursed because of her religion; frozen out even though they needed her skills more than ever. Residual anger warmed her cheeks.

"Anyway, there I was in '29 and the Bureau wanted to do a ten-year review of the Wrigley Field case. Pull together an updated history, stuff for the anniversary, all that. I ended up on the history team. The other agents kept saying, 'Come on, we know what happened, just make it pretty,' and I'd tell them no, let's do this right, let's look at it like a new case. I wasn't very popular. Anyway, we went through tons of material." She paused, blowing out a long breath. "I started finding things that didn't add up."

"Is this where I put on my tinfoil hat?"

She scowled at him. "Just hear me out. Look, I've got to defend the Bureau. We were under incredible pressure right after the attack. Everyone in the country screaming at us for one thing or another. And then all the other stuff."

The other stuff: riots, mosque burnings, Muslims getting beaten to death or shot, women in *hijab* stripped in the streets, mobs torching the beards off Muslim men. That orgy in Buffalo: two hundred dead Yemenis, sixteen blocks burned out. Cops standing by and watching or helping; firemen letting Muslim houses burn. She'd watched from Somalia as it unspooled on the web, terrified for her parents and brother, sick at being helpless to protect them.

"That was a scary, scary time. So I was ready to excuse loose ends, you see? But they kept piling up, and pretty soon I couldn't anymore."

Keep going? She'd hadn't planned to tell him everything in case he decided to get rich by killing her and stealing the story. But now she'd started it was hard to stop, as if she had to purge this huge weight she'd been carrying, the faster the better.

"The first thing that bugged me was what happened on the 21st. The Bureau took custody of the Yemenis from ICE way before anyone had seen the video or even knew what kind of car left the scene. The AG announced it that night—that's what kicked off the worst of it.

"What really got to me was that even with all those records, there were holes. Craters. Canyons. There was *so* much missing stuff. I'd figured the meat of the case was in the classified material, but there wasn't much more there. The guys had ammonium nitrate on their clothes. But they were all landscapers, of course they would. The traffic cams didn't pick up the Impala until it turned onto Clark off Lawrence from the wrong direction. That kind of thing. The way I'm wired, when I find a loose end, I want to tie it off. So I kept trying to track down the lost material, and I put in a request to interview the Yemenis."

After a few seconds of silence, Juan asked, "What did they have to say?"

Nora sighed. "The EAD turned—"

"EAD?"

"Sorry, Executive Assistant Director. He turned me down. I found out later all four of them are dead." She checked Juan's face, covered with his surprise. "Officially, two committed suicide, one died in a fight, the other supposedly of a ruptured appendix. Quite the coincidence."

"Are they really dead?"

Paul chuckled in the kitchen. "Now you're getting it."

Nora shot him a glance, then gave Juan a thin smile. "I have no idea. Probably. Anyway, we put together this whitewash report, which I'm sure was what they wanted in the first place. I went back to my cold cases and FOI requests and monthly polygraphs. And it ate me up that so much was gone. So I kept digging, off the books, but I didn't find much.

"Then I went out for lunch about a year and a half ago, and someone left a note in my purse. A phone number, on *flash paper*, really old-school. It was this old-line agent I'd interviewed for the report. He'd been on the Pile after 9/11 and got some weird kind of cancer from it. Wrigley Field was his last case before he went out on disability. We started talking, and he gave me scraps of stuff from the 10/19 case, and I got interested because I hadn't seen any of it before. Then one day, he gave me this." She tapped the slate, then turned it over to Juan.

"Again?"

"Just watch it. Carefully."

He tapped "play." The screen in her mind played the video, too. Same camera, same street, same buses. The same semi parked, followed by the same sedan. The same driver abandoning the truck.

Only it wasn't the same driver.

This one was white. The three faces in the sedan were noticeably lighter, too.

Juan rewound and replayed those few seconds of video four times. He looked up at Nora. "What the hell?"

Her same reaction the first time. "That's the *original* security footage. Remember how they supposedly couldn't get to it right off because of the rubble? It turns out they found the video eight days after the bombing, in the basement where the recorders lived."

Juan's face crunched in confusion. "Why didn't they announce it then?"

"Are you serious?" Paul asked, a half-laugh in his voice. "The FBI Director had already told the world they'd caught the bombers. The Attorney General called American Muslims 'vipers in our house.' The President said he'd wipe out every last *jihadi* in America, no matter what. My office was getting hundreds of calls a day about the pogroms happening all over the country. The FBI and ICE had already rounded up ten, eleven thousand Muslim men for questioning. Including a cousin of mine, by the way, though they let him go after six days." He turned up his palms. "Do you think the FBI would stand up and say, 'Never mind'?"

"But, cover it up?"

"That's what worked best for all of them," Nora said. "They were stuck with the story they'd created, so they buried the truth and went with the myth. Which included altering the video."

Juan shook his head as if it hurt. "How do you know this agent guy didn't fake up the video himself?"

"He could barely work a cell phone. He invited me up to his house out in West Virginia a few days later. He was dying by then—he'd stopped his chemo—and he said he had a present for me. He had eighteen boxes of paper copies of 10/19 records that got shredded. He also had all these CDs—*CDs*, I told you he was old-school—full of files the Bureau deleted. It was exactly what I'd been looking for. He said he didn't want the secret to die with him, and he was sorry for all the pain it caused… people like me." She recalled Hugh's ravaged face from their last meeting. Dead about a year, now; at least he didn't hurt anymore. Nora held out the slate to Juan. "Here, take a look."

Juan riffled randomly through the hundreds—thousands—of files and folders. From time to time, he'd scratch his head or cup a hand over his mouth. Nora watched him and relived that sucker-punched feeling when she'd learned that everything she'd known about the most important event in the past fifteen years was a lie.

"What's REDCAP?"

She leaned toward him to see the document on the screen. The

Druganic statement from the 23rd, marked TOP SECRET// REDCAP//NODIS. "That's the compartment they created for the sensitive stuff. I'm not read in, so I shouldn't have seen any of it. But what was I supposed to do, burn out my eyes?"

Juan gamely trudged through more files, but he'd slowed as if the weight of it all dragged him down. He finally slumped his elbows onto the counter, staring at the boarded-up kitchen window. "So who really did it?"

Nora tapped and wiped the screen a few times. Pictures of four white men appeared: three square-faced and thick-necked like laborers or bodybuilders, the fourth thinner and darker. She shuddered, just as she always did when she saw their faces. "Dugan, MacRonan, Seybold, and Conners. Paid-up members of the Free Montana Militia. Hooked up with Christian Identity, hooked up with the sovereign citizen movement, anti-everything, highlights in their copies of *The Turner Diaries*, the whole picture. Seybold started mouthing off on the phone a week after the bombing and NSA picked it up. We rolled them up five weeks later. Of course, it was too late by then."

"Why'd they do it?"

"The race war was taking too long to get started. They didn't like the public race-mixing they saw in the big cities. They thought pro sports had been taken over by Jews and nigger junkies and it was ruining good white kids' morals." Juan winced at her words. "So they decided to make *The Turner Diaries* come true. Dugan was a truck driver—that was him in the video. Seybold ran a farm. MacRonan had worked EOD in Iraq. Conners was a painter in an auto-body shop. That's all the brains it took. The Bureau just helped them get away with it."

Juan examined the four pictures. "What happened to them?"

"I hope they're on the bottom of Lake Michigan. The Bureau put them in a place that doesn't exist and sweated their statements out of them. I've got them if you want to read them. It's really sick, sick stuff—they were actually proud of themselves. There's no paper trail on the rest, but the best I can work out, some contractors took the four of them and they were never seen again." Nora slipped the slate from his hand and cradled it against her chest. "Now you know what I did and why they're after me. Sorry you asked?"

Juan nodded, looking lost.

There was more, but he didn't need to know the rest—not yet. What he already knew could kill him.

32

This will be the fourth consecutive national election for which the United States has refused to admit international observers... An estimated nine to ten million otherwise qualified voters have been excluded by voter ID laws aimed primarily at the poor, the young, and racial minorities... Documented claims of voter intimidation, vote buying, and widespread ballot tampering have been ignored to date by government officials.

-- 2032 U.S. Election Assessment Report, Democracy International

TUESDAY, 11 MAY

All the rubble from Wrigley Field seemed to be piled on Luis' shoulders. He trudged across the living room and back, his head throbbing from everything he'd just seen and heard. Could this be real? Would Nora even bother with all this if she was some kind of bad-ass felon on the run? Probably not; she'd just shoot him and move on. But that meant... "If you're right, then it's all a lie," he said, half to himself. "All of it. The laws, the camps, the roundups, the ID checks, invading Yemen. It's all because of a lie."

"Yes," Paul said. He leaned back against the kitchen sink, half-lit by reflected lantern light. "Can you imagine what would happen if the truth came out now?"

Luis tried, but it required hope and trust, which had mostly been ground out of him. "That's your plan? Tell everybody?"

"Pretty much." Nora's folded arms still pressed the slate against her chest. "We've been working with some people in the government in Britain. They're really angry about the NSA hacking the Prime Minister's network. I've sent them about three-quarters of the data over the past year. This is the last of it. It's slow because I can only send a little at a time so the NSA doesn't notice. When I turn over the rest of it, the Brits will give us asylum and new identities. We'll need it, believe me."

"The *Guardian's* already committed to running the story," Paul said. "It'll go global. Even with all our anti-piracy laws and web blocks and everything, it'll get back here."

Nora edged a bit closer to Luis. "I made them promise to wait until I got out with Paul and the kids. Once the story runs, the Bureau will know I leaked. If they can get to us, they'll make us disappear like we never existed. But I guess they already know."

Luis shook his head. "Why would anybody believe it? I remember the conspiracy crazies, blaming aliens and shit. Why aren't you just another nut?"

"Because the crazies don't have this." She held up her slate. "This is just part of it. As far as I know, we have nearly all the case records. MI-5's been comparing our documents to Bureau paper they're gotten from other cases. The *Guardian's* lined up a couple ex-agents to vet the material. It helps that the Bureau's been stonewalling the FOI requests—I know, I'm one of the people doing it—so it already looks like they're hiding something." She hugged the slate again. "Nobody else has this kind of evidence. Only us."

"So all that about Paul going in a camp—"

"Is true." Paul circled into the living room. "That's why we're leaving now and not a couple months from now when she's had time to move the rest of the data and do some more groundwork." He wrapped an arm around Nora's shoulders. "The story has to run by August so there's enough time to affect the election."

Luis had followed them up to now, but this was one step too far. "The election? You seriously think this is gonna change who wins? I mean, it's bad, yeah, but it's ancient history."

"Maybe not so ancient." Nora's words were suddenly wary. She and Paul exchanged a serious look that made Luis think she hadn't told him the whole story.

Paul set his jaw. "The people involved in this… well, let's just say they're pretty senior in the Administration now. A lot of people don't like the way things are, but they've given up on voting. This should give them a reason to vote again. Even if it doesn't work, we have to try. *Someone* has to try. Everyone needs to know."

"There's a passage in the Qur'an I really like," Nora said. "'And mix not up truth with falsehood, nor hide the truth while you know.' That kind of says it."

Luis had gone into this work thinking like them—someone has to try; someone has to fight back. But not one damn thing changed. The utter futility had driven him out as much as that bullet had. He'd never had a weapon as big as this in his hands, though.

His survival instinct—the devil on his shoulder—asked, *how much is it worth?*

Dealing with the FBI himself would be the dumbest move ever. But he could give Nora to Ray in exchange for tearing up his debt. Get out from under in one shot and let the Cartel figure out how to make money off her story.

He glanced at Nora. Her big, dark eyes searched his face. Gifting her to the Cartel meant that one way or another, she'd end up in the FBI's hands, and then she'd be locked up forever or dead. This secret—this truth, if that's what it was—would die with her. The people who built the lie, who'd been taking apart the America Luis had grown up in and loved and fought for, would keep winning and getting richer and wreck things even more.

Then again, maybe they would anyway.

If he helped Nora and he was caught, the FBI might do to him and Bel the same thing they did (according to Nora) to the Yemenis and the militia *tontos.*

With Tavo gone and Ray distracted, maybe now was the time to grab Bel and make his own run south before this insanity blew up in his face. Leave Nora before she got him killed.

Mierda. He had a lot of thinking to do on his two-hour drive back home.

"You two put a lot on one Lotto ticket," he finally said.

"I know." Paul smiled at him. "But think of the jackpot. Will you help?"

33

The United States has achieved energy independence, and is even now an energy exporter, due to the elimination over the past decade of the job-killing environmental, tax, and trade regulations that once prevented America's mining industry from developing our nation's vast reserves of precious resources.

    -- Backgrounder on U.S. Coal, *National Mining Association*

WEDNESDAY, 12 MAY

Sitgreaves National Forest wasn't tore up any more than any other national forest McGinley had seen. Logging roads snaked across the clear-cut tracts; stumps and bare red dirt marked the edges of a lease; spoil clogged the arroyos between the rolling hills. It looked a little like Ouachita up by Little Rock, with less water.

He pounded back his second energy drink to burn off the cobwebs from last night's late courier flight into Tucson. Gennaro had called him yesterday afternoon, said, "We're raiding the mine. You want in?" McGinley hadn't stopped moving until he was on the ramp at Davis-Monthan this morning.

If you're there, baby, he told Carla Jean, *I'm coming for you.*

"You set, Jack?" Gennaro's voice shot through the headset right into McGinley's skull.

"I am. How much longer?"

"Five minutes. Look to your ten o'clock. It's a helluva sight."

McGinley glanced out the window—the second chopper in formation at eight o'clock—then checked his ten. *Jee-sus.* A huge, black crater began filling up the window below the drone gunship leading the flight, spreading out to the base of the mesa out yonder, steps like layers disappearing below the rim. Black haze hung over the mine from the coal dust and diesel exhaust and chemicals and what have you. It was the biggest hole in the ground he'd ever seen.

The chopper nosed down toward the tops of the scraggly dead trees. The ten ICE troops sharing McGinley's space sat up, checking their weapons and gear. McGinley tightened his kevlar's chin strap, pumped a round into his shotgun's chamber, and switched on his data goggles. He felt that buzz he'd gotten in the Army way back when, just before he jumped out of his chopper into Syria to put some hurt on the dirtbag-of-the-day.

They roared over a clearing with a couple prefab metal warehouses in the middle, the ground black from coal dust, trucks and cars parked all over. A technical rolled out toward them, shooting, until *whoosh!* a few rounds from the gunship blew the pickup in half and flared the mounted fifty into the air like a bottle rocket.

Then things got awful busy. Before he knew it, McGinley was on the gravel, sheltering behind a pickup that some asshole by the closest warehouse was taking apart with his AK. Some ICE troops fired back from behind other cars and trucks. Then he heard the gunship's minigun go *rrrrrip* and the asshole disappeared in a spray of red and a couple orphaned legs.

McGinley jogged toward the warehouse behind a trio of ICE troops. Some ol' boy—dirty enough to be a miner—staggered out the door and got beanbagged for his effort. McGinley jumped the man's body and found himself in a melee of miners and guards just inside the warehouse. He cracked a few with his shotgun butt, spotted a weapon, put a round into the guy holding it, and beat a couple more guys to the floor until he broke free of the ruckus and started down a corridor of cubicles screened by ratty plastic shower curtains.

He stopped to take stock. The data goggles showed six troops inside this building, all around the entrance, and another dozen glowing dots around or in the other warehouse a few yards away. The second stick, with Gennaro. Up 'til now, he'd been too busy to think on what he might find in here. Now that was all he could do. It was *time*. He ought to wait for backup, but fuck that. If Carla Jean or her friends were here, he was going to find them *right now*.

Each cube held a cot, a chair, and a whore. Some of them weren't much more than girls. A good number of cubes also had a john, most of them scrambling into their clothes, but that's what McGinley brought all those zip ties for. He'd knock the john flat, zip him up, shine his helmet-mounted light in the girl's face, then move on.

Four cubes in, he found his first blonde. Skinny as Joella, kronked out of her head. He stood there staring at her, almost afraid to look. *Will I even know Carla Jean if I see her?* If the nurses hadn't told him that scarecrow in Otero was Joella, he wouldn't have recognized her. He forced himself to look closer at this one, close enough to see the dark eyebrows and brown eyes surrounded by red. Close enough to smell that she hadn't washed for too long. *Not her.*

He rechecked the ones he'd already passed, then picked up where he'd left off. Lots of Mexes, most so gone they didn't know or care what was happening, each one sadder than the last. By the end of the first aisle, McGinley was fixing to lose his breakfast.

He still had half the warehouse to scout.

Partway down the second aisle, he found a blonde wobbling in the entrance to her cube, wearing near to nothing, looking as lost as could be. McGinley braced himself again, then stared hard at her face. Not Carla Jean, damnit, thank God. He tried to match her to Carla Jean's friends but stopped when the whore grabbed him and started babbling in something that sounded like Russian. He pushed her away, let the disgust shake out of him, then moved on.

Twenty-two whores. Three of them white. None of them Carla Jean or her friends.

He was steaming mad, though, by the time he heard Gennaro's voice in his ear. "McGinley! Get down here to the front. I got something for you."

ICE troops hauled the trussed-up johns out to the parking lot. Four hog-tied Mexes were lined up face-down on the floor near the door. Gennaro crouched by the one closest to McGinley. "Find anything?" Gennaro asked.

"Three white girls, two of them maybe American. Nobody I was looking for."

"Sorry to hear it. This turd here"—Gennaro slapped the prisoner's head—"is the manager of this fine place."

McGinley planted a boot toe in the scumbag's ribs to keep

himself from shooting the little fucker. "Get anything out of him?"

"Not yet. He's asking for his lawyer. I hear the corporate counsel is on his way down here from the HQ building, not that he's gonna get anywhere near here. We got a forensic team and a bus for the hookers coming through the front gate now." Gennaro yanked the Mex's collar down to show off the Z-in-a-circle tattoo on the man's neck. "Big surprise, huh?"

Joella had been on her way here. Maybe Carla Jean or one of her gang had been here. This didn't have to be a total loss. "Reckon you're gonna put him in court?"

Gennaro snorted. "What do you think?"

McGinley nodded. Zetas that ICE got ahold of didn't often make it in front of a judge. Some expensive lawyer would bail them out, or they'd get shanked in holding. Or—McGinley's favorite—an unusual number got dead resisting or trying to escape.

"Ain't nobody left to bitch about scumbags dying in custody," McGinley said. "How's about me and you have a chat with this ol' boy?"

"Fuckin' A, Jack, you always make this big a mess?"

McGinley poured another bottle of water over his arms and head to rinse off the blood. He and Gennaro sat on the tailgate of a shot-to-shit pickup outside the warehouse, watching the whores get hauled onto the ICE bus a few yards away. Them girls looked even sorrier out in the sunshine than they had inside. "Had to get him talking."

"Yeah, but blowing his leg off? Jesus. These were new boots."

The manager had been a tough little pecker, doing nothing but cussing and spitting until McGinley got his attention by taking off the shitbird's right leg with the shotgun. After he stopped screaming, he started talking. The Zeta shit didn't stop until he ran out of things to say and Gennaro put a round between the man's eyes. Yeah, it was messier than McGinley liked, but now he knew a whole lot more about how Zetas moved their whores around. He also had a name to run down: Alcala, a Zeta logistics honcho.

And he knew what became of the women who didn't make it

out of this hellhole. "Reckon there's any call to drag that slurry pond?" McGinley asked.

Gennaro shook his head. "With all the chemicals, the bodies would dissolve in a couple weeks. If she went in there, we'll never know."

Just as well. McGinley was getting used to the idea Carla Jean was still alive out there somewhere. He'd hate to find out different. "You got anything good on Zeta logistics?" he asked after wiping down his arms with a rag. "I mean, better'n what the CIA has."

"We've got some stuff we've picked up. The Zetas push regular combat resupply through Mexican Army logistics, at least the part they control, but they still run this kind of thing themselves. I'll get you into our wiki so you can check it out."

"Thank you kindly."

McGinley watched the bustle around him without paying it much mind. He hadn't quite known what he wanted to find going into this, and now it was over, he still didn't. Twenty-two girls would get to go home if they had homes to go to, though, and half a dozen Zeta fuckers would go in the ground. A good day's work.

"Gonna keep looking?" Gennaro asked.

McGinley slid off the tailgate and slung his shotgun. He watched the bus rumble out of the parking lot with its load of lost women. The lucky ones, maybe. "Reckon so."

34

While everyone knows about government spying, most people don't know that the bulk of surveillance tech used in 2031 belongs to corporations spying on each other or, more often, on you... Walmart is believed to have the nation's second-largest database of individually identifiable behavioral data, right after the National Security Agency...

    -- *"Danger Room: Peeping for Profits," Wired.com*

WEDNESDAY, 12 MAY

Luis ran the shop with half his brain while the other half churned the Nora problem. Did he believe her? Did he believe the 10/19 story? She had so much stuff, too much for a cover story or hoax. Then again, she'd had years to build it. It'd all *seemed* authentic. Was it? Could a cover-up like this stay secret for almost thirteen years?

Maybe it hadn't. He searched for "10/19 conspiracy" on the office slate and came up with over ten million hits. Some of them fingered white supremacists or militias, but the search summaries also showed people blaming the attack on almost every group or organization on Earth. His brain hurt after looking at just a few of those sites.

Should he bail out of this potential disaster? He mulled this into the afternoon.

It was one thing to run Ahmed Average to *el otro lado*. It was a whole different problem to get mixed up with someone on a terrorist watchlist. If he stayed with her and the FBI caught her, they'd get him too. Then what? But if he left, what would happen to her and her family? What would happen to her story?

Is it your problem?

Before he could answer that question, his burner buzzed in his pocket. "Hello?"

"Juan?" Nora's voice, tense. "We're being watched. Can you come?"

Just in case Nora was right, he stopped to check whether the Cartel safe house on Serra Mesa, fifteen miles west of El Cajon, was clear. He discovered an observation post in a foreclosed house across the street: a tiny camera clipped to the roof overhang, a stubby wifi antenna on the chimney to suck up any other cameras' data, and a thin cellular antenna to pump the results out to some central monitoring station. The gear could all be bought on the web and didn't say anything about who was using it.

Half an hour later, Luis crouched in a weedy back yard, peeking through a hole in the fence at the safe house Nora was in.

He wasn't the only one watching the place.

The drone—a slab the size of a chair cushion—buzzed a circle fifty feet over the house. The watchers here were way past remote cameras. They were within a few blocks, no more than a mile. Who were they? The list of just the possible alphabet agencies would take a while to write down, let alone the Cartel's rivals and factions.

The last rays of the setting sun flashed orange off the drone's plastic body. It completely dominated all the approaches to the house. He was pinned as long as it was there. It would need to move soon, though; its haze-gray paint showed it was a daytime drone with only a daylight camera. The watchers would need to swap in a nighttime drone with infrared and night-vision sensors if they planned to keep up their air coverage. The gap wouldn't be enough to get Nora and her family out unobserved, though.

Luis edged away from the missing fence boards, shook out his aching knees. Decision time. *You go in there, you're committed.*

He could leave Nora to deal with these people, whoever they were. If they thought she was a terrorist, they might not want to take her alive. Anyone who got in their way could end up as collateral damage.

An unwanted memory slipped into his brain: Paul's tense face and the kids' wide eyes, all aimed at him as he burst in on them yesterday. Hope's face slowly morphed into Christa's, full of fear and loss, watching him leave home on his way to another run. There were innocents involved. Could he hang them out to dry?

If he did, Nora's 10/19 secret would die with her. Luis couldn't believe it would actually change the election. Still, people had a right to know. They should see who and what their so-called leaders really are.

You can't help them if you're dead.

The drone's whine faded into the distance.

Is it your problem?

Nora stalked from the front door's peephole through the kitchen to the door into the garage and back, her pistol's grip slick with sweat. She'd hardly stopped moving in the nearly five hours since she'd spotted sunlight glinting off binocular lenses in the glassless window across the street. Her head was full of static and conflicting plans and unanswerable questions. *Who are they? What are they waiting for?*

The house had become her whole world—a very small, stuffy, dusty world that with every passing hour felt more like a trap. Juan had said he was coming, but that was hours ago. She had no idea if he was still on his way, or if he'd been arrested or killed. He'd also said he was dropping off the network, and that she should, too. She had and felt marooned.

Nora jumped at the knock on the door into the garage. She would've shot through it if she hadn't heard Juan's voice the moment before she squeezed the trigger. "Nora? You in there?"

Juan's face was flushed even in the bluish light of the LED lantern in the living room, and his breathing was heavy. "There's a drone on you," he panted.

Nora sighed. "What kind?"

"Tactical, a quad-rotor. I had to wait it out."

It took a full circuit—front door to garage and back—before Nora could calm down enough to speak. "How could this happen? How did they find us?"

"There was a remote observation post on one of our other safe houses. I checked on the way here. That means they're probably all blown. Did you go outside?"

Nora squinted through the peephole for too long, hoping to cover the flush she felt creep into her cheeks. "What do you mean, they're *all* blown?"

"Just that. We have to assume they're all being watched. Either the FBI or DEA knew about them already, or, well… it's cartel politics." He filled the doorway between the entry hall and the kitchen. "Did you go outside?"

"Explain 'cartel politics,'" Paul said behind her. Nora glanced back to see him standing in the entry hall, arms crossed, face serious.

Juan arched an eyebrow at him. "Short version? The Zetas grabbed our *capo* about a week ago. They're probably still pumping him dry. Don't know why they'd be here, though. Still…" He turned back to Nora. "We have three dozen safe houses in San Diego County. But these guys are here in person, which means they saw something. *Did you go outside?*"

She wanted to keep ignoring the question but sensed he wouldn't stop asking. "Yes."

"*Mierda.*" Juan paced the kitchen, massaging his neck. "What did I tell you about that?"

"Don't talk to me like I'm a child!" Nora charged into the kitchen after him. She pulled up sharp, trying but failing to smother her anger. "How are you getting us out of here?"

"I can't, not while that thing is up there." Juan stabbed a finger toward the ceiling. "It'll follow us wherever we go." He leveled the finger at Nora. "I told you we have rules here. This is what happens—"

"We aren't your prisoners—"

"Enough!" Paul shouted. Nora and Juan both fell silent. "Corners, both of you." It was the same tone he used on the kids when they fought.

Nora shot some of her resentment toward him—*don't you speak to me that way!*—but he simply pointed to the corner nearest the sink, glaring.

After a few moments of uneasy silence, Juan asked, "Where are the kids?"

"In the back bedroom," Paul said. "All her stomping around with her gun scared them."

"This is *my* fault now?" Nora lunged away from the counter, not knowing where she was going but only that she had to *move* to burn off her frustration.

Paul held up his hand to signal "stop"—something else he did with the kids when they were misbehaving, *the nerve*. "I warned you not to go out there."

Nora spun, clunked her pistol on the counter and stood with her back to the room. She ground her fingertips into the sink's stainless-steel rim, staring at the plywood over the window without seeing it. Her husband was siding with the *narco*. *Perfect*.

"Okay, Juan." Paul sounded far calmer than Nora felt. "What do you want us to do?"

"There's nothing we *can* do. Tomorrow morning, we might have a couple minutes when they switch to their daytime drone. Unless they move on us sooner. Until then…" Juan's boots scraped on the linoleum. "Nora, are these your buddies?"

It took some effort to stop clenching her teeth. She needed to think, no matter how frustrated and scared she was. "I don't think so," she told the sink. "They're not following our playbook. Maybe DEA or ICE? Whoever they are, I don't know what they're waiting for."

"Dark?"

"Maybe. They've got to know it's just me and Paul and the kids. All I've got is my sidearm and an extra magazine."

"That, they don't know. You could've picked up an assault rifle or RPG along the way. It's not hard anymore."

Paul stepped to the door, leaned down to peer through the peephole. "If they want dark, they won't have to wait long." He straightened, looked back to Juan. "What do we *do?*"

Nora felt the weight of Juan's gaze and risked facing him without trying to broil him telepathically. This wasn't his fault. She tried to take all the heat out of her voice. "You should go while you still can."

He shook his head. "They'll spot me. Besides, you people are worth a lot of money to me." Juan turned to Paul. "Pack your stuff. If we get a chance to go, we'll have to move fast."

The pinpoints of light in the plywood covering the window had changed from red-purple to black. If Juan was right, they were out of time. Nora finally turned so she could easily see both men. She said a silent prayer—for all the good it would do—then stepped close to Paul. "Take the kids into the back bathroom and lock the door," she whispered in his ear. "Stay in the bathtub. Don't get up or leave no matter what you hear."

Paul stiffened and drew back. "And you're going to stay out here and get yourself shot?"

Don't do this, please, not now... "I don't plan to get shot."

"Does anybody?" He gripped her arm and pulled her to the back of the living room, beyond Juan's earshot. "I'll put the kids back there, but I'm staying out here to back you up."

"No! You're safer in the back." Nora throttled back the harshness that had crept into her voice. "I don't know what's coming through that door next. One of us has to survive to get the kids out—"

"We *both* need to survive. They need you as much as they need me. And *I* need you." He grabbed her other arm, shook her. "You don't know what's out there? Fine. You need all the help you can get. Give me a gun. I did okay at the range."

"That's different!" Nora broke free. "Paper targets don't shoot back! Do you realize how much training I've had to kill people? Juan's had that training too. You—"

"What if one of them gets past you? What do I do, snap him with a beach towel?"

Nora closed her eyes and sighed. She didn't want to admit it, but he had a point. "Mr. Juan? Do you carry a backup weapon?"

"I did tonight." A moment later, he appeared in the doorway between the kitchen and living room. "Why?"

"It's for Paul."

Juan frowned at him. "You don't have your own?"

Paul let out the first note of a laugh. "With what I do, it's too much of a hassle to carry one. The only places left with gun control are Capitol Hill and around the Mall in D.C." He swept a hand toward Nora. "She's the one with all the guns."

Juan held Nora's gaze and asked a question with his eyes. *Do you want this?* She hesitated, then nodded. Juan pulled a Walther

PPK from behind his back. "Come on over here in the light, Paul…"

She held back, watching the men handle the pistol in the lantern's glare, Juan pointing out the safety and showing Paul a two-point firing stance. She hoped Paul wouldn't try to be a hero and get himself killed. Sometimes he'd try things, like skydiving or deep-sea fishing, that were totally out of character. He claimed it was because he wanted an adventure. She feared it was to prove to her—and to himself—that he was still a man.

He didn't need to. To her, he was the best man in the world. Someday she'd find a way to tell him so he'd believe it.

Juan clapped Paul on the shoulder, finally finishing his lesson. Paul shook his hand. When Juan disappeared into the garage, Nora drifted to her husband's side and took his free hand in both of hers. This was all so wrong—being trapped, being targets, turning such a gentle, loving man as Paul into a combatant, bringing down this threat on their heads. She could hardly look in his eyes. "Please be careful. Stay in the bathroom. Don't go looking for trouble."

Paul gave her a dark look. "You don't think I can do this, do you?"

"It's not that. It's… if they get to you, it means Juan and I can't help you. And you'll have to… to do things you've never done before, to protect the kids. I need to know you'll be there to do that. Promise?"

After a moment, he nodded, then drew her into his arms. She held on as tight as she could, savoring every sensation, hoping this wouldn't be the last time. "Pray for us," she whispered. "I think Allah listens to you better than He does to me."

Paul squeezed her harder. "He listens to both of us. I ask Him nicely, though."

Nora caught the lump in her throat before it could choke her. She reached up and gave Paul the best, deepest kiss she could, in case it was their last. "I love you so much," she whispered when they finally broke apart to breathe. "I wish I told you that more."

"I love you, too." He started to say something, stopped, then slowly stroked her hair. They stood there for a long moment that both lasted forever and went by in a blink. Then Paul scooped up the lantern and disappeared down the hall, leaving Nora alone in the dark.

When Juan returned to the kitchen, Nora was perched on the counter next to the sink, the window open, her face flat against the rough plywood. He asked, "What are you doing?"

Trying not to think. "I drilled a hole in the wood with my Leatherman. I needed something to do." She pointed. "Take the peephole in the door. Is the garage secure?"

"Yeah. Both doors are locked and barred."

They squinted through their tiny portals to the outside world without speaking. Nora could see a narrow slice of the front yard and the street, both empty and silent in the pale wash of the waxing moon. She wished these people would make their move soon so she didn't have to keep obsessing over what would happen once they did.

Then she saw it. Movement. She squeezed her eyes shut for a moment, then pressed her other eye against the hole. She focused so hard, it hurt.

There it was again.

"Did you see that?" Nora whispered. "Edge of the garage. Someone's out there."

35

The glut of combat-experienced veterans and ex-military contractors has democratized the private security contractor (PSC) market... American soldiers-for-hire are now more common than their Russian counterparts were a generation ago... Says Ruslic, "These days, anyone who can buy a Jaguar for cash can rent a tactical team for a couple days."

-- "These Guns for Hire," Forbes.com

WEDNESDAY, 12 MAY

Luis dashed to the back door and pressed his eye to the hole in the plywood next to the latch. A shadow dropped over the backyard fence, then disappeared to his left. A few seconds later, a second and third shadow followed the first. Luis stage-whispered, "Three hostiles heading for the side door."

"At least two out front."

Luis twisted to see why Nora sounded so close. A Nora-shape crouched under the kitchen pass-through, dark-dark gray against the wall's light-dark gray. Luis closed the patio door and took up a position across the entry from her. He drew his pistol, held it with both hands between his knees. His heart hammered his breastbone; sweat drenched his shirt's back and armpits. It'd been years since he'd done an entry, and he'd been on the other side of the door then, with a vest and helmet. The people inside those dusty little houses had felt the way he did right now.

"Think you can shoot federal agents?" Luis whispered.

"I'll shoot anything hunting my family." Nora's voice sounded raspy and tight. "Can you?" He didn't have an answer. "How many rounds?"

"Thirteen. You?"

"Fifteen loaded, fifteen spare." She stopped for some indistinct scratching at the front door. "If they follow the playbook, they'll blow the door, then toss in a flash-bang."

Nora fished a white paper towel off the pass-through, tore off half and tossed the wadded-up remainder to Luis. He stuffed his ears with paper even though it wouldn't do much good against 170 decibels. Then he grabbed her arm and pulled her into the hallway, pushing her into the bedroom to the right. He ducked into the bathroom to his left.

Twin *fooms* like M80 firecrackers in a metal trash can hammered through the house. The front door smashed open. Something crashed on the kitchen floor. Moments later, Luis heard the dental-drill whine of a small motor. He peeked out just in time to see a helicopter the size of a pigeon zip down the entry hall. A recon drone. He ducked back into the bathroom, closed but didn't latch the door, and pressed himself against the wall behind the door.

Boots on tile. "Freeze! Hands up! Don't move!"

The drone-sound buzzed down the hallway beyond the bathroom door. Then came the *clank* of something metal against a close-by wall. The sky ripped apart and slammed the bathroom door against the toes of Luis' boots. His ears filled with static. But he still had his balance and most of his night vision, which might just keep him alive.

Luis wiped his hands on his pants legs, then readied his pistol. The mirror had disappeared from over the sink long ago; no one would see him behind the door from outside. Whoever came in would focus on the room's open area first. That split-second before they checked the other side would be his window to act.

At least five guys—make it six, no one works in odd numbers—on the entry team. Two for each room off the hall. Luis flashed back to the 'Stan. Stack close outside the doorway. Number One pivots away from the hinges; Two pivots toward the hinges; each clears his half of the room.

A shush of boot soles on carpet outside. The red splash of a laser sight glittered off the tub surround's tile. A second swept over the tub apron and the toilet next to it.

Luis drew in a deep breath. Squared his shoulders against the wall.

He kicked the door hard, then put four rounds through it at waist level when it thumped into the men behind it. Full-auto fire smashed tiles from the shower wall and blew away the rest of Luis' hearing. He felt rather than saw or heard a body fall on the floor.

A red thread of laser light glinting off dust and drywall flakes swung his way. Luis crouched an instant before a burst screamed over his head, the muzzle flash erasing his night vision but showing him where the gunman was. He shot twice at the spot where the white-orange flame had been moments before. The laser light tumbled to the floor, then blinked off.

One down. The guy's partner was out there, maybe wounded, maybe just waiting for a clear shot.

Automatic fire sawed through the door, spraying Luis with splinters and chunks of hollow-core sandwich. The door's remains swung against his knee. *There's the partner.* Flashes of gunfire across the hall lit the holes in the door, backed by a thrumming bass line several miles away.

Luis slithered toward the tub, keeping his belly tight against the tile. The smell of blood cut through the dust and gunpowder stink. He reached out to probe the floor to his right. His hand hit something metal: the dead gunman's weapon, the barrel still hot. Now he could see the nearby greenish, glowing outline of tactical goggles on the man's face. He stuck out his hand and tried to pull off the goggles. The strap snagged on the man's helmet.

Something heavy and solid scraped his leg.

He was nearly in the shower when the flash-bang went off. He'd closed his eyes and wrapped his arms over his head, but the inside of his eyelids still turned neon white, and the kick of an enormous horse bounced him off the wrecked shower wall into a heap in the tub. He fumbled his pistol out from under himself, flipped over just in time to make out the red laser knifing toward him through the pink-and-yellow blobs drifting past his eyes.

Find the laser's origin. Aim. Empty the magazine.

He didn't die.

Thirty seconds that lasted an hour passed. The blobs faded to black. Luis poked his head above the tub's rim; no one tried to blow it off. He holstered his empty pistol, crawled out onto a minefield of busted tile and drywall. He reached the first gunman, freed the goggles from his helmet, and slipped them on.

The room turned contrasty green and black. The gunman next to him glowed bright green in the infrared view, the blood from his neck wound showing a softer green around him on the floor. The second guy sprawled face-down on a spreading green pool next to the shredded vanity. Both men wore dark utility pants, long-sleeved tee shirts, combat boots, body armor, gear harnesses, helmets without covers. No patches or insignia from any of the usual agencies. The weapon Luis had touched before the grenade went off was a Heckler & Koch UMP submachine gun, all black, folding stock, used all over the world. These guys could be anyone, from anywhere.

Luis peeked out into the doorway to the bedroom where Nora was. A bright pair of legs stretched along the floor inside. Boots; not Nora. No muzzle flashes. What happened to her?

After stripping the equipment off the second body, Luis strapped on the man's vest and utility belt and slotted a fresh magazine into the UMP. He struggled to his feet, wavering a moment as he unkinked his arms and legs. Nearly every part of him throbbed.

He risked a peek toward the end of the silent hallway. The bright dome of a warm head poked out of the master bedroom. Luis threw himself backward just as a flurry of bullets ripped gashes in the bathroom's doorjamb, splintering the door's hinge edge, spraying him with wood shards.

The kids are down there. Paul's down there.

A muzzle flash bloomed white across from Luis, aimed toward the end of the hall. A stream of white-hot shell casings pinged off the bedroom's wall. *She's alive.* The intensity of his relief surprised Luis.

The firefight boomed back and forth just outside as Luis searched the first gunman he'd killed. He grabbed a stun grenade from the man's utility belt, pulled the pin, then sidearmed the grenade toward the end of the hall. A couple endless seconds passed. Then a flash, a scream of noise, and a howl of pain.

He was out the door and rumbling toward the master bedroom within seconds. Footfalls sounded behind and to his right; he hoped they were Nora's. As he approached the open door, he saw a glowing man-shape pop into view inside, aiming at him. Luis let off a short burst, slammed himself flat against the wall just shy of the door. A swarm of bullets followed a laser beam inches from his nose, tearing at the wall opposite him. The air filled with swirling bits of drywall. Old dust filled Luis' throat, triggering a coughing fit.

Four down. At least one left, holed up in a strong position. How many more on the entry team? Where were they? Reinforcements outside?

Welcome back to the 'Stan.

More beams lighting the haze. More shots, more sharp splinters off the jamb, more flying drywall. A hand gripped his left shoulder; Luis glanced back to glimpse Nora, ready to make this entry. As usual, he'd be Number One through the door. One drew fire first.

I'm too old for this shit. I have a wife, a son. I can't die here.

The doorjamb exploded in his face. By reflex, he pivoted away and shoved Nora back. That may have been what saved her when the wall dissolved around him.

Nora cried "Juan!" when he bounced off the wall and crumpled at her feet. *He can't die yet!* She crouched, stabbed her fingers into his throat. A pulse; still alive, praise Allah. Three flat, glowing circles of white-hot bullets ran diagonally across the chest of his body armor. The IR vision hid the details of the confused textures on his left shoulder, just outside the vest.

A noise. The distinctive *crunch* of a boot kicking a hollow-core door.

The bathroom. *Paul! The kids!*

Nora elbow-crawled through a jumble of gypsum board and ruined lumber to what was left of the master bedroom's doorway. She peeked through a ragged hole. Two bright returns against the wall to the left of the door: one aiming at the bedroom's entrance, the other with his leg coiled to kick in the bathroom door.

The leg pistoned out. The room filled with the *crack* of wood ripping in half.

No no no...

Nora shoved herself forward into the doorway, her body armor slick on the carpet. She rolled on her side, swung the laser designator onto the gunman aiming at her.

...no no no...

He shifted his aim, but not fast enough. Nora loosed a burst into his face. Glowing chunks flew against the wall as his body staggered backward, then collapsed. The other man disappeared inside the bathroom.

...NO NO NO...

She pushed herself off the floor, launched through the bedroom door. Ten feet never seemed so far. Screams. Yelling. Automatic weapons fire.

...NO NO NO NOT MY FAMILY NO...

A body fell heavily.

It sounded like the end of her world.

$$36$$

Nora slipped into the bedroom, the UMP's stock tight against her shoulder. The kids shrieked in the bathroom, but she had to stifle the urge to sprint to them. She had to find the sixth hostile.

She scuffed her feet through the still-glowing shell casings littering the carpet until she could see into the bathroom. Two radiating pairs of legs stretched across the floor. The face-down pair wore boots: the sixth hostile. The face-up pair wore thick-soled work shoes. Paul.

No no no NO NO…

She let her weapon swing free on its sling, yanked her penlight from her pocket. The tiny light was enough to let the goggles' night-vision setting work, showing her more detail than she wanted. The kids huddled in the tub's far corner, clinging to each other, crying. Blood on Paul's face and shirt. Blood on the walls and floor. Shattered tile, bullet holes.

Nora wanted to die right where she stood.

Then Paul groaned, rolled onto his side. *He's alive! Thank you thank you…* He peered at the light, then raised a shaky arm to aim Juan's pistol in her general direction.

"It's me!" she choked through the sobs blocking her throat. "Darling, it's me!"

Nora cradled Paul against her, rocking him, whispering in his ear. She pressed the still-sobbing children to her side with one hand, while with the other she ran her fingers through Paul's hair. Blood dribbled from a wound on the side of his head, the kind that came from a rifle butt and not a bullet. Nora couldn't find any other visible injuries, praise Allah.

Even though he trembled in her arms, Paul wouldn't release his two-handed death grip on Juan's pistol. Every few seconds, he said, "It's okay, guys. It's okay. It's okay." Like a recording, or a broken robot.

"Is he dead?" he finally whispered.

Nora glanced toward the dark lump on the floor next to them. "Yes. You did good." She gulped. "I'm so sorry you had to do that."

He nodded, then winced.

Nora wanted to sit there for a few hours, to comfort Paul and the kids and forget what had just happened. The business part of her brain wouldn't let her. These six hostiles were down, but they'd have backup, vehicles, a recon team maybe. How many more outside? How long before the next wave came in?

"Darling," she murmured after a deep breath, "I need your help."

Paul choked out a garbled laugh. "Who do you want me to shoot?"

"Not that. Juan was hit in the shoulder. I need you to patch him up while I figure out how to get us out of here."

After a few rough breaths, Paul said, "It's not over, is it."

"No, it's not."

Paul and Nora lugged the dead gunman out of the bathroom and dumped him next to his partner. Nora found a small, tube-shaped LED flashlight on the corpse's utility belt, stuffed it in Paul's hand, then scurried back into the bathroom. She lit the lantern Paul had wedged behind the toilet, placed it on the debris-strewn vanity. The room looked even worse in full light.

She crushed Hope and Peter in a hug. "It's okay, Mr. Juan got hurt Daddy's, taking care of him, I love you." It all tumbled out in a rush.

"Is Daddy okay?" Peter asked through his last hiccups of sobs.

"He's fine. He protected you. He was very brave." But there'd be a price to pay later. She hoped it wouldn't cost more than either of them could bear.

Nora kissed them both, then reluctantly pulled away and stood. "I need you to go back in the bathtub for a few minutes. It's safe. Daddy and I will protect you."

Please let that be true.

Nora huddled against the garage's side wall next to the door into the back yard. Juan and her family crouched close behind her. Even bitter with smog, the outside air was better than the stew of mold, dust, blood, and gunpowder in the house. She longed to get out of this horrible place, to get her family somewhere safe. But they were pinned by the whine of a large mosquito.

The drone.

She peeked around the doorjamb into the dark, looking for a tell-tale marker light. The sound was close; she ought to be able to see the drone. With any luck, she'd see it before it saw her.

A dark shape the size of a throw pillow drifted across the not-quite-black background in her NVGs. No light. She switched to infrared, saw the gentle glow of four warm electric motors maybe thirty feet away.

That thing would follow them wherever they went and bring the dogs down on them all.

Nora slid behind the doorjamb and switched off the laser sight mounted on the UMP's receiver. She took a moment to calm her breathing. She'd get one chance at this; the laser or the muzzle flash would warn the drone's operator, and it would never come this close again. They'd all be trapped here until more hostiles arrived.

She carefully slid the UMP's stubby muzzle out the door, aimed at a currently empty piece of sky at the drone's general altitude. Nora wiped dust from her goggles, concentrating on the whine, listening for a change in volume or pitch that would tell her it was moving some way other than left to right past the garage.

The glowing motors edged into her field of view. She inched the barrel up and down as she followed the fuzzy light in the gunsights, trying to draw a bead.

There. She exhaled and fired.

The whine cut off; the glows plummeted. Plastic tinkled on hard ground a second later. They'd be drone-free for at least a few minutes.

Nora swung outside, peeking over the rotting redwood gate. A white panel van and three more SUVs—enough to carry at least another dozen men—had arrived in the fifteen minutes since the last shot. A dark shape on a roof across the street flagged a sniper.

She felt like an antelope surrounded by lions.

She rasped through the doorway, "Go! Straight to the back fence. There's a hole. Don't stop, don't talk."

Paul shuffled out, bent under his backpack, leading Peter by the hand. He looked surprisingly macho in the tactical gear she'd salvaged from the dead men, with a UMP slung across his chest. Juan tottered out of the garage a few seconds later, also geared up, holding Hope's hand.

"Are you okay to walk?" she asked as she hefted Hope into her arms.

He braced against the gate, breathing hard. "Just slow. Go on."

Nora jog-walked toward the back of the yard, hugging the fence, trying not to think about what was happening out front or if the sniper had her dialed in. She pressed Hope's tear-streaked face into her neck. "It's okay, Cupcake. Just be really quiet. We're going someplace safe. Please don't cry." Those thirty feet in the open stretched for miles.

Paul helped her swing Hope through the fence hole into the next yard. "Help Juan," she stage-whispered to Paul, then ducked through the hole herself. She sat the kids together, stroked their hair and murmured comfort to them. Then she broke away to check on the men.

They were ten feet from the fence. Juan's good arm looped around Paul's shoulder. She peered past them toward the street, waiting for gunmen to bust through the gate. *Hurry hurry hurry...*

Then she remembered: half the first team had come over the back fence.

Juan stumbled, but Paul braced him up at the last moment. Nora recognized the grimace on her husband's face: his back had just tweaked out. The men staggered toward the hole.

She heard footsteps and rustling in the yard next to this one. *Faster!*

Juan reached the fence, held onto the hole's edges, then lurched through. Nora yanked him aside so Paul could pick his way through while trying not to bend.

She heard a thump from the other side of the fence. A man flashed past the hole, running toward the safe house. Three more followed. Nora let out a huge sigh of relief.

But they weren't clear yet. Once the hostiles figured out the only people in the safe house were their own casualties, they'd start a search. She had to move everyone out of here… *now.*

She caught Paul's arm. "Your back?" He nodded. "Can you carry Hope?"

"Yeah, or my backpack. Not both. I'm sorry."

"Shh. Get Juan's keys and go get the car. We have to leave right now."

The first explosion knocked them both into silence. Nora dashed to the hole in time to see four men pile through a huge gap in the plywood that used to cover the patio door. More explosions inside—they were using real grenades now, not flash-bangs—and a lot of automatic-weapons chatter. They were clearing rooms by fire. Time was running out.

"Go!" she hissed to Paul. "Fast as you can!"

37

*With the once-formidable Federal and state firefighting
arsenals disbanded or dispersed to budget-strapped local
governments, western states are least able to confront
wildfires just as the number and size of those fires surges...
Record numbers of homeowners evacuated from dwellings
threatened by wildfires or related landslides have opted to
not return or rebuild... "It's almost impossible to sell a
house on a hillside now," says Miley Kendrick, a real
estate agent in wildfire-prone Woodland Hills. "Everyone
knows the insurance companies won't pay fire departments
to protect those properties."*

-- "Wildfires Shape Population Shifts in West,"
LATimes.com

WEDNESDAY, 12 MAY

"Bel?"

"Oh, thank God!" Bel ground her burner phone into her ear.
Half a bottle of cheap wine, a lot of oldies on the iPod (she couldn't
take another go-round of "Bad Romance"), miles paced around the
dining-room table, and *finally* Lucho calls. "Are you okay? Where
are you?"

"Going. To Santee." His voice was drifty, out of focus.
Undecipherable noises rattled in the background.

The lump of ice in her gut grew larger. "What's wrong? Are
you hurt?"

"Someone. Shot me. Through a wall. My shoulder."

Oh, God, no, no, no, no, not again! Not again! "Lucho, I—"

"Hi." A woman's voice. "Your husband got hit in his left
shoulder. It's a—"

"Who are you? Where is he?"

"Um... I'll explain later. It's a through-and-through wound.

181

He's lost a lot of blood. He also took three hits to his body armor–"

Body armor?

"—so he may have a broken rib or two. He wants you to come meet us with your medical bag. We're going to—"

"What's happening? Who are you?" Panic had shorted out most of her rational-thought centers. *Oh, God, what if he dies?*

"We're… his clients. Can you write down an address?"

Bel unearthed a pen and an old notepad in time to copy down an address in Bostonia, and where in hell is Bostonia? "Okay, okay, I'll be there, just, please don't let him die, please—"

"I'm taking care of him as best I can." The woman's voice tried to be comforting, though it wasn't working. "Oh, he also said to take the battery out of your phone before you leave and make sure you're not being followed. We'll see you soon."

"Wait! Give him the phone!"

She heard fumbling. "Bel?"

"Lucho? I'm coming. Hold on, I'll be there soon. Don't you dare die before I can kill you. I love you so much." Bel barely got the words past the rock in her throat. She was already in motion when the connection turned to dead air.

Number 8405 was a flat-roofed, '70s-vintage rancher with gaping-empty windows and a charred palm tree with the top burned off. There were no lights anywhere along this last half of a dead-end street. The headlights revealed to Bel the cracked, rippling mud coating the road and some front yards up the hill ahead. Most of the houses past this point were scorched rubble.

A man faded out of 8405's shadows and edged toward her car. Bel pulled her pistol from the center console, clicked off the safety and held it in her lap.

The man didn't look like a cop. The headlights showed his face to be too soft, his hair a little too long, and it seemed like half the cops she saw now were on steroids, which this guy clearly wasn't. In his tucked-in, black collarless shirt and black jeans, he could almost be going out to a club. But when she rolled down her window at his signal, she still led with her gun.

"Who are you? Where is he?"

The man backed up two quick steps and spread his hands at waist level. No gun. "Whoa. Friend. Are you Bel?"

"Who are you?"

"I'm Paul. You talked to my wife on the phone. Park here. I'll take you to your husband."

Bel followed Paul uphill, passing other burned or abandoned houses. The hardened mud threatened to turn her ankle with every other step. Paul offered to carry her big medical duffel, but instead she handed him the gym bag holding clean clothes for Lucho and his shaving kit.

They entered a long, low-slung ranch house with a stubby garage at the uphill end, boarded-up windows, and dead grass. Inside was overwarm, stuffy, and musty, with a strong overlay of smoke. The carpet had been ripped out who knew how long ago, leaving exposed concrete slab that echoed their steps like a cavern. Paul led her to what had been a bedroom.

"Lucho!"

He sat on a pile of beach towels, his back against the wall facing the door. Harsh lantern light showed his left shoulder, side and sleeve were black with crusted blood down past his elbow and almost to the waistband of his jeans. Bel felt her heart stop for a moment.

A silly half-smile crawled onto his lips. "*Oye, cariña.*"

"You turkey." She charged to his side, dumped her medical bag and thumped to her knees. All she'd thought about during the two-plus-hour drive was throwing herself on top of him and holding him for a few hours, but now she wrestled down the impulse. "Really, getting into a gunfight at your age."

"Sorry."

"Sure you are."

"We tried to keep him from going into shock," Paul said from the doorway. "I hope we didn't make things worse."

"No, that's fine." Bel dragged on some latex gloves, then fished a liter of saline solution from her bag. Going into nurse mode helped her not bog down into worried-sick-scared-to-death wife mode. She checked the use-by date on the foil pack of HemaSafe; it wasn't too expired, so she began mixing the blood substitute into the saline. "Paul, can you bring me some water, please? I need to clean up this crazy man."

Once Paul left, Bel gently peeled off what remained of Lucho's shirt. She gasped at the garish bruises on his chest. She'd seen far worse before, but not on her husband. He gazed at her with a dopey expression and tried to stroke her face. She let him press his palm against her cheek for a moment. She could still smell him despite the dirt and blood and gunpowder: sweat mixed with his soap and shaving cream.

"Stop scaring me, huh?" she murmured. She spiked the IV bag to the wall above his head and ran a line into his right arm. He flinched at the needle, just like he always did. Then she carefully shaved off a square of chest hair, smoothed on a diagnostic patch and watched his vitals on her slate for a few moments. Nothing bad showed up, thank God. "What happened?"

"Got jumped at a safe house." His voice was stronger than on the phone, but still wandered. "We won, sort of."

"This is winning? I don't wanna see losing." The bullet wound under the big, square patches was unattractive rather than ugly, a good excuse for another sigh of relief. "This is gonna sting." She swabbed both sides of his shoulder with alcohol, then sprayed aerosol sulfa into the holes. Lucho squawked both times but didn't flop around too much. "Can't you learn to duck?"

He tried to smile. "If I did, we wouldn't've met."

While she cleaned and dressed his wound, Bel remembered the first moment she laid eyes on a big, handsome, filthy, smelly soldier with a couple nasty shrapnel cuts from an IED. Lucho had no hair, a beautiful smile, and a couple heaping helpings of bad boy in him. She had more attitude than sense back then. They spent their time in her ER cubicle flirting and giving each other shit while she stitched him up. After she told him, "Drop your drawers, soldier," and her fingers lingered with the cotton ball a little too long where she gave him the tetanus booster, she knew she'd have to schedule him for a follow-up. Maybe several.

Twenty-three years later, she was still patching him together.

"Hey." He cupped her chin. "It's okay. Don't cry."

"I'm not crying." Bel sniffed. She'd been pressing a gauze pad against his shoulder for too long. She kissed his hand as she brushed it away, shot her strongest full-spectrum antibiotic into the IV, then sat back on her heels. "Well, your new hole won't kill you. Let's check those ribs." She poked and prodded and grimaced every time he did and tried not to think of all the times she'd rested her head on that chest and listened to his heart beat.

Bel wiped her eyes with the backs of her wrists. "Okay, nothing's moving. I guess your chest's made out of cement—like your head."

Then she kissed him. Long and hard and with every ounce of love she had in her.

38

THURSDAY, 13 MAY

Nora perched on the low concrete planter behind the house and stared down at the sleeping valley. A sprinkle of lights marked the houses and apartments of people back from late shifts or preparing for early ones. Islands of yellow-orange glow showed the intersections the cities managed to keep lit. Above her, stars straggled through the smog and haze.

Hope squirmed in her lap, burying her face and a little fist in Nora's chest. She was too scared to stay with her brother. Peter, like most boys, could sleep through anything. Juan's wife had cleaned Paul's head wound and given him a fentanyl patch for his back. He'd gone back to the former master bedroom to sleep. She didn't envy him the dreams he'd have.

Nora, dead awake, couldn't see sleep anywhere on her radar.

Footsteps crunched the weeds to her left. She drew her pistol, held it next to her right hip, ready. Then Juan's wife appeared from around a corner in a scrub top and jeans, her arms crossed tight over her chest. She stopped.

They eyed each other for a few moments. Nora holstered her weapon. "How is he?"

"He'll live. No thanks to you people."

Nora felt her cheeks flush from the verbal slap. What right did

186

she have to take these chances with the lives of strangers, anyway? "If it means anything, I'm sorry."

"It doesn't. I'm taking him home with me. He needs to stay in bed for a day or two."

This was a flat statement of fact with no possibility of appeal. Nora could think of better places to be stranded than in this shell of a house on a scorched hillside, but it wasn't up to her anymore. "I understand. You're Bel?"

"Yeah. Mirabel, really, but Bel works. You must be Nora."

"I am. And this"—she patted Hope's back—"is Hope. You've met my husband."

"And your boy, too. So, you're the people he's taking to Mexico."

"Yes, if we can get there." Nora checked that Hope was still asleep. "You know, the cartel rep back in D.C. said this would be 'routine.' I wasn't expecting anything like this." She tried to meet Bel's eyes, but couldn't. "I guess you don't really care about that."

Bel shrugged. "Sometimes it's nice just to say it out loud." Her tone was gentler than Nora thought she deserved. Bel's focus rarely left Hope.

Nora scooted to the end of the planter, then patted the open spot. Bel perched on the edge and watched Hope sleep. The moonlight revealed a sadness Nora hadn't expected.

"She's darling," Bel said. "She reminds me of Christa, our daughter, at that age. She's what, four? Five?"

"Four. Juan mentioned—"

"Juan?"

"Your husband?"

Bel chuckled. "His name's Luis. I don't know where 'Juan' came from." Her hand drifted to her mouth. "Um. I wasn't supposed to tell you that, was I? Oh, to hell with it." She gazed at Hope some more, then sighed. "Lucho told me about your husband getting blacklisted. I'm so sorry."

Juan—er, Luis—hadn't told her about 10/19. *Good man.* "It's not your fault."

"Someone has to apologize. God, I sound like Lucho. 'It's the right thing to do, someone has to do it,' all that. He always has to fix everything. He always needs to help." Her voice was wistful, not bitter or complaining, which Nora would've expected.

"You're a nurse. Isn't that what you do every day?"

Bel snorted. "I wish." She stared at her kneecaps. "Truth is, I'm just a traffic cop. I herd people through the ED. They either come out just as sick as they were before, or they get better, but the bills keep them broke for the rest of their lives. Either way, they're screwed."

"You can't mean that." Nora touched Bel's arm for comfort... whose, she couldn't say.

Bel nodded. "On the other hand, my darling husband in there gets himself shot saving people he doesn't know. People like you." She scrubbed her face with her palms. "Listen to me. I'm tired and I'm whining. I hate that. Look, please don't get him killed, okay?"

The plea in Bel's face raised a knot in Nora's throat that went down hard. "That's my plan. Nobody dies."

"Good." Bel watched Hope with eyes filled with remembered pain. After a few moments, she stroked Hope's hair, which Nora normally wouldn't allow but, in this case, felt like the least she could do. Bel stood, brushed off the seat of her pants, then wrapped her arms around herself again. "Keep them safe. Get across. Have a good life. Somebody's gotta come out ahead." She turned and left before Nora could say goodbye.

39

Born out of the events of 9/11 and expanded after the 10/19 atrocity, the TSC maintains the U.S. government's consolidated Terrorist Watchlist—a single database of identifying information about those known or reasonably suspected of being involved in terrorist activity. The Watchlist now contains the names of over nine million suspected terrorists and their supporters.
        -- "Terrorist Screening Center," FBI.gov

FRIDAY, 14 MAY

McGinley spent a couple days on JTF's dime hunting down whatever he could find on Cordero *"El Vendedor"* Alcala, the Zeta logistics weenie the whorehouse manager ratted out at the mine on Wednesday.

He dug up some dirt that was interesting enough—the man apparently had two wives, one in Monterrey, one in Nogales—but not so useful in finding the sumbitch. The CIA said he worked out of the back of an up-armored SUV. Gennaro's crew in El Paso had the usual background intel (ex-Mexican Army, gunrunner, blah blah blah), but the last time anyone had a fix on the man was two months ago. Lots of dope on him moving truckloads of weapons over the border from Texas and Arizona, but only one mention of whores.

Damn good security for a loggie.

The other thing that chapped McGinley's hide was finding out that no one was after Alcala. True, he reckoned that *Los Manosos*—the Zeta supply group—was piddly stuff compared to the people wiping out whole villages at a time or running bargeloads of zip into Corpus Christi. Still, *someone* should want to nail the bastard.

Maybe it was McGinley's job now.

He'd added Alcala's name to his shitbag file and started

working the phone to see what wasn't out on the official wikis. Someone somewhere might have a hard-on for Alcala. Maybe he'd stolen someone else's wife the way he had Carla Jean. All he needed was to find that one other sad sack like himself with that one extra piece of intel to find his way to that Zeta fucker's front door.

McGinley thought he'd escaped clean from the Friday-morning coordination meeting—nothing more than a bunch of pecker-waving by people who hadn't left the damn building all week—until he heard Jorgensen's voice yell, "Mac! Wait up!"

Poster Boy was so pleased with his world he positively glowed. "You've got a snitch called Ojeda, right?"

"That's right. What about it?"

"He's hooked up with Nura al-Khaled."

McGinley stood there chewing on his tongue, trying not to look like a sheep hit by a mallet before its throat's cut. "Where'd you hear that?"

"Need to know, Mac, but it's solid. Did he tell you anything about that? I'm guessing not."

Well, damn. If the Feebs weren't blowing smoke—which was always possible—Ojeda not only managed to get his old job back with the Cartel already, but he'd scored big his first time out. Of course, the dumb bastard should've told McGinley as soon as the deal was done, and it pissed McGinley off to find out this way. "I haven't talked to that ol' boy today. Giving him some room to run, don't you know. So, when I go see him"—which he would as soon as he could figure out what the hell was going on—"what else do you know, so I can hit him with it?"

"Only that he's been working it a couple weeks. He's supposed to get her across the border with her family. Apparently, some big bucks in it for him."

A couple *weeks?* Ojeda had some explaining to do.

"Anyway," Jorgensen went on, "just so you know, we're on him now. We'll lay on full blanket surveillance. We'll bust him when he meets up with Khaled. But I was thinking…"

"That I could talk him into rolling over on her, am I right?" And make the Feebs' jobs easier and cheaper, which they always liked. Jorgensen's smile told him all he needed to know. "Why don't all y'all just give him half that reward you got on her now? Five million makes people real flexible."

"You don't think we're really going to pay that reward to anyone, do you?"

Just like the Feebs to pull that scam. "Well, then, I got me a couple requests."

"Such as?"

"What do you have on Jorge Casillas?"

Jorgensen raised a hand to signal "stop." "Don't go there, Mac."

"All right, then. I want the national security letter on Khaled. It–"

"How do you know there is one?"

"Because this here's a terrorism beef, so what else's it gonna be?"

"Forget it. It's classified."

"Don't you shovel that bullshit on me, son." McGinley pointed at Poster Boy's perfect nose. "I have just as good a clearance as you. If you want me to get Ojeda to flip on Khaled, I need to know more about her than he does, which I reckon ain't much. I got the notion Ojeda's sweet on the rags but not necessarily on terrorists, because, see, he thinks there's a difference. If I can show him what she's up to, well… you catch my drift, right?"

"Jesus." Jorgensen scratched the scar under his chin. "All right, let me make some calls. You might have to get read in. It could take a day or two. I'll see what I can do." He shook his finger at McGinley. "I do this, you better come through, understand?"

McGinley would've liked to break off that finger. "Like you have with Casillas?"

McGinley drained the afternoon's third Dr. Pepper, put his feet up on his open desk drawer, and thought on the big shit-slick opportunity Jorgensen had dumped on him.

He'd soaked up everything he could find on this Khaled

woman in open-source and on the various wikis. If she was a genuine terrorist—with the Feebs, it was hard telling—and Ojeda really was tangled up with her, then McGinley had a shot at grabbing some glory for ICE and some goodwill for himself at the same time. Ojeda was his asset, after all. If McGinley could get to the rag through him, a lot of people in big offices back at Homeland Security would think McGinley was the best thing on two legs. He might maybe get back home and get some help burning the Zetas. Maybe someone could put the screws to the Mexes for some help finding Carla Jean or turning over the rock that Alcala sumbitch was under. He'd spend any points he got from bringing in Khaled for that kind of action, no doubt.

But first he had to drag Ojeda back into the corral, and soon. If the Bureau had "full blanket surveillance" on Ojeda, McGinley had a real small window to act. He had to beat the Feebs to Khaled.

40

The TLPA/McKinsey study estimates a minimum of 2.1 million three-wheeled auto-rickshaws (tuk-tuks) in operation across the U.S., a thousand-fold increase in the past ten years as budget cuts have shut down city bus services. Less than 1% are registered or insured, and each one drives down the rates traditional taxicab operators can charge, threatening their livelihoods.
-- Third-World 'Cabs': The Growing Threat, Taxicab, Limousine and Paratransit Association

FRIDAY, 14 MAY

Luis sprawled on his bed and drifted. He'd done that a lot since Wednesday night. Everything from his hips up throbbed as if someone had gone over him with a baseball bat. The nerves in his left shoulder sizzled. Bel had told him to get up and walk once in a while so he wouldn't lock up, but moving too fast made him dizzy. So he ate codeine-reinforced Tylenol like M&Ms and floated.

The ghosts of the two men he'd killed in El Cajon glared at him while he was awake. When he slept, they merged into a running loop of weird nightmares that dredged up things he'd tried to not think about for twenty years. None of it was restful. The drugs only made it worse.

He'd just jolted out of another bad mental movie when he heard the gentle tap on the door. "A man wants to see you," Alvaro wheezed in Spanish. "He's a *policía*, I think."

"Tell him to go away."

"I did. He won't go."

Luis shuffled to the front door, trying not to move in any of the few dozen ways that hurt. He wasn't surprised to find McGinley waiting for him. "What do you want?"

McGinley crossed his arms and shook his head. "You are one

sorry-looking *hombre*."

"I'm sick."

"Y'all are gonna feel worse after we're done, Ojeda. Me and you need to take a ride."

Luis tried to wake himself up enough to process this, but only made the pounding worse. "I'm not going anywhere with you."

"This ain't a request." McGinley draped his hand over his holstered pistol. "Besides, I guarantee you don't want to talk here."

Outside, the Neighborhood Watch guys stopped shoveling gravel out of a pickup into a pothole to watch Luis stagger out to McGinley's medium-gray Santana. McGinley drove out of the neighborhood as if he was trying to escape the hill fire. Once they hit the low-rise suburbia of Fairhaven Avenue, he slowed so the road hammering wouldn't destroy both their spines.

"Remember that pow-wow we had last Monday?" McGinley growled. "The one where I told you I'd kill your job and throw your pretty wife out of the country and put the old folks in a camp if you fucked with me? Well, you need to think on that right quick, 'cause you have fucked up more ways'n I can count."

How'd he find out? "I don't know what you're talking about."

McGinley tsked and shook his head again. Then, without warning, his right fist backhanded Luis just below his ribs.

The Disneyland fireworks show filled Luis' eyes. He jerked forward to double over, but the seat belt's shoulder harness caught him short and snapped against the bruises McGinley hadn't hit. Luis hung there, half bent, coughing and gagging as he fought to catch a breath.

"Let's try this again. Tell me about Nura al-Khaled." Luis lost the lungful of air he'd managed to claw down. "I never reckoned you for a traitor, Ojeda. It's one thing to move all them women and kids and old folks around. That's almost touching. But a real live terrorist? I'm disappointed in you."

How did he find out? How much did he know? Luis used his breathing problem for cover as he tried to figure out what to say. He wasn't in any condition to get smacked around.

"I'm waitin'."

Luis finally sat up straight. "Is this ride so you can dump me in the landfill?"

McGinley laughed. "*Amigo*, I don't gotta dump your body. I can just shoot you while escaping." When he stopped at the light on Grand just south of I-5, the car was swarmed by ragged little kids trying to sell mints and paper flowers. They scattered when he flashed his badge. "This ride is so our friends in the FBI don't listen in." He glanced at Luis, probably seeing the shock. "Oh, yeah. They know about you and al-Khaled. I reckon they already climbed so far up your asshole you can't feel 'em no more."

Ay, chingado. Luis remembered what Nora had told him—blanket wiretaps, drones, super-SWAT teams. If McGinley was right, it was "game over." They might already have Nora, or they'd have her soon; then they'd come for him. The Cartel might pay for a lawyer assuming any of this got to a courtroom six or seven years from now. In the meantime, he'd be an old man in some jungle of a prison, getting older fast. "They on Bel too?"

"I reckon so, just to be thorough. When they get a mind to, the Feebs just go to town. That's the upside of working for the last civilian Federal agency with any money."

"How long?"

"Well, I just found out this morning, but I ain't first on their mailing list, if you know what I mean." He stopped to let a mixed group of Latino women and kids—faces half-covered by grubby surgical masks—cross the road on their way to a street market set up in front of a dead gas station. "Let me tell you how this works. It can go two ways. One way is you keep being cute with me, and the Feebs bust you and your new girlfriend and put you in some military prison somewhere and forget about you, and your wife goes in a camp because she must be in on it, and maybe your son gets bounced from the Marines, and your folks end up living in a tent. How's that sound to you?"

Luis worked hard to keep his face blank even though his heart was about to seize up. This *tonto* wanted him to lose it. Luis wouldn't give him the pleasure. "They don't even do that kind of shit in Russia anymore."

"Maybe not. The other way—you'll like this better—is you tell me where al-Khaled is, and I bust her, and since you're my CI and you led me to her, you get off with maybe a couple days in holding just to make it look good, and you retire and you and your pretty wife and your folks get to live your lives in peace."

"Until the Cartel kills me for being a snitch. What do you get out of Option Two?"

McGinley smiled that predator smile Luis last saw at the ID check. "I get to put a genuine terrorist in a cage. ICE gets more money in the next budget, which means maybe I get a raise. And I get to cornhole the Bureau, which I just love to do, 'cause them arrogant sumbitches are always in my chili playing 'I've Got a Secret' and I can't tell you how irritating that is."

Option Two sounded a lot better than the first one. Except for the part about the Cartel feeding him to the sharks, and that he didn't believe McGinley would let him go so easily. And the part about giving up Nora. But since this cracker was talking about options, the Feds didn't have her yet. Luis might have some room to bargain a way to keep himself and his family out of jail.

"One problem." Luis tried to find a way to sit that didn't hurt and kept his face turned away from McGinley. He watched the busy sidewalk as the car nosed through the tuk-tuks and pedicabs jamming Fourth Street in Santa Ana's Latino business district. "Someone else already made a play for her. Not the FBI."

"Who?"

"Not sure. They sent two teams of contractors to hit a safe house in El Cajon. The first team was going for a capture. No shooting until the people inside started shooting back. The second team was in full kill-them-all mode."

"You ain't got nothing to do with all this, right?"

"Just telling you what I know."

"What makes you so sure they were contractors?"

"They didn't wear uniforms and they carried no IDs. That's how I figure they're not FBI or any of your other friends."

McGinley chewed this over for a few moments. "Reckon they were cartel?"

"That's my guess." Not that Luis needed to think about Zetas again—ever—but they were popping up too much lately. "The first six were Anglos and didn't have Zeta tats. That's why I'm saying contractors and not *sicarios*. They're trying to keep it at arm's length."

"And it ain't your boys because, well, why bother? They already got you."

"Yeah. Where'd the FBI get their information about Nora?" Luis winced the moment he said her first name and not her last.

McGinley raised an eyebrow at him. "'Nora,' is it? Well. I don't know where the Feebs got their intel, but since y'all are first-name buddies and all, maybe it's true." He threaded through the northbound traffic on Main, heading away from downtown and La Paloma into patchy low-rise commercial buildings and a blight of vidboards, pawn shops, tire- and slate-rental stores, and payday lenders. The gold late-afternoon light didn't make the area any more attractive. "Do you know a Jorge Casillas?"

Distracted by the FBI bombshell, Luis took a moment to surface and answer. "Who?"

"He's been visiting with your good friend Esquivel."

"Who is he?"

"He's a fixer." Another predator smile. "For the Zetas."

Getting shot was less of a shock. It couldn't be true. Luis figured McGinley wasn't above lying his ass off if it suited him. Ray had been beating the drum to stand up to the Zetas, to fight back when they invaded Norte territory. He'd offered to lead a unit himself. No *way* would he be a Zeta patsy.

And no way would he sell out Luis. They'd been like brothers for over twenty years. Ray had been best man at Luis' wedding. He was Christa's and Nacho's godfather.

"Awful quiet over there. Got nothing to say?"

"That makes no sense. Maybe Ray's trying to turn him."

"Anything's possible, I reckon." McGinley's voice made it obvious how likely he thought it was.

Luis said, "What I don't get is, why would the Zetas care about Nora?"

"The reward maybe? Ten million dollars ain't nothing to spit at."

Ten million? Luis squashed the near-instant urge to turn in Nora himself. That's what these people wanted. Besides, they'd bust him and he'd never see a dime. "A day's revenue from Texas? Big deal."

They skirted a rear-ender standoff in the right lane—two men pointing guns at each other and screaming over a few shards of busted plastic from their cars—and passed a two-story $3 store bustling with cars and shoppers. Luis remembered it had been a bookstore back when those still existed. It also reminded him where they were. "You better hang a U up here if you don't want to get stuck in traffic. It's rush hour."

McGinley shot him a dark look but bulled his way into the turn pocket anyway. "You got something to tell me?"

Try it? Luis had nothing to lose. "Nora's not a terrorist."

"That so."

"She's an FBI agent and—"

"A *what?*"

McGinley's pop-eyed surprise made Luis want to laugh, but he bottled it up. "You heard me. I know, that part didn't make the news. She's running because she found out some stuff she wasn't supposed to."

"What kind of 'stuff'?" McGinley's words were coated with skepticism thicker than the breading on fried chicken.

How much should he tell McGinley? The man probably wouldn't buy it anyway. But if Luis could kick up a little doubt, get McGinley to poke in a few of the wrong places, he could buy himself enough time to get Nora over the border. What happened then, he had no idea. "It's about 10/19. Those Yemeni guys? They didn't do it. It—"

McGinley wheeled on him, his face going red. "What kinda shit is this, Ojeda?"

"Just listen. It was some militia assholes. The FBI blamed the Yemenis because everyone wanted it to be Muslims. She found out and now they're trying to stop her from going public."

"Jee-sus." McGinley shook his head. "That what she told you? You fell for that?"

"You fell for this she's-been-a-terrorist-for-thirteen-years story on the news?"

For once, McGinley didn't have a comeback.

"You should see what she's got. Case files, interviews, video, photos. That's only part of what she found. Don't believe me? Look her up in the Bureau directory. Ask your FBI friends if you can read into REDCAP. That's the SCI compartment for the 10/19 intel. Or look up the Free Montana Militia and see where it went."

McGinley fell back into his seat and started torturing the steering wheel as he stared out the windshield. "You didn't happen to get names for them militia boys, did you? Your tinfoil hat didn't get in the way?"

"Funny. Um… Dugan, Conners, Seybold. There was a fourth one, Mac something, I can't remember."

McGinley considered this. "I got a deal for you, Ojeda. I'll look into this. You find out what Casillas is doing with your buddy Esquivel, and you keep tabs on al-Khaled. You don't move her without telling me. Understand? That's as good as this gets right now."

"What about the FBI?"

"Let me wrassle with them. Maybe they'll bend a little if they think they're gonna get what they want. You just do as you're told. Deal?"

Compared with Option One, it was a great deal. But Luis could see a million things go wrong with it. With full-court-press FBI surveillance hanging over him, he had no idea how long Nora would go free. If he didn't agree, he was pretty sure his life and his family's lives would be over very soon.

Luis took a deep breath, preparing to jump off the high diving board. "Okay. Deal."

41

> *Large discount retailers are expected to continue their strong performance through 2032 as their market base of subprime-income customers continues to grow… Walmart, Target, BigLots!, $2.99 Only and other national chains now anchor 81% of regional shopping centers, replacing bygone mid-market retailers such as Sears, JCPenney, Dillard's, and Macy's.*
> -- Sector Outlook for 2032, *National Retail Federation*

FRIDAY, 14 MAY

Luis' brain had jolted from dazed to hyper-alert during his ride with McGinley. He'd talked the Fed into dropping him at the $3 store; he had things to do and calls to make, and if the FBI was all over his home, he couldn't do them there. Now he stood in the parking lot, hands shaking, imagining that every person he saw was an FBI agent.

Get it together, he scolded himself. *Lose yourself in the crowd.*

He gimped across the street to the struggling Main Place Mall and entered the huge Target where Macy's used to be. The bright lights and colors jangled his eyes but seeing the busy bargain shoppers helped lower his heart rate to only mildly panicked. Yes, the FBI could still track him on the store cameras, but first they had to know he was there. *Keep moving.*

In the electronics department, he selected a nicer Kenyan-knockoff Huawei smartphone and three five-packs of 15-minute phone chips. Once through the self-serve checkout, he plunged into the scrum in groceries, woke up the phone, and brought up Skype using the store's wifi. He was as anonymous as he'd ever get; the Feds would have to parse every one of the dozens of data streams inside the store to find his. Good luck with that.

As he wove through the food shoppers, he left a message for

Ray asking for a meet, then asked Nathan for a full scan of the house. He called for a Cartel car; his truck was probably a rolling sensor net by now. Nora picked up on the second ring.

"Since when?" she asked after he told her the FBI was after him.

"No idea. Not too long, or they'd have picked me up by now."

She was silent for a few moments. Then she sighed. "I'm sorry. This is my fault."

"We'll figure out whose fault it is later. You need to go dark. Pull the batteries out of everything that's got batteries. Check your burner for messages every two hours but go to a different house every time. I'll get down there when I can."

He wanted to call Bel, but he didn't know when she'd last swapped chips in her burner. The FBI must have her phone tapped. He'd tell her tonight if he survived the day.

Luis browbeat his big sister Lourdes over the phone until she agreed to put up Alvaro and Graciela in Denver for a while. She was pissed, but it was time for her to take care of someone other than herself for a change. He needed to take their parents out of play. He could already hear tonight's conversation with them—especially Dad—and didn't look forward to it.

Had Tavo known about Salma? He probably knew she'd been Ray's girlfriend, but not about her makeup work with the travelers. She deserved a warning anyway. "It's me," he said when she finally picked up. "How long would it take you to leave the country?"

"Why?"

"It's time."

A lot of dead air followed. "Really? Because of Ray?"

"Because of him, and because of me. The FBI knows about me. It's time to get out while you can. Before you go, I need you to do me a favor. Remember Tyler from the shop?"

"The cute one with the plastic leg? Sure I do."

Luis told her what he needed. Any eavesdropping shoppers would be confused.

"You know I can't say 'no' to you. Okay, one last job, then off to my permanent vacation." Ice clinked against glass in the background. "Hey, handsome… come with me. Keep me safe. We could find a little beach…"

That sounded wonderful for a split-second, until Luis reconnected with reality. "You know I can't. I have a wife I'd like to keep. You'll do fine. Just be careful, okay?"

"You are *so* straight." Salma paused. "Lucho? Watch out for Ray. I know he's your friend, but he's into things—"

The rest of Luis' brain-fog burned away. "What do you mean, 'into things'?"

"Just… be careful. He's got big plans for himself, and I'm not sure they include any of us. Don't get in his way. And get out of this thing with Nora before she gets you killed. Please. I like you better alive."

"So do I." *Watch out for Ray* echoed in his brain. He'd push harder, but he'd gotten all he would from her about it. "Take care."

"I'll tell you where I land. Maybe you can come visit sometime, huh?"

"Maybe." Which sounded like *goodbye*. He'd never see Salma again. Probably for the best, though it didn't feel that way. "Take care of yourself. *Vaya con Dios*."

Getting to Ray's house through the early-evening traffic was more of a trial than Luis had expected. Newport Beach PD hassled him for driving while brown inside the sixteen-foot steel pillars of the city's wall, reminding him why he didn't go there this late.

Warm, indirect lighting popped the white walls of Ray's house against the waning sunset. The neighbors' indoor lights were far brighter than the five-watt fluorescents Luis was stuck with at home. The trickle of the little fountain next to Ray's front door reminded him these people could also afford to fill their koi ponds and big swimming pools and water their landscaping.

At least this time, Ray's blonde was fully dressed in her black maid uniform. "Good evening, Mr. Ojeda. Ray will be down in just a minute. Can I get you something?"

"Iced tea?" he said when he stepped inside. He couldn't risk a beer in his half-drugged condition.

Luis followed the blonde through the cream limestone and white marble to the kitchen. *Maids know everything*, his rational voice told him as he watched her pull together his drink from the endless cabinets and the huge fridge. Schmoozing her for information meant shouldering past his resentment, though. "You're Keira, right? Like the actress?"

"Yes. She was my mom's favorite."

She didn't look at him, and her tone was polite-verging-on-frosty. Had Ray told her Luis' opinion of her? "How long've you been here?"

"Three years and some."

"Huh. I'll bet you guys have been busy lately." No reply. He'd run out of small talk. *How do you like sleeping with Ray?* No, that wouldn't lead anywhere he wanted to go. *Get to it, then.* "Hey, a guy I know said he'd been by here. Jorge Casillas? Know him?"

The maid hesitated just a moment while stirring his drink. Her jaw got a little harder. Then she recovered, put on a tight smile, and handed him a tall glass of tea with perfect ice cubes and even a sprig of mint. "I'll go see what's keeping Ray."

Luis stood sipping his tea at the floor-to-ceiling living-room window, switching his attention between the glowing-turquoise infinity pool, the soccer and baseball games on the huge databoard on the wall over the fireplace, and the window-washing robot's silver slab as it crawled across the glass. After a few minutes, he saw Ray's reflection ambling down the stairs behind him.

"What do the neighbors think of all these guards?" Luis asked.

"They're down with it," Ray answered in Spanish. "Half of them have live-in muscle. Safest city in the state and they have juiced-up ex-soldiers walking the Sharpoo. Come on, let's sit." Ray muted the databoard with a sharp gesture and sprawled into an armchair. "You don't look so good, *hermano*."

Luis perched on the flat, hard-as-a-rock couch, trying not to bend. He switched to Spanish. "There's a reason. How often do you sweep this place?"

Ray laughed. "Seriously? Every day. Vibrators on the windows, ultrasonics outside to fuck with parabolic mikes. Why? What's going on?"

"You know about El Cajon, right?"

"What about it?"

Luis described the attack on the safe house, killing the six gunmen, his escape, his suspicions about who sent them. Ray nodded and made the right noises, but it seemed to Luis that he wasn't as surprised or concerned as he ought to be. Had he heard this already?

"Sorry you got hit," Ray said. "You okay? Bel taking care of you?"

"Yeah." Lucho shifted, wished he hadn't. "Feels like I walked in front of a truck."

"Where's the *bruja?*"

"Safe for now."

"Come on, *hermano.*" Ray spread his hands. "Let me help you. I can give you men, supplies, whatever. You don't have to lone-wolf this. She's in one of our houses?"

Why was he suddenly being so helpful? "No. The one in Serra Mesa's being watched, too. We've gotta figure they're all burned, that the Zetas got it out of Tavo. But there's a bigger problem. The FBI knows I've got Nora."

Ray fell back into his chair, an *oh, shit* look on his face. "How do you know?"

"McGinley told me. Nathan's ripping bugs out of my house right now."

"McGinley? Why would he tell you?"

"Because he wants to bust Nora himself." Luis leaned forward without thinking. Every muscle from his hips up screamed at him for it. "We can't blame this one on the Zetas. There's a serious fucking leak in your organization. I'm telling you nothing until you fix it." Luis turned away from Ray's mouthful-of-pickles expression, watching the guards pace outside for a few moments. "Who's this Casillas guy who keeps visiting?"

Ray bolted upright. "None of your bus—"

"Fuck that, Ray!" Luis said it with far more heat than he'd ever used on Ray before. "You're meeting with a Zeta fixer at the same time his people are torturing Tavo and his hired help's trying to kill me and kidnap my client. Who is he?"

Ray lurched out of his chair and stalked across the room to the bar. Luis wondered if he'd crossed the wrong line; Ray was more-or-less a *capo*, now. He watched Ray pour a healthy slug of tequila, drain half, then refill. Bracing himself to kill Luis?

"Okay." Ray turned back to Luis. "This doesn't go past the kitchen, got it? You'll know why when I tell you."

Luis pointed up to the bridge across the living room. "How about your girlfriend?"

"That's why we're using Spanish, so she doesn't understand. Yes, Casillas is a Zeta. For now. He feels unappreciated. Once we get our leadership settled, he's going to flip to us and bring over a chunk of the Zetas' California business. We're planning his move."

This sounded like science fiction. "People who flip on the Zetas die."

"Yeah, usually. If we can keep him alive and take his network, it'll be huge. People will figure out they don't have to roll over for those *cabrones* anymore. That's why I can't talk about it with you or anyone. If they find out, he's dead in a real bad way, you know?"

"Uh-huh." This didn't sound right. Why would they meet here—especially now—where the Zetas could keep tabs on him? On the other hand, Luis had worried Ray might try something like this. What did Salma say? *Ray's into things.* Luis struggled off of the sofa and lumbered stiff-legged toward the bar. "How do you know this guy's for real?"

"I just do. Look, he's a nasty little prick and I'd rather throw him off the cliff than work with him, you know? But we need a win, *hermano*. We're getting our asses kicked." He poured another three fingers of tequila and downed half in one shot. "Be chill about this. Don't tell McGinley. ICE and DEA are full of snitches. Understand?"

Luis didn't say anything, just set his empty glass on the bar. He spent a few uncomfortable moments peering into Ray's eyes. "Were any of the other safe houses hit?"

Ray's attention wavered between Luis and his glass; the booze won. "I don't know. I'll have to get a team on it. Why?"

"If they only went after El Cajon, they were targeting Nora. If they hit everyplace, they were just after whatever they could find."

"Good thinking. I'll get a survey done." Ray squeezed Luis' uninjured right shoulder. "Keep the faith, *hermano*. Don't shut me out. You know I won't let anything happen to you, right? After all this time?"

42

Fifteen years ago, the American expatriate community in Boquete was a few thousand strong and notably white and gray-haired. Today, over sixty thousand Americans of all ethnicities live in this Panamanian mountain city, making it the world's largest foreign concentration of U.S. citizens. Most of these newcomers are working-age refugees from El Norte's pollution, politics, and decay...

-- "Best Destinations for U.S. Expats,"
Money.USNews.com

SATURDAY, 15 MAY

God, this sounded like such a bad idea. But Bel couldn't see any other options, and neither could Lucho. They'd talked it over until way past midnight. She snuggled closer—it was weird to be on his right after twenty-plus years on the other side of the bed—and whispered, "Are you sure?"

"Yeah." His fingertips stroked up and down her spine, leaving a little trail of tingle.

He'd said it was safe in the bedroom, that his tech guy had put in something that blocked transmitters and vibrated the windows. Having the ceiling fan clacking away at takeoff speed made things even harder for any eavesdroppers, plus it moved the air enough that she and Lucho could stand to cling together even in the heat. This room was more secure than anyplace else they could go. For all that, she couldn't shake the creepy feeling that someone might be listening.

"If we do this, I don't know what'll happen," he murmured in her ear.

The feel of his skin on hers had her heart going crazy and scrambled all her thoughts. He was still too fragile to make love, damnit, and she desperately wanted to. The way this was going, she didn't know when she'd get another chance.

She kissed him. "I feel like I'm never going to see you again."

"That's not gonna happen." He pecked her forehead. "Make sure Mom and Dad get on the plane tomorrow morning. I need them far away from any blowback. Will you do that?"

Bel smiled a little. "Are you kidding? I'm *so* about putting Graciela in a different time zone. You have no idea."

He smiled, too, but only for a moment. "Dad's pretty scared. He doesn't want to be away from you. He thinks you're some kind of magic healer."

"I am. Didn't you know?" The joke fell with a *thud*, even for her. Bel and that old bat Graciela managed to stay more-or-less civil with each other, even though Lucho's mom had wanted some pretty little no-attitude *mamacita* to cook for him and start pushing out lots of grandkids. Alvaro had adopted her the second time he saw her. She'd miss him. "There's nothing I can do for him now anyway, except maybe hold his hand."

"Sometimes that's enough."

The more she thought about the two of them escaping, the more complicated the idea sounded. "The FBI isn't going to just let you go, even if you get Nora over the border."

"I know. We may need to hang out down south for a while until we see what happens when Nora gets her information out."

"That could take a long time."

"I know." He traced her cheekbone with a fingertip. He looked so sad. "I'm sorry, *cariña*. I didn't want this. But I can't give up on Nora. I can't let her get caught. And I can't leave you up here in danger."

Bel rolled on her side and propped her head on her hand, looking down on him. She absently smoothed the tape holding the gauze pads over his shoulder wound. She would've been happy to stay like that for the next few hours, but a question had been gnawing at her ever since they'd started talking. "What happens if we can't come back?"

He didn't answer for a long time. Then he slipped his hand into hers and intertwined their fingers. "We start over someplace else."

"But what happened to all that about the Cartel hunting us

down? Did they change their minds?"

"The way things are going? I don't know if there's going to *be* a Cartel a couple months from now. Tavo's dead, or he's going to be soon. Hard telling what'll happen to Ray."

Bel set her chin down on their clasped hands. This might be over? She desperately wanted to believe it. All she could think about for the past two weeks was Lucho being a slave to the Cartel for the rest of his life, however short a time that might be. But maybe—one way or another—they'd get to grow old and fat together after all.

An idea flew straight out of Bel's mouth before she could think it through. "Let me come with you."

"I'd love to." Luis pulled her against him, stroked her hair.

She burrowed her face into the soft part of his throat and hung on tight. She wanted him to stop right there, but something in his voice told her to wait for the *but*.

"But I can't. It's too dangerous. I don't want you anywhere near Nora. I don't know what's going to happen with her, but whatever it is, I won't expose you to it."

"But you'll expose her to it."

"She's just a traveler. You're my life."

That felt as good as his skin pressed against hers. "So, I just go to Tijuana and wait for you in a hotel? That's it?"

"That's it. Whatever bags you pack, put them in your car when you load up Mom's and Dad's so the FBI won't figure out you're skipping. Nathan'll meet you at the airport and clean out any trackers before you leave. You got paid yesterday, right?"

"Yeah. There's not much left, but we'll have something. What are we going to live on?"

"We'll work that out later." He pulled her face to his and kissed her. "Right now, we have to worry about not getting caught."

No problem. All they had to do was get past the FBI. And the Zetas. And the desert. And that asshole Ray. And that violent wilderness south of the border, where so many people had died.

⬡

Luis finished stuffing the two banker's boxes with clothes, his field gear, and his rolled-up backpack. The vidframe on the dresser caught his eye. Each picture dissolved into the next. When that photo of Christa appeared, he tapped the screen to pause and traced her face with his fingertip. *I'm sorry*, mija. The next photo showed Nacho's boot-camp graduation, his impossibly fit, brown, young-looking son in his olive service-dress uniform, standing between depressingly old-looking versions of Luis and Bel. *Forgive me*, mijo. He slipped the frame into a box.

He turned to take mental snapshots of the room. When would he be here again? When would he sleep in this bed—he ran his palm over the geometric-print top sheet—with Bel again? Ever? Lead weights piled onto his heart. This house wasn't much, but it was his and he and Bel had done a lot of living and loving here.

The next part went by way too fast. Luis carried the two boxes out to his truck, then returned to the living room to say his goodbyes. Alvaro perched on a dining-room chair, clutching his ragged bathrobe around him. Graciela stood in the kitchen entry dressed for work, arms folded, holding a spatula like a club. Bel paced circles near the front door. Nobody smiled.

Luis kissed his mother's cheek. "Lourdes is looking forward to seeing you guys."

"No, she isn't," Graciela snapped back in Spanish. Luis instantly felt like he was eight years old again. "You're abandoning us. Don't lie to us too."

He took in what he hoped was a calming breath. "Not now, Mama. Please don't."

His mother jabbed her chin toward Bel. "Did *she* talk you into this?"

"No. I talked *her* into it. You want to stay? Fine. Say 'hi' to the FBI for me."

Graciela glared at him. "You're just like your father."

Luis pulled her into an awkward hug, the spatula grinding into his ribs. She was like a bird's nest in his arms, but one made of steel wire instead of straw. "That can't be too bad," he whispered in her ear. "How long have you been with him?"

Alvaro took both of Luis' hands in his own and murmured, "Don't forget us." Tears wobbled in his eyes.

Luis nodded, unable to work up any words other than "I love

you." He embraced his father for what he hoped wouldn't be the last time.

Then it was Bel's turn. The others found someplace else to look as she and Luis stood by the front door, staring into each other's eyes. Holding hands turned into a hug, which became a tight clinch, which led to the best kiss they could give each other.

He pulled back to say *I love you.* Before he got a sound out, she placed her index finger across his lips and shook her head, breaking loose a tear.

43

*From over 11,000 stores in the U.S. in 2016, Starbucks
now has 670, concentrated in a small number of very
wealthy areas... The best one-line explanation for
Starbucks' disappearance from the U.S. market comes
from Morgan Choudhoury, an analyst for HSBC Global
Asset Management: "You can't sell $10 coffee to people
making $3 an hour."*

-- "Starbucks' U.S. Business Worth Beans,"
BusinessInsider.com

SATURDAY, 15 MAY

The snitch screeched out of the drive-through lane behind the boarded-up Starbucks onto Broadway and disappeared past the dead Chula Vista Center mall. As McGinley moseyed back to his car, he decided this ol' boy was worth keeping. He was a goddamn kronker and smelled worse than a wet goat, but it was well worth paying to hear the things he had to say about the Zetas infesting San Diego County.

McGinley's dataspecs flashed an incoming call. Unknown number; Ojeda already? "McGinley here."

"Special Agent Jack McGinley?" A careful voice, no accent. "With JTF-30?"

"Only one I know of. Who're you?"

"Special Agent Friday Tranh, with the HSI Phoenix field office. Are you the one who's interested in Cordero Alcala?"

McGinley leaned back against his Santana's fender and paid a lot more attention to Friday Tranh. "Why, yes I am. Do you have intel on him?"

"We may have his vehicle. A green Cadillac Olympia with extra armor, right? Would you like to see it?"

Agent Tranh just became McGinley's favorite person. "I surely

211

would. Where is it?"

"In Mexico. About two hundred yards from where I'm standing."

The Border Patrol outpost sat in the middle of fuck-all noplace: a square of double-wides and a gravel helipad surrounded by desert, spitting distance from the fence. San Luis Rio Colorado, the nearest town, was over thirty miles west as the crow flies, if there were any crows stupid enough to be out in this wasteland.

McGinley didn't pay it much mind. He was glued to the fence, his binoculars were glued to his face, and he had Alcala's SUV square in his sights.

It hunkered in the middle of eight other vehicles, most of them blown to hell. A semi burned to its chassis; another one jackknifed; a third one with its trailer's side looking like a kid's connect-the-dots picture; a couple shot-to-shit deuce-and-a-halfs; a black SUV on its roof; and two raggedy-looking RVs, all scattered on either side of the Mex Federal Highway 2.

"There were another eleven tractor-trailers in the convoy." Tranh stood close to McGinley. He was one of those sharp-faced little Vietnamese who look like they're made out of glass until you tangle with them and they bust you in half. "Also, another seven military trucks, with MRAPs on either end. After the airstrike, the survivors loaded on the other vehicles and continued westbound."

"When was all this again?"

"Oh-five-forty-three." Tranh's mirrored dataspecs stared at McGinley. "You're also interested in the RVs, aren't you?"

McGinley recalled what he'd told Tranh on the phone, that this was part of a human-trafficking investigation. It was in a very specific kind of way. "That's right. When do we head out?"

The sound of a huge hummingbird zipped overhead. A haze-gray drone gunship zoomed over the fence and started to orbit the wrecks. It reminded him of a baby version of the old Apaches.

"Our air support is here, so we go now." Tranh marched toward the line of four tan Border Patrol BRV-Os waiting to go through the big, open gate in the fence. "Stay in contact. This is the main supply route between Juarez and Mexicali. The Zetas and MU run a lot of traffic through here to resupply their forces near San Luis. Another convoy is due in an hour, so we have forty-five minutes on site."

"Roger that." McGinley was of no mind to get caught alone on the wrong side of the fence. He set his phone to count off the time.

The kill zone smelled like diesel and burned rubber and barbeque gone bad. McGinley choked a bit, blinked his eyes clear, then stepped off toward the green Olympia sitting catawampus on the shoulder about thirty yards away. He settled the borrowed tactical goggles on his face, switched on the data feed. Little green dots spread out over a wireframe map.

The SUV's left front wheel bent under the nose, and as he got closer, McGinley saw the windshield was shot out and the hood had a big hole at the front. Cannon fire, most likely. He also noted the fancy titanium rims and the dollar-bill-green paint that looked near a mile deep.

He circled to the passenger's side, yanked open the front door. *Jee-sus.* The survivors may have skedaddled, but the dead stuck around. They'd been baking for most of the day. He turned away from what was left of the driver, pushed a pair of foam earplugs up his nose, snapped on some latex gloves, and got to work.

And found nothing. Well, not exactly *nothing*: Alcala (if he'd really been here) left behind a big cooler full of water and beer and soda (McGinley helped himself to a Coke). He ate Mex food out of a Styrofoam clamshell. Someone left gas receipts under the custom-leather front passenger's seat. The Olympia's GPS and black box might be useful, but Tranh's boys were busy scooping up all those. He stood for a spell staring at the back seat. *You got away this time, boy. Not next time.*

The closest RV—a clapped-out Itasca a dozen yards away, its paint half gone from sand and sun—had managed to high-center itself on what was left of a cinder-block wall around a little ruined shack. Antifreeze and oil made a mess under its nose. One of Tranh's boys was already under the hood, pulling the black box.

McGinley ducked through the side door, leading with his pistol. Inside smelled like booze and perfume and sweat. There was beer in the little fridge and ten twelve-pack cartons of rubbers under the sink. Girl shampoo and soap in the tiny toilet and shower. A couple 200mg kronk tablets on the stained carpet next to the tore-up bed in the bedroom. The Zetas could run three or four whores out of each RV—one in here, one out on the sofabed, another in the drop-down bunk over the driver's seat—line up the johns outside and move them through like a factory.

For a moment, McGinley saw Carla Jean on this bed, eyes dead, some Mex grinding away at her. Then he scrambled outside to leave his lunch next to the oil patch.

He leaned back against the RV's slab side for a few moments, letting his mind clear. He'd been ignoring the radio chatter coming over the goggles, but he finally realized Tranh was calling his name. "Yeah, McGinley here."

"The convoy is moving faster than we expected. We have to leave in fifteen minutes."

Shit. McGinley spat to clean out his mouth. He reset his timer. "Roger that."

Back inside the Itasca, McGinley tore through every drawer and storage hole. He found a bushel of flimsy lingerie, some crappy-cheap clothes made in Texas or Angola, and more long, black hairs in more places than he could count. Not a picture or scrap of ID. The high point was leaving, getting away from the smells and the pictures in his head.

He jogged to the Winnebago two dozen yards away. He couldn't tell what was wrong with it and didn't really care; he had eight minutes left and so far, he'd found shit.

The air inside was rank in a way that snaked through the plugs in his nose. Then he saw why: a Mex girl on the sofa, all black and bloated, her head at a weird angle, an arm bent in a place arms don't bend. The girls must've been thrown around like the fuzzy dice on the rear-view when the RV went offroad, and this one broke her neck. Damn shame.

He ignored the flies and the stink and rifled the drawers and cabinets like a machine. Some pot, more booze, more undies, more rubbers, junk food, spray-can air freshener, zip ties, a half-used first-aid kit, a flashlight. A pink see-through lighter he pocketed.

A plastic hair brush… with blond hairs in it.

McGinley sagged on the edge of the bed, staring at the brush.

A tangle of medium-blond hair, at most six inches long. Shorter than Carla Jean's, but that was a long time ago and who knew what she looked like now, anyway? Her color, though.

"Agent McGinley?" Tranh's voice in his ear. "Our time is up."

"Copy." He tore apart the rest of the bedroom, emptied the drawers on the bedsheet, went through every scrap of clothing, every comb and lipstick tube, searching for something that was Carla Jean's. It was just him being a damn fool—she wouldn't have anything left over from when she was taken—but he had to check. He *had* to.

Nothing. Just the brush, and the hair.

He dropped the brush into an evidence bag and shoved it into a back pocket. He snagged a mostly full tequila bottle off the floor, rushed past the dead Mex girl and burst outside. The heat and sun and dust were a far sight better than what was in there. Two BRV-Os rolled down the highway toward him; two others dragged roster-tails of dust back to the fence.

McGinley jogged down the asphalt until he reached Alcala's SUV. He stood for a moment considering the shiny wheels and fancy paint. *You pimping sumbitch. I will find you. If this here's Carla Jean's hair, I'll find her too and let her kill you. Slow.*

A BRV-O clattered to a stop behind him. He didn't turn until he heard a door open.

Tranh's dataspecs frowned at him. "We have to go, Agent McGinley."

"Are y'all done with this?" McGinley aimed a thumb at the Olympia.

"We have the GPS and data recorder, yes."

"Good." McGinley shoved open the hood, poured the tequila over the wrecked engine block, then fired it up with the pink lighter. Between the booze and the leaking gas and oil, it caught right quick. McGinley climbed into the BRV-O next to Tranh and watched the smoke as they pulled away. When they were halfway to the fence, the Olympia's gas tank cooked off. That fireball felt better to McGinley than anything he'd done for a long time.

"Why did you do that?" Tranh asked.

"Practicing. For when I meet up with the fucker who owns it."

44

SATURDAY, 15 MAY

Luis waved goodbye as Nathan pushed through the office's entry into the night. Tyler stood next to Luis, considering the cardboard flat on the counter. Eight bugs and three miniature cameras lay piled on the cardboard, dead. The keylogger software and the trap door infesting the office computer had vaporized when Nathan's bag of digital tricks got after them. Two audio bugs and a tracker puck from Luis' truck crowned the pile.

"FBI's gonna be pissed," Tyler said.

"They'll get over it." Or not. The Bureau would treat him the same either way. "They'll replace all that shit tonight after we leave. Watch what you say tomorrow."

"Roger that."

They stood quietly for a few moments at ninety degrees to each other, arms crossed, both gazing out the locked front doors. The street was empty. The Feds didn't need a physical surveillance team—they could track the truck with a drone and not have to worry about losing it in traffic. They may have tagged the cab's roof with infrared paint for a drone's benefit; he wouldn't know until it started to yellow after a few days in the sun. Any other watchers would be using NVGs from a distance. Exactly what Luis had hoped.

Luis scuffed away a dust bunny with the toe of his boot. "Sure you want to do this?"

"Yes, sir. You've been good to me. Gave me a chance."

And hadn't regretted it. Still… "You know this might not turn out so good for you."

"You get three squares in jail, right? A mattress? Toilet?"

"As far as I know."

Tyler shrugged. "Bonus."

They filed into the storage room. There between parts racks

stood Luis' backpack, filled with the contents of the two now-empty banker's boxes. Tyler dragged his pack from a nearby corner. Other than dirt and wear, the two were identical; Luis had bought the pair three years back and gave one to Tyler to replace the ragged thing he'd been hauling.

"Ready?" Luis asked.

"Yes, sir."

Luis handed Tyler his button-down shirt and khakis, then climbed into his old ACU trousers and boots. He swapped a semi-new long-sleeved black tee shirt for the dark-olive one Tyler had worn to work. Tyler's everyday costume wasn't a lot different from what Luis wore when he ran travelers over the border. They were roughly the same height, but Tyler carried at least thirty fewer pounds. Luis' work clothes hung on him. Nothing they could do about that.

"Now it's beauty-parlor time," Luis said.

They crowded into the bathroom—the only mirror in the shop—and Luis broke open the box Salma had sent by courier that afternoon. He scanned the several pages of printed instructions. He'd asked for idiot-proof; she'd taken him seriously. He pulled a wig from the box and handed it to Tyler. "Put some hair on, will you?"

The wig was a good match for Luis' hair—not quite as much gray (Salma was maybe being kind) but the right texture and length. Tyler slipped it over his bristly buzz cut, cocked his head this way and that. "Hm. Feels weird."

"You're getting off light." Luis handed him a set of electric hair clippers. "Know how to use these?"

For the next hour, Luis followed Salma's instructions to turn himself into Tyler and vice versa. He couldn't stop scratching his new quarter-inch brush cut. At the end, they stood side-by-side in front of the dirty mirror, shaking their heads in amazement. Tyler had Luis' nose and eyebrows, filled-out cheeks and fuller mouth. Luis had covered much of his hair stubble with Tyler's battered old Angels cap, and now had a longer, slimmer nose, lighter eyebrows, and thinner lips.

"You're darker than me," Tyler said.

"Not that much, with your tan. Doesn't matter. It just has to look good enough on night vision. They won't see color." He hoped he was right. If he wasn't, they'd find out in a bad way. "Let's go."

People pay to live here, Luis thought. Tyler pulled the truck into the driveway to the derelict self-storage place that was now his home, in a grimy light-industrial area of Costa Mesa three long blocks from the shop. Half the roll-up doors yawned open, revealing people sitting on lawn chairs or old sofas in the faint rectangles of weak light spilling out of the storage cubes. People looking for a chance at night-shift work stuffed themselves into a couple of already-overloaded temp-agency minivans.

"All the way back." Tyler held out a shiny-new padlock key. "Fifth one on the left. C105."

Luis took the key. "Anything I should look out for?"

"Nope. They're all normals. More or less."

Once he stepped outside, Luis would become Tyler. Tyler would drive to Luis' house and sleep in the garage. As far as the FBI was concerned, nothing would've changed. Before dawn tomorrow morning, Tyler would drive to work as Luis, then become himself again. Luis should have vanished by then. At least, that's how this was supposed to work.

"Thanks, Tyler." Luis stretched out his hand. "If I can't get back, I'll put in a good word for you with Xiao if you're interested in running the shop."

"Sure." Tyler shook his hand. "Good luck. Watch your six."

Luis didn't even look back when he heard the truck pull away. He trudged into the storage yard with his backpack slung over his good shoulder. He didn't have to try hard to limp; his body had stiffened from his injuries. Music spooled out of cheap speakers attached to phones and streamers, a sampling of every genre from the past twenty years. He returned waves and nods along his way to Tyler's narrow storage cube.

It wasn't much: a plastic patio chair, a battered bathroom vanity with a slab of plywood on top, an old Red Cross cot, a tiny microwave. Great home for a wounded veteran… and he was doing better than some Luis knew of.

If Luis didn't play this right, this could be his next home.

He called the car service for his ride south.

$$45$$

SUNDAY, 16 MAY

Nora wanted to say "no." The word wouldn't come out.

Just enough early-morning light straggled through the open door leading from the garage to the back yard for Nora to see the dark circles under Luis' eyes. He looked odd with his hair chopped off. Paul watched them from the doorway leading into the house, leaning against the doorjamb, his arms folded.

Nora drifted to the door and caught some pale sunshine on her face. This was so wrong. They'd sworn they'd leave together: a full family, nobody left behind. She couldn't protect them if they split up, and she had to—it was her job, her duty. Leave them to a stranger? No way.

But…

Luis had risked his life in the firefight at the other safe house. He'd taken a bullet. What more did he have to do to prove himself to her?

She hadn't slept right for months since she and Paul had made this decision and hardly at all here in California. More than anything, she had to know her family would be safe, even if she was caught or killed. She'd put up with whatever the Bureau decided to do to her, but she couldn't live knowing Paul or the children were in a camp or prison or…

Nora finally asked, "Will this work?"

"It should," Luis said behind her. "It's your picture up on Fox, not theirs. You're the one they're after. So let's get Paul and the kids south the easy way, and me and you walk out, okay?"

"How would this work?" Paul asked. "What do we do when we get across?"

"I'll have a guy meet you, get you holed up in a motel. I've worked with him a lot. He's good, I trust him. Then when me and Nora get over, he'll come get us and you guys move on."

"How long will we be apart?"

"Day or two. Depends on how far we have to go."

He made it sound so simple. Nora's angels and demons had a screaming match inside her head. She turned to face Luis. "Can you guarantee they'll be safe?"

Luis shook his head. "I can't guarantee *we'll* be safe. Beto's a good man; he'll take care of them. That's the best anyone can do right now."

Paul stepped down onto the garage floor, his face set. "I say we do it."

"Paul!"

He held up his hand. "Just wait. It's easier on the kids. I'm all for easier. And it's not as risky for you. I'm all for that, too." He approached her, arms out. "Just let go. It'll be fine."

Paul was right, but she hated the idea. Nora stared at him for what seemed like hours, her head about to burst. Being separated terrified her. The way things were, though, she might be endangering the most important people in her world right now, just by being near.

Let go. She hadn't let go since the day she'd married Paul. How could she let go of the other half of her life?

How could she not?

46

While other nations enjoy more online amenities and services, no one is as utterly dependent on the Internet as Americans are…With no paper mail, no paper bills, no paper checks and no access to humans at the bank, the financial lives of average Americans exist entirely online…The leverage this gives Comcast, AT&T, and Verizon – the last three providers of broadband access in the U.S. – is hard to overstate… Losing Internet or email access means you essentially cease to exist.

-- "Shackled to the Net," Wired.com

Sunday, 16 May

Bel watched with a growing load of sadness and guilt as Alvaro and Graciela hobbled their way through the glass security tunnel leading to the scanners for John Wayne Airport's Terminal C. Just before they passed into the semi-opaque frosted part at the end, Alvaro gave her a look that weighed a thousand pounds. She only just held herself together. Her gut told her she'd never see Lucho's dad alive again. This—the abandonment—would kill him.

She hurried through the pairs of patrolling guards into the nearest ladies' room and found an empty stall. She stood facing the door. It'd been years since she'd been in an airport, and the overall grubbiness surprised her; luckily, sitting on the seat wasn't on the program. She pulled her burner phone—a junky little Nigerian iPhone 21 copy—from her purse and slipped in the battery. She held her breath as it booted up. *Please be there please…*

One text waiting: "Im ok."

Bel closed her eyes and let out a huge sigh. She'd slept in her clothes on top of the bed the night before just in case the FBI came through the windows. The burner had sat inches away on her nightstand, luring her to connect to Lucho. She hadn't dared turn the thing on until now in case the FBI was watching for it.

She longed to call him, to hear his voice, but she didn't have a number. He'd left his personal phone on the dresser. It was a reminder of how out of reach he was. Where was he? Had he crossed the border yet? Was he safe?

Bel stared at the text for a few more moments, touched her fingertips to the letters. She then erased the phone's memory the way Lucho had taught her. She removed the chip, snapped it in half, then flushed it down the toilet.

The morning was already bright and hot at not quite eight. She trotted to her car in the parking structure, eager to get going. Traffic would still be Sunday-morning light; maybe she'd get to the San Ysidro crossing by lunchtime. It would cost a fortune in tolls to take the Interstate all the way, but now that she and Lucho had decided to do this, she wanted to get it over with.

She twisted the key in her car's ignition. In an instant, a huge, black SUV filled her rear-view mirror. Stormtroopers in black swarmed her from all sides.

The room was small, beige, barren, overcooled, and smelled like industrial cleaners. Kind of like one of the hospital's exam rooms. Bel stared up at the black camera bubble in the corner above the single steel door; it stared back. The rigid, white plastic chair put pressure on all the wrong parts of her butt and thighs without providing any back support at all—also like the hospital. She wanted desperately to get up and pace, but her wrists were zip-tied to an eyelet poking out of her side of the laminate tabletop.

Three hours had gone by like three months.

Her whole body had burned with outrage and embarrassment when the FBI stormtroopers threw her on the garage's concrete and trussed her up like a pig. Since then, her anger had melted into a dull throb in her back and a fog of fear everywhere else. What was taking so long? What were they doing? Would she ever get out?

Through the fear, she held on tight to one floating piece of debris from the wreck of her life: she was still at the airport, not on her way to some dungeon somewhere. Yet.

The loud *clack* of the door's latch release jolted her out of her haze. A sharp-featured but otherwise unmemorable man in a black suit paced in, carrying a stainless-steel tray. The door whispered closed behind him, locking with another gunshot-like crack. He placed the tray in the exact center of the table. It held her personal and burner phones and her slate, each in a plastic zip-lock evidence bag.

Evidence. That must make her a criminal.

The man arranged himself in the chair opposite her, crossed his legs and straightened the crease in his slacks. He watched her coolly, blinking occasionally like a basking iguana.

"Who are you?" Bel wished her voice wouldn't shake so much.

"Special Agent Symonds." Symonds' voice was low, deliberate and almost eerily calm, as if this was some kind of exercise.

She couldn't keep from staring at her things on the tray. "What do you want?"

"My people are searching your home right now. Is there anything you wish to tell me, Mrs. Ojeda?"

You bastards! Bel clamped her mouth shut until she could trust it not to bury her. "Do you have a warrant?"

"Not one that I can share with you."

She took a temperature reading from the man's turquoise eyes. No heat at all. She was used to living and working with people who flew their emotions like flags over their heads. Symonds' detachment disturbed her more than if he'd been stomping around and screaming.

He lifted her slate from the tray, turned it in his hands the way he might an unusual piece of driftwood. "It's remarkable, isn't it, Mrs. Ojeda? The things we can learn from something that looks so simple. Our technicians will find everything you've hidden on this. We've locked your email accounts, your autopays, your medical records. You have no secrets, you understand. So, Mrs. Ojeda… do you have anything to tell me?"

"You locked our autopays? How do we pay our bills?"

"I wouldn't worry about that." Symonds didn't even look at her. "We'll unlock them if there's no evidence in them. In three or four months, perhaps."

Months? By then the bank will have taken the house. Maybe

that was the point. The panic she'd tried to smother started burning through the mental blanket she'd thrown on it.

"Of course," he went on while he placed her slate on the tray, "you don't have to worry about your mortgage since we've seized your house—"

"You *what?*"

"—as the proceeds of criminal activity. They won't foreclose until the property is cleared." Symonds leaned back in his chair. "These days, that takes a year to eighteen months if we don't file charges. If we do, it's an average of seven years for a federal case to go to trial. A shortage of judges, you see." He put a finger to his lips. "But I forgot: this is a national security issue. There won't be a trial. We'll simply sell the house after we close the case."

Bel's face couldn't burn any hotter if someone had thrown flaming gasoline on it. Could they actually take the house and *sell* it? No trial, no appeal? But even as her mind screamed against what Symonds said, she pictured all those people packed off to prison camps. Not just Muslims, but also the "fellow travelers" who complained or resisted. A bucketful of fear doused her anger and left her pressing her knees together so Symonds couldn't see them shake.

Symonds narrowed his eyes. "Mrs. Ojeda." He pitched his voice low enough that she had to lean forward to hear him clearly. "I've told you this so you understand you have no power at all in this situation. Do you understand?"

Even though it killed her to do it, Bel nodded once.

"Very good. All this is a huge headache. You can probably imagine that. The Bureau can be very accommodating if you're innocent bystanders and you cooperate with us. What I'm saying is, you can make this go away by answering one simple question." He leaned toward her. "Where is your husband, Mrs. Ojeda?"

She'd been waiting for that. Give up her husband—the man she'd loved for twenty-three years—and life would go on. But even if she'd consider this deal—which she wouldn't—she couldn't do what Symonds wanted. She could only tell this man the truth. "I have no idea where he is now."

Symonds fell back into his chair and let out a disappointed sigh. He shook his head, maybe imagining all the paperwork she was forcing on him. "The Bureau has some leeway in what to do with unindicted family members living in a seized house. If you cooperate, we can let you stay pending resolution of the case. If you don't? Well, eviction is so easy these days. Since you're all material witnesses, though, I imagine it's simply easier to take you into custody. For your own protection, of course. Once people learn your husband is harboring a wanted terrorist, it's hard telling what they'll do, isn't it?"

She wished he'd yell or kick the chairs or even pull his gun on her. She could understand that; she could deal with it. She handled irate people every day at work. But this bland detachment—talking about what could happen to the ants on the sidewalk—grabbed at some dark, scary place inside her.

"The last time I knew where Lucho was," she said, no strength left in her voice, "was when he walked out the front door yesterday morning."

"You've had no contact since?"

"None." Thank God she'd flushed the chip in her burner.

"Did he say where he was going?"

"No."

"Do you have any idea where he may have gone?"

"South somewhere. He could be in Mexico by now, I don't know." *Please let that be true.*

The agent shook his head. He checked his watch, then returned to Bel and parked his palms on his knees. "Mrs. Ojeda, would you be willing to contact your husband? Explain the situation to him, persuade him to turn himself in? Would you do that to save your house and your family?"

Bel's anger roared back, hotter than ever. How could she give in to this kind of extortion? Lucho had told her Nora's secret; the FBI was just trying to cover its own ass, and the asses of a bunch of high-up people, and the lie that put them all where they were.

She opened her mouth to hit him with this but grabbed the words at the last moment. If he knew she knew the truth, she'd never see daylight again. She had to play along, get loose from these people, so she could try to go south again.

"I can't if you take my phone and slate." Bel tried to sound as beat down as she could. She couldn't give in too easily or he wouldn't believe her.

Finally, a reaction: a spark of interest flitted through his eyes. "If we left them?"

"I don't know his phone number. He left his real phone. I think he's using some other one."

"I can give you a list of the numbers he used before ten PM last night."

Bel pretended to think it over. She'd have to leave messages at all those numbers—the FBI would be listening—but she knew he'd use each one only once, then discard the chips. He'd never hear whatever whining she poured out for the FBI's benefit. With any luck, this would stall these bastards long enough for her to think of something else. Whatever that was.

"Okay." She faked a sob and let her head hang in mock shame. "Okay, I'll do it. Please don't put me in jail."

For the first time, Symonds' face changed. His lips turned up in a tiny smile. "That's a very wise decision, Mrs. Ojeda." He waved his left hand. A few moments later, the door clacked again and a sallow-skinned agent in a midnight-blue FBI windbreaker strode in, unzipping a black vinyl case the size of an old paperback book. It opened as he approached.

Bel's stomach collapsed at what she saw. "No. Please."

Symonds stood and gave her a broader smile. "We can't take any chances now, can we? Put your face on the table, Mrs. Ojeda. Please don't make this any more unpleasant."

47

Traditional snowbirds have disappeared from towns throughout the Southwest, replaced by growing bands of the destitute who spend their last dollars to reach the southern border in search of a miracle… A lucky few land low-paying jobs in Mexican border towns, often selling medicine or liquor to fellow Americans. "The pay's better down here," says Taylor Sharp, 52, formerly of Indianapolis, now a part-time salesclerk in a Mexicali carnicería. "They still have a minimum wage."
* -- "Seasonal Migration Becomes Year-Round Headache,"*
LATimes.com

SUNDAY, 16 MAY

As he drove down State 186 in the Cartel's Santana past Andrade's pair of trailer parks, Luis pictured refugee camps from the 'Stan. Banged-up RVs covered with sunshades; travel trailers up on blocks; laundry turning yellow in the coal smog from Yuma across the Colorado. The oily red sludge in the canal alongside the road made his eyes burn.

Luis fed another ten bucks into the Quechans' treasury for a parking space at the border lot's north end and a quarter-mile hike to the line of maybe four dozen people waiting to pass the little guardhouse at the border. Once he'd have been the baby of the crowd; now there were all ages, seniors down to a few bawling infants, decent clothes to rags, some clearly sick, others drooping in the lunchtime heat or from general weariness.

He paced through the parking lot until he could see the CBP booth just shy of the vertical metal bars of the fence marking the border. He lounged against a swaybacked pickup and watched the line inchworm past the bulletproof glass. He timed a few: fifteen or twenty seconds each. Usually at a crossing, Customs and Border

Protection would take a Level 1 scan off everyone's ID, checking whether it was valid and the embedded picture matched the one on the front. Any red flags got pulled aside for special attention. Once past this checkpoint, the only speed bump was the bored Mexican cop waving people through on the other side of the gate.

Luis timed over twenty crossers until he picked up a pattern. Most people got through with a Level 1. But three women—all between 20 and 40—were put through a Level 2 and maybe a face scan. CBP had gotten smart in the past week; now they were looking specifically for Nora's type.

He hiked back to the car to find all four doors open. Paul napped in the back seat with a kid under each arm, while Nora—in her blond wig and one of Paul's white undershirts tucked into khakis—paced behind the car like a tiger past feeding time. "Well?" she demanded.

"They're scanning young women. Paul and the kids should be fine."

Nora nodded, swallowed, then turned her eyes toward the crossing. The morning's drive from Bostonia had been tense and quiet. Even the kids picked up on the grown-ups' mood and just huddled against their mother.

Luis opened the trunk with the button next to the steering wheel. "It's time. It won't get easier if we wait, and I want to get to our crossing before dark. Paul? Wake up."

Paul scrubbed his face with his palms, then scooted the kids out of the car and rounded to the trunk. He wore his last facial appliance, along with a brown-and-black plaid work shirt open over a white undershirt and faded jeans they'd bought at a thrift store in El Centro. Luis had told him not to shave, so Paul's looks had gone from well-scrubbed professional to refugee. The black eye and bruised cheekbone from the safe-house fight finished the picture.

Once Paul and the kids had shouldered their backpacks, the whole family stood in an aimless knot at the trunk. Nora and Paul just stared at each other while the kids looked around with wrinkled noses. Luis backed off to give them a little privacy. Finally, Nora and Paul grabbed each other and held on like their world was about to end—which it was—then kissed hard and long.

She knelt between her children and hugged Peter first, then Hope, then both. Luis wanted to tell her *You'll scare them*, but let it go.

Finally, they were done. Luis adjusted Paul's backpack straps. "Okay, this should work fine. Remember, Beto will pick you up at *Farmacia* Colorado. It's maybe five minutes down the road past the gate. He'll show you a copy of your ID. There's a liquor store across the street where you can get drinks. They'll take dollars. Questions?"

Paul glanced at his wife, who stood with her arms folded like a coil of wire around her ribs. "How long before this Beto shows up?"

"He might be there already, or it could be up to an hour. It depends." On the road from Mexicali to here, on roadblocks, on fighting, on Zetas. None of which these people needed to hear about. "Call when he shows up. I'll let you know if he's delayed. Okay?"

Paul nodded. "I always wanted to see sunny Mexico."

Hope screwed up her face. "I don't wanna go without Mommy."

Before Luis could come up with a good lie, Nora knelt next to her daughter. "It's okay, Cupcake. I'll be coming in a little while. I just need to do something first." Hope pouted and hung her head, which meant—if she was anything like Christa had been—this issue wasn't settled. Nora gave her another hug, then guided her to Paul's outstretched hand.

"Wait for us to hit the end of the line," Luis told Nora. "Then go park on the shoulder north of the entry station. You can watch from there." He set off after Paul and the kids, not waiting for Nora's reply.

They shuffled along without speaking. Paul didn't seem to be in any hurry. This was when it all got real, Luis figured; everything had been reversible until now. He'd had a few travelers back out at the last minute, usually natives who hadn't known any home other than America. It was sad to watch. Both he and they knew they'd end up in a camp.

Could he do it? Leave the country forever? Despite what he'd said to Bel, Luis had asked himself that question for years and never could answer it in a way he believed. Screwed up as it was, this was his home. He'd given it a lot of sweat and blood.

"What's your name?" he asked Paul as they approached the end of the line.

"Patrick Ramirez." He rattled off the cover address and phone number. Showing off, or nerves? Paul's jaw locked tight and sweat rolled down his forehead. He'd picked up Hope after she'd started to whine, carrying her with his arms crossed under her butt, her arms around his neck. His grimace told Luis the weight wasn't helping his sore back any.

"I'll carry her if you want."

"No, I'm fine. Thanks." Paul hefted Hope. "What if they stop me?"

"They're not looking for you. Even if they are, you don't look like you."

"That's not what I asked. What do I do if they try to stop me?"

Luis couldn't read Paul's eyes behind the Gargoyles, so he tried to decode his tone. Paul had been quiet and serious since the safe-house fight. He'd kept a dead gunman's Beretta even though Nora had tried to take it from him. He'd been all for this plan. But now the points of his jaw were white, and his voice was tight and borderline harsh. Was that the pain? Fear?

"Go as fast as you can through the gate," Luis finally said. "Hide in the closest crowd. Any CBP or Border Patrol guards will come at you from this side. They won't chase you across the line and they won't risk shooting into Mexico." Luis clapped Paul's non-Hope shoulder. "Relax. Just be natural, you'll do fine."

They fell in behind a gaunt man and woman, both with sun-brown skin chapped from too much time outside, and a downcast boy about ten with ratty hair and rattier clothes. Probably inmates of a trailer park up the road. The line spasmed forward. The kids turned whiny in the midday heat. Paul put Hope down in order to drag the water bottles from his backpack.

"Nora says you were in the Army," Paul said. "Did you see any action?"

"Two tours in Afghanistan."

"Wow, that long ago." He fussed with Hope for a moment. "Ever kill anyone?"

So that's what this was about. "A few. It was a war, after all."

"How long did it take you to get over it?"

Luis thought carefully before he answered. "You don't get over it. You just file it away. Eventually you stop thinking about it." *While you're awake.* "You did what you had to."

Paul nodded, his lips disappearing into a line.

Luis drifted a few feet away from Paul, being there without crowding him, letting the man get used to flying solo. About thirty feet from the CBP post, Luis took Paul's hand. "Good luck. See you soon."

Paul managed a repeat of his sincere handshake. "Please take care of my wife, will you?"

"Believe me, I want you guys together just as bad as you do. Now, breathe. You'll be fine." Luis waved to the kids, then retreated up the road to Nora and the waiting car.

Customs and Border Patrol Officer Aransky waved through a family of walking skeletons and grabbed a swipe from his water bottle. The A/C just barely held its own, as usual, and the scene outside his bulletproof glass made him feel even hotter. Heat waves rolled off the road through the crossing and from the entry station's low roofs, fuzzing the world.

He pushed the lever that shoved the ID drawer open outside. "IDs in the tray, please."

A younger guy—messy black hair, stubble, undershirt—dropped his white ID in the drawer. Then he started fiddling with something below the window bottom. Aransky stood and craned over his counter to find two little kids, a boy, and a real cute little girl, standing next to the guy. Two more cards clinked into the aluminum tray.

Aransky hauled in the drawer and ran the checks on his computer. Patrick, Peter, and Hope Ramirez from someplace in Riverside County. Long way to go to get to a dump like this. He keyed the external mike in time to hear, "—wanna go with Mommy." The little girl.

"Mommy's coming soon," the guy said. He sweated like he had a shower going in his hair—okay, it was hot—and looked like he'd been in a fight. With Mommy?

"When, Daddy? I want Mommy!"

Aransky leaned back on his barstool. He saw this once or twice a week. Things get tough up north; Mom or Dad decides it's better south of the border, then packs up the kids and ducks out without the spouse. They looked a lot like this bunch. He leaned into his microphone. "Are you the children's father, Mr. Ramirez?"

The guy's eyes got big. "Uh, yes, yes I am."

"Where's their mother?"

"She's coming later. She had things to do."

Jesus, that's what they always said. These three carried backpacks; this wasn't just a day trip. Aransky gripped the counter and keyed the alert button with his thumb. "Do you have her permission to take the kids over the border?"

"Uh, yeah, of course. She's coming too, just later."

"Can I see it?"

"See what?"

"Her written permission. You're supposed to have it." Not that he enforced the rule unless things looked squirrelly. Like now.

Ramirez dragged his sleeve across his face. "You're kidding. I've never heard of that. I'm their father."

Aransky glimpsed Navarro trotting across 186 toward them. "Mr. Ramirez, could you stand aside so Officer Navarro can sort this out? Thank you." He passed the IDs back out in the drawer.

Ramirez' mouth dropped open when he noticed Navarro. The little girl was still going on about her mom. Poor thing. The boy peered up at his dad, then at Aransky, then back, looking like a confused puppy.

Ramirez reached for the girl's hand. That's when she bolted.

⬤

Nora perched on her knees on the front passenger's seat, pressing the eyepieces of her green-gray compact binoculars into her face so hard that her eye sockets ached. She could just barely see Paul and the children at the guard post through the Ford's back window. She'd been counting seconds since they moved into position. "It's taking too long."

"Yeah, it is," Luis said. "But the ID drawer's open, so they passed the scan. What's the holdup?"

"Is that Border Patrol coming up?" An officer in khaki utilities marched into her view, his hands gripping his equipment belt's buckle.

"CBP. They wear the same field gear."

Go! she wanted to shout to Paul. *Get away!* She'd been on the edge of nausea all morning and now only an extreme act of will kept her tiny breakfast in her stomach. This had to work. It couldn't not work. They had to get across. *Why aren't you* moving?

Hope dashed into the street.

"No, Cupcake! No!" Nora screamed. She lunged for the door handle, but Luis got to her first, yanking her hand back.

"The cop's got her," he reported. "Christ, Paul, get out, get out… he's across, he grabbed Peter, they're across, goddamnit, Paul…"

Nora broke Luis' grip, tried again for the door. "I've gotta get her! Let me go! I want my baby!" Both of Luis' arms clamped around her. She kicked at the dash and tried to throw a punch, screaming and swearing, and he snagged her right hand and forced it between her thighs and dragged her back against him, dodging her flailing head while she wailed "No no no no NO my baby my baby oh no my baby…"

…and then she doubled over in her seat, sobbing into her knees, thumping the dash with her fists. Luis stroked her hair, murmuring, "It's okay. We'll fix this. It's okay. Shhh."

They had Hope. They had her daughter. It would never be okay. This was her fault for not letting dead things stay dead, for dragging her down here, for agreeing to this idiot plan, for not being there, for *everything.*

"We'll get her back," Luis said. "I swear we'll get her back."

Nora pushed herself upright, clearing her eyes on the heels of her hands. Her whole body burned with helplessness turning to rage that choked her. "If we don't, I'll kill you."

48

*Although no official statistics are available, studies
accomplished in academia and by private marketing firms
suggest the average non-agricultural workweek in the USA
has increased to approximately 61 hours, a level found
nowhere else in the developed world and last seen in the
USA in 1890.*
-- "Box 9. Industrial Productivity: Comparing the Data,"
Global Employment Trends, *International Labour
Organization*

SUNDAY, 16 MAY

McGinley lumbered to his feet and stretched. The sounds of
half a dozen other people burning their day off doing the JTF thing
drifted over the cubicle tops. He'd already gone to see the old
mission with the birds and spent ten minutes or so watching surfers
get covered with crude oil. The sooner he wrapped up something
here, the sooner he could go home. His real home, where he knew
the bugs and humidity and could see something green for a damn
change. Get back to Job One: kicking Zeta ass and looking for
Carla Jean.

So he might as well work.

The national security letter for this al-Khaled chick made for
interesting reading. The Bureau said she was hooked into every
major terrorist threat from 10/19 on. Yemenis, Saudis, Paks,
Iranians, whatever; she was there. Which made no damn sense at
all. Much as he hated just about everything that came out of that
fucked-up corner of the world, he wasn't dumb enough to believe
those people all got along and sang whatever the rag version of
"Kumbayah" was.

Then he made the mistake of trying to square her sheet with
the Bureau's story. Not only was she a Feeb, but her papa was some

big businessman in the D.C. area. He was on the Virginia Republican Committee until 10/19. ROTC? Military police? She must be some kind of liberal rag, but that didn't square with the whole *jihadi* thing.

The Feebs *said* she got radical in Somalia, but she didn't get there until a few months before 10/19, and she was supposed to be part of that? They *said* she was mixed up with those Saudi boys in Dallas, but she was at Quantico then. Neat trick. The rest happened while she was at Bureau headquarters in D.C. Well, okay, he could almost go with that—except D.C. had turned into a fortress and everybody knew every phone inside the Beltway was monitored 24/7.

If Khaled went bad in Somalia, why didn't the Army notice? It was still the Army back then, not contractors, back when psychotics weren't so popular. But she was a genuine hero—Bronze Star, MSM, ACM. Would someone in al-Qaeda's pocket put herself out like that? So maybe she flipped later, when she got kicked out because the contractors were cleaning women out of the Army. That might piss her off. But no—she joins the Bureau. As a mole? Pass all the background investigations and polygraphs and that whole round of shit they put their people through? And nobody found out?

McGinley would love to talk to someone who knew the Khaled woman, really *knew* her, but that wasn't too likely and the Feebs would whack his pecker for getting in their chili. This investigation was an Office of Professional Responsibility production. Knowing the Bureau the way he did, he doubted anyone in D.C. would talk to him about it. OPR was Internal Affairs, or "the Inquisition" as the Feeb guys called it when they had enough liquor in them.

Then there was REDCAP. And REDCAP smelled like a pig farm.

Those four Yemeni fuckers from 10/19? REDCAP. Twelve, almost thirteen years ago, and they were still Top Secret? The Free Montana Militia vanished three months after 10/19; seven years of the usual intel, then zero. Why? REDCAP. Dugan, Conners, Seybold? REDCAP. The bomb forensics? REDCAP. Case notes? REDCAP. Witness statements? REDCAP.

The Bureau was either protecting a source or method, or a

result. All the tech they had back then, you could buy on the Internet now, and the methods were on the spy shows on the web. Locking down everything to protect one or two sources made no damn sense at all, not after this long. But if they were hiding a *result*...

Maybe Ojeda's new rag girlfriend wasn't full of shit after all.

That idea just chapped his ass.

McGinley's phone rang. He checked the screen: the SAC. "Yes, sir?"

"Mac, what are you doing in the Bureau's shorts?"

McGinley rubbed the spot above his ear where he knew the headache would start. "Sir?"

"I got a call from one of Mazarik's people. They're saying you've been trying to get into SCI data since yesterday. Are you?"

"No, sir, I'm not trying to get into SCI data. I'm trying to run down something I got from a snitch, and it all turns out to be SCI. Ain't the same thing."

Long silence on the other end. "Whichever way it is, back off. The Bureau wants to shut you down. I've got it covered now, but if you do it again, they'll come after you. Understand?"

That was awful strong for only hiding sources or methods. "Sir, how do I know if something I need is classified 'til I look for it?"

"Don't overthink this. Stay in your lane. Do you understand?"

McGinley really wanted to say "no," but he'd learned early on that throwing rocks at things bigger than him is a good way to get a stomping. "Yes, sir. I understand."

But that didn't mean he'd stop.

49

The DM3000 product line provides a complete, easy-to-use desktop DNA analysis solution for clinical or law enforcement applications… No small clinic or detective bureau can afford to be without one of these industry-leading systems.
-- DM3000 Field DNA Sequencer/Analyzer, Bio-Rad Laboratories

SUNDAY, 16 MAY

Back in the parking lot, Luis scanned the CBP compound from the Santana's driver's seat. His binoculars brought the signs close enough to read. The two-lane entry station and its service building sat at the south end. It had a tall, flat overhead structure on white posts flanked by a squat tan building not much larger than a double-wide.

Hope had vanished into that tan building across the street half an hour ago. She hadn't come out, and no CBP vehicles had headed north since then. Luis had counted nine CBP troopers so far: one at the southbound exit booth, two going over the southbound traffic, two (one with a dog) inspecting the northbound vehicles at the entry station, two at the pedestrian entry booths, a roving supervisor, and the guy who'd snagged Hope. Call it an even dozen, just to be sure.

"What's your plan?" Nora snapped during her hundredth circuit around the car.

"What's yours?"

"Go in there and get her out."

"And get yourself killed or arrested? Good plan."

"Start talking, then."

Her constant circling was getting on his nerves. Worse, it might draw attention. "Keep pacing like that and you'll melt."

Nora glared at him without stopping. "It's not your daughter they took."

"I wish I still had a daughter for them to take."

She ducked her head. "Sorry."

Luis couldn't really blame her for being anxious and angry; he would be too. But he needed her to think since he'd drawn a blank. He flexed his aching shoulder, screaming now after fighting with Nora.

"I thought these IDs of yours were supposed to work," Nora snarled.

"It wasn't the IDs. The guard gave them back. If they'd failed, CBP would keep them." Luis replayed the scene at the crossing for the hundredth time. "Paul was jumpy as a cat around a vacuum cleaner, though."

Nora whirled on Luis. "Don't you dare blame this on Paul!"

"Just saying. It wasn't the IDs."

After stalking a few more laps around the car, Nora stopped at the open driver's door, arms crossed, her big sunglasses reflecting two tiny pictures of Luis. "You know how the system works. What are they doing to her?"

He set down his binoculars. "First thing, they'll run her ID to figure out who Mommy is. That takes a Level 2, so they may already know she doesn't exist. They'll know for sure when they drill down into Mommy's records. So, assume her cover's blown. Next they'll try a flash DNA search—"

"They can't do that without a warrant or parental consent."

"Get real. That's like saying you guys can't search a house without a warrant. They'll try to get a family match. Those take forty-five minutes or an hour to finish depending on how far the search has to dig. I know you guys are in the system, so that's when all the flashing red lights'll go off. So, they may not know yet who she really is, but they know she isn't who her ID says she is. I'll bet she hasn't memorized the cover identities, has she?"

Nora snorted. "She's four. What do you think?" She stared across the street at the tan CBP building. "So we have fifteen minutes or so before they know she's my daughter."

"Something like that." Put that way, the situation looked even worse.

He hadn't brought it up, but he hadn't heard from either Paul or Beto. Half an hour wasn't long enough to start worrying, but Luis was surprised Paul hadn't called to find out what happened to Hope. He'd take one bad omen at a time.

"Open the trunk," Nora ordered.

"Why?"

"I need my dress."

"Why?"

"I'm going in there to get Hope."

"You're out of your fucking mind. They'll bottle you up in a minute."

Nora thrust an angry finger at him. "Then come up with a better plan. Right now she's just a lost little girl with a flakey ID. Once they get her real name, it's too late."

She stood straight, shoulders back, waiting. Luis didn't have a comeback. It wouldn't work; she'd get caught, and he'd have only a few minutes to get away. But he didn't have a better idea. If they waited, Hope would end up at the ICE detention center in El Centro or the transit camp at MCAS Yuma and either way, they'd never get her out.

He popped the trunk.

Sweat rolled down Nora's back and sides as she neared the CBP building's single glass door. The sweat made the sundress' yellow elastic top cling even more than usual. Against her better judgment, she'd pulled up the skirt a couple inches and hid the extra material behind a wide belt; now the hem hit mid-thigh. She wasn't ashamed of her body—she'd worked hard to keep fit—but hated flaunting it this way, having men leching on her boobs and legs.

At least they weren't looking at her face.

An electronic bell binged when she pushed through the door into the air-conditioned office. A wood-and-laminate counter split the space lengthwise. Linoleum and plastic chairs lay to her left, metal desks and computers to her right. A young CBP officer slumped on his stool behind the counter, fiddling with a bulky ruggedized slate.

"Mommy! Mommy!"

Nora's heart shot into her sinuses. She turned just in time to see Hope bound off a plastic chair next to the desk closest to the entry and come running toward the counter. "Cupcake!" Nora trotted to the counter as fast as she could in these stupid wedge-soled canvas shoes. In any sensible outfit, she'd just vault the thing. "It's okay. I'm here now."

A graying, balding CBP cop—captain's bars on the epaulets of his dark-blue uniform—slowly climbed out of his desk chair and ambled to the counter. "Are you this little girl's mother?"

"Yes, I am." She grabbed Hope's outstretched hand and shook it. "I hear she was a bad girl and ran away from Daddy. Isn't that right, Cupcake?"

"I'm sorry, Mommy. I was scared."

The captain touched his splayed fingertips to the countertop and spent several moments examining Nora. She'd done a terrible job putting on her makeup—she'd done it in about thirty seconds in the car's rear-view mirror—and hoped she didn't look too sketchy. She gave the cop her very best smile. "She wasn't too much of a problem, was she, officer?"

He gave her an old-cop smile, the same kind the veteran agents at the Bureau used: a sliver of teeth, a couple crinkles at the corners of his mouth, no change in his gray-blue eyes. "She was fine, ma'am. She doesn't have any ID, though."

"Oh, dear." Nora tried to mold her face into something that looked like frustration. She'd never been an actress and she'd spent a lot of her adult life masking her emotions from the men around her, so she had no idea what actually came out of her effort. "My husband must have it."

"I see." He spent way too much time looking at her face, his eyebrows creeping closer together every second. "I'm sorry, ma'am, I have to ask. Have you been here recently? You look very familiar to me."

"Oh, no, it's been over a year." She tried for an apologetic smile but wasn't sure which muscles were supposed to go where. "I just have one of those faces, you know?"

The cop nodded. "May I see your ID please, ma'am?"

Nora let go of Hope even though every nerve in her body told her to hold on. She fumbled her fake ID from her wallet, steadied her hand, passed the card to the cop. "I think it still works." Her voice had climbed an octave since she'd walked in.

The cop ambled back to his desk, then fed her ID into the card reader attached to his computer. Nora squeezed Hope's hand again. Just those few minutes apart had filled Nora with a terror she hadn't ever felt, not in combat, not with the Bureau. Her hands still trembled, and her heart pounded. Or was that from waiting for these cops to notice she was about to fly apart?

"I was so worried," she told the younger cop on the stool to her left. He nodded.

"Nicole Ramirez?" the captain called out.

"That's me."

"Could you confirm your address, please?"

She recited the fake address, trying not to let her voice squeak with strain.

"Thank you, ma'am. Any idea why the girl would say your name is Nora and you live in Virginia?"

She needed to gulp down the boulder in her throat, but the younger cop still watched her (although maybe he was watching her boobs; she couldn't tell). She coughed out a little laugh. "Oh, dear, did she?" The captain lifted a graying eyebrow at her. "We just recently moved. She hasn't gotten used to our new—"

"Mommy, that's—"

"Hush, Cupcake. I'm talking to the nice policeman." Her brain scurried to pull her train of thought back onto its tracks. "Sorry. Anyway, our new neighborhood looks a little like where we came from." *Why Nora? Why Nora?* "And… um, do you have children?"

"Yes, ma'am." He hadn't taken her ID from the card reader yet. That meant a Level 2 scan. What had Luis said? A 50-50 chance it would work. She tried to decide if she could pull Hope over the counter while she held a gun on these two cops. How far could she get before they shot her?

"Well, when they were little, did you ever tell them stories before they went to bed"—she could smell the smoke from her brain straining to lie so much so fast for so long—"maybe you made them up, and you and your family were in them, but you had adventures? My husband does that, and my character is named Nora, and—"

"Mommy! That's—"

"Shhh, I'm talking, don't interrupt—"

"But Mommy—"

"Hush! Don't make me tell you again." Nora flashed a genuinely frazzled smile at the older cop. "Well, you know how kids are."

The captain focused on his screen, scrolled the display with his forefinger. He scowled. "She also said you're a detective."

Nora glanced at her watch. They'd had Hope for fifty minutes. When had they done the DNA scan? How much time was left? "That's my character in the story." She was trying and failing to sound patient. "I—my character—finds treasure and things. Hope loves it."

The captain aimed a long, penetrating look at her. His eyes were like pale marble, hard and unrevealing. "Your husband ran from one of my officers. Do you know why he'd do that?"

She'd had time to think of an answer to this one. "He's very nervous around police. We've had some problems with the contract cops in our area. Some bad arrests, a couple of beatings. They don't like Latinos."

"I see." The captain's fingers drummed his desktop for a few moments. "Ma'am, would you mind letting me take a DNA sample I can compare to the girl?"

More time, plus they'd have positive proof she'd been there. She was already on camera. "Is that really necessary?"

"We need to make sure you're really her mother before we release her to you. You understand, of course."

"Of course. You'll need hers too, I guess."

He took a clear vial from his top desk drawer. A long, sterile swab ran its length. "We already have hers. We're running it through the system to find a parental match. If you want, we can wait for that to come back, but it may be another ten or fifteen minutes. We can do a match here in about five."

Ten or fifteen minutes left… maybe. She caught a real breath for the first time since she climbed out of the car. "Oh. Well, in that case, sure."

He took the sample from the inside of her cheek and fed the swab into a low, boxy machine in an off-white case with a video screen on top. A DNA analyzer; she'd seen them in police offices all around the country. The cop poked at the screen and stabbed some buttons. Yellow lights flashed on the control panel and the machine peeped.

Five minutes. She had to stand there for five minutes and smile and pray that Hope didn't say the wrong thing and that their scan of Hope's DNA didn't come back early. And not pass out from not being able to breathe.

"Excuse me, officer?" she said to the younger cop on the stool. "Can my daughter sit up here on the counter? It's hard to keep bending over like this."

The younger cop mulled this over for a moment, looking first at Nora, then Hope. Then he swiveled his stool and said, "Cap'n?" The captain nodded from his desk. The younger guy slid off his stool, paced to Hope, clasped his hands under her arms and said, "Here you go. One, two, up!" Hope's rear thumped onto the countertop.

"Say 'thank you' to the nice man," Nora told her.

"Thank you."

"What brings you out here to Andrade?" the captain asked.

Once again, she was prepared. "My husband needs some dental work done. We wanted to stay away from Tijuana, and one of our neighbors recommended a dentist in Los Algodones, so"—she shrugged, hoping she wasn't laying it on too thick—"here we are." Nora gathered up Hope in her arms, snuggled her so if her daughter said anything, no one would hear it.

Four minutes.

Cars stuttered through the two lines outside the window, getting their trunks checked and their tires sniffed by a big black-and-brown German Shepherd-looking thing. Nora suppressed a shiver. Dogs had always scared her. She didn't know if it was tribal—"dog" is an insult to most Arabs—or just hearing her little school friends talk about getting bit, but she'd never wanted anything to do with a dog.

"You shouldn't have run away from Daddy," Nora murmured into Hope's ear.

"Sorry." Hope pushed out her lower lip. "Don't leave me again, Mommy. It's scary."

"I won't. You're staying with me."

Three minutes.

Out in the southbound traffic lane, the two CBP officers worked over an old sedan with skin cancer, checking the trunk and under the hood, running the occupants' IDs. Could Luis just drive her over the border here? She could meet up with Paul and Peter and they could all go together. Her ID had passed the Level 2 scan, after all. Was it 50-50 every time, or if it works once does it always work?

Two minutes.

An officer working the northbound lanes banged through the door. His M4 carbine, slung muzzle-down across his chest, clanked off the push bar. The big black-and-brown German Shepherd-looking thing panted in after him. "Captain? The repeater just fritzed out again."

"Aw, shit. Hold on." The captain lurched out of his chair and disappeared through a door into the back. He'd miss the test result. How long before he came back?

The dog settled on its enormous rear just behind Nora. She tried to ignore the *huha huha huha* of its panting and the bursts of warm air against her bare calves.

The dog's handler scooped the ball cap off his close-shaven head, drew a sleeve across his forehead. "Hot out there, huh?" he asked Nora.

"Yes, hot. Nice in here." The lead the handler clutched in his left hand was thick as a man's belt, but it looked like a shoestring to Nora. *Get that creature away from me...*

"Try it now," the captain's voice boomed from the back room.

Dog Cop checked his field reader, tapped it a few times. "No, sir. Not yet."

A *yawp* noise made Nora glance down and behind her. The dog's huge mouth gaped open in a yawn. A mammoth tongue, T-Rex teeth. That thing could swallow Hope whole. It finished its yawn, lapped at its lips (*do dogs have lips?*). Its round, black eyes gazed up at her with an expression that said, *Are you dinner?*

She squeezed Hope a little tighter.

"Mommy, you're hurting me."

"Sorry, I'm sorry."

One minute.

Nora stuck her right hand into her purse, wrapped it around her pistol's grip. She had no problem shooting a dog, none. She just hoped she could put it down before the thing ripped out her throat.

"How about now?" the captain yelled.

"Hold on." Dog Cop fiddled with his field reader, thumbing it off and on, waiting for it to reboot. "Nope."

Just fix the damn thing!

The analyzer peeped. The flashing green light on the control panel burned a hole in Nora's vision. A cold dog nose snuffled at her leg. "Officer?" she said to the cop on the stool. "I think my test is done? Could you check, please?"

Once again, he climbed off his stool, then paced to the analyzer. He prodded the screen with a thick finger, leaned closer to read the red and blue bar charts and callouts. "Hey, Cap'n, she passed the test. Can she go?"

Nora felt her knees turn to rubber bands. *Passed.* She picked Hope off the counter, sidestepped the dog (his eyes said, *Dinner and a snack?*), called out, "Thank you, Captain!"

"What?"

"She passed. Can she go?" The cop squinted at the captain's computer. "You got an alert, too."

"Uh, yeah, let her go. What's the alert?"

Dog Cop held the door open for Nora as she hurried out. She looked right and found the Santana parked at the compound's north end, flashers on. She hitched up Hope, said, "Put your arms around my neck, Cupcake," and quick-stepped toward the car as fast as she could without turning an ankle on the damn shoes.

"Miss?" The voice behind her sounded like Dog Cop. "Miss, could you come back?"

The alert. They'd identified her. She wound up into a trot, wished she had some sensible shoes.

"Mommy, slow down! I can't hang on!"

"I can't slow down," she gasped. Hope weighed a ton and Nora was already off-balance.

"Halt! Put down the child and show me your hands! Now!"

She kicked off her shoes, yanked up her skirt and started to run. The asphalt seared the soles of her feet. *Don't look back don't stop don't slow down go go go…*

A shot. She ducked around an outbuilding. Her shoulders ached as if they were about to come apart; her arms burned with Hope's weight; her feet were on fire. Hope screamed and cried and clung to Nora's neck so hard, Nora started to see stars. An alarm moaned to life behind her, the first note of what sounded like an air-raid siren.

Ten yards to the car. Luis stood in the open driver's door, gun in one hand, waving her forward. She focused on the open back door, dark like a cave, shelter, safety. *Go.*

Another shot, yelling, running feet. The dog booming. *Is it chasing me?*

In the car.

Luis hit the gas before she could close the door. It slammed shut when the car surged forward, tires screaming and smoking. Hope's crying filled the cabin. Nora tried to soothe her with one hand, strapped herself in with the other. Child in one hand, weapon in the other.

"You okay?" Luis said over his shoulder.

"Fine." Nora lowered her window, stuck her head out, and lost the last of her breakfast.

50

One of the many ironies of America's current economic situation is that a great number of its Red Indian tribes are now materially better off than their non-indigenous neighbours... With economic power has come a new willingness to aggressively exercise their sovereignty, as they eject non-aboriginal service providers and become in fact the mini-states established by treaty in the 19th and 20th centuries.

-- "United States: Native Uprising," Economist.com

SUNDAY, 16 MAY

Luis could see flashing light bars in the rear-view as he roared past the southernmost trailer park. It was a couple miles to the checkpoint at the main entrance to the reservation and the Santana was nudging eighty. They might make it to the tollbooth.

He caught Nora's eyes in the mirror. She crushed a crying Hope against her body with both arms. Luis didn't know whether he ought to be impressed by her guts for walking into that trap, or be pissed that she'd blown cover and signaled to the entire border where they were. He'd figure it out when he got a moment. "Change," he barked.

"Into what?"

"Something else that makes you look female. Switch wigs, lose the nose and chin."

"I'll look like myself."

"We'll deal. Just don't be the woman on the cameras back there."

They charged through more desert, then passed the second trailer park. He saw Nora lock Hope into a seat belt, then haul her backpack onto the seat and start to pull out clothes. "What happened?"

"They got an alert on me. On Hope, I guess, just as I was leaving."

"You got the IDs back?"

"Mine's still in the reader back there. Paul has Hope's."

"Oh, great. Hope's backpack?"

"In the office."

"And you were on camera for a good fifteen minutes."

"Forget the cameras—they have my DNA. I had to prove I'm Hope's mother."

"*Ay, chingado.*" Luis shook his head. The only way it could've worked out worse was if she'd killed a cop. "You didn't shoot anybody, right?"

"No." She pointed to the rear-view. "Could you turn that away?"

Luis wrenched up the mirror so it filled with headliner. "I'm too busy to perv on you right now," he growled.

They flew across a canal and into the gentle rise leading to I-8. Sand berms blurred by to their right, and the tan-stucco-and-tile casino grew fast at their ten o'clock. The flashing lights disappeared behind a corner.

Luis spied the wide driveway to the left. He stomped the brakes and wrenched the wheel. The car drifted with the scream of rubber over a small rise—Nora and Hope both squawked as the car went airborne—and into the ocean of asphalt surrounding the casino. Just as Luis stuffed the car into an empty spot in a full section of parking, the two CBP vehicles charged past the driveway on their way to the bridge over I-8.

Nothing but the ticking of hot metal broke the silence for a moment. Then Nora said, "A little warning?"

Luis started to look back but glimpsed her clutching something bright pink to her chest and stopped. "Just get dressed."

"Are we going inside?"

"No. We can't stay long. They'll figure out we're not on the highway and come looking for us." Luis grabbed his binoculars from the glove box and scoped the tops of the nearest three light poles. No visible cameras; a lucky break. He pushed open the door. "Back in a second."

The heat seared his nostrils. He swept the lot with his

binoculars until he found the white casino security mini-SUV cruising two aisles away. Beyond the lot's far north edge, perhaps a hundred yards off, he watched a black-and-white California Highway Patrol car roll up the offramp, its light bar blinking red and blue. The roadblock was building up.

Luis dropped back into the driver's seat and jacked his burner into the car's data console. The Cartel's license-plate app appeared on the phone's screen. It had been years since he'd last switched states on the e-plates, and it'd been a pain in the ass. With one eye on Security and the other on the phone, he managed to find the right menu, selected "Arizona," and searched for a pewter Santana within a year or two of this one. The "Searching…" notice pulsed endlessly.

He found casino security again—in the next row over, moving faster than he liked. "Come on," he grumbled at his phone. "You slow son-of-a-bitch."

"What are you doing?" Nora asked.

"Changing the plates."

An Arizona number appeared on the screen. He confirmed it, then lurched outside and hurried to the car's nose. Last time he did this, the app hadn't replaced the front California tag. It hadn't this time, either. *Come on…*

He sensed movement behind him. A white SUV with a flashing blue-and-white light bar eased down the driveway.

CBP was on the scene.

Luis kicked a rock into the aisle. Why couldn't those *tontos* come a couple minutes from now? Why did Hope have to run? Once he got that out of his system, his analytical mind shoved its way forward and started throwing off ideas for getting past the roadblock. He didn't like any of them, but he'd have to settle for the least-bad solution.

Security trundled down the next aisle over. Luis had a couple minutes to act, no more. He rapped on the left rear window.

It whirred down, revealing Nora's anxious face. Her hands gripped the top of the door. She'd changed into a lipstick-pink tank top, jeans, and the black version of her blond wig. "What's happening?"

"CBP's here. Get out. You and Hope are going in the trunk."

"We'll fry!"

"It won't be that long. They're looking for a guy, a gal and a kid. I wasn't on camera. You and Hope need to disappear. Get out."

Nora closed her eyes, sighed, then nodded. She leaned to her right—"Come on, Cupcake, we're going to play hide-and-seek"—then turned back to him. "Are we clear?"

Security's flashing yellow light rounded the corner at the end of the next aisle, heading for this one. CBP's blue-and-white lights blinked their way down the next aisle on the other side. "We're clear. Move."

He helped Nora into the trunk while keeping an eye on the lights. Hope squirmed and kicked when he picked her up, wrenching his crippled shoulder. "No! I don't wanna go in there!"

Nora reached up to grab one of Hope's flailing legs. "Raja! Behave!"

Hope froze, her eyes growing huge. Luis handed the girl to Nora, dropped Nora's backpack next to his, rearranged the flats of bottled water and their weapons and tactical gear to make more room, then eased shut the trunk.

Security swung into the end of his aisle.

Go slow, Luis told himself. *Fast means guilty*. But slow meant Nora and Hope would roast in the trunk. In this heat, dogs and kids left in a car could die in a few minutes.

He strolled to the car's nose, ready to break the LCD screen if he had to. The white-and-blue California license plate was gone, replaced by the red-gold-blue Arizona sunset design. He let out his held breath, wiped his forehead on his sleeve.

Once he started the car, he did a quick sweep for anything that said "woman" or "little girl." The blond wig peeked out from under the passenger's seat. Luis cursed, shoved it farther under cover. He backed into the aisle at walking speed. In the rear-view, he caught a quick red flash—Security's laser scanner, swiping his plate. Luis hesitated a moment, then pulled away.

No siren, no chase.

Breathing again, Luis steered out onto State 186. Up ahead at the mouth of the overpass, he could already see the flashing lights of the other CBP vehicle and the CHP cruiser. Waiting.

A muffled little-girl shriek leaked out through the back seat. Luis yelled, "Quiet back there!" He unbuttoned his shirt as he approached the roadblock, then slipped on his old CBP ball cap. His palms poured sweat like faucets. *Chill. Be the rock.*

The CBP trooper waved him down. When the trooper edged his way to the Santana's driver's door, Luis lowered his window and held out his fake ID. "Hey, mon, what's happening?" He threw a little *cholo* rumble into his voice.

The trooper ignored the ID, peering into the car. He gestured to the window behind Luis. "Open that." Luis did as he was told. The CBP guy scoped the back for a lot longer than an empty seat needed. Did he see the wig? Did something else roll out on the floor?

Then the CBP guy slid to the car's rear, glanced down. Luis' shirt felt like he'd been swimming in it. One sound, one thump out of Nora or Hope…

The trooper paced back to Luis' window. "Where did you come from just now?"

"The casino, mon. Won some bucks."

"Where are you going?"

"Winterhaven, mon." Luis gave the man his best hazy smile. "Temptations, you know?" The local strip club.

"I know it." The CBP guy stared at Luis' sunglasses and cap for a few moments, then shook his head. "All right, move on." He waved at the CHP unit, which backed up enough to leave a car-sized gap to drive through.

Yes! Luis flicked a salute to the trooper. "Sure thing, mon."

He drove the mile to the reservation's toll crossing at the maddeningly slow speed limit, paying more attention to the mirror than the windshield. Nobody followed. The horizon danced in the heat blazing off the desert. The data screen on the dash said the temperature was 109. "How you guys doing?" he yelled.

"Just get us out of here." Nora's voice was thin with an edge of desperation.

"Hang on. Almost there."

A teenaged Quechan in a Lakers jersey took the ten-dollar bill from Luis' outstretched hand without bothering to look at his face. The kid waved him across the two-lane bridge over the American

Canal, the only swatch of blue or green in sight.

Luis rolled through a few minutes of rocky desert and creosote before he pulled onto the dirt shoulder. Only the rattle of light breeze in the brush and the rumor of I-8 to the south broke the silence. He threw open the trunk lid, hoping not to find fried people.

Nora glared up at him. She'd pulled off her wig and was soaked from the waist up, surrounded by a half-dozen empty water bottles. Poor Hope looked like a drowned kitten.

"That wasn't fun." Hope frowned at Luis.

"No, it wasn't." He helped both the women out of the trunk.

"Let's not do that again, okay?" Nora peeled the tank top away from her body and flapped the bottom to get some airflow. "Are we safe here?"

Luis opened Nora's backpack and pulled out the wadded-up sundress. "Sort of. We're on tribal land. They hate ICE and CBP, so any cooperation is gonna come slow and hard. We're both the right color to be here, not like down the road in Arizona. We're good for a little while. Grab the wig from inside?"

Nora fetched the wig, holding it like a dead animal. "Now what?"

"Now we do what I didn't want—we try to go overland with her." He nodded toward Hope, who walked in circles a few feet away with her arms flapping like wings. "That's all we can do now. We'll never get close to another crossing." Nora turned her eyes away from him. "I know a place. There's a flat part and a mountain part. Depending on how lucky we are, we may be able to cross over the flat part."

"Okay."

"Two problems. We have to go into Arizona to get there." Nora grimaced. "Second, it'll take us into Sonora."

"So?"

"Godawful desert, for one thing. But worse, it's Zetaland."

Nora shook her head wearily. "There's noplace else we can go?"

"Just you and me? Sure. With her? This is the closest place where we have a prayer of getting across even semi-easily without having to climb a wall or do any mountaineering. It doesn't get any better farther east and the California border's been locked up for years."

"Mommy?" Hope peeped. "What's Zetaland? Are there rides?"

Nora gave the girl a faded smile. "No, Cupcake, it's not like that. It's not a nice place."

"Oh." Hope squirmed. "I hafta go potty."

"Okay." Nora sighed and aimed a tired look at Luis. "Any bathrooms near here?" Luis pointed to a mound of sagebrush a few yards away. "Right. Do you have any tissues?"

"Napkins, in the glove box."

Once mother and daughter disappeared behind the weeds, Luis shoveled the dress and wig into an orange trash bag in a pile at the shoulder's edge. Then he slid his burner out of his shirt pocket, inserted the battery and checked for messages. None. Four calls to Beto, four messages, and nothing back but silence. Paul hadn't answered Luis' call, either. Going on ninety minutes since Paul and Peter busted across the border and no word from anyone. What happened? The FBI and DEA launched cross-border raids without warning the Mexican police. Did the Feds get them?

Worse yet: did the Zetas get them? If so, how did they know where to find them?

One disaster at a time, Luis told himself. He didn't want to think about the implications.

If the Zetas could find Paul, they could find Nora, too.

51

...However, international attention has yet to turn to the fates of over 5,000 Catholics, Episcopalians, and American Friends (Quakers) held in federal prison camps as a result of their work in the Sanctuary movement... Pope Matthew continues to engage the U.S. Government to gain the release of these prisoners of conscience despite the rupture of diplomatic relations between the U.S. and the Vatican, which the President has referred to in fundraising events as the "whore of Babylon."

-- "Seeking Shelter for Sanctuary,"
CommonwealMagazine.org

SUNDAY, 16 MAY

The supermarket-sized thrift store hunkered in an older part of Yuma—not that there were many newer parts—surrounded by faded, half-empty single-story commercial buildings. Luis surveyed the cars in the parking lot: old, sad, coated with desert sand. None of them were cops.

They'd jounced over farm roads and a sagging bridge to get into Yuma without having to deal with the Arizona Highway Patrol roadblocks. Nora, now revived after two Quarter Pounders, a large fry, and an iced tea half as big as she was, had pointed out that Hope would need something better than a tee shirt and shorts to wear on the crossing. As much as Luis didn't want any contact with the locals, he had to agree. He'd followed Nora's directions via MapQuest, scrupulously following the speed limits and traffic lights. The local cops wouldn't be able to see them through the Santana's tinted glass to pull them over for driving while brown, but a bullshit speeding stop could turn into a disaster.

The lettering on the thrift store's front windows spelled out for Luis the kind of trouble they'd find inside. "I think we need to move on.”

“Why?”

“See that? ‘100% American.’”

Nora’s mouth twisted. “I don’t know about you, but I’m 100% American.”

“That’s not what they mean.”

“I know what they mean.” Nora’s hands balled into fists. “Idiots like these are chasing me out of my own country. I’ll be damned if I let them keep me from buying a coat for my daughter.”

Luis sighed. Normally he’d agree, but not here and not now. “You don’t have an ID, remember? Your picture is on TV. Everybody in there is armed and half of them are probably zipheads or kronkers. You really want to pick this fight?”

The expression on her face said *hell, yes*. But after a few moments, she sighed. “Where do we go, then?”

“Look up ‘sanctuary’ and ‘Yuma’.”

They pulled up across the street from a small Catholic church in a moldering residential area out back of downtown. The church’s thick Pueblo-style stucco walls had shed chunks of tan paint and lost others to racist graffiti; steel mesh shrouded the stained-glass windows on the front and sides. A many-times-painted wall stretched along the sidewalk to another stucco building, perhaps a community hall. A wooden sign near the church’s main doors read “San Antonio de Padua.”

“What’s here?” Nora asked.

“Sanctuary for anyone who isn’t popular. That’s us right now. Food, shelter, medical care sometimes, whatever. They usually have a handout box of clothes. It’s almost summer, so warm clothes probably aren’t going fast.”

Inside they found white plaster walls, worn dark woodwork, and afternoon light streaming in the stained-glass windows. The mesh cast gridlike shadows on the designs and cut the sun into streamers that highlighted every grain of dust in the air. Judging from the time and the dozen shabby people drifting out, vespers had ended.

Luis left Nora and Hope at the back of the central aisle, found the font, touched his fingers to the holy water and crossed himself. Decades of Sunday Mass had turned into muscle memory. What was being here like for Nora? He'd been with her and her family at all hours of the day and night and had seen them pray only once, which was odd for Muslims. He'd often had to plan traveler movements around their prayer schedules. Maybe they waited until he was gone, or maybe they weren't too observant.

An old woman pushed through the squeaking door of an antique confessional in the left side aisle. He crossed to it as quietly as he could and caught an alarmingly young, blond priest as he stepped out of his half of the booth.

The priest peered up at Luis, his head tilted to one side. "*Bienvenidos a nuestra iglesia.*" His accent was one Luis had never heard laid on top of Spanish before. The gentle light didn't mask the moonscape of acne scars over his high cheekbones or the scar splitting his upper lip.

"Father, do you provide sanctuary here?" Luis asked in English.

"Yes, yes." The priest smiled. "Sanctuary, yes. I am Father Jedrik." Jedrik had some kind of Slavic accent, not heavy but obvious. He shook Luis' hand in both of his. "The woman and child, they are with you, yes?"

"Yeah. They need a restroom, and we need warm clothes for the girl. We have money."

"Of course." The priest steered Luis down the aisle. "Money is not needed for sanctuary. But the church…" He smiled and shrugged.

After Jedrik led Nora and Hope away, Luis slumped in a back pew, part praying for grace that night, part wondering what happened to Paul and Beto, and part figuring what he'd do with his half of the Khaled family once they made it to *el otro lado*. It was also time to start calling Bel to see if she'd made it to Tijuana yet.

He was betting that the buses still ran on Federal Highway 2— the two-lane road that paralleled the border—mostly because the buses always ran, through war and famine and floods and plague. Lacking Beto's help, they'd have to take a bus to Mexicali at least. If the road was still open. If the Zetas weren't looking for them. If they made it across the desert at all.

Heavenly Father: Hope's only a little girl. Please don't make it too hard on her.

Jedrik slid onto the pew next to Luis. He sat straight, his hands folded in his lap. His black shirt was tucked into a pair of boot-cut blue jeans. "Your friends are changing clothes and washing."

"That sounds like a great idea. I'd like to do that when they're done."

"Of course. You go across the border, yes? It is why you want warm clothes, I think."

"Yes."

"Which way, I may ask?"

"El Camino del Diablo." A series of desert tracks used by the Indians and the Spanish after them to cross some of the nastiest desert around.

Jedrik pursed his lips. "This is hard for the little one, but not as hard as other places. You go on west side of mountains, yes?"

"We haven't decided yet." Luis waited to be struck by lightning for lying to a priest. When no fireworks appeared, he asked, "Can you tell me anything?"

The priest rocked slightly on the pew, nodding each time he swung forward. "There are airplanes over the fence, of course."

"Manned?"

"No, the other. Drones. With guns, very bad. But." He drew a line in the air with his forefinger. "Where El Camino crosses the state highway, yes? Police patrol to catch people."

"I doubt they catch many incoming."

Jedrik shook his head. "They do not look for that now, I think. The police, they find people, not white people, driving at night to go across the state, yes? Take their things. They put these not-white people in the jail until they pay big fines." Jedrik bit his lower lip, looked down at his hands. "Then by canal, um, *jak mówisz…* Border Keepers, yes? Be careful, bad people."

Those assholes. "They're still out there?"

"Yes. I hear rumors. Bodies buried in the desert, under rocks, yes? Bad things happen to women, evil things. Please be careful."

Luis sighed. The bigger threat came before they even hit the border. He filed this intel away, hoping not to have to use it. "Thank you, Father."

"God bless you, my son." The priest rose, placed a hand on Luis' shoulder. "I will pray for you and your friends. They are Muslim, yes?" Luis nodded. "The Holy Father says we can pray even for them. God will hear and decide." He smiled. "Hope is a very good name for a little girl, I think."

"Yeah, it is. Father… will you hear my confession?" It had been two years since he'd gone to confession. If there was ever a time to do it, this was it.

"Yes, yes, of course. You have a hard journey ahead. You must prepare."

52

SUNDAY, 16 MAY

McGinley slumped in the recliner, mostly ignoring the baseball game playing on the little wall-mounted databoard. Denver against... San Jose? Where the fuck was San Jose? And who cares? Of course, there wasn't a Rangers game tonight. Enough damn soccer on, though.

He shut off the game and moseyed out to his apartment's balcony to lean on the rail. From the fifth floor, he could see over the marina out to the ocean. A couple fires burned in the concrete circles on the beach. If he listened real close, he could hear the surf.

Carla Jean loved the water. No matter how deep he was in the doghouse, all McGinley had to do was take her to the Gulf for a weekend and all was forgiven. He could see her splashing in the water, all tan in one of her little bikinis. Grinning like a kid with a Christmas pony, her hair flying in the wind. He'd give a body part to see that smile again...

His phone rang. He sighed, checked the screen, then stood bolt upright. "Yes, sir?"

"Agent McGinley? This is Arthur O'Hanlon."

ICE Deputy Director O'Hanlon. Jesus, it got kicked all the way up *there*? "Yes, sir, I'm Jack McGinley. Are you calling about my report?"

"Yes, I am. I have Mel Devereaux on the line"—HSI Executive Assistant Director Devereaux, McGinley's boss' boss' boss, *well, shit if this ain't special*—"and I wanted to get back to you as quickly as possible." No joke: it was past ten D.C. time. "How certain are you that your confidential informant is in contact with Nura al-Khaled?"

"Well, sir, he told me, and he gets nothing out of lying except me on his butt some more. Also, like I said in the report, the Feebs—sorry, the FBI—are pretty sure he's got her, too."

"Can you bring him in, Jack?" Devereaux said.

"I might, sir, if'n I can get the FBI to back off his family some. Get some goodwill, give him a reason to play ball. He's real attached to his family, sir."

"I'm sure he is." O'Hanlon again. "Agent McGinley, I'm authorizing you to pursue this in any way you need to. I'll deal with the Bureau. You'll report directly to Mel. I'll backbrief your chain in the morning. If you need anything, ask Mel. I expect you understand how important it is to the agency's future for you to bring this woman in."

"Yes, sir, that I do." Plus the bloody nose it'll give the Feebs.

"Very good. Go get her, son."

"Jack?" Devereaux said. "I'll get a tac team ready to go for when you nail her."

After years of swimming upstream, McGinley didn't know whether he could stand the sudden downpour of support and "Jack" this and "go get her" that. But hell, he'd take it and run. Maybe for once they even meant it. "Thank you, sirs. I'll get on it first thing. I'll take her down."

53

Approximately 55% of Arizona's population left the state during the 2020s in response to the collapse of the state's finances following that decade's wholesale cuts in Federal spending, as well as the catastrophic loss of surface water due to prolonged droughts throughout the West... Many of the remaining Arizonans interviewed for this story approve of the result...

-- "Arizona's Cities Are the New Empty Places,"
LATimes.com

SUNDAY, 16 MAY

Nora rocked side-to-side in the second-row seats as the aged Expedition squeaked and rattled its way eastbound on Old U.S. 80. The SUV's shocks and struts didn't soak up the assault from the huge potholes and remaining chunks of asphalt. This couldn't be a good sign. If the paved roads were this bad, what were the dirt ones like?

She twisted to look through the back window. The mountains showed black against the lingering red-and-yellow photochemical sunset painted across the western sky. Bright patches of sun burned on the mountains to the south. They'd be going through those soon.

This desert was so unlike the green fields and forests of home. Miles and miles of undeveloped land, scrub brush, sand, and the occasional spindly tree or saguaro cactus. Only occasional power lines proved human civilization had arrived. It looked more like Somalia than America.

She and Luis had stolen the Ford 4x4 from a scabby used-car lot in Gadsden, a paved patch in the desert hard against the Colorado River southwest of Yuma. They left the Cartel's Santana in a grocery-store parking lot a block north of the San Luis crossing. She and Hope stayed in the car while Luis went inside to buy more water and energy bars. "Isn't that overkill for grocery shopping?" she'd asked, pointing to the submachine gun slung across his back.

"Here? No. And I won't get hassled."

While waiting, she'd had too much time to think about what hadn't happened yet. Paul hadn't called, and neither had Luis' man. Luis finally admitted he'd been trying to reach them without success. Where was her husband? Where was Peter? Had something happened to them? Those worries had worn grooves inside her brain ever since. No wonder she'd been semi-sick to her stomach for an hour now.

Hope poked Nora's body armor. "Why are you wearing that, Mommy?"

The same reason she had her UMP on the floor at her feet. She looped her arm around Hope's shoulder and pulled her close. "So we'll be safe."

"Can I have one too?"

"They don't make these for little girls." Actually, they did now—she'd seen them on the Internet. That it made sense didn't lessen the essential wrongness. Kids got caught in gun battles, too. Mass shootings had become so common—she saw the raw figures at work—that the Bureau had to keep bumping up the definition of "mass shooting" (over twelve fatalities now) so the statistics wouldn't be too embarrassing.

"How come?"

"Because their mommies are supposed to protect them, like I'll protect you." Nora scrunched her daughter in a one-armed hug and kissed the top of her head. She caught Luis' eye in the rear-view mirror. "How much longer? I think I'm going to be an inch shorter after this."

"A couple miles to the turnoff, then about thirty miles cross-country."

A flash a hundred yards or so ahead revealed a side road intersecting the highway. There was enough light for her to see dust billowing behind a big, white pickup with its brights on. A low-profile light bar on the roof, a dark stripe cutting diagonally across the door, big tires, heavy brush bars. "Is that…?"

"Yuma County Sheriff."

The Expedition slowed gradually. Luis flicked the high beams, the signal to go ahead, but the pickup waited at the intersection. They passed the dirt road's mouth. Nora glanced back in time to see the truck pull onto the highway to follow them. She squinted in the headlight glare. "Are you going the limit?"

"I don't even know what the limit *is*. I haven't seen a sign since we got off the Interstate."

Nora recalled the priest's warning that the local cops would pull over non-whites to extort money. They probably liked not having a posted speed limit; that way, it could be anything they wanted it to be. She saw herself up against warlords and bandits in Somalia and became uncomfortably aware she was in a stolen vehicle. "Do you think that car lot reported us?"

"They were closed. I don't see how they'd know so soon."

Cameras, alarms, witnesses; that's how. After a couple minutes, they passed a jumble of run-down houses, trailers, storage tanks and junk straddling another dirt road. A sprinkling of distant window lights marked more settlement. She mentally urged the cop to pull off to patrol, but he didn't.

At the next dirt road, a sign the size of a sheet of plywood was propped up on wooden posts behind a sagging barbed-wire fence. The caricature of a hook-nosed Arab in a *kaffiyeh* with red crosshairs over his forehead and "Open Season – No Limit" in big, faded black letters. She'd seen several "Terrorist Hunting License" bumper stickers in Yuma. Out here, they probably meant it.

"What's the plan?" Nora wished her voice was steadier.

Luis didn't answer for a few moments, which didn't make her feel any more confident. "I can't say I want to shoot cops, but we may have to. These guys carry assault rifles. They'll stand off and blow this thing to pieces if we let them."

"I didn't hear a plan in there."

"There wasn't one."

"You're just full of good news. How long before we turn off?"

"A mile or so."

A shootout with police. That was even sicker than body armor for children. She was a law-enforcement officer; she wasn't supposed to kill other cops. But a few nights ago at the safe house, she'd been ready to do just that to protect her family. Maybe it was all about incentive. Or maybe she really was turning into a terrorist.

The glare from behind suddenly disappeared. The police truck blazed past, rocketing into the darkness ahead of them. Nora sagged in her seat, relieved beyond words that Hope wouldn't end up in the middle of a firefight.

The sunset's yellows had shifted to reds, and the reds to purple. The road ahead slowly faded into the night that closed in on either side of them. The road moan fell in pitch as the Expedition slowed. "Turn's just ahead," Luis announced.

A blast of light filled the road ahead of them. Headlights, floodlights, strobes. The police truck blocked the highway.

"Hold on!" Luis yelled.

He screeched onto a cross-street running south toward the now-black mountains fading into the night sky, then stomped the gas. Nora grabbed Hope with one hand, the back of the driver's seat with the other, and leaned into the turn.

A few seconds later, headlights and floodlights filled the rear window. Nora's insides fell into a heap between her hips. The lightwash revealed a huge orchard to her left and vast nothingness on her right, not even little yellow fireflies of windows to comfort her. "Is this the right road?"

"Yeah. That doesn't give me a good feeling."

Are they herding us? "How far are we going?"

"A couple miles until we hit the range boundary."

"Then what?"

"Then we find out if there's Border Keepers down there."

Desert scrub replaced the orchard. Telephone poles whizzed by to her right. The mountains were faint shapes now, some marked by tiny blinking red lights. The truck was so close behind them, its lights so bright, Nora could read her watch as if it was daylight. This felt more like the prelude to an ambush every minute. It made a certain twisted sense that if these cops were bandits, they'd make their move after nightfall… which had just happened.

"What if you just stop?"

Luis flicked his eyes to the rear-view mirror. "That close, they'll rear-end us."

"Maybe it'll disable the truck."

"Not with the brush bars that thing has. It'll end up in your lap."

An overpass appeared ahead, a dark strip with a lighter area underneath. The tire roar over the broken pavement grew so loud Nora could hardly hear herself think, which was fine, since her thoughts were growing more morbid by the minute. When they emerged on the other side, Luis reported, "I-8, in case you care."

"Mommy, I'm scared."

Nora gathered Hope in her arms and hugged her as tight as she dared. "It's okay to be scared," she whispered into Hope's ear. "It means you're thinking."

"Are you scared?"

Which was better: the obvious but reassuring lie, or the awful truth? "Yes, I am. Even mommies get scared sometimes. Just hold on to me."

The tire noise went hollow; moonlight flashed off a thread of water on either side. "The canal!" Nora cried. "That's the canal the Border Keepers should be at, right?"

"No. That's in a couple minutes."

They crested a small rise, then the wrecked asphalt ended and all at once they were on dirt, the wheels thrumming on washboard. The cops' lights dimmed in the dust plume, then slid to the road's centerline. Luis corrected to stay directly in front of them. They moved, he moved. They slithered all over the road, banging over ridges, crashing into dips, the cops' truck just a few yards behind them.

The cops fell back.

Luis slowed, then stopped on a bridge. A silvery canal ran straight beneath them.

"They're giving up," Nora said. "They're letting us go."

"I don't think so."

The dust-caked windshield exploded with light.

"They brought us to the Border Keepers."

54

The Minutemen movement dissolved after the effective end of illegal immigration into the U.S. in the mid-2020s. A number of its more extreme adherents formed loosely organized, often violent splinter groups to pursue their own agendas. These groups initially took different names, but by 2027 had come to be known collectively as "Border Keepers," after the largest and oldest of these organizations, based in southwestern Arizona.

-- "Border Keepers," Wikipedia

SUNDAY, 16 MAY

Luis said, "I'm going to roll down the rear window. Tell me what the cops are doing." He kept his eyes focused on the instrument panel, trying to avoid the floodlights turning the windshield white.

The window whined down. "They've blocked us in," Nora said. "They're about ten yards back, pulled across the road, lights off. It doesn't look like anyone got out."

"Okay." They'd let their buddies at the other end of the bridge do the hard work, then take their cut. "How well can you see right now?"

"Well enough. I've got my NVGs on. Why?"

"Check out the cop truck and see if there are any corporate logos or 'operated by' stickers."

After a few moments, Nora said, "Provided by AFT Worldwide.'"

Contractors. Figures—a broke-ass county like this couldn't (or wouldn't) afford real employees. "If they come this way and look hostile, open up on them. Shoot to wound if you can. Think of them like buzzards, not cops."

"That's easy for you to say. Do you know how much training

I've had to *not* shoot cops?"

Luis threw off his harness, twisted in his seat and motioned to Nora. When she leaned in, he grabbed her body armor's shoulder strap, hauled her close and rasped, "Let me make it easier for you. Everybody outside this car wants to lynch me, rape and kill you, cook and eat Hope, and steal everything we have. Any questions?" Nora swallowed, then shook her head. "Good. Cover our six."

He released her, settled back into his seat, and tried to think of the next move. First, he had to be able to see. The windshield washer had fluid (thank God) and the too-old wipers managed to scrape away most of the sludge without disintegrating. The whiteout resolved itself into a supernova of light surrounded by blackness, not a huge improvement but enough to get an idea of what was out there. Based on the lights' grouping and spread, they had a Jeep or something like it. Two guys, maybe three, all armed to the teeth based on his previous collisions with Border Keepers. Not bad odds.

Luis never had a beef with the old Minutemen. His dad hated them, but Luis wasn't bringing people in, he was taking them out, and the Minutemen were down with that. A couple even helped him get a van full of travelers out of a ditch once. But once its thug faction mutated into Border Keepers, they became a real pain in the ass.

What he remembered of these *pendejos* was they liked to dress up in camo and drink beer and carry guns and pretend to be warriors. Like a lot of other superpatriots, most had never managed to put on a real uniform and actually serve the country they supposedly loved so much. They wouldn't be used to anyone shooting back. But they loved their guns and could probably hit what they aimed at as long as they were sober enough.

The cops were another thing, though. Ex-military of some flavor; they'd know what they were doing. The odds swung back to the bad guys' favor.

Nora said, "I'm waiting for that plan."

"So am I. Where's Hope?"

"On the floor, scared to death."

Smart girl. Luis noticed a man-shaped silhouette flit past the lights. Those guys out there would start to move in pretty soon and things would get uglier than they already were. He didn't want to start a bloodbath. Right now, the contractor-cops were in vulture mode, waiting to pick over the spoils. If bad things started happening to their buddies, they could not only get involved but also call in more cops and trackers and maybe drones and all kinds of shit that would make getting away a fantasy instead of just a dream.

The Expedition sat in the first ten yards of a paved bridge forty or so yards long. The Jeep parked nose-on at the bridge's other end a bit to the left of center.

An idea crept into Luis' brain. "How do you feel about low-speed crashes?"

"They're better than high-speed ones." Nora sounded distracted.

He rolled down all the windows—broken-glass management—and switched the Expedition into four-wheel-drive. "Get on the floor on top of Hope."

"What are you doing?"

"Getting us out of here." He strapped in, shifted into neutral, revved the engine. If this worked, they'd be out of this trap without purposely killing anyone. If it didn't, they'd die soon, and not well.

I'm sorry, Bel. This wasn't the plan. I love you.

He hunched behind the steering wheel and jammed the shifter into drive. The big, grippy tires launched the three-ton beast forward. Yellow flashes popped beside the floodlights. Bullets pinged against the SUV. The windshield starred until it was opaque. Then he saw the man-silhouette again, rushing toward the Expedition with what looked like a shotgun. Luis shoved open his door just in time to catch the man full-on and *thump* him off into the darkness. The lights filled the disintegrating windshield, safety glass rained in on Luis, Hope shrieked her lungs out and…

…he twitched the wheel to the right, glanced off the Jeep's front bumper. The Expedition shuddered and screeched, but the lighter car whipped back and around in a cloud of dust and a clatter of loose gear.

They were clear.

Luis slewed the SUV around a sharp left-hand turn that fed into a hairpin. He could barely see through a windshield pocked with a couple dozen holes the size of dimes. He had to sit up to wrestle the wheel over, hoping that wasn't when the lucky shot would come whizzing through the back window. They bucked and dived over the uneven ground, every landing a slam he felt in his butt all the way up into his skull. The seat belt's constant pummeling of his left shoulder was like being punched on his wound over and over until he finally couldn't feel anything anymore. Nora and Hope squawked at each jounce.

When he finally skidded around the end of the hairpin onto a due-south stretch of dirt road, he slowed so he could roll up the windows and give Nora a chance to get off the floor. "You two okay?" he shouted over the chaos.

Nora wiped a dark stain—blood?—from under her nose with her wrist. She buckled up, then pulled a sobbing Hope onto her lap and cradled her. "Okay enough, I guess. Can you roll up this window?"

"It won't. They probably shot it." He fiddled with the headlights, low beams, high beams, but only the right side of the road lit up; the left lamp must be broken. He settled on a speed that compromised between progress, no visibility, and spinal injury. Hope's crying brought back memories of Christa at that age, scared of the dark and the monsters in it. "Is she hurt?"

Nora didn't say anything long enough for Luis to check her in the rear-view mirror. Her head bent over the girl. Between chassis noises, he caught snippets of motherly cooing.

The world behind them was dark and dusty. Risk a stop? He couldn't go on without being able to see what was coming. He let the Expedition glide down to a walking pace before he applied the brake.

"Why are we stopping?" Nora asked.

"I can't see." He pulled the magazine out of his UMP, ejected the chambered round, then beat the remaining glass out of the windshield frame with the weapon's stock. Another check in the mirror; still clear. He stepped outside, brushed the glass chunks off himself and his seat, shook out the floor mat, then made a quick round of the Ford. Several holes in the body; the left front fender bent back; a hole through the grille (but not the radiator, he discovered when he checked under the hood); a person-sized dent in the driver's door; the driver's side-view mirror hanging by a couple wires; left rear window blown out. Tires sound. Not bad.

He looked back. A white glow grew steadily brighter in the distance.

"They're following us." He labored back into the driver's seat. His chest and left side were a single bruised mass of pain. Within seconds they were back up to what passed for speed on this rutted dirt road.

"The cops or the other guys?" Nora asked.

"Don't know. Don't care right now."

Luis pulled his night-vision goggles from the center console, jammed them on his face, then snapped off the headlights. His view through the empty windshield frame turned black-and-green. He hoped losing sight of the SUV's lights would make their pursuers give up and go home. It didn't.

The glow turned into a blob of light that slowly grew in the rear-view mirror. These guys probably had way more experience driving out here, covering this road many times more than Luis had. Their Jeep was a better match for the road than the big, heavy Expedition.

The bad guys were going to win this race.

They busted past the crossroad marking the border of Goldwater Air Force Range and the start of the Camino del Diablo. Their hunters didn't stop. A mile ground by, then two, then three, and the blob of light expanded behind them bit by bit. A couple bugs careened into Luis' forehead—*damn, that hurt*—and many more hurtled past his ears on their way out the open back window. Only the gale rushing through kept the dust from choking him.

"Is there someplace we can hide?" Nora yelled above the wind noise.

"Not for another few miles. An old airstrip."

"How many miles?"

"A few. Five or six maybe. I don't remember—I didn't come out here much."

Nora craned her head over her shoulder. "I'll bet they do."

Another mile. Tracked vehicles—probably Marine AFVs—had left behind a churned, lumpy trail Luis recognized from the 'Stan.

It rattled the SUV from nose to tail. His brain joined the throbbing rhythm in his chest and shoulder. Fighting the steering wheel shot bolts of pain up his arms. Hope finally stopped crying and lapsed into a stunned silence. Luis wished his head would do the same thing.

He swerved around an abandoned truck wheel and tire in the road. Beside it lurked a hole a couple feet wide and deeper than the NVGs allowed him to see. He tried to avoid it, but the SUV's left front wheel charged in. A heavy *crack* filled the cabin. The Expedition heeled over, then spun. The front airbag punched Luis full in the face. Before he could finish yelling "Goddamnit!" the SUV crashed down on all fours in a cloud of dust.

Luis slapped the deflating airbag out of his face. He shook his aching head, trying to take a deep breath. It didn't hurt more than usual. The bridge of his nose hurt like a son of a bitch, though, and all he could see was static. He realized his NVGs were broken and flung them away, blinking to drive off the flickering stars.

The followers. He twisted to look. Their lights were brighter, no more than a mile away.

Nora held her neck in one hand, Hope's hand in the other, and turned her head in big circles, grimacing. "Are you okay?" she asked, winded. Hope cried like a colicky infant.

He shook his head, a huge mistake. "We've got to get away. They'll be here in a minute."

She nodded, handed him her H&K, then unbuckled and stepped out. Luis kicked open the driver's door, then shuffled across the road into the sparse scrub. Nora trailed a few steps behind him with Hope in her arms. They'd stumbled no more than thirty yards when their pursuers' vehicle closed in. Luis dropped to his face and wriggled his body into the loose dirt, trying to create cover where there was none. Nora joined him a few seconds later.

He tapped Nora's shoulder, then pointed to Hope. "She needs to stay quiet."

"We already had that talk. Where are your NVGs?"

"Busted. Where are yours?"

"They flew off when we crashed."

The Jeep stopped a few yards behind the crippled Expedition. "Not the cops," Nora whispered.

A robust roll cage replaced the Jeep's roof. Two bumper-mounted floods were dead on the left side. The full brunt of the two remaining floodlights and two roll bar-mounted spots focused on the Expedition, making it flare against the dark. Seeing the lights edge-on lessened their impact, though, and Luis could make out two dark male figures in the Jeep. He passed a UMP to Nora. "See them?"

"Yes."

"Can you get them?"

"With this thing? No. There's too much in the way. At least they don't have NVGs."

"Not on, at least." Their own lights would blind them. Then again, they were already blinded; they'd been staring into all that candlepower shooting off the Jeep's nose. The rest of the world would be a black smear to them. "I'm gonna move over that way to get a second angle on them. If you get a shot, take it."

"Right."

Luis pushed himself up on his elbows, cradled his UMP on his forearms, then crawled what his tortured body told him was three miles but what was really about twenty feet. He collapsed, panting, his left arm on fire. He was way too old to be doing this commando shit.

"Where are youuuu?" a young male voice called out. He laughed. "Come out, come out!"

Tonto. Luis settled, snapped off the UMP's safety and switched to single shot. He didn't want to damage the Jeep any more than necessary. He'd need it if they weren't going to walk the next twenty-some miles to get to the jump-off point.

The Jeep's driver hopped out and wandered into the floodlights. He was a youngish guy in a Nomex flight jacket and tiger-stripe utility pants, head shaved, toting an evil-looking assault rifle with a carelessness that would've had Luis' old platoon sergeant knocking the kid's ass all over the compound. Luis couldn't see what happened to the other guy.

Tiger Stripes swaggered to the open back door, poked his rifle muzzle inside, then repeated his act with the driver's door. Luis heard muttered conversation through the still air. Tiger Stripes strolled to the open back window, peeked in, then hauled out

Nora's backpack. He dropped it on the road, crouched, opened it, rummaged. "Woohoo! Hey Ern, check this out!"

He pulled out something, then spread it open and held it up in the light. A bra. "Hey bitch! Come out and try this on for us!" He stood, waved the bra over his head. "Come on, babe! Give us a show!"

One shot. Tiger Stripes staggered, then collapsed against the Expedition's tailgate before sliding to the ground. Luis shook his head. *Don't mess with her undies.* He felt exactly the same lack of remorse he remembered from watching Taliban go down so long ago.

A short burst ripped out over the SUV's hood. Luis tried to spot the shooter but couldn't see anything in the absolute dark behind the bright. He rolled out his left shoulder, sighted in on the right-hand spotlight, and squeezed off a round. No effect. He tried again and the spot exploded like an old-time flashbulb in the movies.

The second guy returned fire, a one-second burst that plowed up dirt a few yards in front of Luis. Nora let off another round, and Luis crawled another ten feet closer to the road. Aim, fire: the leftmost floodlight blew out. The SUV was half as bright as it had been a couple minutes before. Leaving some lights on made these guys easier targets but kept Luis from getting his night vision back.

He switched to full auto, waiting for answering fire. He got it, but not over the Ford's hood. The guy had crawled into the SUV and shot through the open back door. Dirt geysered a few feet to Luis' right. He had Luis' range.

Nora loosed off a burst. The bullets clanged into the SUV's body. Luis struggled into a crouch, scurried ten yards closer to the road, then dropped. The gunman lobbed a few rapid, single shots back at Nora. Saving his ammo? Whatever it was, he was still shooting at Hope. Luis pushed back into a crouch, put a short burst through the back door, then ran for the road while the gunman pounded a few rounds into the place Luis had been.

Luis had planned to stop at the road's edge, but momentum and adrenaline carried him all the way to the crippled SUV's tilting nose. He slung his UMP and drew his Sig; this would be like clearing a room. He poked his head above the hood, wincing at the

Jeep's blaze of light.

Another few shots from inside—spent casings pinged off metal—then several from Nora's direction—*clank clank clank*, shattering glass. Luis slid around the SUV's nose to the unlit side away from Nora, stopped at the open front passenger's door. In the stillness, he could hear the gunman squirming on the second-row seat, less than six feet away.

Should he just kill this *tonto*, or give him a chance to surrender? Taking the moral high ground out here in the middle of the desert wasn't the smartest move. But then, Luis liked to think he was better than this scum. He swallowed to reopen his throat. "It's over. Give up and you get to live."

The guy answered by shooting wildly over the front seats with a pistol. Luis crouched by the front wheel, cursing himself. So much for surprise. Then his anger took over. *Try to do the right thing and he shits on your shoes...*

Luis swung upright, aimed through the passenger's window, and fired five times through the seat back. He heard a sharp cry, then the thud of a weapon hitting the floor. Luis lurched to the open rear door, grabbed the gunman's ankles, and dragged him out onto the dirt. He searched the man, took a sheathed buck knife off his belt and a little .22 backup pistol from his ankle holster. Then he stood back to see who'd chased him across the desert.

The man's American-flag ball cap covered most of his thin white hair. Decades of sun and heat lined his face. A dark red splotch spread over the message on his tan tee shirt's chest— "Undocumented Border Patrol Agent"—while another crawled across the upper right thigh of his faded Wranglers.

"You stupid son-of-a-bitch," Luis grumbled. "You couldn't just let it go."

The old man squinted up at him. "You speak English?"

"Of course I speak English! I was born here! I'm as American as you!"

The old man coughed out a laugh. "You'll never be as American as me, *mojado*."

This asshole probably voted. No wonder the country was so fucked up. "Maybe. But I'll never be as stupid as you are, either."

Luis yelled "Clear!" into the night. While he waited for Nora to reappear, he hauled the dead Border Keeper next to his buddy beside the SUV, then kicked dirt over the blood in the road so Hope wouldn't have to see it. He shifted the backpacks and groceries to the cargo area behind the Jeep's back seats. He was about to go looking for the women when Nora's shape hobbled out of the darkness, Hope trailing behind her. "What's wrong? Are you hurt?"

"Uh-huh."

He reached her in a few strides, wrapped an arm around her shoulders and half-carried her to the Jeep. He caught Hope, lifted her into the back seat, then gave Nora a scan. Other than being coated with dirt and bits of sagebrush, she looked fine from the front. "Where…?"

She braced herself against the Jeep, gulped, then pointed at her rear. He swiveled her toward the light reflecting off the Expedition's tailgate. The seat of her jeans was ripped just above her left thigh and a dark trail of blood reached to her knee.

"It really hurts." Her voice was as tight as her grimace.

"I'll bet. Can you sit?"

"I don't know." She peered at his left shoulder. "You're a mess."

The left side of his shirt was caked in a blood-dirt mix that was slowly turning to cement. Nora brushed some dirt off his forehead, then held up blood-smeared fingertips for him to see.

"Where are they?" she asked. Luis pointed toward the SUV. "Let's get away from here."

"We both need to get patched up."

"I don't care. We can stop down the road. I don't want Hope around dead people."

"Neither do I. Can you get in?"

"I'll try."

He grabbed a water bottle from behind the back seat, then returned stiff-legged to the old man. The blood had oozed farther across his chest and leg. He watched Luis place the water bottle in the dirt next to his head, then gasped. "You're not going to kill me?"

"I'm not like you." Luis straightened as best he could. "Maybe your cop buddies will find you before the desert kills you. *Vaya con Dios*, old man."

The man's face pruned in disgust. "Speak English, you wetback fuck."

Luis was too tired and hurt too much to be angry. "Fine. Go to hell."

55

SUNDAY, 16 MAY

If she hadn't had Hope to worry about, Nora wouldn't have been able to bear the next two miles. Even at their much-reduced speed, the Jeep's every bump and jolt shot spears of blinding light into her eyes. She'd never been wounded in all her years in the Army and the Bureau. To get shot down *there*, now, almost by accident by some wacko, seemed too random to be truly random, as if it was punishment for doing all this to her family.

But she did have Hope to worry about, so she did what she could to comfort the frighteningly silent little girl wound up in a tight ball against her, sucking her thumb. The past few days must have plowed huge gashes across her daughter's psyche, ones Nora might never be able to fill in. The truckload of guilt already piled on Nora's shoulders grew heavier. All she could do was hold Hope and rock her and try not to throw up from her own pain.

When Luis stopped and turned off the Jeep, the relief was almost sensual. Nora sighed, peeled off her body armor and leaned back in her seat, gazing at the millions of stars in the crystalline sky. With the road and engine noise gone, the world fell nearly silent except for the gentle ticking of cooling metal and the occasional rattle of brush in the spotty breeze. A coyote yipped far, far away.

"Was that one of your friends?" she asked Luis.

"Could be." He undid his seat belt and shifted to look back at her. "How is she?" Nora shrugged; it was far too early to tell. "How are you?"

She wanted to say something brave but didn't have it in her anymore. "About to scream."

"Yeah, I feel you." He pushed open the driver's door and slowly, carefully levered himself out onto the road. After a big stretch, he unlashed and removed his body armor. Then he staggered to the Jeep's back end, rustled through a backpack, and handed her a white plastic first-aid kit, then an olive-drab military med kit like the one she'd carried in the Army. Finally, he passed her several bottles of water and a larger white plastic box. He held up a flattened roll of what looked like blue paper towels. "Bonus. The knuckleheads had something useful."

Luis went over each kit's contents, then they went to separate ends of the Jeep, Luis in front, Nora to the back. Hope tried to grab her on the way out—"Mommy, don't leave me!"—but Nora managed to get her to stay in the back seat. Pulling down her pants was pure agony, the now-stiff denim scraping over what felt like every nerve ending in her entire rear. Once she unclenched her jaws, she clamped her penlight between her teeth and surveyed the damage as best she could through the blood. The wound was on the downhill side of her left cheek, almost impossible to see.

She wet a couple blue towels and scrubbed her leg and hip until she could see skin instead of dirt and blood. That bought only a few minutes. She couldn't clean or dress the wound if she couldn't see it. Of all the places to get shot...

Now what? She knew what she needed to do but couldn't get the words out right away. This would be far more intimate than she'd ever wanted to be with Luis, no matter how trustworthy he'd turned out to be, no matter what he'd sacrificed for her. No man (other than a doctor) had seen her undressed since she'd married Paul, and only a couple before that. But if she didn't get help, blood loss and infection would race to knock her over first. *Forgive me, Paul.* "Luis? I need your help."

He appeared a few moments later, shirt off, blood smeared on the left side of his chest and upper arm. He pulled up short, blinked. "Um..."

"Don't get any ideas. I can't... I can't see it. Can you...?"

Luis worked his jaw for a moment. "Okay, sure. Um... I'll fix that, and you can change the dressing on my back, okay?"

"Deal."

They consolidated all the first-aid supplies in the back of the Jeep. She handed Luis her penlight. He turned it in his fingers. "We have the spotlight. I'd rather run down their battery than—"

"Not in front of my daughter."

"Good point." He knelt behind her, tugged on the edge of her panties—another fireball of pain—pressed gentle fingertips around the burning area. "Okay, the good news is, it's a grazing shot. The bullet didn't go in. The bad news is, it left a pretty good gash. It's gonna hurt to sit for a while, and it'll scar up unless you get it fixed."

What would Paul think of a big scar on her rear? "Can you make it so I won't bleed to death?"

"I can do that." She gasped as the elastic in her briefs hit the wound's edge. "Sorry."

She leaned forward against the Jeep's tail, bent slightly at the hips, and did what she could to ignore the fact that a strange man was washing and prodding her almost-bare rear. Luis was incredibly gentle and didn't try to touch her out of bounds. She kept her briefs out of the way with one hand while with the other she passed him what he called for, which kept her brain busy.

When he asked for the povidone bottle, she braced for what was next.

"This is gonna hurt a little."

She couldn't catch her first scream in time when the iodine solution hit her wound. She grabbed a paper-wrapped bandage roll from the supplies and bit down hard on it. The pain couldn't burn hotter had he turned a cigarette lighter on her.

Hope's head peeked up over the back seat. "Mommy, what's wrong?"

Nora pulled the bandage from her mouth. "I'm just fixing an owie, Cupcake." Her voice sounded like she was being strangled.

"Can I help?"

"No, no, no, just sit down. I'll be done in a couple minutes, okay?"

A few minutes later, she felt Luis stand and sigh. "Okay, all done. Grab some Avelox tabs from the mil kit. Take one now, then one every twelve hours. It'll screw up your digestion, but that's better than gangrene in your butt."

She reached back to probe the dressing. It felt neat and secure, far better than she could have done on her own. He'd had practice. "Thanks. I need to change. Can you…?"

When he went away, she put on new briefs, patched the hole in her jeans with the Jeep's duct tape, and reassembled herself as much as possible. She called to him. Luis had tidied his front more thoroughly, but his back was a horror show. He took her place at the Jeep's back end while she washed and cleaned both sides of his shoulder wound. It was odd and a bit disturbing being this close to a half-dressed man, touching him, feeling his warmth. There was nothing romantic or sexual about it—blood was *not* a turn-on for her—but the intimacy unsettled her. Once again, Luis behaved like a gentleman. How wrong she'd been about him at first.

"All done." She stepped back, proud of her handiwork.

Luis tried to rotate the shoulder, but Nora could tell from his wince and sharp sucked-in breath that it hurt a lot. "Thanks," he rasped. "Good job." He took a pair of white tablets from a baggie and slugged them down with a gulp of water, then carefully pulled on a long-sleeved black tee shirt he'd draped over the top of his backpack. He handed her a small folding shovel. "Dig a pit and bury all the waste so the animals don't get into it. I'll get the supplies squared away."

"Okay." She twiddled the shovel for a moment. Her cheeks warmed despite the breeze. After everything, *now* she started blushing. "We don't have to tell anyone about this, do we?"

56

Caption: "U.S.-Mexican border between Mexicali and Nogales. The bright white line is the border fence. Wider light pools are the locations of patrol bases along the fence."
-- "Latest HD Earth Photos from China's Tiangong Space Station," SkyandTelescope.com

MONDAY, 17 MAY

Well past midnight, and still on the road. The farther south they traveled, the rougher the going, especially once Luis turned off the Camino del Diablo into the Cipriano Pass to cut west through the mountains. Now they did well to maintain an average fifteen miles an hour. The moon had already passed its zenith and had begun its long dive toward the horizon.

As usual, the day's warmth had bled off quickly into the cloudless sky. The Jeep's heater kept their legs warm enough, but Luis was still glad for his field jacket. No one realizes how cold a desert can get even in the summer until they experience it themselves.

"How much farther?" Nora asked, her voice sleepy.

He glanced in the rear-view mirror. Nora huddled glassy-eyed in a heavy, dark sweatshirt and windbreaker with the collar turned up, her fists clutched between her thighs. Hope, wrapped in a beach towel, had finally settled down again after a couple episodes of night fright. Poor thing. She'd be one messed-up little kid once this was over, even with devoted parents like Nora and Paul. This trip had been expensive on a lot of different levels.

"Fourteen, fifteen miles or so. Another hour. How're you doing?"

"Okay. That Tylenol works pretty well."

"It's got codeine in it."

"You *narcos* get all the good drugs."

He checked to see if she was serious. She wore a tired-dopey smile; probably not. "Actually, you can get it over-the-counter in Mexican *farmacias*."

"Hm. Why are you working for those people? Someone like you?"

"What do you mean, 'someone like me'?"

"You're a…" She trailed off. He glanced in the mirror, caught her chewing her lip. "You're honorable and smart and kind and reliable. Why are you mixed up with them?"

Wow. He had no idea he'd gone up so far in her opinion. "I was moving people south on the side when the cartels discovered they could make money doing it. A friend of mine worked for the Nortes and he hooked me up."

"You deal with them even knowing what they are?"

"I don't mess with the other stuff. I know, that's not an excuse. Look at who you work for. The things they do, what they're doing to you right now. Can you really complain about the Cartel?"

"That's different."

"How? You and ICE put four hundred thousand innocent people in prison with no trial. You have border guards shooting women and children trying to get out—"

"That doesn't really happen. That's—"

"It did to me. My last run before this. A couple contractors not too far from here shot me and mowed down four of the five travelers with me. That includes a woman and her daughter, about Hope's age." No reply. "I could work for an oil company and shovel some more gunk on the nice beaches we used to have. I could work for a broker and screw people out of their retirement money so they have to live with their kids, like my folks do. That's legal, I guess. The Cartel bought out my business. Now I'm tied to them. It sucks, but there it is."

They bounced over more ruts for a while. Finally Nora said, "Sorry I asked."

"Yeah." Now he felt guilty for unloading on her after posing a question he'd asked himself about a million times. "Look, I don't love them. They do some really evil things. I guess my point is that a lot of big companies do really evil things, and their stock goes up and their CEOs get to have dinner with the President. The cartels are just big companies now."

"You don't want to get laid off by them, though."

"No, that gets kinda rough."

They rounded a ridge and left the pass. The whole southern horizon was a straight black line against a midnight-blue band of sky. A few scattered bumps broke into the blue in the far distance. Stars shimmered like dewdrops at dawn.

"You going to miss the States?" Luis asked.

"I don't know. Probably. I was born here." She sounded wistful, as if she'd mentioned an old lover. "But it's not really my country anymore. It's decided it doesn't want me."

"They don't want you blowing the whistle on them."

"Oh, it's more than that. I've never been 'American enough' for a lot of people." Luis could hear the quotation marks around her phrase. "I took a lot of static in the Army for being what I am. It's been a lot worse since 10/19. I see how people look at me when I tell them my last name. People we thought were friends won't visit anymore. Nearly everyone in our mosque has moved or got sent off to a camp. I can't tell you how many polygraphs and background investigations I've been through at work in the past ten years."

"Try being Latino in Arizona or Alabama or Kansas."

"At least they think you're just trying to steal their jobs, not kill their children."

"You'd be surprised."

"Maybe." When she didn't continue, Luis glanced in the mirror. Nora stared up into the stars, her eyes big and sad. A few moments passed. "You know the funny thing? Other Muslims didn't think we were 'good Muslims.' We were never really hard-core about it when I was growing up. We'd do Friday prayers and Ramadan and paid our *zakat*, but we belonged to a pretty liberal mosque. I mean, look what I did—joined the Army, became an FBI agent. What good Muslim dad lets his daughter go crazy like that?"

"So what happened?"

"Well, 10/19, of course. We might as well have been fundamentalists, the way—"

"No. To you. The hats, your clothes, the way you are around

Paul. You changed. Why?"

Nora gave him a closed-lip smile, looked down, rearranged Hope's towel. She stayed silent so long, Luis figured the conversation was over until she spoke. "I went on a *hajj* with my family. I was just out of the Army, out of Somalia. I'd done some bad things, seen a lot of bad things, and…" She turned her gaze back up to the sky. "I guess I was looking for something. Going to those places, seeing all those people who believed so much… it makes things more real. It would be like you going to the Holy Land. It made me want to be better. And now, with the kids…"

Hearing all this was far more intimate than seeing Nora with her pants down. It was like holding something very fragile in his hands. He could see himself years ago at the baptismal font, welcoming Christa into a church he'd abandoned when he enlisted. He'd wanted to be better, too. "Are you? Better?"

She shrugged. "I hope so. I'm still not a very good Muslim. It's hard to be, here, now. But I try. Someday I'll find my place. It just won't be… here."

Luis shook his head. Such a waste. Nora and her family were the kinds of people the country needed—and was losing. "I hope you do."

She sighed. "Thanks. There've been some good people, ones who reached out to us, who tried to help. People like that priest back in Yuma. They're the only reason I can still hope things will get better someday." Her face didn't reflect any of that hope, only fatigue and disappointment.

"Maybe you can get that started with your information."

"Maybe."

As the track neared the mountains to their left, it cut across more and rougher networks of water channels left behind by decades of runoff. Down, up, slide, jolt, rinse, repeat, until Luis' teeth threatened to bail out of their sockets. Then at the last moment, he'd come to a flat, open patch that would last a few hundred yards until the next spider's web of stream beds threw itself in his path. A faint glow appeared along the southern horizon: the border fence and its lights. Luis' hands were numb from the constant vibration, not the cold. The ache in his shoulder and back screamed for codeine he didn't dare take.

The dashboard clock read "3:19" when Luis stopped in a wide, dry streambed and turned off the engine so he could hear the now-deafening silence. He tumbled out of the Jeep, stretched, twisted to break up the stiffness, and shook some feeling back into his hands and feet. After a few minutes, he leaned into the Jeep to tap Nora's leg.

She startled awake, shook her head hard, sneezed. "What is it?"

"We're here."

"Here where?" Her eyes swept the land around them, focused on the fence to the Jeep's right. "Is that the border? It's so close."

"About a mile." Close enough to make out the individual light towers and follow the brown line into the hills. He pointed to their left. "My original plan was to go up there. About a three-mile hike and some rock climbing to get to the border, no fence, no guards. That was before we were all casualties. How much walking do you think you can do now?"

Nora winced as she shifted in her seat. "Not three miles, not uphill. Hope will never make it either. What's Plan B?"

"It's not much better." Luis pointed straight ahead into the mouth of a narrow canyon. "We follow that track about a mile up to the fence, and unless they've blocked it off, do some mountain-goat action on the rock faces to get over. We come out at almost the same place as Plan A. It's another couple miles to the highway and a bus stop either way. The problem is, this gets patrolled by drones and there's motion sensors down here."

"Can we drive to the fence?"

"It's rough. A lot of erosion and rockfall. Driving this thing will take longer than walking, and it'll give them a great big heat blob to see on IR."

She nodded. "Unless there's a Plan C with a helicopter, I vote for Plan B."

They divided the surviving water bottles and energy bars between the two backpacks. Nora strapped on her body armor and submachine gun, then Luis helped her with her pack. "I'll drive the Jeep up there so they'll think we took Plan A and waste time looking for us in the wrong place. Walk straight toward that notch in the hills. It'll be a bit rough for the first couple hundred yards, then you'll hit what passes for a track. Follow it to where two big stream beds come together. That's the fence line. No lights on that part. If I haven't caught up by then and it's quiet, hang out and rest. If you hear a lot of noise behind you, get over the fence however you can. Take cover and wait. If I don't show up by dawn—"

"What are you talking about, 'if you don't show up'?" Nora growled. "You're dumping us here?"

"No, I wouldn't do that. The standard Border Patrol response if they see activity out here is to send a gunship. I want you guys to go on by yourselves and be safe. Follow the stream bed down to the highway, then go east. There's a roadhouse kind of thing there. Call this number to get picked up." He recited Ray's latest burner-phone number. "This is all for just-in-case. Once I dump the Jeep, I'll be right behind you. Understand?"

The moon was just bright enough to pick out Nora's glare. "Don't you give up on us now."

"I told you, I won't do that. Get going. Dawn's in about two hours. I want us over the line by then."

They'd made good time over the first couple hundred yards past the steep black slopes towering above them. Nora got them through the jumbled water channels and rockfall without any mishaps other than scraped palms and lots of dust. Even Hope had managed to not cry or whine, though she had every reason to.

Then on level, open ground, Hope stepped in a hole.

She went down hard, face-first, with a *thud* that curdled Nora's stomach. The following silence was the worst part, that endless moment between a child's fall and the howl of pain that follows. Nora gathered Hope in her arms just in time to get a faceful of her daughter's first shriek.

Nora cuddled the girl against her, rocking, shushing, stroking her face and hair. She freed up a hand to shine her penlight at the hole. Not deep, but just the right shape to catch someone unaware.

"It hurts! Mommy, it hurts it hurts…"

Nora pulled up Hope's denim pants leg; no blood (*praise Allah!*), no protruding bone, nothing hanging at an unnatural angle.

A sprain, she hoped, maybe just a twisted ankle, *please, please…* Nora ran her fingers along Hope's leg, feeling for knots or give or a pain reaction. When she reached the little ankle, Hope screamed again and jerked her leg away. Her cries echoed off the rock walls all around them.

Why now? They were so close. All the problems, all the close calls, all the lost sleep and bad food and boredom and being dirty and scared. They'd gotten through it all. Safety was just a few minutes away… and *this* happens. Hope's crying kicked holes in Nora's heart.

The frustration and fear and fatigue of not just today, not just these past two weeks, but from months and years climbed up her throat. She threw her head back until she stared at the cold, distant sky. "Why are You doing this?" she screamed. "Why don't You care anymore?"

The stars fuzzed out. Parts of her snapped deep inside and trickled from her eyes.

"I'm sorry, Cupcake, I'm sorry, I'm sorry, I'm so sorry…"

She fought the tears, tried to shove away the sobs sandpapering her throat. She had to keep it together for her husband and son lost in the unknown somewhere out there, for her tortured daughter, for her parents driven from their beloved, adopted homeland. She'd fought for so long she could barely remember how to let loose, how to cry. Her heart struggled against her, dredging up all the things she shouldn't have done but did, all the things she should've done but didn't, all the tears she hadn't shed because she had to "be strong." Her Hope was broken, and her hope clung to her fingertips, slipping away.

She crushed Hope's face to her throat. "Forgive me. I'm so sorry. I let you down…"

Her daughter pushed away; a little blurry face aimed up at Nora. Then a little hand pressed Nora's cheek. "Mommy, (sniff sniff) don't cry, you're scaring me. Why are you crying?"

"Because I'm so sorry I hurt you."

"I'm sorry I fell down. Please don't cry."

They swapped apologies between their sobs until Nora realized *she's me, she's four-year-old me.* The sheer absurdity kicked her into a hard, coughing laugh. She laughed with tears sheeting down her cheeks and off her chin, with Hope pleading, "What's so funny?"

"I… I'm just… I'm really, really tired… and it just all… it all caught up." Nora forced down a few deep breaths. "I'm sorry. Let me wrap up your ankle, okay, Cupcake? I'll stop crying."

"Promise?"

"I promise." She fought her way out of her pack, snuffling all the way, got the Ace bandage out of the first-aid kit, then went to work on Hope. She stopped every few seconds to wipe the tears from her eyes with a McDonalds napkin. When she wasn't biting her lip in pain, Hope peered at her, confusion and some alarm plain on her face. *She's never seen me cry. Peter hasn't either. How many years since I cried in front of Paul?*

An odd, discordant note broke through the sound of her own sniffles and Hope's tiny "ows" and the cool breeze through the underbrush. Something Nora didn't understand until she remembered what it meant.

The buzz of a large bee. Red and green stars passing across the sky. A drone.

57

The Office of Air and Marine (OAM) protects the American people and the nation's critical infrastructure through the coordinated use of integrated air and marine forces to detect, interdict and prevent acts of terrorism and the unlawful movement of people, illegal drugs and other contraband toward or across the borders of the United States.

-- "About Air and Marine," U.S. Customs and Border Protection (cbp.gov)

MONDAY, 17 MAY

It hadn't taken long for Luis to remember how to do this—how to read the fine shadings of light and shadow, how to avoid the worst of the thorns, how to decide whether that round patch ahead was a hole or a rattlesnake. He moved ahead not necessarily comfortably—his shoulder and chest hurt too much for that—but with confidence. He had to be catching up to Nora and Hope.

A noise behind him made him slow and cock his ear back. A high-pitched whine bounced between the rocks all around him. The sound of a mosquito close to his ear... except mosquitoes didn't live out here. Luis looked up in time to see marker lights pass a few hundred feet overhead. Nobody cruised this part of the border for fun.

The lights tilted, then cut a circle across the sky. The whine got more effort behind it, broadened, echoed harder off the rocks.

A drone had spotted him.

Luis' instinct was to run to the canyon wall and hunker under a rock, try to wait it out. But it wouldn't do any good. The drone could watch him for hours. Now it had found him, a gunship drone would be on its way. Nora and Hope were out there somewhere. He had to get to them before the gunship did.

He angled toward the canyon's south wall, hoping to pick up the track. He ignored the echoing whine, trying not to think about the lights circling over him. Once he cleared the worst of the rough ground, he eased into a jog even though it made the backpack straps slap against his shoulder wound. The moonlight shone just bright enough to turn the ground into a minefield of dips and bumps and cracks, any one of which could swallow a foot or snap a leg.

After a few minutes he stopped, cupped his hands around his mouth and shouted, "Nora!" His voice bounced from rock to rock; hers didn't. More trotting, more jinking around holes that didn't exist, more shying from snakes that turned into sticks. He stopped, called out again. No answer. *Where are they?* He looked up to the drone; now the lights drew a long ellipse, with him at one end.

It had found them.

He pushed himself faster, cranking down the backpack's straps to keep it from battering his kidneys as hard as it had his now-numb shoulder. His brain flew back to double-timing across open Afghan fields to avoid giving the Taliban easy targets. He'd been twenty years younger and a lot fitter back then, and the Taliban hadn't had air support on its way.

When he saw the drone's track become more circular, he dropped into a shambling walk, panted, then yelled "Nora!" again.

"Here!" A tiny voice, splintering on the rocks. Then a faint blue-white pinpoint arced back and forth. Nora's penlight.

Luis' lungs were broiling by the time he reached Nora. She stood astride the track, her H&K cradled in her right arm, her left arm swinging the penlight. The relief in her face mirrored what he felt. He staggered to a stop, braced his palms on his knees, and sucked down as much air as he could.

When he finally stood straight, Nora asked, "How long before the gunship comes?"

"Hard to say. It depends on how far away it was when they chopped it here. Could be five minutes or an hour. We've gotta keep moving." He noticed the tear tracks in the dust coating Nora's face, and Hope sitting on the ground with her left shoe off. "What happened?"

Nora hung her head. "Hope stepped in a hole. Her ankle's

twisted or sprained." She looked up, grim-faced. "She can't walk."

Luis could only shake his head. "Whatever. We'll take turns carrying her. Come on."

They could manage only a fast walk; jogging bounced Hope too much and made her cry. The first time Luis took Hope from Nora's arms, he dredged up all the comforting dad things he used to say to Christa when she got hurt or was scared and murmured them to Hope, who kept her arms wrapped tight around his neck. He glanced back over his shoulder a few times to try to catch the gunship's blinking marker lights, to see if they were about to be blasted into paste. The sky remained clear.

Up ahead, he spotted the fence.

They plunged into the dry riverbed, then back up over the bank, and within a couple minutes they arrived at the "separation barrier": eighteen feet tall, eight iron posts supporting each six-foot-long, four-foot-tall flat steel panel at the top, stretched across what used to be the river's outlet into Mexico. Dry brush and dead parts of trees piled against the base. This end ran directly into a sheer cliff—no climbing possible. The other end, about four hundred yards away, ran into a steep slope that used to be climbable from this side.

Engineers had pounded the ground flat along the fence, but enough junk had built up that Luis and Nora couldn't keep on the path. They swerved onto and off the embankment, skirting the debris at the risk of tripping in the shadows. He looked back again.

A blinking red beacon flanked by marker lights bobbed maybe a mile away. The gunship. Infrared sighting, a minigun mounted in the nose, more maneuverable than a manned chopper. He didn't want to be caught in the open by that thing.

Three hundred yards. They dropped into the riverbed that meandered in and out of the fence line, hopped over rocks and ruts, and scaled a low rise. Nora tried to run while carrying Hope but could manage only a fast hobble. "Nora! Let me take her!"

Nora sideslipped to him, panting and sweating. Luis grabbed the girl from her, draped her over his good shoulder, and moved as fast as he could toward the end of the fence. He could see it in the gloom: a rock shelf, then a slope of scree tucked into a sharp angle against the fence's top. They'd be partly exposed until they reached the top, where they'd stand out like torches in a dark back yard.

The gunship whirred overhead, swept out into Mexican airspace, then clawed through an impossible bank to line up for another pass. It was half the size of a Blackhawk and a lot quieter. The sound was more like the beating of a dragonfly's wings, if the dragonfly was the size of a Cessna.

"Against the fence!" Luis shouted. He cut right to snug up against the rusty metal stakes. The drone pilot would still be able to see them but couldn't count on hitting anything but the fence; he'd wheel around for a clear shot to conserve his ammo. They might just have a chance.

Luis checked on Nora, who was slowing, the wrong speed adjustment. "We're almost there!" he yelled. "Keep moving!"

The gunship zoomed past, practically scraping the fence top.

Luis staggered to a halt behind a shallow outcropping, folded into a crouch and slid Hope off his shoulder. She took one look at the drone—now hovering fifty yards away, its blunt snout resembling a giant evil insect—then turned and threw her arms around Luis' neck. "Make it go away! It's icky!"

He patted her back. "Okay, sweetheart, don't worry." The rock shielded them more-or-less. Her mom, however, was still in the open, her limp worsening with each step. "Keep coming!" he barked. "Just a few more steps! Come on!"

She leaped into the niche just as the drone opened fire. The hoofbeat pounding of bullets churned the ground just feet from them, drowning the minigun's ripping-cloth racket. The noise stopped as suddenly as it started, leaving behind a drifting cloud of dirt and shredded sagebrush. Hope squealed.

Nora pressed closer into Luis' arms. "Now what?"

"Your leg's bad?"

"My leg's fine. My rear feels like an alligator's eating it."

Same as Luis' left shoulder. "Can you climb?"

"With that thing out there? Will it let us?"

"I'm going to try to blind it." According to things he'd seen online, multiple high heat sources and smoke confused the night-vision cameras and thermal targeting sensors. He'd never tried it; he hoped the geeks were right. "Get the flares out of my backpack."

While Nora rummaged, Luis watched the gunship slide from

side to side, trying to get a better target picture on them. It could hover there for hours and had no incentive to leave. A Border Patrol team was probably already on its way to clean up the mess the drone would make.

"How many do you have?" Nora asked.

"Should be three."

"I've got two..."

Luis checked the area around him. About six feet above him, he spied a crack in the rock just about the right size for the end of a flare. A thick layer of dry brush crowded the fence's base, and creosote and greasewood studded the ground just beyond their hide. Promising.

Then something else caught his eye. The iron posts normally had less than six inches between them. But the six-foot-wide section ending at the foot of the slope had either gone in crooked or had settled, leaving a gap of a foot or so that stretched from the ground to about five feet up. Way too small for a normal-sized man to get through. But maybe...

"Got it." Nora handed the three flares to Luis.

"Look over there. Think you can fit through that?"

She squinted along Luis' outstretched arm. "I'd have to take off my vest and backpack, and I couldn't get my pack through it."

Luis turned Hope around so she could look out. "Hope, do you think you could get through those bars over there?"

Hope shook her head in that overbroad way littles have. "I have an owie on my leg."

Luis craned to look up at the slope. "There's no way we'll get her out up there. I can't lift anything above my head, and you can barely walk. It's through the fence with her, or we wait for them to come get us."

Nora pointed toward the gunship, still waiting patiently for them. "What about that?"

Good question. The gap in the fence was maybe four feet away, but all in the open. Hope could use the posts to prop herself up. It would be slow, but doable. It all depended on the guy at Davis-Monthan AFB in Tucson or Creech outside Las Vegas, the guy looking at them through a video screen right now and waiting for them to come out to play.

"There's a guy flying that thing," Luis finally said. "A real CBP guy, not some whacked-out 'roid monster of a contractor. He's not going to shoot a little girl."

"Are you *crazy?*" Nora snatched Hope away from him, folded her arms around her like a shield. "You're betting my daughter's life on that."

"You got another plan?"

Nora looked at the gap, then the slope. It was so high and steep. She didn't know if she could make it up there, far less pack Hope over the top. "Do we have a way out?"

"Yeah, but only if she goes first."

She peeked at the drone. It drifted up and down in the light breeze, looking like some giant prehistoric insect. If it wanted, that thing could make Hope disappear with a single burst from its gun. If it did, Nora might throw herself out there too, just to get it over with. Then she remembered Luis' words: *there's a guy flying that thing… he won't shoot a little girl.* True?

Nora measured the slope again. Every time she did, it seemed higher, more impossible. The gunship blocked the only other way out.

There's a guy flying that thing… She had no choice. She had to believe some humanity was left in the world. "All right." Her voice was little more than a whisper. "If you're wrong—"

"I know, you'll kill me. If I'm wrong, I'll want you to. There's a white undershirt in the bottom of my pack. Can you get it?"

Nora plunged into his backpack again, yanked him around probably more than necessary but enough to beat back some of her fear, then plunked the rolled-up tee shirt into his hand.

"Okay. She should wave this as she goes." He handed it back to her. "It's probably better if Mommy tells her what to do."

Nora unrolled the shirt, then knelt and grasped Hope's shoulders. "Okay, Cupcake. I need you be really brave, okay?" *Braver than I am.* "I need you to wave this at that big… bug out there—"

"But Mommy—"

"Shh. Listen. Go along the fence to that hole, then go through to the other side. Lay down on the ground and look at the stars. I'll come get you in a couple minutes. Okay? Can you do that?"

"The big bug will get me."

"No it won't." Nora shot a glare at Luis. "It's just going to watch you." *Please let that be true…*

Hope leaned into Nora. "I'm scared."

"So am I, Cupcake." She hugged her daughter hard, then kissed her forehead. "Remember what I told you." She held the hug as long as she dared, whispered, "I love you," then turned Hope around. "Okay, wave the shirt at the bug."

Luis stood and slid forward to the outcrop's edge.

"What are you doing?" Nora hissed. "Get back."

"I'm not far enough out to be a target. I want to show the pilot how short Hope is."

Hope hobbled to the fence, stopped, waved the shirt again.

The gunship bobbed, yawed to the right a fraction, as if watching.

Nora stood, hands over her mouth, eyes riveted. *Please don't shoot my baby please oh please don't I'm begging you shoot me not her please…*

Hope half-hopped, half-limped from one post to the next. At each, she stopped to wave the shirt.

Nora hadn't been able to make her lungs work since her daughter lurched into the open.

Hope reached the gap. She stared at the drone, eyes round and unblinking. She waved the shirt again.

The gunship sideslipped a few feet to its right. Luis grabbed Nora's arm, pulled her back into the niche. She didn't resist.

Hope turned to face Nora and Luis. "Mommy?"

"Go through the hole!" Nora called out. "Go through and get away from the fence! Now! I'll be there soon."

Hope's little chin wrinkled. She nodded. Then she slipped through the gap.

Nora sagged against the rock wall, gulping down a huge breath. Her heart started beating again. *She's safe. Praise Allah, my baby's safe.*

"Ready?" Luis said. He gripped her right arm, squeezing

gently. "Time to follow her."

"How?"

"I'm going to light the brush on fire. The heat'll wash out our IR returns, and the smoke and light will turn the pilot's night-vision picture white. I'll give you a boost up on the shelf, then hand you a flare. Light it and stick it as far up in the scree as you can, then get up the slope. Drop your pack over the side at the top of the fence, then work your way down. Be careful going down—it's nasty. I'll be right behind you. Got it?"

The whole scheme sounded insane. The gunship would tear them apart. But what choice did they have? "Will this work?"

"Sure."

"Liar. Let's get it over with."

Luis twisted off the first flare's top. "These are bright. Don't look straight at them." He struck the flare's end against the top. The night turned end-of-the-world-Sun-exploding white. Then she heard a *foom*, and immediately the smell of roasting plants filled her nostrils. She heard and felt Luis disappear, then that evil ripping sound of the drone's gun and the thunder of bullets plowing the earth just a few feet away. *Be careful be careful I can't do this alone…*

A minute later he stood next to her, breathing hard. "Ready?"

No. Smoke filled the little niche, her sinuses, her head. "Yes."

His idea of a "boost" was to hook his shoulder under her pack and stand up fast with his good hand pushing up on her crotch. She didn't have time to object. The narrow ledge that had been above her head a moment before was now at mid-chest, and she automatically planted her palms and levered herself up just like on the Army confidence course. He thrust a flare into her hands the moment she stood. She sparked it and stabbed the end into the loose rock to her left.

Nora climbed. She crawled up the loose rubble, stomping her boot toes into the mess and swimming upwards, sliding back a foot for every three she advanced. She could just about hear the drone's rotors beating away behind her, angry and confused, its gun hammering the rock and the dirt. She looked back just once, saw Luis a few feet behind her, scratching one-handed against the slope, the inferno below bathing them both in reds and yellows through a fog of smoke that, despite its pleasant woody smell, burned her throat and eyes.

The rock just above her head exploded, splashing fragments into her face before she could drop and hug the slope. Had it found her? Was she about to die? But the burst didn't repeat, and she scrambled through the hole with an extra jolt of desperate energy.

She looked to her right and saw only desert. She'd passed the top of the fence. She braced herself, tore off her pack, then rolled it over the side. It bounced down to the ground below.

Luis wasn't joking about the downhill side. The rocks slid out at the slightest touch and more followed them from above. Stones pinballed off her arms and legs. Those flares could have been burning against her wound. Blood dripped into her eyes from a hurt she didn't remember.

The slope collapsed underneath her with ten feet left to go. She screamed involuntarily as the entire patch of rockfall she clung to turned liquid and careened down, throwing her head-over-heels against the desert floor, then pelting her with stones. She curled into a ball, covered her head with her hands, and waited for the pummeling to stop.

Eventually, it did.

She lay there aching in a hundred places, coughing, blood seeping into her eyes and out her nose. Every part of her smelled of smoke and grit. She waited for the gunship to find her in the open and finish her off. It would probably hurt less.

Footsteps on gravel, then jumbled rock. Luis' voice in mid-grunt: "There you go." Then strong, dusty fingers brushing her hair and face. She opened her eyes.

Hope kneeled next to her, wide-eyed. Then she flopped her face onto Nora's stomach and wailed out her fear.

Luis squatted behind Hope. "You okay?"

Nora struggled up on one elbow, finger-brushed the dirt from Hope's hair. The gunship hovered on the other side of the fence, its underside glowing red in the reflected firelight. "What's he waiting for?"

"He's watching, but he won't shoot. He missed his chance." He smiled. "*Bienvenido a México*. We made it."

58

Eleventy-bazillion dollars blown on recording every phone call in America, McGinley seethed, *and all a body has to do is buy a goddamn Nigerian phone from Walmart and it's all just shit.*

Ojeda was in the wind. He hadn't returned a single one of McGinley's calls, though it was hard telling what number the man used now. He'd dropped off the Feebs' radar Saturday night—they were real quick to tell McGinley that, like it was his fault—and a Border Patrol report had him and Khaled and a child on the border a few hours ago. Supposedly tried to shoot down a drone, which sounded like pure bullshit. The Feebs said Mrs. Ojeda was cooperating, which McGinley *knew* was bullshit. That woman wouldn't turn against her man no matter what got done to her.

So McGinley lied and said it was all part of a plan and he had an agreement with Ojeda, who was due to check in that morning. The Feebs said they'd leave things be. That's where it stood a few hours ago. If the sorry sumbitch didn't surface pretty soon, McGinley would have enough egg on his face to keep Waffle House going for another year.

A news alert popped up on his screen. McGinley stabbed it with a finger. As the Fox News video played, he felt his face get redder and hotter. Those goddamn Feebs had lied to him.

59

Monday, 17 May

It used to be a truck stop and roadhouse: a flat-roofed, cinderblock building a little larger than a double-wide, its daisy-yellow paint peeling, the front roof overhang sagging between its pipe supports, derelict trucks and RVs in back, a graffittied, once-silver propane tank on one side. Now it was a refugee camp, a stop on the trail of misery between Mexicali and Nogales.

I guess we're refugees. Luis sat at a plastic picnic table in a patch of shade cast by one of the half-dozen Red Cross tents laid out in two rows east of the bar and café. The tent's skirts were rolled up, as were those of three others, turning them into canopies; the bath tent and clinic were fully enclosed. The three dozen or so other people at the camp stayed away from him, peeking at him from lowered eyes or carefully turned heads. Probably the pile of body armor and weapons on the ground next to him put them off. If he was a *sicario*, he was a target, or they were.

The *chilaquiles* were pretty not-bad, though he tried not to think about what exactly was in them or on the grill that made them. The coffee—black, Americano style—was hot enough to kill whatever swam in the water. After a day of eating not much more than energy bars, anything hot and filling was a feast.

A familiar thrumming behind Luis made him twist to scan the sky. A conga line of a half-dozen helicopters threaded westward over the mountains south of the camp. He figured they were headed for the distant rumble to the southwest. Someone was fighting someone down there, and had been long enough to get artillery involved.

"Blackhawks?" Nora's voice asked.

She stood across the table from him, more-or-less clean—they'd both been dust-gray from top to bottom when they stumbled out of the desert a few hours ago, and he still was—eyes bloodshot, hair damp, wearing a wrinkled black button-down blouse and fresh blue jeans. Her hands linked under Hope's butt, forming a sling.

"Yeah. How you guys doing?"

Nora plopped Hope on the nearest plastic chair, unloaded her own pack and perched carefully. "They cleaned and repacked my wound and gave me a tetanus booster. They say I'll live. They also said you did a good job, by the way. Miss Cupcake here"—she ruffled Hope's hair; Hope scowled—"has a bad sprain, but only a sprain."

"What's that?" Hope pointed to Luis' food. A pink tee shirt and blue sweatpants had replaced her cross-country clothes.

"It's called *chilaquiles*."

"What's that?"

"Breakfast. Want to try some?"

"Is there pork in that?" Nora asked.

"Nope. Chicken."

"Okay," Hope said. Luis cut a little-girl mouthful and held out his fork. Hope chewed for a while, swallowed, and smiled. "That's good."

"I'll bet if you ask your mom, she'll get some for you."

Nora frowned at them both. "No, thanks. I got MREs from the Red Cross people. I'll stick with those."

"Chicken. Save those for the trip. Between the meds and the power bars, your gut's gonna be screwed up for a week anyway. Get something hot in you." Luis gathered a big-girl mouthful and held it out to Nora on his fork. "Here, try it. Don't look like a wimp in front of your daughter."

Nora scrunched her face at him but took the food. "Hm. Where'd you get that?"

"In there." He pointed to the roadhouse. "Let me finish and I'll get you something."

"Well… okay." Nora watched while he ate and gave Hope another bite. "What do we do now?"

Luis had already worked up his to-do list. It felt good to be able to plan ahead again, not just react. "I'll call Ray once I get cleaned up. He may be able to send someone out to get us, but if there's fighting, maybe not. We may end up on the bus to San Luis or Mexicali. The next one comes through at 10:40-ish."

"Are the buses still running with all the fighting?"

"Looks that way. One came by eastbound while you were getting cleaned up. Anyway, I'll see if he's heard from Beto or Paul. If he hasn't, I'll ask him to send some guys out to look."

Nora propped her elbows on the table and put her face in her palms. Luis could hear her breathing deeply. After a moment she looked up, her eyes even more tired and sad than before. "Okay. Are we safe here?"

He shrugged. "Safe enough. Nobody messes with the CRM. Everybody—"

"The what?"

"*Cruz Roja Mexicana.* Everybody needs them too much. It's like they don't mess with the banks or breweries or distilleries. If someone does, everyone tracks them down and makes them suffer. Thing is, we can't stay here forever. We still need to get you guys to England, right?"

She nodded. After a few moments, she reached out and took the hand he rested on the table. "Thank you."

Holding her hand felt weird. Not bad, just strange. "For what?"

"For keeping your promise."

"Why wouldn't I?"

Nora gave him a tired but genuine smile. "It's rare."

Luis stood in the shadow of the tiny boxlike chapel just to the west of the roadhouse, showered, re-patched, in his other set of clothes. Even though the normals stayed away from him, he didn't need eavesdroppers, and he didn't want Nora to hear if he had to unload on Ray.

Three rings, then Ray's voice. "*Si?*"

"It's me."

A moment passed. "God damn, *hermano*, you finally call. You know the FBI's after you?"

"I told you that."

"No, I mean *seriously* after you. It's on the news. There's a reward."

What? McGinley was supposed to get them off his back. "A

reward? How much?"

"Five million. Careful, or I'll turn you in myself."

What made him worth five million bucks? If it was Nora, then the FBI was even more desperate to get her back than either of them imagined. "If you do, split the reward with Bel. Hey, why I called. We're over the border, off CF 2. Can somebody pick us up?"

"Been there long?"

"A few hours. Can someone get us? We're not in great shape."

"You've got the *bruja*, right? And the other kid?"

"Answer the fucking question."

Ray sighed. "Look, it's tough getting through San Luis right now, you know? Truth is, the Zetas have it, since Saturday. We've got a full-up battle going on a few miles south of there. If you can get through San Luis, I can have someone waiting for you on the other side. Better yet, make it Mexicali."

Luis kicked at the gravel as he tried to decipher what he heard in Ray's voice. He sounded distracted, but also a shade pissed off. "Sorry to ruin your morning, *compa*."

"No, no, it's not that. I just moved down here last night. It hasn't been a great morning." By *down here*, Luis assumed he meant Baja. "The Zetas are kicking our ass and the FBI just raided a bunch of our safe houses. There's a million things that need doing and I'm way behind. Help me out here, okay?"

You wanted this, Luis didn't say. Then he rewound a sentence. "Wait a minute. They raided the safe houses? Were they after Nora?"

"Fuck if I know. That's like eleven on my top-ten list, you know? Just get on the road."

"Fine. I'll call you when we land somewhere. You hear from Beto? I can't reach him."

"Beto? Yeah. He's in Mexicali with the *bruja's* husband and the boy. He couldn't get through to your number. They're fine."

Couldn't get through? Since Sunday morning? No voicemail? And Nora had been trying to call Paul's burner, also with no success.

Something crawled up Luis' neck. It wasn't a bug.

McGinley was on his way back to the JTF building from Camp Pendleton's Navy Exchange when his phone rang through on his car's comm console. "McGinley."

"Can you talk?"

He damn near drove the car into the ditch by the road. McGinley had been waiting for this call but didn't really expect it anymore. "Ojeda, you dumb sumbitch, we had a deal!"

"And the FBI has a reward out on me, so I guess you broke it."

The man had a point. McGinley pulled into the nearest parking lot he could find so he didn't drive into a tank or some such. "You listen. I talked to them, and they said they'd back off. Someone on their end put that reward out on you. I knew nothing about it 'til this morning. I reckon you're on the other side now?"

"Yeah, we are. Guess you saw the drone footage."

"I did. Slick move, burning the brush like that." And in a way it impressed him, at least a little. Ojeda dreamed up a plan and made it work when most folks would be crapping their shorts. "Where are you? We still have an agreement, *amigo*. I can come get your new girlfriend in a few hours. Take her off your hands for you."

"Making deals with you guys hasn't gone so well. Question: who has Tavo?"

That didn't make a lot of sense, and McGinley had to stop to think on it for a few seconds. "The Zetas do. One of my snitches sold me some bullshit about a double, but—"

"Are you sure?" Ojeda's voice sounded like he had a burr under his saddle. "The FBI suddenly knows a lot about the Nortes. They just knocked over the Cartel's safe houses. Haven't touched them for years far as I know, now they go after a bunch of them. Did they raid Zeta safe houses too? Also, they found out about me and Nora a few days *after* Tavo got snatched. Hardly anybody knew about that—Ray, me, and Tavo. Does the Bureau have him? If they don't, how are they getting this intel?"

McGinley leaned back into his seat, letting this roam through his mind while he watched the drilling rigs in the lake-flat Pacific a couple miles offshore. The picture of the dead runners from Barstow. The Feebs stiff-arming him about Casillas. The sudden discovery of a "terrorist" right in their own HQ. True, the Feebs were plugged into the NSA and their own ungodly mess of surveillance and wiretaps and what all. But the timing… the *timing* was a skosh too convenient.

"What do you want from me, Ojeda?"

Something big and diesel rumbled through Ojeda's end of the line. He was outside by a road, not that knowing that meant a damn thing. "Get answers to my questions. You want to know what they're up to; I know you do. Make us both happy. I'll call back in a few hours. They're pushing me into a corner, McGinley. Me and Nora can just disappear."

That slick bastard. The hell of it was, he was right. McGinley wanted to know what kind of game the Feebs were playing. He and Ojeda maybe had more in common than he'd thought.

60

SafeTrax offers a full line of implantable GPS tracking chips that are completely safe for use in humans. Imagine the peace of mind knowing that by using a simple, easy-to-use app on your slate or phone, you can at any moment locate your young children or an elderly loved one to within five feet anyplace on Earth.

-- "About Our Products," SafeTrax.com

MONDAY, 17 MAY

Bel strapped on the Taser and a fresh pair of latex gloves to prepare for her first round in the Pit this shift. The tracker lozenge the FBI planted between her shoulder blades itched like crazy. She finally understood why so many chipped kids showed up with their backs all torn up—it was all she could do to keep from rubbing on a doorjamb like a bear against a tree. Beyond the constant irritation, it was humiliating to be on an electronic leash like an animal or a child. All her FBI watchers would let her do was pretend that today was a normal day.

Only half her brain focused on Out There; the other half worried about Lucho. She'd checked her burner phone as soon as she got to work and found a new text: "Ok in mexico." Ever since, she'd fought the urge to call the number that sent the message. He might not be using it anymore and the FBI was sure to be listening to hers. She kept the burner on. There was no way they'd be able to find it in the hundreds of cell phones in the hospital—or at least she hoped they couldn't—and she didn't want to miss a call from Lucho if he managed one.

The Pit was the usual disgusting, chaotic cesspool. She'd ferried three casualties into the ED for treatment before she was even a third of the way around the waiting area. She paused at the double doors after ushering the third patient through, surveying the mob with a heavier-than-usual load of hopelessness. Would this ever get better? Would anyone ever fix this train wreck? The only answer she could believe made her want to kick a wall in.

Flashing and movement drew her focus to the small databoard attached to the square pillar in the room's center. Fox News had some kind of bulletin going on, not that that was anything unusual. The whirling shapes resolved into two red stripes, the one across the top of the screen blaring "TERROR ALERT." She never made it to the bottom of the screen to see what the other one said.

In between them was a close-up of Lucho's face.

"What are you going to do?"

Bel had asked herself that once every five seconds, in between thinking *oh, God* and trying to convince herself it was all a big mistake, which didn't work. Now she watched Ros check the stalls in the women's staff restroom to see if they were alone. "I don't know."

Ros had towed her away from the ED doors and to the bathroom before a doctor found her channeling her inner deer-in-the-headlights. Bel had started out standing, but soon slid down the tile wall by the sinks until her butt hit the floor.

Ros squatted in front of her and slapped a palm down on each of Bel's kneecaps at Bel's chin level. "Want anything? Some tranqs, maybe?"

"No. Thanks, though." Bel couldn't turn off her brain even though the idea sounded great. She had to think.

"It's not true, right?"

"God, no! Lucho's not a terrorist. It's... oh, I don't know. Complicated."

"I'll bet." Ros sat back on her heels. "Where is he? Have you talked to him?"

"Not yet. He's out of town." He'd never felt so far away, and she'd never felt so alone. How much could she trust Ros? They were friendly, but not in a sharing-deepest-secrets way. Ros had her own agenda.

"He's not having an affair, is he? With that Arab—"

"No! It's not an affair, just business." She failed again to get down a deep breath. "Look, Ros, thanks for getting me out of there, but you shouldn't—"

"Get involved?" Ros crossed her arms and snorted. "I owe you, remember? Besides, they probably already think I'm a terrorist. I'm sick of this 'terrorist' shit. Half the country's a terrorist. Listen, *qin*, us old-timers have to stick together. The kids don't remember how things used to be. We need to show them."

She had a point. Ros' union work had probably earned her a file with some spooky agency somewhere. "I guess they think we're both troublemakers now."

"No shit. Do you have somewhere to go?" Ros' voice softened.

"You mean, not home?" She could go home. She could go anywhere. She wouldn't get far—the FBI could follow the tracker chip and haul her away any time they wanted. "There's nowhere I can go," she finally said. "I won't go to your place, though. That's like telling the cops to arrest you, too."

"How will they know?"

"Because..." Bel hadn't wanted to admit this to anyone, but Ros deserved to know if she was going to get involved. "They put a tracker on me."

"They chipped you?" When Bel nodded, Ros shook her head and made a disgusted noise. "Those bastards. Stand up, let me see."

Bel climbed to her feet, turning to face the wall. Ros hiked up the hem of Bel's scrub top and tugged down her athletic bra's backband. Bel felt a cool fingertip gently probe the raw lump.

Ros let her go. "Okay, wait here. I need to go score some supplies."

"What for?" Bel pulled down and smoothed her top.

"To get that thing out of you. I'll just be a sec."

"Ros, no!" Bel grabbed Ros' arm. "The FBI did this. You'll–"

"Fuck the FBI. You. Saved. My. Life. Last week, remember? So let me do this. You're gonna try to get away, right?"

Bel would be on the run sometime soon. It was an instinct, like breathing. She nodded.

Ros pulled her arm free. "Then that tracker's gotta go. You can carry it if you want, but at least you'll be able to dump it when you have to." She took Bel's face in both her hands. "I need to fight back too, *qin*. For Zach. Now stay put and come up with a plan. I'll be back in a few."

"Okay." Bel needed a plan. She hoped she'd have enough time to make one. And she prayed she'd have the courage to use it when she had to—which could be very soon.

61

MONDAY, 17 MAY

The Chinese Golden Dragon bus was less than ten years old, but its suspension felt twice that. Every pothole and ridge shot straight into Nora's tortured rear. Luckily, the highway had been maintained better than the ones up north, so they hit fewer shocks than they would in the supposed "developed world."

Nora and Luis filled two seats near the back of the bus on the left. Hope sat on Nora's lap, fascinated by a landscape unlike any she'd ever seen, watching out the window as the tan hardpan and sun-broiled balls of shrubs blurred by. The rusted strip of border fence underlined the rugged tan-gray mountains visible through the windows on the other side. They'd pass a roadside shrine from time to time, its white cement and faded plastic flowers marking someone's end. Nora answered the "Mommy, what's that?" questions without knowing much more than Hope did. Luis slumped asleep to her right, his chin doubled under his drooping head.

They'd sold their body armor and UMPs to a man who sat in the roadhouse's corner booth. He'd tried to trade for marijuana, then zip, but Luis managed to get money out of him after a lot of haggling in Spanish. It seemed crazy to give up that gear, but Luis explained it would only hurt them. "They sometimes stop the buses at roadblocks." The idea that still twirled Nora's stomach. "If we have this stuff, whoever finds it will kill us right there."

He'd also made her put on the black wig, some makeup, an apple-green, sleeveless button-down top and dark jeans. "Aren't we done with that?" she'd pleaded. "They don't get Fox down here."

"Actually, they do. I don't know how far the net's stretched. Where we're going, we could walk across the border in about ten minutes. So can they. Let's play it safe."

Two convoys of Humvees and armored fighting vehicles had raced past them going west in the half-hour since they'd boarded the bus. She couldn't tell who they belonged to and it hardly mattered. They also passed through a cluster of burned-out semis, military trucks and RVs straddling the road. Now she didn't resent the costume so much.

The land gradually became slightly less sterile. Power lines appeared, and soon they trundled down a recently repaved four-lane highway. Buildings appeared—a gas station, a junkyard, some kind of construction yard. Then the bus slowed. She peered over the seats in front of her to see a pair of dark Humvees parked in a vee across the westbound lanes. Off to the right, a white banner covered with Spanish draped a fence. She wondered if the big red "Z" at the bottom meant what she hoped it didn't.

Nora fell back against her seat, her heart turning over faster than the bus's engine. A roadblock. She'd read the stories about drug gangs stopping buses and slaughtering all the passengers, leaving the bodies roadside or dumping them in some city street.

She elbowed Luis. His head popped up, eyes blinking. He checked the view out each side. "Yeah?"

"There's a roadblock. We're stopping."

He peeked down the center aisle, then leaned in close to her. "Zetas," he whispered. "This is their turf now."

"Mommy, are we there yet?"

Nora gave Hope a squeeze, more for her own comfort than her daughter's. All those pictures of innocent dead Mexicans came back to haunt her. "What do we do?"

"Chill. They might not even come on the bus. If they do, they'll probably be looking for mules or anyone who might be an enemy."

"Like us?"

He chewed his lower lip for a few seconds, thinking. "I doubt it. I'm too old, and you have Hope."

The bus stopped, pulled forward a few feet, stopped again. The air brakes hissed. Nora reached under her shirttail to finger the butt of her Glock nestled in the small of her back. If these people wanted her, they'd have to fight her.

"Why did we stop?" Hope asked.

Nora brushed Hope's hair off her face. "Because some men outside are looking for something." *Us? Do they know about us?*

The door opened. A man in gray tiger-stripe utility pants, body armor and a black hood trudged up the stairs, an AK-105 slung across his chest. He stopped to talk to the driver.

Nora glanced to Luis. He still slumped in his seat, but his face had gone quiet and watchful, and his eyes were locked forward.

The hooded man edged down the aisle. His right hand curled around his carbine's pistol grip; his left carried a slate. He'd stop, look at a passenger, hold up the slate, then move on.

Luis leaned against her and wrapped his arm around her waist. She was about to push him away when he whispered, "Your name is Mirabel. You're my wife. I married you in *El Norte* and took you to Nogales. You're deaf; you lip-read only English. We're going to El Centro to visit your parents. We're on the bus so we don't have to drive across Arizona. Got all that?"

A legend in thirty seconds? "What about Hope?"

"Her name's Esperanza. She's our daughter."

The hooded man had made it halfway down the aisle. His head swept left and right, pausing here and there to check his slate. He argued with a young man, dragged him out of his seat and pushed him toward the door.

"Undo your top couple buttons."

"Are you crazy? What—"

Luis clamped a hand across her mouth. "If he's got your picture, we need to give him something else to look at. Do it."

Nora glanced up—the gunman was only a couple rows away now—swallowed her principles, and loosened the top two buttons on her shirt. The resulting wedge of skin wouldn't be much of a distraction. She clamped her teeth hard, undid the next one, and spread the open collar to show off her cleavage. There: if that didn't do it, the guy was gay.

Hope squirmed in Nora's lap, frowned at her as she exposed herself. "Mommy—"

Nora pressed her fingers against her daughter's lips. "Hush. Don't say anything. Do whatever I tell you, agree with whatever I say, even if you don't understand. Okay?" Hope scowled but nodded. Nora kissed her. "Good girl."

The gunman stopped next to their row. He looked to his left at the two young women in the seats across the aisle. Luis stole a peep at the man's slate, then cozied up to Nora and nuzzled her ear. "Your photo's on the slate."

The lightning bolt she'd felt hovering over her head struck. *They want me. They want to kill me.* Her hand burrowed behind her back to get to her weapon, but she managed to stop it just in time. That was the fastest way to end up as part of a mass execution.

The gunman turned. His focus fixed on her face, slid down to her chest, then slowly worked its way back up. He held up his slate so he could see both it and her face at the same time. Then he asked her a question in Spanish.

I'm deaf. What do I do? After a moment, she cocked her head, then looked to Luis. He turned to face her and said slowly in English, "What is your name?"

The guy spent too much time looking at his slate. She remembered the deaf girl she'd known in college and pretended her mouth was full of peanut butter. "Mirabel," she told the gunman.

Luis explained something to the man in Spanish while Nora looked on with genuine ignorance. She picked up the word "*esposa*"—wife—and place names. The gunman examined her cleavage while he listened, forcing her to turn her head away. They couldn't afford to have this scum see the hate and fear she felt crawling into her eyes.

The tone of their words changed. The gunman became demanding, Luis defensive. Then a rough hand yanked her head around. She slapped it away without thinking, only to find herself face-to-face with a now-angry Zeta. Her anger fed on his. She'd blow his head off if he touched her again.

No. That's Nora the Terrorist talking. Give him fear. You have to play the part.

She flooded her mind with every sad image she could scrape up—Paul and Peter hurt, Hope abused and frightened, her parents disgraced, that moment of hopelessness in the desert—and felt her eyes fill. She let her chin go floppy, clutched shut her shirt's open throat. Then she let loose a strangled sob and pushed her face into Luis' chest. He wrapped both arms around her and Hope and rocked them, stroking her back, strong but not hard. It was more comfortable than it ought to be. He grumbled something at the gunman that sounded like the Spanish version of "Look what you've done."

Nora had a fuzzy view of the man's chest out of the corner of her eye. He stood there, his hands moving aimlessly, until he threw them up in frustration and stomped down the aisle toward the back of the bus. He returned a minute later, but only for a few seconds before he turned to march up the aisle toward the exit.

The engine rumbled and the bus rolled past the roadblock.

Once she stuffed her fear into a lockable closet, Nora pulled away from Luis, flashing him a self-conscious smile. She dabbed at her eyes with the bunched curtain next to her before she closed up her blouse.

"Mommy, are you okay?"

"I'm fine," Nora whispered. "I was just pretending to make that bad man go away."

"You pretend good. I thought it was for real."

The city grew up around them—palm trees in the median, tilt-up concrete buildings in the industrial park, the Bimbo bread distributorship (*really? Bimbo?*), used-car lots, junkyards, all of it with the border fence as a rusty backdrop. Nora noticed other, less homely things: lots of late-model SUVs, big pickups, Humvees, and military trucks parked at major intersections; the occasional knot of soldiers or masked gunmen around a building; the burned-out shells of businesses and homes.

She peeked at Luis now and then. He'd saved them once again, been brave again. She was so lucky the Cartel chose him for this. She avoided his eyes, though, fearing she'd crossed some kind of line by throwing herself on him the way she had. It wasn't until they passed a scorched *Policía Federal* station that Luis whispered, "You played that great back there."

Nora risked a look. He gave her an encouraging smile. "I didn't go too far?"

"It was perfect." He patted her hand. "Remember that. We may need it again."

Twenty minutes later, the bus groaned into the back lot of San Luis Rio Colorado's central bus station, a stained white building with a peaked roof. Nora noted the uniformed cops using their batons to shove back a jostling crowd along the station's wall. "What are the police like here?"

Luis had already stood in the aisle and had to duck to peek out her window. "If they're still here, they work for the Zetas. Assume any uniform you see is crooked."

The crowd's shouting sounded ugly and desperate. The other passengers avoided looking at these people and their scraps of luggage, pretending not to hear. Nora stuck close to Luis as he retrieved their backpacks from the baggage hold under the bus. "What's happening?" she asked when they edged into the middle of the lot.

Luis, his back to the crowd, cocked his head and focused on the noise. "They're afraid they won't get on the bus. It sounds like they think the company sold too many tickets."

"Would they do that?"

"Yeah. Come on—we're going around front."

A mob ten or twelve deep boiled around the bus station's white-and-green façade, spilling into the street. Men and women and children of all ages shoved and battered each other with suitcases and bags to get a few feet closer to the entrance. A hooded gunman by the doors ripped out a burst into the air from his AK, sending the nearest people screaming backwards into others who had no interest in moving away. Nora didn't need convincing when Luis towed her around the corner to a bus-stop bench. "Stay here. Have your weapon handy."

Nora perched in the canopy's tiny patch of shade, one arm around Hope, her other hand clutching her Glock behind her. Hope stared at everything with huge eyes—the soldiers crowding the restaurant on the next corner, the sandbags piled in front of the police station across the street, the Mexican flags, the white banner hanging from an electrical cable crossing the street, twitching as cars drove underneath.

She'd seen this scene before, in Somalia. One army leaves, another arrives, and the normal people try to get out of the way. She never thought she'd be one of them.

Luis fought his way out of the scrum and grabbed Nora's arm. "Let's go."

"What about Mexicali?"

"We're not getting there on a bus. It's gonna get ugly in a few minutes. We need to go."

He led Nora and Hope across Calle 5 and north toward Francisco Madero, a big commercial street running through San Luis' downtown. The sounds of more shooting and screaming followed them, but Luis refused to look back. More Zetas had just arrived at the station, and he had no interest in finding out whether they had his picture, too.

"Why didn't we just book straight through to Mexicali?" Nora asked after they'd limped a block. "Why'd we get off the bus?"

"Because it wasn't one of our options. If Hope wasn't so damn cute, the driver might not have sold me tickets to get here."

"So now what?"

They reached the intersection with Francisco Madero. The gunfire back at the bus station sounded like firecrackers at a Fourth of July parade. Luis parked Nora under the overhanging roof of a party-dress store—creampuff dresses in sherbet colors—then stepped into the street to snag one of the white taxicabs cruising for fares. They used to line up at the bus station, but not today.

After the third taxi slowed, then sped past, Nora called out, "You're trying to catch a cab?"

"Yeah."

"Why don't we rent a car?"

"You saw how it was back there, right? You think there are any rental cars left here?" A fourth taxi raced past. Then he understood: the drivers didn't want to pick up a man traveling alone. He might jack the cab, or the Zetas might pull them over and kill them both. He motioned to Nora. "Come out here."

She raised an eyebrow but hobbled to him. "Is this where I pole dance so they'll stop?"

"Not yet. Just make sure they can see Hope."

The fifth taxi, a four-door Nissan hybrid, stopped within seconds. Luis leaned down to the driver's window. "How much to get to Mexicali?" he asked in Spanish.

The driver, a roundish middle-aged guy in a green-and-white-striped Santos Laguna tee shirt, gave Luis a classic double-take. "*¿Estás loco, señor?* You see what's happening here?"

Luis edged in closer, his shoulders filling the window. "Yeah. That's why me and the wife need to get out."

The driver's face lost some of its color. "I can't. They're stopping cars going out."

"Yeah, and I'll bet you know how to get around that, too." The driver looked away, chewed on a lip. "A hundred bucks American, cash, and a tank of gas at the other end."

That got the driver's attention. He checked his mirrors, looking around for anyone who might be watching. "You got it? Now?"

Luis peeled five twenties from the much-shrunken roll in his pocket, folded them in his hand, then showed the driver the bills in his palm. The driver reached for the money, but Luis slammed his fist shut. "When we get there, *compa*. After you take us out of here so we don't have Zetas hassling us. *¿Comprendes?*"

The driver peeked past Luis at Nora and Hope. Luis hoped Nora was using her most pathetic look on the man. Finally, he said, "Okay. Get in, now."

Nora didn't say a word until they were twenty minutes into their ride, heading southwest toward the farm roads leading to Baja. She whispered, "Once we leave here, are we safe?"

Luis considered that for a moment. "You're safe when you land in London. I don't know what's going on in Mexicali. This was Norte turf two years ago. Now look at it."

She nodded, her face grim. "Paul and Peter are there?"

"That's what Ray said."

"How do we find them?"

He had to think about that one, too. "I'll call Ray once we're there." He hoped Ray would finally give him a straight answer. "We'll get them back. I promise."

62

"Goddamnit! You shoot these terrorists, or I'll shoot you!"
-- Off-duty Oakland PD sergeant to a squad of riot police
responding to a longshoremen's strike at the Port of
Oakland; video shown on YouTube.com

MONDAY, 17 MAY

The loudspeaker scratched out, "Code Orange, Code Orange. All available ED staff to Reception. Code Orange."

Bel had just left an exam cube—the day's fourteenth case of listeriosis—and stood in the middle of the aisle, processing this order. Nurses and doctors popped their heads out of green curtains. Confused looks, then shock. Bel joined a stampede of nurses through the double doors leading to the Pit. A mass-casualty incident had just hit the ED.

Outside, Bel found half a dozen dirty, bloody men in blue overalls lying on the floor at the Reception booths or helping each other through the outside doors. The tear-gas fumes rolling off them stung Bel's eyes half-closed. She dived toward the nearest prone man—gunshot wound, lower abdomen—and demanded, "What happened? What is this?"

"Strike," he grunted, his eyes screwed closed against the pain. "God *damn!* At the plant. We walked out. Set up a line. They got cops or something." He stifled a scream. "It hurt bad, nurse, please, it hurt bad…"

Bel swept the area for staff. No doctors around yet, of course. As head nurse for the department, she had to get things moving. She pointed to Sindee, the nearest nurse. "You're Staging Manager. Get gurneys, as many as you can. Set up stations in the back hall. We'll have to treat them there." She pointed again. "Dakota! Triage, now!" She stood, slapped her hand against the nearest Reception window, startling the clerk. "Code Orange the whole hospital, stat!"

Training, instinct, and anger took over. She was back at Bagram, helping the night duty nurse, suddenly facing half-a-dozen DUSTOFFs hauling in casualties from a patrol gone bad. She got Dortmund with the Taser to herd the regular waiting patients either outside or into the back of the Pit. A young doctor appeared at the ED doors; she pinned him with a pointed finger. "You! Ops Section Chief! Get treatment organized. Go!" He went.

Sirens outside. It hadn't registered until now that she hadn't heard a single ambulance arrive. The plant and the cops hadn't called for transport, as usual. The approaching sirens weren't the whoop of ambulances or the honking of fire engines; they were police cars. More wounded? Or more trouble?

Doctors and nurses poured into the Pit from the hospital entrance. Three guards—fucking worthless rent-a-cops—huddled in one corner, waiting for someone to tell them what to do; Bel got them cleaning up the jumble of abandoned cars blocking the dropoff lane. The team fell into the rhythm it had learned in all those training exercises, leaving Bel to direct traffic and untangle problems. She checked her watch; twelve minutes since the first Code Orange and no sign of Benbow, the department head who was supposed to be Incident Commander. Probably with Admin, figuring out how to get someone to pay for all this. *Fuck him.*

Three dead so far, twenty-eight admits, ten critical, more coming in. Burns from microwave cannon, burst eardrums from sound guns, tear-gas burns, blunt-force trauma, one poor kid maybe sixteen with his legs crushed. The gunshot wounds she'd seen on the criticals told her the cops had shot to kill, not wound. The cries and screams and moans filled the Pit past bursting. Every new casualty raised the heat on Bel's rage. They did this kind of shit in Russia, Saudi Arabia, Ethiopia. This was America, or was supposed to be. Used to be.

A cop filled the doors leading outside. Midnight-blue utilities, black tac gear, white helmet with a shiny black face shield, studded gloves, four-foot baton. No badge, no name tape. Of course; off-duty. The plant had hired them.

He grabbed the nearest worker—a Latino man with a bloody bandage around his arm—and flung the man to the floor. When the worker tried to push himself up, the cop smashed the baton across the back of the man's head.

"Noooo!"

Bel launched herself at the cop, staggering him back against the doorframe before he clipped her with his baton's handle and sent her spinning into the nearest line of chairs. Fuzz exploded in her eyes; she tasted blood. She struggled up on one elbow in time to watch the cop smash another worker against the wall and beat him into a pile on the floor.

A pair of meaty arms cradled Bel. Dortmund. "Bel, you okay? How many fingers?"

She spat out a mouthful of blood, counted the six fingers she saw wavering in front of her and divided by two. "Three. Gimme your Taser."

"No, Bel, don't—"

"Give it to me!" She struggled out of his arms, stood on rubber-band legs, shook her head clear. *God, that hurt.* Dortmund frowned his disapproval, then slapped the Taser into her outstretched hand.

Don't think. Do. A wiry old guy spun away from the cop's baton and crashed into her. She held him up—just barely—and waited for the cop to come after them. Just as he raised his baton, she swept up the Taser and shot him in the leg. He dropped like a set of car keys.

The buzzing, yelling, groaning crowd fell silent for a moment. Bel stood, wobbling, still aiming the Taser. The old guy staggered away from her. Then a female voice behind her whooped, "*Maha! Bring it!*" and the lull broke under a new wave of noise.

A pair of guards stood in the corridor leading to the hospital's main lobby, their eyes wide. Bel popped the cartridge from the Taser, then pointed to the guards. "You two. Get him out of here and keep the rest of them out. This is a hospital, not a cage match."

That might not last long. Through the glass doors she saw a trio of cop-thugs pounce on a couple of workers from the plant, batons swinging up and down until both men lay still on the ground. Other cop-thugs swarmed the parking lot, going after anyone in a jumpsuit, smashing car windows. She stumbled through the doors into the outside heat to watch, horrified, then turned and lost what little breakfast was left in her stomach.

She straightened to wipe her mouth on the front of her scrub top. A thin, bedraggled guy stood a couple feet away, aiming his old-style phone at the carnage. "Please tell me you're recording this," she said.

"Oh, yeah."

"Please tell me you're going to post this."

"You bet. You okay, lady?"

She couldn't focus and her stomach had turned itself inside out. "I'm better now."

Bel returned to the Pit. She waved off Dortmund before he could fuss over her and began to help Dakota with the triage. They ran out of gurneys; orderlies used backboards to move the non-ambulatories into the treatment area. She focused so hard on the job that she brushed off the tugging on her sleeve until someone slugged her shoulder. "What?" she barked.

It was Ros, goggles on her scrub cap, mask pulled down. "They're here. The FBI."

Bel stood, peeked through the windows. Three big, black SUVs blocked the dropoff lane. Men in FBI windbreakers pooled on the sidewalk, listening to an agent who pointed and yelled words she couldn't hear. She surveyed the shambles around her. "I can't leave, not with—"

"You have to. Let's go." Ros grabbed a fistful of Bel's sleeve and dragged her through the ED's double doors. "Where's the tracker?"

"In my pocket."

"Lose it, and your badge."

Bel dropped the little paper-towel-wrapped bundle into a half-full trash bin in the treatment area, then followed it with her ID and its embedded tracker. Rocketing, colliding priorities filled her brain. She and Ros rushed through the bustling doctors and nurses toward the back door. Gurneys and stretchers lined the corridor beyond, tended by more nurses and doctors and techs and orderlies, the moans and pleas bouncing off the linoleum and the metal doors to make the sound of a suffering army.

Bel and Ros got partway down a corridor leading to the back of the hospital when Bel pulled up. "Wait. I have to go to the locker room. I need my stuff."

"There's no time."

"I have to pee, too."

They trotted through the halls—running would draw too much attention—passing the usual foot traffic as well as other people rushing because of the Code Orange. They fit right in. In the locker room, Bel quickly emptied out, grabbed her purse, gym bag, and spare clothes, thought a moment, then took the lock, too. She'd never be able to come back, and who could tell if she'd need a lock someplace? Ros stood by the door, staring at her watch, barking "Hurry up!" every minute or so.

They breezed into the short hallway leading to the double sliding doors that opened into the parking garage. A security guard stepped out from behind his counter, held up his slate. "Excuse me ladies. We have a security alert. You have to scan out."

Had the FBI turned out building security to look for her? Bel nudged Ros away so they could pass on either side of the guard. Ros nodded, moved ahead, and pulled her staff ID out of her collar. Bel pretended to dig hers from her purse. The guard turned to catch Ros' scan. She fumbled it, opening the clip that held the card to its blue-and-white lanyard. Ros and the guard stooped at the same time to pick up the ID. Bel swooped around them and scurried out the doors.

"Wait! Miss, wait, you have to…"

Bel angled for the stairwell. Running feet slapped concrete behind her: Ros, closing fast. The guard dithered at the open doors, not sure whether to chase them or call for help.

Bel and Ros charged up the steel stairs, their footsteps clanging up the concrete shaft. Ros cut for a door covered with a gigantic blue "3". "Where are you going?" Bel demanded. "I'm on four."

"I'm on three." Ros grabbed Bel's arm. "Stop bitching."

They race-walked partway up the nearest ramp and stopped at a beat-up, burnt-orange Kia two-door hybrid with blacked-out windows. Ros tossed a set of keys at Bel. "Get out of here before they lock this place down."

"Your *car?* I can't—"

"Just shut up and take it. They'll be watching yours. It's old and there's no batteries left in it, so it's slow as hell, but it gets great mileage." Ros grabbed Bel's biceps. "You have to get away from these bastards. Consider yourself paid back."

Bel hugged Ros hard, wishing she'd spent more time getting to know this woman instead of shying away because she was always throwing herself in the way of danger. "Thank you, thank you, thank you," she murmured. "I'll let you know where I leave it." She pulled away, dragging her car keys from her purse and handing them to Ros. "Blue Chevy Breeze. Its batteries are dead, too."

Ros squatted next to the open driver's door as Bel cranked on the engine. "When you get a couple miles away, stop someplace with no cameras and take the plates off. There's another set underneath. The screwdriver's in the glove box."

"What? Fake license plates? Ros, what—"

"The union, remember? Think I want these people keeping track of where I go?" She stood, shoved the door closed, then swept her hand toward the aisle. "Stop fucking around. Get out of here."

The world started crashing in on Bel all at once. She was a fugitive and she'd involved this other person. This friend. "You be careful." She tried not to let her voice break. "Thanks."

Ros nodded. Her chin looked stiffer than normal, her lips flatter. "Don't get caught."

63

Monday, 17 May

"Lucho?"

"Bel? Where are you? Are you okay?"

"The FBI caught me on Sunday. I just got away. I don't think they know where I've gone yet. What's that noise? Are you in a car?"

"Yeah, on the way to Mexicali. Be there in an hour maybe. Are you okay?"

"No, I'm terrified! I'm going south. San Clemente's coming up in a few minutes. You still want me in Tijuana, right?"

"Yeah. I think we're done up north. I want you here with me, okay?"

"I want that too. Especially so I can choke the living shit out of you for getting us into this, you big… big…"

"Hey, hey. Don't cry, it'll—"

"I'm not crying! How do I do this?"

"When you get to San Ysidro, park at the border-crossing lot and walk in. It's easier to escape if you're not tied to a car. They may not have red-flagged you yet, but if they try to stop you, run like hell. They won't touch you on the other side. Take a taxi to the central bus terminal in La Mesa and stay there until I can get Ray to pick you up. Don't use your credit cards until you're over the border. Got all that?"

"Yeah. Yeah, I've got it."

"I love you. See you soon."

"I love you too, you stupid *mojado*."

◡

"Ray, it's me."

"*Hermano!* Where are you?"

325

"On the road. Look, Bel's on her way to TJ. Can you pick her up?"

"I can send guys—"

"No. You. She's not getting in a car with someone she doesn't know, not down here. She'll be at the La Mesa bus terminal in a couple hours. I need you to bring her to Mexicali."

"You don't want much, do you? Why Mexicali?"

"That's where Nora's husband and son are, right? I need you to get them hooked up. Beto's still dark. Come on, Ray, you owe me. My life up north's done because of all this. I need to get this wrapped up so me and Bel can figure out what to do next."

"It's not so easy for me to travel anymore. I'm *capo* now, remember? It's like a parade for me to go anywhere. All the security and shit, you know? This takes time."

"Then stop wasting it. Sorry I'm breaking your balls, but that's what's been happening to me over the past few days and I'm sharing the pain. Call me when you've got her."

"Shit. All right, let me work it. I may not make it to Mexicali until tomorrow. I'm not driving the roads at night. That's just stupid, you know?"

"Whatever. Me and Nora will hole up somewhere. Don't let me down, *compa*. This is my wife. Mother of my children, love of my life. Protect her."

"Right, right. Don't worry, *hermano*, I'll get her personally. I'll take good care of her."

64

McGinley might be a country boy, but he wasn't stupid. If he asked Jorgensen where he got his information, Poster Boy would shut him down like he always did. But that wasn't the only way to get answers.

An old buddy from FLETC who now worked south Texas said, "Naw, the Bureau hasn't gone near the Zeta houses we're sitting on. Haven't heard they're doing anything like that down here."

Casillas had been seeing Esquivel since the 5th, four days after Villalobos headed south. Esquivel made his run for the border yesterday. Did Casillas follow?

McGinley got into an FBI wiki—he had his ways—and checked their intel for Pacifico Norte. Wouldn't you know, the safe-house addresses for Southern California were right there, dated May 13th. Nine days after the Zetas (supposedly) snatched Villalobos.

The Feebs got their panties in a wad about Ojeda on the 14th. If they'd developed their intel from watching Khaled, Ojeda should've popped up over a week before.

In fact, intel on the Nortes had grown like kudzu over the past few days if the dates in the wiki were right, which they ought to be for what the Feebs paid for the damn thing.

He went through the wiki looking for that shot of the Barstow runners' heads on a Mexicali curb. He couldn't find it, but he turned up a passel of others just like it—fresh heads, red blood, no watermarks. They all came from unnamed confidential informants.

He leaned back in his chair, crossed his boots at the ankles and swirled what was left of his first post-lunch Dr. Pepper in its can. Maybe the Feebs had gotten smart all of a sudden, or maybe they'd done their homework after their girl ran off to the Nortes.

327

Or maybe they had a source in the Zetas. CIA's turf, but those two never played nice.

Or maybe they had a piece of grabbing Villalobos. Contracted it out to people who made it look like Zetas. Maybe they were sweating the man in a black site somewhere.

That attack on the El Cajon safe house Wednesday night? Ojeda was convinced it wasn't the Feebs, that it was a contract job put up by the Zetas. But why would the Zetas want a pain-in-the-ass like Khaled? Was it another false-flag op by the Bureau? If it was, why do it that way?

The only people who'd benefit from the Bureau going *jihad* on the Nortes were the Zetas, and those evil fuckers were nobody McGinley would wish on anyone, even these Left Coast pinheads. Unless…

Naw, that was stupid.

The Feebs were assholes, but they'd never hook up with the Zetas.

65

A growing number of Americans are turning to an unlikely source for their banking needs: civil war-wracked Mexico... Unlike American financial institutions, Mexican banks impose virtually no fees on account holders, pay interest on even small balances, and due to the influence of the drug cartels, are extremely unlikely ever to go bust or lose depositors' money...

-- "United States: Bank Run for the Border,"
Economist.com

MONDAY, 17 MAY

Luis crouched in the shadow of a cinder-block wall, sucking down a cold Coke he'd bought from a burrito truck at the nearby corner. Walking even a few hundred yards in this afternoon heat had burned up most of his remaining energy. Across the street, the fortress-like Public Security Secretariat for Baja loomed over its surrounding rock gardens and cactus, circled by troopers in full combat gear. If anyone traced his phone calls, he hoped they'd scratch their heads when they saw he was a few yards from the state's top cop shop. The Norte *narcomantas* he'd seen coming into the central city made him hope the cops still belonged to the right side.

He'd stashed Nora and Hope in the Crowne Plaza a couple blocks away. Nora's face went orgasmic when she sat on the crisp white linens covering the king-sized bed. No wonder; she'd been sleeping on floors for eight days. Luis gave her the obligatory "don't leave the room, keep your gun handy" speech and left when she announced she and Hope were going to take a long, hot bath. That was more information than he needed.

Now that they were more-or-less safe, he could use his whole brain to worry about Bel and, if there was any room left, figure out

329

what to do next. Nora's family was still cut in half; he had to bring it together again before he could call the job done.

He had plenty of time to obsess over that. Now was Bel's time. He checked his watch; she should be over the border and at the bus station by now. Luis slid the chip he'd used last time into his phone so she'd know who was calling, powered up, then selected her number from his call history. One ring, two, three, four. The default voicemail greeting, an electronic female voice saying to leave a message.

Luis banged the back of his head against the wall. Why didn't she answer? She should be there by now. If Ray did what he promised, she should be with him. *Please, God, don't let anything happen to her. I need her.*

Then his rational brain kicked in. Her phone's battery might be dead. No reception. It's on vibrate and she didn't feel it. Any number of reasons, none he should worry about. But it was way too much like Paul and Peter falling off the edge of the world when they crossed into Los Algodones, still out of touch after more than a day.

Half an hour and three more calls later, Luis' rational brain couldn't drown out the scary things screaming in his head. He swallowed the rock of fear in his throat, called Ray, and left a "call me" message.

Fifteen minutes later, his phone buzzed. "Hey, *hermano.* What's up?" Ray.

"Did you get Bel?"

"Sure did." Ray's voice was more cheerful than it'd been for the past three weeks. "A few minutes ago. She made it okay."

Dios mío, thank you, thank you… "How is she? She's not answering her phone."

"She's fine. Mad as a wet cat, you know? Say, you don't sound so great."

"I'm wiped out. I'm not tracking. Let me talk to her."

"When she comes back out. She made me stop so she can do some shopping. I guess she didn't have time to pack much. But I'll have her call you when she's done, okay?"

Shopping? Now? Luis felt the fiesta in his brain go still. This didn't make any sense. She would've called the moment she got the chance. "Where are you?"

"At a Walmart not too far from the bus station. Look, we can make it to Mexicali before dark. I'll meet you there, we can wrap this up. You have the *bruja*, right?"

"Uh, yeah." Luis could barely string words together, his mind was racing so fast. He knew that Walmart. They had great cell coverage. They had flash rechargers that shoppers could use free. This was wrong. "Um… tell Bel I love her and, uh, have her call me. Right away."

"Will do, *hermano*. See you soon."

But she didn't call. Luis paced the halls of Mexicali's central bus station for three hours, waiting for Bel or Ray to reach out. He would've liked to go back to his expensive hotel room, but the last thing he wanted to do was have a cell phone he'd used broadcasting its location nonstop in a room next to Nora's. He needed to lose himself among normal people doing normal things. The noise and bustle also helped distract him from thinking about how his wife had been swallowed by Tijuana, and how his best friend might have arranged the swallowing.

His rational brain finally started breaking through the worry-induced static. Even if Bel's phone was dead, Ray's wasn't, plus the senior Cartel guys carried secure satellite phones. Bel would've demanded to call Luis as soon as Ray showed up with a working phone, no matter how much she needed to go shopping.

Luis logged into their joint Mexican checking account—still open; the FBI would have to work pretty hard to grab it since the cartels owned the various banking regulators—but couldn't find a current debit for Walmart or any cash withdrawals since yesterday. Their American Visa account said "contact customer service," meaning it was already frozen. The Mexican one from their bank had no activity for today.

Unless Ray gave her money, Bel hadn't gone shopping. Would he do that? Maybe, but Luis doubted Bel would take it. She'd be pissed enough that she had to spend a couple hours in a car with Ray, far less let herself be in his debt in any way.

So what, then?

Something Ray said started echoing in his mind: "You have the *bruja*, right?" For someone who'd wanted to wash his hands of Nora, lately Ray had been awfully interested in Nora's status and in "helping" Luis with her. Ray claimed Nora's husband and son were safe and secure but had never quite managed to cough up a phone number for them. Then there were the leaks to the FBI. And the ten-million-dollar reward for Nora. And Ray hadn't seemed all that concerned about McGinley, had he?

Was Ray a snitch for the FBI? An eight-figure payday could turn almost anyone's head.

Luis sagged onto a bench and rubbed at the pounding in his temples.

What was waiting for him at the end of this road?

66

"It's me," Luis said into his phone. "You called."

"Hey, *hermano*, I'm in town." Ray didn't sound as cheerful as he had a few hours before. Had Bel been beating on him, or was something screwed up? "We should get together. Bel's anxious to see you."

But not enough to phone? "What happened? She didn't call."

"Yeah, sorry about that. The coverage is shit between TJ and here, you know? Come on out to the house. You remember where it is, out in San Pedro? I'll send a car."

Cell coverage wasn't that bad out there, and the sat phone worked everywhere. None of this passed the smell test. Luis stared out his hotel-room window at the lights of downtown Mexicali and tried to make a snap decision about whether to trust his oldest friend.

"I think I'd rather do this in public." He felt himself hollow out. "Nothing personal, I'm just jumpy down here. Meet me at the food court in Plaza Chachanilla in an hour."

Ray didn't answer for a few seconds. When he did, his voice was tight. "Is there a problem? You don't trust me anymore?"

"I don't trust anyone anymore. Come meet me at the mall, *compa*. And don't bring a bazillion guards. You'll scare all the shoppers away."

Ray's end of the line went silent; he'd muted. Luis paced the room, wondering who Ray was talking to. "Okay. For you I'll do this. We'll be there in an hour. Why don't you bring the *bruja*, too? We can get everyone hooked up at the same time."

"See you in an hour." Luis cut the connection before he could say the wrong thing—whatever that was.

What was that he'd heard in Ray's voice?

333

After eight on a Monday night wasn't a high-traffic time for the mall in general or the food court in particular. Shoppers dotted about a dozen tables under the food court's barrel-vaulted skylights, now black with night. The arches and ceiling coffers were bright with desert candy colors—hot golds and rusty reds and sunset pinks—and sometime in the past two years, someone had set a desert landscape in tile across the width of the floor.

Luis sat with his back to the trickling old-school hacienda fountain, nursing a *jamaica*. He should've bought something to coat his stomach, which was doing aerobatics, but doubted even that would help.

He kept his eyes moving, searching the crowd for a glimpse of Bel and Ray. At the same time, he made a note of every military-age man he saw, every set of camos, every Anglo, every dark suit and short haircut. Who would come with Ray? Nortes... or Feds?

A few shoppers stared past Luis, then quietly melted away. He glanced over his shoulder. A half-dozen *sicarios* marched toward him in a hexagonal group. Desert camo; Nortes. In the middle, two men: Ray, wearing expensive-looking slacks and an iridescent green shirt, and a smaller, skinnier guy in dark-blue *caballero* clothes and a black cowboy hat. No Bel.

The lead bodyguard approached Luis from behind, ordered "Stand up" in Spanish, then frisked him with a force and attitude Luis had last run across in a Newport Beach cop. Apparently satisfied, the gunman stepped back. Ray and the cowboy circled the table, Ray smiling, the cowboy's face closed and unreadable.

Ray stuck out his hand. "God damn, *hermano*. What happened to your hair?"

Luis didn't hide his reluctance to reach out and take Ray's hand. "Where's Bel?"

"She's here. Don't worry. We're just checking things out first."

Meaning Ray had her under guard someplace. Protection, or as a hostage? Luis fought to keep his rising anger and alarm under wraps. He nodded toward the cowboy. "Who's this guy?"

"This is Jorge Casillas. We talked about him, remember?"

Casillas didn't offer to shake hands, which was just as well since Luis probably wouldn't have anyway. They spent some time measuring each other with their eyes. "Why's he here?"

Ray tapped his palms on the back of the swiveling metal chair before him. "He's part of this now. Let's sit." He waited for the other two men to take their seats around the square table before he settled in.

Luis had rehearsed this while he waited. Ray would expect him to be his usual trusting self. It was time to change things up. He jabbed a thumb over his shoulder at the bodyguard, still just a couple feet behind him. "Lose the gorillas, Ray. This is our business, not theirs."

Ray narrowed his eyes. "I don't like how you're demanding things all of a sudden."

"I don't give a fuck what you 'like.' Lose the gorillas or I walk."

After a moment of thin-lipped glaring, Ray waved away his *sicarios*. They spread out in a loose circle around the table, the closest about twenty feet away, watching the rapidly thinning crowd.

Now Luis could pull back a little, keep things unbalanced. "Good. Where's Bel?"

"Like I said, she's close. We've got her."

"Who's 'we'?"

Ray leaned back, crossed his legs, smoothed down his slacks. "You have the *bruja?*"

"Yeah. Answer my question."

"She's here?"

"No. What happened to her husband and son? What happened to Beto?"

"Her people are… secure. Beto… well…" Ray turned his eyes down to the table.

"Jesus. You killed him. You killed Beto. You son-of-a-bitch."

"No, I didn't."

Luis swiveled to face Casillas. "You did it?" Casillas shrugged. "Ray, tell me something. Who's running the Cartel? You, or him?"

"It's complicated."

"Bullshit. One-word answer. You or Casillas?" But the answer was right there in Casillas' thin, empty smile. What it meant for all of them turned his insides as cold as his iced hibiscus tea. "Is he part of the 'we' who has Bel?"

Ray tried on a reassuring smile that didn't quite take. "Look. Things have changed. We… had to change along with them or we'd get run over, you know? We… we were losing the war. You know what the other takeovers were like. All the leadership dies. Their families, their maids, their… pets, hundreds of people, you know? And there was no point. They knew they were beat, but they had to do the whole macho thing and go down in flames."

Chingado. You sold us out. "So you're a hero."

Ray shook his head. He even looked apologetic, but Luis couldn't bring himself to forgive him. "No, not a hero. I just saw reality. Tavo was going to take us all down with him, *hermano*. He was going to get us all killed. I had to stop the craziness."

"So you shopped him to"—Luis hooked a thumb at Casillas— "*his* people."

"Yeah. It had to be done."

"Then they made you *capo*." Ray didn't answer. Just as well. "Congratulations, Ray. I hope you two'll be happy together. Now give me Bel and Nora's people, I'll get Nora on a plane, and that'll be done, and *I'll* be done. I'm out of this. I retire."

"It's not so easy, *Señor* Ojeda." Casillas spoke Spanish in a voice so low, Luis had to lean forward to hear it, which was probably the point. "We need the woman. Khaled."

Luis glanced toward Ray, who nodded. "Why?"

"It's not your concern. Bring her to us, then you and your wife can go."

"Or?"

Ray winced.

Casillas shrugged again. "Or we kill you and your wife, your son, your mother and father and brother and sister and anyone who belongs to them. We burn your home and your business. In the end we get the woman anyway, because she can't hide forever, and we know she can't move by herself here. Your choice." He cocked his head, touched his phone pod, then murmured something Luis couldn't catch.

Everything inside him went dead. Knowing this could happen was one thing; hearing Casillas recite the whole litany with a smile on his face—even a fake one—was terrifying. Luis took a couple deep breaths. "Nice people you hooked us up with, Ray."

"That's why we need to be their friends, you know?"

Talk about an offer he couldn't refuse. Luis leaned back, staring at Ray without seeing him. He couldn't force himself to look at that psychopath Casillas. Random thoughts crawled through the sludge in his brain. "What do you want her for?"

"It's none of your concern," Casillas repeated. Now he sounded irritated.

Ray raised a palm toward Casillas. "Jorge, let me tell him."

"It's not his business, Ramiro. He knows what he—"

"Please, let me. It'll make a difference." Casillas shrugged and sat back. Ray leaned toward Luis. "We're going to turn her over to the FBI."

Luis sat stunned for a few moments. "What for, the reward? Are you nuts?"

"No, not the reward. They were never going to pay it anyway. You see, the Bureau and the Zetas… have an… understanding."

Stunned again. Luis sat there with his mouth hanging open. He looked toward Casillas, who nodded, then back to Ray. "The FBI's in bed with"—he pointed—"*them*."

"That's harsh. They share some intel, give the Bureau access to prisoners. If someone from another cartel goes into Zeta territory from *El Norte*, they give him back to the Feds. The Zetas and the Bureau lay off each other up north. That kind of thing."

That was how the FBI found out about Luis. "Why would the FBI bend over for *them*?"

Ray spread his hands. "It's more than just the Bureau. It's higher than that."

"Higher? The government is hooked up with the Zetas?" After a while, Luis just couldn't be surprised anymore.

"I don't understand why this is difficult for you, *Señor* Ojeda," Casillas said. "*México Unido* is winning the war. When we merge with Pacifico Norte, we'll control almost three-quarters of our nation. The *Americano* leaders, they are realistic men. They understand *México Unido* will be the next government of México." He looked into Luis' face and smiled, showing some seriously unmaintained teeth. "That so-called government in the *Distrito Federal*, they're"—he made a dismissive *pfft* sound—"*socialistas.*

México Unido represents capitalism and Christianity—"

"While you cut off people's heads and burn buildings with women and children inside."

Casillas waved that away. "Tactics. In the old days, the *Americanos* were happy enough when soldiers *El Norte* equipped led by officers *El Norte* trained shot *Mexicanos* in the street because they made protests. Their leaders understand us, as we understand them. We can do business together."

The sad part was, this was the first thing Casillas said that didn't shock Luis. He could see those *idiotas* in Washington "doing business" with the Zetas. Their kind of guys. Then he thought of McGinley. "Not everybody's on board. ICE is still after you."

"That will change soon."

"So Nora's just something to keep *El Norte* sweet? That's all?"

"Oh, no," Casillas said. "She's very important, to us and to the *Americanos*. You see, we've been talking to their State Department for two years, maybe more. We have an agreement. Her escape created a problem, and an opportunity. So now, when we surrender her and her family to their *Federales*, the agreement will be completed."

"Meaning?"

"Meaning," Ray said, "the U.S. recognizes the Zetas as the legitimate government of Mexico."

Luis let his head fall back until he could stare at the floor mural's distorted reflection in the skylights above him. Of course they'd recognize the Zetas. Endless possibilities for all that drug money, all those weapons sales, the oil, maybe slave labor making a comeback where nobody would see it. "So those really were Zeta contractors at the safe house in El Cajon."

"Yes," Casillas answered. "We need to finish this quickly before the moment passes."

"That's why we need you to give us Nora," Ray said.

"You asked about your wife, *Señor* Ojeda," Casillas said. "Please look behind you."

Dread began to drive out the chill that filled Luis' mind and body. He sat up and swiveled the chair until he could see behind him.

Three men in suits stood close together about ten feet away. A trail of blood trickled from one's nose, another's coat had a torn shoulder seam, the third favored his right leg. In the middle of their group stood Bel: blackening eye, bloody lip, hands behind her back. She mouthed *I'm sorry* at him.

"Your wife is very spirited, *Señor* Ojeda," Casillas reported. "She stabbed one of my men. I respect that. It's why I won't have her raped and killed yet. If you give us Khaled, you can have your wife and you're free to do what you want. But if you don't… well. Do we understand each other, *Señor* Ojeda?"

67

Nora was glad they'd retreated to the bathroom. She was on the verge of losing her room-service dinner. "Oh, Luis, I'm sorry, I'm so sorry, I never wanted this…"

"I know." Luis sat rigid on the toilet, torturing a towel in his fists. "Ray sold us out. Now those *cabrones…*"

She turned to the sink to splash some cold water on her face. Not only had she risked her own family's lives; she'd now dragged someone else's family into danger. She couldn't allow that. She stood there dripping into the basin, her forearms pressing into the marble counter, trying to bring some order to her thoughts. "You have to give me up."

"No. Then those assholes win."

"You *have* to." Nora grabbed a towel from the counter, turned and tried to focus on Luis while her face was coming unglued. "I can't let them do anything to Bel. I'd never forgive myself. You have to give me to them."

Luis glared at her. "That's stupid. You know what they'll do to you. This is between me and them, and that's how I'm gonna settle it."

"It doesn't matter. I'm not worth an innocent life." And by saying it, she realized the truth in her words. She let go of the— *what is it, vanity?*—that had made her inflict all this pain and fear and suffering on the people she loved and now on people trying to help. Now her only worth was as a bargaining chip. "The people in England have most of the important intel. It'll take them longer to go through it without me, to figure out what's there. I won't be able to explain it to them. But they'll work it out and they can still publish."

"In time?"

Nora tried to remember the plan she'd worked out, when

everything had to be done in what order to have the greatest effect. It all seemed so silly now. She'd tried so hard for so long to keep control over her life and everything in it. Ever since she'd arrived at Dulles almost three weeks ago, though, her entire world had been flying apart, the pieces shattering against walls and cutting down innocent bystanders. It had to stop.

"Call your friend. Tell him I'll come. But I need you to do something for me. Ask if they'll let Peter go. The Bureau doesn't want him. I need you to take my children to my parents in Marseilles." As she said the words, her heart came undone and she couldn't stop the tears sheeting down her face. "Please don't let them be brainwashed by some Christian zealot. Promise me you'll do that."

"No, it's not over—"

"Promise me! I know you'll keep your promise. Save my children. Please."

Luis' chin grew harder. "*If* I can't save you and Paul—*if*—yes, I promise I'll get the kids out. But there's one more thing we can try before you give up. Remember McGinley?"

"That ICE agent? What can he do?"

Luis pushed himself to his feet, whacked the towel into his palm, then stared straight at her face. His eyes were harder and deadlier than she'd ever seen them. "I'm going to find out."

68

MONDAY, 17 MAY

"McGinley here."

Ojeda's voice. "What did you find out?"

"Hello to you too, *amigo*. It's a little late for you, ain't it? What I found out is maybe you're as smart as I first thought. There's something going on, but damned if I can root it out."

"But you agree the FBI's got some kind of back-door thing going on?"

"Well… shit. I reckon so. Can't prove it, though."

"You interested in knowing more?"

"What've you got?"

"In a while. Do you think I'm a terrorist?"

"I think you're up to your neck in Cartel business, which pisses me off. And I *know* you're wrapped up with that Khaled woman, which pisses me off more. But a terrorist? Well…"

"Come on, McGinley."

"Aw, hell. No. You're not the type."

"Thanks. Is Nora the type? You've seen her record, right?"

"I've seen it."

"You believe the Bureau's story on her? That she helped with 10/19 even though she was in Somalia?"

"What do you want, Ojeda?"

"The Bureau's lying to you about Tavo, and they're lying to you about me. We agree on that. So you think maybe they're lying to you about Nora?"

Silence.

"McGinley, are you there?"

"Yeah, I'm here. What do you *want?*"

"It's time you met Nora. Listen to what she has to say. I think it'll expand your mind."

"Hell, son, now you're talking sense. I've wanted to get to her ever since I heard—"

"No. This isn't me handing her over. This is me setting up a meeting we all walk away from when it's done."

"And why do I want to do that?"

"Because I'm going to tell you some things straight from the Zeta's mouth. Things you're gonna want to confirm. And then I'm gonna give you a target that's way better than a whistleblower. If you play it right, you can come out a hero. Are you ready?"

69

TUESDAY, 18 MAY

Not even nine A.M. yet and the traffic going into Mexicali was no faster than McGinley could walk, so he parked in a clip-joint of a lot a few hundred yards north of the line and hoofed it across. The CBP troop at the checkpoint counter just waved him through when McGinley badged him. Just like that, he was in Mexico. It always amazed him how easy it was to get in, and how hard to get out.

He spotted Ojeda standing on the corner next to the ramp to the tunnel under López Mateos, the main drag into town, with palm trees and a white iron picket fence behind him. McGinley did a quick sweep for Ojeda's backup, if there was any. They could be anywhere in this dogpile. Cars and people everywhere, but he didn't see any guns except on the Mex police, so he figured he was as safe as he'd get.

He dodged the swarm of taxis and delivery trucks rounding Zorilla into López Mateos and strode to within a couple paces of Ojeda. God *damn*, the man looked bad. Huge bags under eyes that looked like roadmaps, buzzed-off hair. "You look like shit, *amigo*."

"Didn't sleep."

"Me, neither."

"Probably not the same reason." Ojeda held out a hand, palm-up. "Give me your phone."

No use arguing with the man. McGinley twisted the phone pod off his ear and dropped it into Ojeda's palm. Ojeda fiddled with it, popped out the battery, then stowed it and the battery in a foil pouch like the kind that come out of MREs. "I hope you cleaned that out."

"Don't worry." He shoved the pouch into a shirt pocket, then took a little black box with an antenna from the other and waved the thing all over McGinley. Looking for transmitters; good thing he hadn't worn any or he'd be taking clothes off out here in the middle of everything. Ojeda finished and tucked away his toy. "Let's get a taxi."

They rode through everybody's idea of a border town—one-story storefronts, every other one a *farmacia* or dentist or *cambio*, arches, big ads and little neon signs, yellows and reds faded by the sun and too much time gone between coats of paint. Buildings from the Twenties or Thirties, curved corners and details around the windows they just don't do anymore. It reminded him of some country towns back home, the ones that never got rich enough to tear down everything old.

"You ever notice," he asked Ojeda, "how hard it's getting to tell Mexico from America?"

"It's not that hard. The roads down here are better, and there's no Ryantowns in the parks."

True enough. Buses, too. McGinley couldn't recall the last time he'd seen a city bus back home. "How far are we going?"

"You'll find out. I need your weapon."

"Did you see a weapon on me?"

"Mind if I check?" McGinley sighed and scooted to the front edge of the back seat. Ojeda ran his hands around McGinley's belt and lower legs, then pulled the S&W Bodyguard backup pistol from its ankle holster. "I guess this is a toy, then?"

"Forgot I had it."

They passed a city park—strange to see one of those without company logos all over like a NASCAR racer—turned right onto a commercial street where half the buildings were behind scaffolds, then stopped at a church, white with brown trim and a fancy bell tower. "We're here," Ojeda announced. "Hope you don't hate Catholics as much as you hate Muslims."

McGinley reckoned he had that one coming, so he let it go. He expected the church would be one of them Mex fever dreams full of carved saints with blood all over them and gewgahs on every flat surface, the kind of place that gave little kids nightmares. But this one was different: plain white walls, simple wood pews, one icon over the altar, small, clear windows above the big arches between the side aisles and the church's nave. A sprinkle of people sat in pews toward the business end of the place.

Ojeda said, "I gave some money to the parish in the Cartel's name. They'll leave us alone. Keep your voice down. Try not to swear too much."

McGinley snapped, "I know how to behave in church."

He followed Ojeda to the right side aisle, where a woman sat next to a little girl. It wasn't until McGinley got a few feet away that he recognized her. The woman stood when he reached the end of her pew.

"Special Agent Nora Khaled, FBI." She held out her hand to shake. "Thanks for meeting with me."

He looked in her eyes—big, dark, flat, hard—and decided to skip the handshake. "Special Agent Jack McGinley, ICE HSI." He nodded toward Ojeda. "Your boyfriend here tells a good story."

"Good. This is my daughter, Hope."

Of course she'd pick a name like "Hope." It probably was really some weird rag thing that sounded like gargling. But she was a cute little thing—like her mama, if he had to admit it—with thick black hair and eyes that covered half her face. He bent to get down to her level. "Pleased to meet you, Hope."

"Are you Mr. Luis' friend?"

"Mr. Luis and I do business from time to time."

"Are you Mommy's friend?"

He most certainly was not, but a bitty thing like her wasn't part of any of that. "I just met your mama. We're gonna have us a talk."

The girl tilted her head and frowned. He had that effect on women. "You talk funny."

"Why, yes I do." When he stood, he caught Khaled watching him and her little girl, one of her eyebrows cocked up. "You always bring your daughter to your meetings?"

"No, but I wasn't going to leave her alone in the hotel. I also thought it might help if you saw that we start out as children instead of being hatched as full-grown *jihadis*."

Ouch. "I appreciate that you're more-or-less human, Mrs. Khaled. You wanted to talk? Let's talk."

"Luis?" Khaled hauled her daughter off the pew and passed her to Ojeda, who held her against him with his right arm. McGinley noticed for the first time the girl's missing left shoe and the Ace bandage wrapped around her foot. Khaled touched the girl's arm.

"Cupcake, I need to talk to Agent McGinley for a while. Stay with Mr. Luis and be a good girl, okay?"

"Okay, Mommy."

Jesus. Just like normal people. Maybe that was her point. Her jeans and tee shirt made her look like any young mom he could see anywhere. Her English was probably better than his; no accent anywhere to be found. Put on a little makeup and lay off the triceps some, maybe grow the hair out a skosh, and she'd even be half-pretty. In short, nothing at all like what he'd expected.

"Let's sit," she said. She pulled a slate out of a little blue-and-black gym bag behind her, switched it on, and set it on the seat between them. Then Khaled looked deep into his head with those big, brown eyes of hers. "Remember 10/19?"

McGinley slumped in the pew, one boot propped on the knee rest, Khaled's slate on his thigh. If this was fake, it was *real* good, and someone had worked it for a long, long time. He recognized the forms and screenshots and all the little details. He hadn't yet seen anything that looked off.

He remembered the crackpots and freaks who came out from under their rocks after 10/19. All those wild conspiracy theories—the Trilateral Commission did it, the Mossad did it, the CIA did it, the Chinese did it, the Russians did it, space aliens did it. He didn't remember a single one about a bunch of peckerheads from Montana doing it. But here it was.

Damn.

He didn't look up when Ojeda settled a foot or so away, just shuffled through a few more files. He wouldn't figure it out now; hell, he might never figure it out. If nothing else, Khaled made a damn good case that those Yemeni boys weren't the perps. He wasn't solid yet on the militia angle, but it fit. That meant nothing that happened since made a damn bit of sense.

"It's a lot to take in," Ojeda said.

"That it is, *amigo.*" McGinley sighed, switched off the slate and set it aside. "What did you and the little one talk about all that time?"

"I told her about the saints here. Taught her some Spanish."

"She teach you any Arabic?"

"Nope. She doesn't know any. Nora hasn't decided yet whether to go the old-school way with the kids or put them in English Qu'ran class."

"Didn't know there was such a thing." He'd never met a rag who didn't speak some kind of rag language. Now he had. He slid lower on the seat. "I reckon there's a lot of things I don't know. That's quite a woman, there."

"Yeah, she is."

McGinley heard something in his voice and stared at him. "You ain't sweet on her, are you?"

"No. I'm very married." Ojeda sat up like he'd been bit. "And the Zetas have my wife."

No wonder the man looked all used up. McGinley recalled Ojeda's wife at her hospital, her death-ray stare cooking him where he stood. She was a tough one. For Ojeda's sake, he hoped she was tough enough. "I am truly sorry to hear that."

Luis nodded. "What did you find out about what I told you?"

"Well, that's why I didn't get no sleep last night, that and driving way the hell out here. I woke up a bunch of people back East who likely never reckoned they'd get asked the things I was asking. Not a one of them would tell me 'yes,' but they wouldn't say 'no' either, so that makes me think the answer's yes, it's true."

"How do you feel about that?"

"What are you, a shrink? It makes me mad as hell. Just the thought that anyone would deal with those…" He remembered where he was and broke off. "I'm in a church, so I can't tell you exactly what I think of Zetas, but I reckon you already know."

"Probably the same as me."

"And they lied." McGinley sat up and leaned in toward Ojeda, shaking a finger. "They *lied* about 10/19. That was a sacred event and they played politics with it." He shut his mouth before all the things he'd been thinking picked that time to jump out. The more he thought about it, the madder he got. Ojeda didn't need to know that.

"So you believe Nora." McGinley nodded. "Glad to hear it."

McGinley scoped Ojeda's face, looking for tells. "What do you want?"

"I want my wife back. Nora told me to trade her for Bel, no questions. I told her you might be able to help us turn this into a win."

"How so?"

"I can hand you the new *capo* of Pacifico Norte."

His old buddy? Really? McGinley leaned in closer, looking for the con in the man's eyes.

"And that Casillas guy?" Ojeda continued. "I think he's way more than just a fixer. I can give you him, too. And I wouldn't be surprised if there are more senior Zetas at this meet tonight. You've got warrants out on all those guys, don't you?"

"We don't. DEA does, I'm sure of that. You know, this can get awful messy. Zetas don't go nowhere without a whole army."

"Then bring your own. Bring the DEA, Border Patrol. Everybody except the FBI."

"The Mexes get sore when we come down here to straighten things out. A snatch-and-scoot's one thing—we do them a lot—but a big hairball like this might rile someone."

"Who runs this city? The Mexican government? Not for a long time. It's either the Nortes or the Zetas, maybe both right now. Who's going to complain?"

McGinley folded his arms on the back of the pew in front of him and thought a spell. It wasn't a terrorist bust, but it wasn't hog slop, either. Then again, even if he did bring in Khaled, it wouldn't be a righteous terrorist bust. The doubts he'd had a couple days ago had turned more solid. The Bureau was up to its neck in all this, and he didn't doubt they'd stampede one of their own if it suited them.

"Let me guess… your plan is for Khaled to get away."

"Something like that."

He could, of course, just forget that part and arrest her anyway. He glanced her way, nose-to-nose with the girl a couple pews over. She must've sensed him because she looked up and met his eyes. They were softer and maybe sadder than they'd been before.

"She told you to throw her under the bus to save your wife?"

"Yeah. Several times. She asked me to give her up and get her kids out of here."

This was *so* not what McGinley expected. "When and where is this here get-together?"

"Tonight. Don't know the time. I have to call Ray to tell him I'll bring Nora, then I'll find out. Or I guess you can track the Bureau's guys. Are you in?"

This could be a crowning moment of awesome, or it could turn into an enormous pile of shit. "I gotta talk to some people." Including himself. "Keep me informed and I'll tell you what's cooking."

"Don't take too long. When it happens, it'll happen fast. Nora and I have to do something, even if it means turning her over to the FBI. You know what the Bureau will do to her. They'll either kill her like the Yemenis or disappear her like the militia idiots." Ojeda nodded in her direction. "Take a look, McGinley."

McGinley already had. He stood. "Don't you put this on me, Ojeda. I'll be in touch."

70

TUESDAY, 18 MAY

The *Museo Sol del Nino* was the perfect place to hide—cool, cheap, full of kids, and loud enough to make eavesdropping improbable. And fun.

Nora needed fun.

They'd abandoned the Crowne Plaza after Luis' meeting at the mall. He'd explained that the Zetas' *La Dirección* cyber unit might find them through his Cartel credit card. So they left with their backpacks, took a cash advance from the lobby ATM, and checked into a fleabag motel in the old town. That morning, they left their stuff with the front desk, met with McGinley, then took off.

With her aching rear, Luis' injured shoulder, Hope's twisted ankle, and the heat, wandering hadn't lasted long. The science museum was a godsend. They watched a 3D movie about whale sharks in the Gulf of California, started an earthquake in a miniature town, and ate tacos and churros at the café. They took turns carrying Hope—even for such a little girl, she got very heavy very fast. The way Hope chattered at Luis, the way she looked at him, Nora could tell they were becoming fond of each other.

That was good. He might end up being her only way out of this mess.

Luis and Hope sat on a patch of gray industrial carpet surrounded by red and white pieces of machines, trying to build a robot that would walk a mechanical dog. On the other side of the carpet circle, a pair of Mexican moms and their three kids raced with them to come up with a working robot first. "Come on," Luis said to Nora. "Get in here and help."

She was in the middle of yet another mood downswing and wanted to stay in her own bubble. "Oh, no, that's okay—"

"Get in here. They're kicking our butts."

Which was how she learned that the best way to pop a mood

bubble was to sit on the floor trying to get wheels on a mechanical dog-walker.

Hope got her contraption going and hobbled after it as it led a yapping plastic dog across the floor. Nora and Luis sat side-by-side watching her encounter with one of the competition, a long-haired little girl a couple inches older than her wearing a pink dress. Nora felt everything inside her sink. After tonight, would she ever see her daughter again? Her son? Her husband? Anyone?

"Stop looking at your watch," Luis growled.

"I can't help it."

"Give it to me." He held out his hand.

"Why?"

"Because you'll drive yourself crazy, and me with you. Come on, give it here." She slipped off her watch and placed it in his palm. He dropped it into a shirt pocket. "Just let time happen. You can't stop it, so don't worry about it."

"Is that some kind of ancient Mexican tribal wisdom?"

"No, it's ancient infantry wisdom. I'm worried as hell about Bel, but I can't help her now and I won't be able to if I shut down, which I will if I worry enough."

She'd caught the haunted look in his eyes from time to time, especially when he'd seen someone who resembled his wife. "I know the feeling."

"Look, McGinley'll come through. That 10/19 stuff got him all wound up, and he's pissed about the Bureau and the Zetas hooking up."

That was nice, but… "It's not up to him, is it."

"True. But as unpopular as you guys are? The chance to make a big bust and leave the FBI with shit all over its face has gotta appeal to somebody."

"I hope you're right." She'd convinced herself of it about a dozen times since the meeting, and she'd completely written it off another dozen times. She watched her daughter giggle with the other girl. Then she noticed Luis watching Hope, saw the pain and longing in his eyes. "How old was your daughter?"

"Seventeen." His voice came at her from a great distance. "Her name was Christiana. Christa."

"Was it an accident? Was she sick?"

"Oh, it was no accident." His words crackled with anger. He closed his eyes and took a deep breath. "Sorry. She got pregnant. That part was an accident. Bel was buying the Pill for her on the gray market. She must've got a bad batch."

"Gray market? Why?"

"Insurance won't pay for birth control or prenatal or delivery. Anyway—" he threw up his hands—"the last thing we wanted was Christa the teenage mom, so we were gonna adopt out the baby."

"And Bel could do the prenatal care."

"Yeah. Except it went wrong. Christa was hurting and bleeding. Bel finally hauled her into the hospital after hours and traded a resident a case of good tequila for running an ultrasound. It was a tube baby. 'Ectopic' I think they call it."

Nora, being obsessive, had researched every possible complication of pregnancy when she was carrying Peter. She once again appreciated how lucky she'd been with both her boringly normal pregnancies and her father's doctor friends. "That's treatable."

Luis nodded once, an ironic smile on his lips. "Yeah, in the rest of the world. They give the mom some drugs and she aborts. End of problem. That's illegal back home, though. Even to save the mother. Bel couldn't get the drugs because they're controlled."

"But… she knows doctors, right? She couldn't get help?"

He snorted. "Yeah. Her doctor buddies. Nobody wanted to lose his license or get shot by some nut for doing an abortion. Lots of help."

She waited for him to finish the story. He didn't. "What happened?"

"We waited for Christa to miscarry. Guess that's what usually happens. Except she didn't. Or, she did finally, but it broke something and she started bleeding like crazy and the doctors… couldn't…" He closed his eyes, swallowed.

Nora brushed his sleeve. "I'm sorry."

He nodded again, opened his eyes. "Yeah. Thanks." He gestured toward Hope. "When I look at her, it's like looking at Christa again. Same hair, same eyes. And…"

They sat quietly side-by-side, watching Hope play with the girl in pink. Luis' story made Nora even more frightened of losing her daughter. How do you survive that kind of pain? How do you go on? After a long while, she asked, "What are we going to do with her?"

Luis sighed. "I figured we'd take her back to the cathedral. Leave her with the priest. She's been there with us, so it's familiar, and they have nuns to take care of her. We can leave instructions who to call if we don't… you know."

She nodded. "That sounds good." She didn't know whether she'd be able to let go when the time came. Nora glanced at her bare wrist and saw the afterimage of her watch. Four hours left. "When we're done here, can we go someplace where I can see the sky?"

He looked at her for a few moments, eyebrows bunched, lips pursed. "Sure. It's going to be hot."

"I don't care. I want to see the sky. I don't know if I'll ever get to see it again."

Luis nodded, understanding. Then he wrapped his arm around her and pulled her close so she could lay her head on his shoulder. She didn't resist. This might be the last time anyone would ever hold her.

71

Luis thumbed his phone's "end call" button and let out a long exhale. "That was McGinley."

Nora paced past him, arms crossed tight, jaw hard and square. "And?"

"Still waiting for the go-ahead and the location."

"Is he coming or not?"

"Hard to tell. He's got three tac teams in Calexico though—one ICE and two DEA—and a Border Patrol gunship drone on tap. If they turn it on, they can be here in a couple minutes."

"If." Nora had gone gloomy the moment the elderly nun plucked Hope from her arms at the cathedral. Beneath her Disneyland cap, her face was as dark as he'd ever seen it, noticeable even in the streetlight wash and the Cineopolis sign's glare. She paced fast and compulsively back and forth on an unvarying twenty-foot line.

The parking lot behind them rapidly filled with cars trying to make the first evening showtimes in the big blue box of a multiplex. Not all the sunset was gone yet, and what was left colored the Public Safety Secretariat building's concrete face. Luis bet not even the Zetas would do anything evil to them across the street from the state cop headquarters.

He probed the hard lump at the top of his butt through his jeans. He'd hidden Nora's Glock—the smaller of the two pistols they had available—in a cocoon of toilet paper that disguised its shape. It looked like he had a somewhat larger butt than usual. He hoped the people coming to get them wouldn't be thorough with their searches.

A white Range Rover approached, slowed, then lurched to a halt behind three diagonal-parked cars. A horn blared behind the SUV, then stopped when a man holding a stubby, suppressed

355

Krinkov—AKS-74U—rolled out the passenger's door. He made an angry gesture with his left hand—*go around*, cabrón—while he gripped his assault rifle with his right. *That's right. Rush it, get sloppy.*

The gunman waved Nora forward. Luis followed on her heels, but the *sicario* held up his hand to halt Luis between two parked cars. The man gestured for Nora to hold her arms out at shoulder height. He quickly searched her waistband, calves, and ankles, then peeked down the back of her shirt to see if she had anything taped to her back. He patted her front pants pockets, then reached around and squeezed her breasts through her blousy purple shirt.

"Hey! Stop that!" She tried to break away, but the *sicario* cuffed the back of her head with the heel of his hand.

"Just stand still," Luis said. "He's not getting fresh. He wants to see if you have anything hidden in your bra."

Apparently satisfied Nora wasn't a threat, the gunman pushed her face-first into the Range Rover's side and expertly handcuffed her. He yanked open the back door, shoved Nora inside, then motioned to Luis to step forward.

Luis tried to dial down all his reactions, breathe slower, calm his heart as the man's fingers slid around the inside of his waistband, patted his front pockets, and clapped his ankles. He hoped the light was bad enough to not pick out the pistol's outline in his pants seat. The gunman pulled Luis' phone from his shirt pocket, jacked out the battery and stashed it in his pants. Done with his thankfully less-than-complete search, he pushed Luis into the back of the SUV. Moments later, they were underway.

First hurdle crossed. Luis had passed his search and was unrestrained. Neither the driver nor the gunman riding shotgun could see much in the dark back seat behind them. Now Luis had to pay attention to where they were going as well as try to fish the pistol out of his pants, all without drawing attention to himself.

He maneuvered his hand inside the back of his trousers, touching the paper-wrapped bundle of gun. He hadn't counted on the paper rustling so much. The guys up front might not be able to hear it over the road and engine noise and the A/C's whoosh, but did he want to find out the wrong way? "Hey, *compa*," he said to the driver in Spanish. "How about some tunes?"

The driver shot him a glance, then shrugged. He fiddled with the console in the center of the dash and turned up *banda* rap, among Luis' least-favorite kinds of music. Still, it was noise.

Luis wiggled the pistol free and set it down butt-up behind him. He waited for a repeat of the obnoxious trumpet fanfare to cover the main wad of tissue ripping away from the weapon. Several traffic signals whizzed by as he stripped away the rest of the toilet paper. Finally, he was done. He slid the weapon's nose into his waistband as the trombones blatted out their final notes.

Now he could watch, and plan, and simmer. These *cabrones* had Bel. A flashback from last night: Bel bloodied and scared in the hands of those killers. She'd stabbed one of them, but what had they done to her for revenge? Was she still alive? Did she wish she wasn't?

No, she had to be alive. Bel couldn't die. She was the one person who'd managed to make him into a better man. He needed her the way he needed air.

He'd been a punk kid. Not gangs, but angry at the world. At the cops, for hassling him because he was brown and wore a hoodie. At how his dad broke his back day after day and brought home hardly anything while the *gabacho* owner lived in a big house and gave money to politicians who wanted to throw people like Luis and his family out of the country. At how Alvaro kept telling him, "You better go to college, or you'll end up like me."

Even back then, college was a mirage for a kid in a two-minimum-wage household, getting dimmer with every tuition hike. So he joined the Army, the only way a poor kid could afford college. He was an angry soldier in his first tour in the 'Stan. He took out his anger on the Afghans—some who deserved it, some who didn't—got a couple medals, a couple reprimands. It was like he belonged there.

On his second tour, two things happened. He met Ray, the big brother he'd always wanted. And he met Bel. She was the first girl who never let him run her over, the first one who didn't fight fair, the first who'd tell him exactly what she thought of his attitude. Before he even felt himself falling, he was crazy in love and planning babies and houses and careers and wasn't angry anymore. She'd given him a future and made him smart enough to take it.

Nobody—*nobody*—was going to hurt Bel or take her away from him.

The SUV stopped in front of a chain-link gate. Their headlights picked out a *sicario* opening a padlock on the other side. Luis squinted into the lightwash on a green sign next to the gate: "*Aduana de Mexicali, Baja California, Área Restringida.*"

Mexican Customs. Brilliant. No one would look for them here.

They cleared the gate and drove past what must have been a couple hundred seized cars, trucks, RVs and a few semis, the headlights flashing off dusty windows and dirty chrome. *Sicarios* lurked in the shadows, the moonlight picking out the barrels of their assault rifles and their NVG lenses. A couple FBI windbreakers went by. Up on a nearby rise, he recognized the floodlit crossing station where he'd met McGinley that morning. They finally stopped at the end of a prefab metal warehouse that appeared to be an unintended shade of dirty tan, flanked on its long sides by shiny black, white and silver SUVs. The guests.

Bel was in there. Luis could sense it, feel it inside him. She was there, and he was going to get her out.

"Okay," the driver said in Spanish. "This is it."

"Yes it is," Luis said. Then he drew the pistol and shot both men in the head.

72

McGinley was near to certain he'd wear out the soles of his boots on this airport ramp before those peckerheads in D.C. made up their minds about anything. The big do down south was about to start. Of course, if Ojeda didn't cough up the location, nobody was going anywhere.

"Sir?" The comm tech leaned out of the oh-so-subtle black van a few feet away. "The CI's back on the scope."

About damn time. McGinley jogged to the van and ducked his head through the side door to look at the screen. The tech pointed to a green crosshairs on the road map of Mexicali. "Is he moving?" McGinley asked.

"No, sir. I mean, a little, a few feet here and there, but that's all."

Well, well. Ojeda was just on the other side of the line. "What's that place he's at?"

The tech switched the map to a satellite image, used his fingers to zoom in. "Can't tell, sir. Lots of cars, a couple warehouses. A storage yard?"

McGinley's phone rang. He checked the screen, then barked, "Where the hell are you?"

"Mexican Customs impound lot off Zorilla," Ojeda whispered back. "Right on the border. I can see the crossing from here. Are you coming?"

McGinley stepped away from the van. Mexicali lit up the sky maybe three hundred yards south, staggering distance after a good drunk. Hell, his team could *walk* there if they took a mind to it. "I'm working on that. Has the dance started?"

"I don't know. We just got loose from our pickup. There's *sicarios* all over the place and some FBI. Someone's going to find the bodies we left. There's not much time."

I know that, McGinley was about to say, but he reckoned Ojeda knew he knew and the man was in the middle of it down there. "We're in the air when we get clearance, not before. You got any more names you can feed me? Sweeten the pot?"

"We haven't been inside yet. Everything's guarded. We didn't want to start anything until we knew what you guys are doing."

"I could throw a rock and hit you, but I gotta get some ol' boy out of his cocktail party to tell me I can do it." He heard his voice getting all parade-ground and stopped to bring himself down. This was the higher-ups' fault, not Ojeda's. "I reckon what I'm saying is, if there's something you gotta do, you do it, don't wait on us. We'll help if we can. Right now, you're on your own, *amigo*."

Ray followed Casillas around the Zeta side of the warehouse, meeting the people who would run his life from now on. Casillas introduced him to Zambreño, the deputy *presidente* of *México Unido*, the Zetas' political front, and Salgado, the commander of western-sector security forces. There were representatives of *Los Halcones*—the group that supervised product distribution—and *Los Mañosos*—now the security forces' logistical branch, in charge of buying weapons and ammo. All wore designer suits and ties, looking very official and respectable. Getting used to it, Ray guessed.

He glanced across the cement floor to the other side of the warehouse. The *El Norte* delegation, a bunch of dark suits, clustered behind a screen of FBI SWAT heavies. There was supposedly a State Department guy over there, and a Bureau Deputy Executive Assistant Director, some kind of White House rep, and all their horseholders and advisors.

All they needed now was the star of the show.

Casillas nudged Ray away from one of the Zeta suits. "Ojeda and the woman haven't arrived yet." Ray had to lean in to hear him.

"Your guys were handling that, not me."

"I'm aware of that. They were collected at the agreed time and place, but we've heard nothing since. I need to know: can Ojeda be trusted?"

Could he? The old Lucho was dependable as the sunrise, but this new version Ray had dealt with for the past couple weeks? He'd taken this job way more seriously than Ray had ever expected. That could be bad news. Casillas didn't need to know this; not yet, at least. "If he says he'll do something, he'll do it. He won't do anything stupid while you have his wife. They're crazy about each other."

"While *we* have his wife," Casillas corrected. "You have to remember you're a part of our family now." He touched his phone pod, murmured a message, then gripped Ray's shoulder. "Speaking of family, we need to talk soon about finding you a wife. Someone respectable. Someone who could be, shall we say, First Lady of Baja."

What?

"You can have mistresses, of course. That's understood. But you need someone suitable for a wife. We'll talk when this is done."

A *wife?* They'd taken his power, his house, his friends, Keira. Probably his freedom. Now they were going to marry him off? It wasn't a joke; Zetas didn't have a sense of humor. As Casillas towed him toward yet another suit, Ray felt the walls closing in on him.

Luis and Nora crouched behind a dust-caked, twenty-year-old Freightliner semi parked nose-on to the warehouse's end. They'd taken the guards' weapons and body armor. The Range Rover sat in the middle of a line of abandoned cars.

How much of McGinley's message should he tell Nora? Hearing that the cavalry might stay in the stable could make her throw away her guns and walk into that warehouse. He didn't know if he could stop her or if he should even try. Bel was in there, waiting. Ray had said he could get the boy out, but Luis didn't believe Ray could deliver on anything anymore.

A phone buzzed in his pocket. He pulled it out; it had been the driver's. "*Sí?*"

"The boss wants to know where you are." A low voice, speaking Spanish.

Just what Luis had been afraid of. "Yeah, we're on López Mateos." He pitched his voice lower and roughed it up as much as he could. "Some *tonto* in a truck got in a wreck right in front of us, you know?"

"How much longer?"

"Fifteen minutes, maybe twenty. We're stuck. We're by the Teatro, you know? No way around."

"I'll tell him."

Nora nudged him as he put the phone away. "What was that?"

"They're checking up on their boys."

"What about McGinley?"

"Talking to Washington."

"Oh, great."

They couldn't just sit. Someone would find the bodies or discover there was no wreck. Then the place would come unglued. "Let's recon. Maybe we'll see something useful."

Nora grumbled, "Maybe pigs will fly."

When the Zetas came for Bel and Paul and Peter in their cement prison, Bel had a plan to not get trussed up like a turkey.

The gunman at the door told them to lay face-down on the floor and put their hands behind their backs while his partner snapped handcuffs on each of them. When he got to Bel, she took the left cuff without a sound, but when he touched her right wrist she screamed in Spanish, "Ow! That hurts! Please, not so tight, my wrist hurts, please."

The guy crouching next to her hesitated. She looked up to the *sicario* by the door—frowning, half-confused, she'd blown his programming—and pleaded, "Come on, please, just a little loose, okay? Please? My wrist hurts so bad."

Maybe it was her face—she'd made Paul describe it to her, as horrifying as it felt—or maybe the helplessness she'd thrown into her voice, but after a moment the guy by the door nodded. The gunman next to her loosened the cuff until she could tell there was a good quarter inch or so of play all the way around. Perfect.

Their blindfolded ride in the back of a van took maybe twenty minutes. Every stop, turn, and curve doubled her full-body ache. Guards led them outside, then into what must have been a large building that echoed with their footsteps, then into a stuffy, smaller room that smelled dusty. They looped her handcuff chain around something that felt like metal shelves, then slammed and locked the door. After a while, she heard the muttering of voices outside.

Bel slid down the metal corner post of whatever she was locked to until she could reach her blindfold. She tugged it up so she could see out of the eye that wasn't swollen shut from last night's beating. Knowing the guy she'd stabbed had died had made the beatdown easier to take.

They were in a storage room. She, Paul, and Peter were each chained to one of three metal shelf units that were bolted to the back wall. A window covered with brown paper was set into the wall facing her, next to the door. The backlight on the paper revealed the concrete floor's general grubbiness and the rust patches on the shelves. A dead light bulb hung from the ceiling in a metal cage. Random junk littered the floor and some of the shelves.

Including pipe. Three-foot pipe segments on the shelf behind Paul, a couple still with fittings. Weapons.

She slid back up the shelf's corner post until she could touch her right cuff with her left hand. She carefully worked the cuff off, scouring the skin on her thumb until she was finally able to slip it free. The only good thing about having big wrists and little hands. She picked her way across the floor and scraped up a bottom corner of the paper to peek through.

The big, echoing room was a warehouse. A bunch of Latino guys in suits milled around, shaking hands and talking. Behind the talking suits were rows of tall metal shelves full of crates and a few odd items—a set of golf clubs, a baby stroller, a dismantled toilet. *Sicarios* in gray camouflage and black hoods stood to the left with their guns ready. She couldn't see a way out. *Damn it!*

There was Ray, over on one side of the talking suits, with a little guy dressed like an urban cowboy. The same guy who was at the mall? She wondered whether she could ask to see Ray and try to talk him into letting her go. No, that wouldn't work. She'd treated him like shit ever since he got Lucho tangled up in the Cartel. Too bad she'd never learned to smile and shut up.

She tip-toed to Paul. "Are you okay?" she whispered.

He nodded. "How did—"

Bel put her fingers to his lips. "Shh." She checked his cuffs—too tight for him to get out—then moved to Peter. The poor little guy was trembling, and his blindfold was wet. She whispered, "It's gonna be okay," then gave him a hug.

"Where's daddy?" he whimpered.

"Right here," Paul stage-whispered. "It's gonna be okay, buddy. Just hang tough."

She could get Peter out of the handcuffs easily, but what then? She wouldn't leave without them both. She had no idea what to do once she got past the door and there was a lot of firepower out there that wouldn't be glad to see them.

Bel was about to go back to her shelf when she decided to find out if she could see anything different through the window's other corner. She peeled up the paper's edge to find herself looking at more suits. But these were different, dark and stodgy instead of the flashy, stylish outfits the *narcos* wore. And all these guys were Anglos. Then she noticed their guards: dark blue utilities, helmets, M4 carbines. "FBI" in yellow on their body armor.

FBI? Here?

Nora steadied the steel drum while she watched for guards. Luis balanced on top of the barrel, trying to wipe clean a spot on the window so he could see inside. A dusty semi-trailer screened them from the road, but gunmen patrolled everywhere, and it was just a matter of time before someone spotted her or Luis or both.

Luis had surprised her in the car. He took out those two men without any hesitation. He'd been such a calm, steady presence that she'd never imagined he could turn into a stone killer just like that. Then she remembered the cartel safe house and how he'd become Action Hero when they were attacked. If this was how he reacted when someone he cared about was in danger, she was glad for all that time he'd spent bonding with Hope.

The *clack* of a fake camera shutter made her look up. Luis held his phone's back against the window; the screen's glow washed over his face. She braced the barrel with both hands to keep it still. Two more *clacks*, then Luis hopped down next to her.

"What did you see?" she whispered.

"A bunch of American government types and a bunch of Cartel guys. I didn't see Paul or Bel." He used his index fingers to type on the screen. "There—just sent them to McGinley."

Boots scraped on gritty concrete to Nora's left. She spun, bringing up her stubby rifle. Two chatting cartel gunmen stepped out of the moonlight into the semi-trailer's shadow. Both faced the wall and got busy with the flies on their camo utility pants. She stood like a rock, kept her breathing light enough to not drown out the sound of them peeing against the metal warehouse wall. She mentally rehearsed what to do if either of them spotted her. Luis became a large stillness next to her, his rifle also ready.

The nearest guard finished, shook, buttoned up. He pulled a water bottle from his thigh pocket, unscrewed it… and dropped the cap. It clicked against the warehouse's concrete apron. "*Chingado*," he grumbled.

Look down, Nora told him. *Not over here.*

The gunman scanned the ground around his feet, looked to his right, froze. He and Nora locked eyes for a moment. "*Ay—*"

Nora shot him once through the dark hollow of his left eye. The suppressed rifle made a *thud* sound, like dropping a sandbag. The man crumpled, his rifle clattering against the cement. Another *thud* told her Luis had killed the other guard before the first one had finished falling.

They dragged the bodies farther into the shadows and relieved them of their extra ammunition. Nora knew she ought to feel bad about this—she'd killed someone in cold blood who didn't have a chance to defend himself—but she couldn't. They'd have done the same to her. As far as she was concerned, she was back in Somalia and these people were Shabab. The Army had stopped trying to capture the Somalian radicals before she got there; the unofficial order was "kill them all." She and her unit had done just that, not that it had helped in the end.

"Let's go." Luis pointed toward the warehouse's far end.

"How long are we going to wait for McGinley?"

"Until he shows up, we run out of time, or we figure out how to do this without him."

As much as she wanted to, she couldn't argue with that.

McGinley checked the pictures on his slate, then forwarded them to the intel weenie in the van with the comm tech. "Run facials on these. You're already late."

Good work, Ojeda. The two pictures of that mob of Mexes might just shake something loose back in D.C.

"Sir, this third shot's of Americans."

"I don't give a damn," he snapped. "Do it anyway." He turned to the comm tech. "Chop the gunship to that yard for a look-see. They can stay on our side of the line if they want. Tap the video and drag it over here."

A couple minutes later, the better of the two beauty shots of the cartel boys flashed on his slate. Over half the faces were tagged with names and links to their files. He poked at a couple with vaguely familiar names. The guest list for that hoe-down had some heavy hitters.

Then he saw it: "Alcala." Weasel-faced bastard was smiling right into the damn camera, like he knew it was there. *I'm coming for you, son.* "Intel! Send that thing to O'Hanlon and the DEA."

The comm tech said, "Sir, the gunship feed is coming to you."

McGinley poked the throbbing red icon on his slate. An oblique infrared view of the customs yard filled the screen, with a targeting reticule in the center and readouts at the bottom for altitude and heading and distance to target. Bright little green bodies went this way and that, most of them not in any great hurry. He whistled; there sure were a passel of them. Two heat sources moved along at a good clip by the half-bright warehouse. Ojeda and Khaled?

His phone beeped: O'Hanlon. "You got the intel, sir?" McGinley asked. "Are we a go?"

Ray kept looking at his watch as he paced. The driver's fifteen-to-twenty estimate was blown. What happened? Where were they?

In the center of the floor, Zambreño and the State Department guy had a laugh. Their helpers stood next to them, eyeing each other. A few yards away, a couple FBI suits had a conference with Salgado and two of his aides. The uncomfortable looks on all their faces made Ray glad he wasn't part of it. Too bad there wasn't a bar.

Casillas walked in a tight circle behind Ray, chin in his hand, talking to his phone pod, his mouth a thin slash. Ray knew what bad news looked like.

Done circling, Casillas stalked to Ray's side. "Our men just found the vehicle we sent for your friend and the woman." He put a lot of weight on *your friend*. "Both the driver and guard are dead, and their weapons are missing." Casillas grabbed Ray's arm. "You assured me your friend would be no trouble."

"You took the man's wife and beat the shit out of her. What do you expect?"

Casillas glared at him. "What would he do now? Where would he go?"

Ray never expected this. He tried to think. "Lucho knows what'll happen to Bel if he fucks us over. He's going to try to get her out. It's the only thing that makes sense."

Casillas nodded. "We'll have to eliminate her, then." He reached for his phone pod.

"No, wait." *Shut up*, he told himself. But he couldn't erase twenty-plus years with Lucho, not this way. Killing Bel would destroy him. No, not destroy; it would turn him back into what he was before he met Bel. "You kill her, there's nothing left to control him. He'll come straight at us and take down everyone he can. We need her alive."

Casillas narrowed his eyes. "I hope for your sake this is true." He paused, scowling. "Call him. Tell him he's making a serious mistake. We can motivate him without killing his woman." He tapped his phone pod. "Put a guard with them."

Nora and Luis had to take cover every few seconds as they worked their way down the warehouse's side, behind derelict cars or new cartel SUVs, pallets of shrink-wrapped crates or empty steel drums. More guards appeared every time Nora looked up. Finally, with the end of the warehouse ten yards away, she and Luis sagged to the ground behind a rusted twenty-foot COSCO shipping container. She leaned against the metal siding and let her head fall back.

This was useless. They were spending more time hiding than moving.

She unfastened her neck chain, wrapped it around her fingers, and stared at the blocky pendant in her palm. This was now the most valuable thing about her.

"You okay?" Luis whispered.

"There's something I didn't tell you. Something about the 10/19 cover-up."

"And why are you telling me now? Here?"

She peeked past the container to the road. Four guards paced through the tiny slice of outside she could see. "Because I don't think I'm going to make it."

Luis frowned. "Come on. We're almost there."

"And then what?" Nora dialed back her volume; even whispers could carry. "There'll be more of them there. McGinley isn't coming and we can't fight all these people by ourselves. We don't know where Paul is or even if he's alive." She had to stop to fight with her stomach over that idea. "So someone else needs to know."

Luis shook his head, a disgusted look on his face. "You're just tired. Don't—"

"No. I'm realistic." And exhausted, and scared, and feeling very alone, even with Luis next to her. Everything she'd felt in the hotel room the night before had come back ten times as strong. She held up the pendant. "Just listen. There's a folder called '12/5/19 AG meeting' at the root. It has an audio recording, a transcript, and notes from a meeting between the Director, the Attorney General, and a White House lawyer right after we rolled up the real bombers. Give it directly to the *Guardian*, not to the Brit government. If their government gets it, they'll use it for leverage and nobody else will hear it."

"Why? What's so special about it?"

"The Director briefed the AG in that meeting about the militia creeps and gave him two options. Either they could announce the new arrests, or they could stick to the story they already had going. The AG picked option two."

"How'd you get that?"

"There was a fourth person in the room—Hugh, the old agent who gave me all this stuff. Officially, he was there to help the Director with the materials. But the Director had him wear a wire so if this blew up, he could take the AG down with him. When Hugh heard their decision, he got so disgusted he started making copies of everything in case it was destroyed."

Luis shrugged. "Good for him. But, so what?"

Why didn't he see it? "Do you know who was AG in 2019?"

"I don't know who it is now."

Ah. Living in the Beltway bubble, it was easy to forget that hardly anyone on the outside kept track of who did what inside. "He ran for office twice, both times as the guy who caught the Wrigley Field Four and solved the Muslim problem in America. Does that help?"

Juan just stared at her.

"In 2022, he ran for Senate in Texas and won. Then in '28 he ran for President. And won."

Luis closed his eyes and rested his head against the warehouse wall. He was surprised at how unsurprised he was. Of course the President was involved. That's why Nora wanted this to screw up the election. "Thanks a lot. No pressure here."

"Sorry." She pulled the pendant loose from her hand and held it up so he could see. "Keep this for Paul. I don't want these people getting it."

Luis ducked so she could fasten the chain around his neck. When she was done, he touched the square chunk of silver, still warm from her hand. "You're sure?" She nodded. "Okay." He slid the pendant into his shirt.

"If Paul doesn't get out—"

"He will, don't—"

"If he doesn't, there's an address on the root of the folder tree.

Get the data there." She clutched his forearm. "Now give me up. We tried. There's nothing more we can do."

Luis stared through the container, deciding what to say. Surrendering her to a quick execution or a lifetime in a dungeon was so wrong. He'd been sure he'd worked it out, that McGinley would back them up, that they could pull it off somehow. But he couldn't see it now. She was right; they couldn't win against this small army the Zetas had brought, and who could tell which side the FBI would come down on?

"They're not going to be real happy with me killing their guys," he said.

"Then blame it on me. I grabbed one of their guns and shot them both, then I ran away. You didn't tell them because you wanted to find me yourself and keep your word to them. If you want, I'll hit you so it looks like I attacked you."

"This is crazy—"

"No, *this* is crazy." She waved toward the other side of the container. She'd put on her determined face, the one that told him she'd made up her mind and nothing would change it. "I'm tired. I'm done running. All I want is to make sure my kids are going to be okay." Nora handed her rifle to him, then unfastened her body armor and yanked it off. "Call your friend. Tell him you caught me."

Disbelief, anger and relief fought a cage match inside Luis. She was right, but she was dead wrong. There had to be another way out of this, not this… "Nora, I—"

"Don't. I've made up my mind." She leaned in, kissed his cheek. "You're very sweet, and I can't thank you enough for how hard you've worked at this. I'm not going to let you destroy your life for me. You and Bel and my kids need to live. Do this last thing for me, okay?"

He looked into her eyes. They were calm, at peace. Arguing would only piss her off and make her do something even more stupid. He turned his head away, pulled out his phone and tried to call McGinley. Voicemail. *I guess that's it.* He disconnected without leaving a message, sat staring at the screen for a few moments, then punched in Ray's number.

"Yeah?"

"Ray, it's me. I—"

"What the fuck are you doing?" Ray hissed. Voices buzzed behind him. "They're going to barbeque me! Where are you? What are you trying to prove?"

"Outside. I've got Nora." One last shot. "You didn't let the boy go. She figured the deal was off, so she capped the guys who picked us up and ran. I just found her again."

"They won't let the kid go until they have her. And why'd you even let this happen? You know they have Bel. What, you're trading her in for Salma?"

"No. If the deal with her was off, then it was off with me, too. Look, are you and your boys going to ante up? I'll trade Nora for Bel and the boy."

"I can't make deals—"

"Then get me someone who can. She's good with this, she'll go quietly. She just wants her kids safe, and she doesn't want me to take the fall for what she did." Saying that made him sick to his stomach. Alvaro had always taught him to take the hit if it was his to take. "Straight-up swap, her for them. You guys can have your lovefest and we'll disappear."

Ray sputtered for a moment. Luis had never heard him do that before. "Jesus. Hold on." His end of the line went silent.

"What did he say?" Nora asked.

"He's checking with the new boss." Even if they agreed, would they stick to it? If it was just Ray—the old Ray—Luis would be more confident. Anything could happen with these Zeta *pendejos*. His brain started reeling off the dozen ways this could go bad.

"You there?" Ray's voice.

"Yeah."

"Bring her in. Any door will do. We'll give you the kid, you give us Nora."

"What about Bel?"

"They're holding onto her for a while. Make sure you behave."

"Goddamnit, Ray, that's not the deal! You said—"

"That's the deal you get now," Ray growled. "I had to stop Casillas from killing her a few minutes ago. We're done bargaining. Take it and shut up."

Casillas wanted to kill Bel? That *cabrón* was a dead man.

But what would stop him from killing them both after the FBI went home, just out of spite? Nothing.

Saying "okay" was the hardest thing he'd told anyone for a long time, but he did it anyway.

"What was that?" Nora's voice was drained of any feeling.

"They'll give me Peter when I take you inside."

"What about Bel?"

He stood, reached out a hand. "Come on. They're pissed, we can't push it anymore."

"*What about Bel?*"

"Never mind. That's between me and Casillas. Let's go." Luis helped her to her feet. "You'd better hit me so I have a story to tell them."

Nora nodded. She shifted Luis so his back was against the building, then drew her pistol, gripped the slide, then whacked the butt into the side of his head without any warning. Luis staggered, lost balance but managed to brace himself against the wall. He leaned forward and planted his hands on his knees, waiting for the stars to clear. "You didn't say anything about hitting me that hard."

"It has to look good if they're going to believe you." She dropped her gun belt onto her body armor. "Are you okay?"

"I guess." He straightened, shook his head clear. "I should cuff you so it looks right."

"I understand." She turned her back, held her wrists together behind her.

Luis handcuffed her loosely, then slipped the key into her back pocket. "In case you change your mind." He drew his pistol. "Let's get this over with."

They picked up their first shadow as soon as they stepped out from behind the container. Then another. And another. Two more stood at the back door. Four AK-104s and an AA-12 automatic shotgun pointed straight at them. Sweat poured into Luis' eyes and soaked his shirt; blood trickled into his ear. He steered Nora with her wrists, keeping his pistol aimed in her general direction. *Do nothing fast*, he reminded himself. *Keep your hands out.* "*La puerta, por favor*," he called out to the two *sicarios* before him. They yanked open the door just seconds before Nora reached it.

Inside they found themselves at the end opposite the gathering, looking down a wide central aisle between ranks of massive shelves. Three dozen faces stared back. Nora halted; the door slammed behind them. *Committed.* She took in a deep breath, stood straight, squared her shoulders, then marched down the aisle as if she was on parade.

Luis felt a twinge of pride mixed with sadness. *You go, girl. Go out a soldier.*

A gunman in Mexican Army camo appeared at the aisle's end, pushing Peter ahead of him. The boy still wore what he had at Andrade—jeans and gym shoes and a light tee shirt. The moment he saw his mother, he broke away from his keeper and pelted down the aisle, crashing into Nora face-first, throwing his arms around her. "Mommy! You're okay! Daddy's here, too, we were scared for you, but it's okay now, it's okay…"

Nora knelt slowly, leaned into her son's hug. Luis holstered his weapon and stepped back, giving them room. Peter went on, pouring out all the fear and doubt and relief from the past couple of days. Nora murmured to him over his words. Her arms strained against the handcuffs.

Peter peeked behind his mother's back. His eyes rounded. "Mommy, why are your hands tied?" That seemed to be the first time he noticed Luis. "Why did you do that? Why did you tie her up? Let her go! Let her go!" He rushed Luis and beat his little fists against Luis' body armor. Luis took the pummeling without a sound. He deserved this. It shouldn't have come to this.

"Peter!" Nora twisted to face her son. "Peter, stop!" The boy kept pounding Luis' chest, then shifted to kicking his shins. *Damn, the kid can kick.* "Butrus!" Peter stopped in mid-kick, shrank from his mother. "Come here, sweetie." The boy edged toward Nora, glancing back at Luis with confusion diluting the anger in his face. When he reached her, she said, "Listen to me. He did this because I told him to. I—"

"Why?"

"There's no time to explain. I need you to go with Mr. Luis and do exactly what he says. I—"

"I don't wanna! I'm gonna stay with you and Daddy! We gotta stick together, you—"

"No!" Peter flinched. Nora closed her eyes, took a breath, then said in a much gentler tone, "I need you to do this for me, sweetie. I need you to obey me. You need to stay with Mr. Luis. He'll keep you safe. He'll take you to Hope, okay? Sweetie, promise me?"

Peter looked from Nora to Luis, fear now chasing away the remaining anger. "I promise."

"Okay." Nora's voice wavered. "Now give me a hug."

Luis looked away, trying to swallow the sorrow climbing up his throat. He couldn't watch Nora say goodbye to her son for the last time, not after having already seen her give up her daughter. It was too easy to imagine himself or Bel doing this, if they even got the chance.

She whispered to Peter as he clung to her. He sniffed. A moment later, Luis felt a tug on his body armor. He looked down to find Peter next to him, his eyes spraying tears down his cheeks, his face fighting with itself. "I'm sorry," he choked.

"So am I." He squeezed Peter's shoulder, then stepped forward to help Nora stand. She resumed her parade-ground posture, then strode the last few steps to the soldier, leaving Luis behind.

Just before the man led her away, she looked back over her shoulder at Luis. He wished he could say something to comfort her but couldn't think of a thing. Then she mouthed *thank you* and marched away.

73

Ray could breathe normally for the first time in half an hour. The *bruja* was finally under control. Luis had brought her in (*maybe I won't have to kill him*). Casillas had given Ray a tiny, approving nod (*maybe he won't kill me*). The *jefes* had started to smile again. *This might work out.*

Nora marched down the aisle like this was a freaking front-and-center, chin up, chest out. She could put on a show, he had to give her that. Once she and the Mexican Army captain reached the clearing between the FBI and the cartel men, she stepped into a crisp parade rest.

A scuffling and door-slam at the head of the room got everyone's attention. A *sicario* dragged Nora's husband toward her by the elbow. Ray switched back to Nora in time to catch the crack in her mask—a hard swallow, lips pressed flat, pain around her eyes. The guard pushed the husband next to Nora. She swiveled her head, whispered to him. The husband nodded, then looked at the ground.

Salgado marched up to Nora and her husband, gave them the hard eye, then faced the FBI gaggle. He wore freshly pressed and starched tiger-stripe battledress and his old Mexican Army ribbons; maybe he thought that would buy more respect from the *Yanquis*. "Good evening, *Señores*. We have captured these two fugitives in our land." His English was slow and accented, but clear. "We know they interest you. We give them to you in the spirit of cooperation and friendship." He prodded the husband. "Identify yourself, please."

"Paul Khaled." The man wouldn't look up. He barely raised his voice, but his face was dark and angry.

Salgado reached out to touch Nora, but the look she gave him stopped him in mid-move and should've fried his brain. She turned her head, staring straight at the FBI honcho. "Special Agent Nora Khaled. Counterterrorism Division, Federal Bureau of Investigation. And a proud American."

Luis watched Nora walk away beside the guard—the man hadn't touched her or needed to—then squatted next to Peter.

The boy's eyes locked on his mom. "Where's she going?"

"She has some business with those men up there." Luis put an arm around Peter, but the boy shrugged him off. "I need you to do something for your mom and me."

"What?"

"I need you to hide. Find a place back here where nobody will see you and don't come out except for me or your mom or dad or Bel. Understand?"

"Why?" Peter fixed Luis with the most intense look he'd ever seen on a six-year-old. He sure was his mother's son. "Where are you going? Mommy said you have to stay with me."

"She said I have to protect you. It's not the same thing." Luis once had discussions like this with Nacho and recalled seeing Bel's brand of stubborn on his son's face. Explaining without falling back on *because* was some of the hardest work he'd ever done as a dad. "I think some bad things might happen here, and I need—your mom needs—to know you're safe so we can deal with it. That's why I need you to hide. Can you do that?"

Peter checked on his mother. Nora had reached the end of the aisle and now stood at parade rest. "Where's my sister?"

"She's safe. She's with some nice people who're taking care of her. I'll get you to her when we're done here. Peter, we can't talk about this anymore. Please go hide. All right?"

They both watched a guard shove Paul next to Nora. The bit of strength in the boy's face wobbled. "Are you gonna help Mommy and Daddy?"

"I'm going to try."

Doubt clouded Peter's eyes. He stared at Luis in a way that made him wonder if the boy was X-raying his soul. Then Peter turned and trotted to the nearest set of shelves.

Someone talked loudly outside, but Bel couldn't make out the words. The guard stood across the room. She could hear him breathe, smell his cigarette. When he moved, something on his web gear clinked—a D-ring against his weapon, maybe.

It was just her and the guard now. She'd barely held herself together as they dragged Paul and Peter out of the room. When they took her away, what would they take her to?

Footsteps and clinking approached her. She could feel the guard stand way too close to her. "What's your name, *mamacita?*" he said in Spanish.

Go to hell. He must have heard that, because the slap came a moment later, slamming her against the metal post behind her. She tasted blood and saw stars the blindfold didn't shut out.

He grabbed her jaw. "What's your name, bitch?" He had a young voice that hadn't yet been scoured by cigarettes and booze and life.

"Rosa." She couldn't bear to hear his voice say her real name.

"Huh." His hands squeezed her breasts through her shirt. The fear she'd felt when Paul left came back about ten times sharper. *No, not this. Not this.* The guard chuckled. "*Ay,* mama, you ain't bad for an old one, huh? Let's see those *tetas.*"

Bel wanted to scream when he pulled her shirt up to her armpits, but clamped her mouth shut and instead grabbed her right handcuff with her left hand. Her bound arms pinned her shirt hem above her breasts. The guard's hands roamed over her—"*Ay, mama, ¡que buena!*"—then his fingers wrapped around the chest band and ripped her bra upwards. She ground her teeth as the underwires scraped over her nipples.

The cuff was stuck.

She couldn't do anything until she could get her hand free, even as he groped her, pinching her nipples, saying stupid dirty things about the girls. The cuff was definitely tighter now. Maybe her hand had swelled; maybe she'd accidentally closed the cuff when she put it back on. She twisted, feeling the burn of skin coming off the base of her thumb. *Get off me!* her mind screamed, both at the hardware and at the pig molesting her.

"You look good for an old woman, *chica*," the rodent crooned. "Too bad about the bruises." She felt his fingers fumble at the top button of her jeans. *Not this not this not this no no no...* "Let's see what you got down here, huh? You want to show me, huh?"

Bel tore more skin off the base of her thumb. *Just a little more, come on, get off...*

The worm unzipped her, grabbed her jeans and panties on each side, and yanked them to her knees.

She flashed to that shower cube at Bagram: that asshole technician crowding her into the corner, grabbing at her. She'd fought him off with sheer fury and terror, but she'd had both hands free, and he wasn't packing a gun. The same fury and terror flooded her system now.

"*Ay*, mama, all clean and smooth down there, huh?" His hand forced itself between her legs. She tried to crush his fingers between her thighs and got another slap for her effort. The cuff was so close to coming off, just another fraction of an inch. *Off! Now! NOW!*

"I know what you want, mama, huh?"

I want your cock to fall off I want you to burn to death you cockroach you termite...

"I got it right here. You want it? I know you do." He wrenched her sideways, grabbed her hair and forced her to bend over.

The cuff tore a chunk of skin from her thumb, then flew off.

Bel swung her left hand behind her, slammed the handcuff against what felt like his face. He spat "What the *fuck?*" and let go of her hair.

She ripped off the blindfold, grabbed a length of pipe from the next shelf over, and swung backward as hard as she could. The elbow joint at the end crashed into his neck—"You fuckin' *bitch*, I'm gonna *kill* you!"—and spun him around so he tripped over his own feet and went down on his knees. She shuffled forward a step, changed up her grip, then slammed the pipe between his legs. He howled, collapsed on the concrete.

He swore at her. He could still talk. He could still breathe. That cockroach.

Bel hiked up her pants, then lunged forward. Someone growled the filthiest language she'd ever heard, curses in two languages, rising and falling with the pipe she plowed into his head and shoulders and upstretched arms as she showed that *asshole* what it was *like* to be *afraid* for your *body* and your *life* and to be *treated* like a slab of *meat* you *culero* you *hijo de puta* just *chingate guey* you *pedazo de mierda...*

The voice was hers, only not like she'd ever heard it before. When she looked down, the guard's head was a misshapen pile of raw hamburger and the pipe dripped blood on the floor. She couldn't see where the blood landed because there was so much.

The pipe clanged on the cement. She stumbled to the other corner, fell against the wall, then barfed her dinner of bottled water and takeout fried chicken. Long after everything was out, she heaved and heaved until she could barely breathe or see or feel.

She'd never killed anyone. Ever. She'd wanted to—everyone wants to sometime—but hadn't because normal people don't do that. Good people don't do that.

That cockroach was going to rape you.

I killed a man.

He was going to rape *you!*

The debate in her head faded into fog. She straightened, wiped her eyes. Put herself back together again as best she could without being able to feel anything in her hands or feet or anywhere else on her body. She slid the cockroach's pistol out of his back waistband, then picked up his AK. A bottle of water from the flat by the door. A peek out the window: Nora and Paul, flanked by two FBI SWAT guys. How nice.

Bel slumped to the floor against Paul's bookcase, the AK across her knees, pistol by her side. No way out for her now. When they came in and saw that... *mess* over there, they'd kill her. Maybe she'd take a few with her.

I'm so sorry, Lucho.

That's when she heard the first explosion.

Luis heard the familiar drumroll of a Blackhawk an instant before an explosion blew out two of the warehouse's windows. The sounds outside bounced loud and clear through the windows and off the metal roof: Blackhawks thrumming a couple hundred feet overhead, AKs firing, the ripping-canvas noise of a minigun, shouts, screams.

Hijo de perra. McGinley came through.

Luis had hung back from the gathering at the end of the warehouse, trying to get a feel for the layout and puzzle out where Bel was. The agreement between *México Unido* and the U.S. lay on a folding table in the clearing's center. Luis tuned out Zambreño's rambling speech about new beginnings and ultimate triumphs, and now the State Department suit—gray-haired, round-cheeked, some kind of Southern—went on about cooperation and good neighbors.

Now Luis tried to listen to everything.

Gunmen on both sides shuffled, glancing between their own, checking their weapons. Some American suits whipped out their phones. So did Salgado's aides and Casillas. Ray had drifted a few feet down the aisle from the pack of Zetas. Nora stared straight at Luis.

He nodded to her, drew his pistol, then scuttled to the shelf unit closest to Ray. Smoke and the giant-hummingbird whir of a drone gunship blew through the open windows. The State Department suit had stopped babbling, though Luis couldn't tell what he was doing now. He didn't care. He was going to find Bel, and nothing was going to get between him and his wife.

Luis slipped around the end of the shelves, quick-stepped forward, then grabbed Ray's collar with his right hand. His left ground the pistol's muzzle into the back of Ray's head. Luis dragged him behind the shelves. "Where is she?"

"Jesus, Lucho, let me go!"

"Where's Bel?"

"Get that thing off"—Luis knocked the side of his head with the pistol—"Fuck! Chill, will you?"

"*¿Donde esta Bel?* Understand me now?" Luis tightened his grip on Ray's collar.

Ray choked as his tie knot bit into his throat. "For Chrissakes, it's me! We can talk! Just let me go."

"Like you just let Bel go? Like I had to blackmail you into letting the kid go? Drop your piece." A few seconds later, Ray's pistol clattered on the floor. "Now, last time. Where's Bel?"

Ray's neck bloomed red around his collar. He reached up to loosen his tie; Luis slapped down his hand. "Front of the room." Panic shook his voice. "Left-hand window. There's a door, it goes into a storage room. She's in there."

"Her and who else?"

"A guard."

A bolt of anger ripped through Luis. "You left her in there—*alone*—with one of those animals?" He jammed the pistol's muzzle into Ray's ear. "I oughta shoot you now."

"It's okay! It's okay! They won't hurt her, I swear!" Ray reached back to peel Luis' hand from his collar, but Luis whacked his wrist hard with the pistol. Ray slumped. "Let me go. We can talk. Jesus, *hermano*, why can't we talk?"

Because there's nothing left to say. Luis whipped Ray's belt off his suit slacks. "Hands behind your back." He strapped Ray's wrists together, then yanked his tie around so the tail draped over Ray's back. He grabbed it like a leash. "We're going to get Bel."

"Are you fucking *loco?* Our guys'll kill you if the Feds don't."

"You're in front. Figure it out." Even as Luis' anger built, he marveled at what he'd done to Ray over the past few minutes. He didn't regret it. It was too late for that. "Listen to me," he growled. "I've loved you like a brother for half my life. You're godfather to my children. That's why you're not dead right now. But you're not that guy anymore. I don't know who the hell you are. You lied to me, you sold me out, you kidnapped my wife. We're done. It's over between us. If I ever see you again, I'll kill you. *¿Comprende?*"

Ray nodded. "I did what I had to. I'm sorry, *hermano*."

Luis looked everywhere but at Ray. This would hit him later when he had time to think. Right now, he had only two goals: rescue Bel; save Nora. "Too late. Let's get going."

A billow of orange flame lit the empty windows. The walls rattled. Nervous voices in English and Spanish buzzed at the warehouse's front. Then another familiar sound from outside: the turbine whine of a Blackhawk hovering low. Boots on the ground, coming up.

Ray nodded toward the cartel side of the warehouse. "That way. Behind our guys."

"Your guys. Lead the way."

Every gunshot, every explosion knocked away a piece of Nora's sense of defeat and hopelessness. She'd brazened it out, thrown all the go-to-hell attitude she had left into her words and the way she'd carried herself. But it ran out, and she'd stood through all the posturing and chest-thumping with a glaze over her brain. The little ceremony around signing the MOA between the Zetas and the State Department had made her want to vomit.

Now the Bureau guys around her shifted and muttered and switched off their carbines' safeties. "Who the fuck is out there?" she'd heard a headquarters flunky grouse in between threatening people on his phone. The Mexicans swirled like bees, half of them barking into phones, their thugs slowly spreading out in case this turned into shooting.

She'd almost cheered when Luis hauled away that Esquivel swine. Luis was still on her side. McGinley had done his part. She began fishing for the handcuff key in her back pocket, just in case. But knowing that a lot could still go wrong kept her from building up too much hope.

The sounds changed. A firefight, M4s, and grenade launchers; McGinley's people had landed. Nora nudged Paul with her shoulder. "Get ready to drop. I'll tell you when." He nodded.

"Hey," her QRT agent snapped. "No talking."

She sized him up in a moment: young, built like a cinder block, eyes bright on some kind of supplement. Ex-contract soldier, probably. "Those are our guys out there," she told him with all the fake confidence she could scrape up.

"Al-Qaeda?"

"ICE. Border Patrol. DEA. They're going to clean up the mess the brass made."

"Shut up."

"Those people over there?" She nodded toward the Mexicans. "They cut the heads off women and little kids—"

"Shut up, bitch—"

"That's who D.C.'s hooking up with. Do you feel good

about—"

The guard backhanded her, not hard but enough. She'd normally draw on anyone who did that to her, but the handcuffs spoiled that fantasy. Instead, she shook it off. "When our guys come in, who're you going to shoot at? Them, or your new buddies over there?"

The QRT guy leaned down to sneer in her face. "You, you fucking traitor."

She couldn't help smiling at the maniac uncertainty in his eyes. "The traitors are the ones running our country."

Before he could answer, the door behind the Mexicans exploded.

◆

Luis and Ray both hit the cement when the loading door came rocketing into the warehouse in a cloud of flame and smoke only yards away. Luis' ears filled with static.

Battle sounds pounded the air—pistols, AKs, carbines, screaming, shouting, bullets crashing through metal, shattering glass. Luis crawled past Ray to peek past the last shelf unit. At least four bodies were on the ground—two *sicarios*, a cartel guy in a suit, and an FBI SWAT trooper. Smoke grenades spewed between the factions; legs in black ran along the front wall.

The front wall. The storage room. Bel was back there. Bullets were flying everywhere. They'd go through that wall like tinfoil. The longer he took, the more likely she'd be hurt.

When the last of the stick of ten SWAT guys scrambled through the door, Luis crawled back to Ray. "Let's keep going. We'll be behind the assault team. Get up."

He pushed off the floor, grabbed Ray's leash and duck-walked into the open using Ray as a shield. Bullets chinked through the metal wall behind him. A bleeding *sicario* staggered out of the haze; Luis fired blindly into the man's center of mass, putting him down.

The smoke burned Luis' throat, stinging tears from his eyes. Ray kept stopping, forcing Luis to jab his pistol into the back of Ray's head to goose him along. Luis felt a tug across the back of his body armor—a bullet, a hair too close. *Keep moving. Save Bel.*

They'd just reached the front wall when Ray screamed and dropped, clutching his chest. Luis crouched behind him, pulled Ray's coat away. Blood bloomed across the right side of his chest. Not fatal—not yet—but he was out of the fight. Luis tore off Ray's tie and used it to bind his ankles. No matter what, he was going to pay for what he'd done.

A brief gap in the murk showed Luis the storage-room window—smashed—and the door—peppered with over a dozen bullet holes. *Oh, God, Bel, stay down*, cariña, *I'm coming…*

The next moment, Luis was flat on his back, his chest on fire.

Casillas crouched next to the shelves, staying low, watching the Zeta delegation fade away or get shot down. Half these *idiotas* had pulled out their guns and started shooting at the *Yanquis*, for all the good it did them. He wasn't that stupid. Pose no visible threat and you're not a target; the *Yanquis* probably thought they'd get to arrest someone. Not like his Zetas, who knew the simple fact that anyone left standing was an enemy who needed to be put down.

He wanted nothing to do with a *Yanqui* prison. He could hear fighting outside. Loyal *soldados* were out there. He had to get out, rally the men, fade into the *barrio*. The gringos wouldn't dare follow them into that maze.

A hostage. He needed a hostage.

Casillas stared at the storage-room door.

He knew exactly where to find one.

74

Bel pressed herself flatter against the concrete than she'd ever thought possible, crossed her arms over her head, and waited to die. The window disintegrated in a few seconds. Bullets clanged through the wall, cracking into the shelves above her. Smoke wafted in. Hot shrapnel peppered her neck and arms. Her ears throbbed with the noise.

Please, God, let me see Lucho again. Let me see my son. Dios te salve, María. Llena eres de gracia…

Someone rattled the doorknob, trying to open the door. She'd piled junk against it, but there wasn't that much. Whoever was out there really wanted to come in, slamming into the door over and over, each time pushing it open a bit more.

"Lucho?" she yelled. "Is that you? Lucho?"

If it was Lucho trying to get in, he'd answer her. If it wasn't him, it was bad news. She readied the rifle she'd taken from the guard she killed and aimed at the door.

The door splintered and fell off its hinges. A man stumbled in, coughing, a whorl of smoke following him. He stepped over the pipes and pallets Bel had piled up, leaving the haze behind.

The man she'd seen with Ray at the mall. The little one with the cowboy clothes. The bastard who'd put her in here.

He spotted her a moment later. Drew his pistol.

She blew him out the door.

⬤

Nora had her cuffs off in seconds after the DEA charged in. She'd picked up an M4 from a fallen QRT agent and started sniping Zetas through the smoke. A D.C. flunky tried to grab the carbine from her hands, but she clipped him with the butt. He

385

toppled on his rear, sitting dazed until a bullet took him out. No loss.

Then Paul screamed.

He'd dropped flat behind her when the shooting started. Now he clutched his thigh, blood forcing its way between his fingers.

Oh no. No. Big arteries. He'd bleed out. She had to get him out of here.

She slung her carbine, grabbed Paul under his arms, and tried to drag him down the central aisle while staying as low and small as she could. He outweighed her by a good sixty pounds and the position was awkward and stole a lot of her strength, even though the adrenaline had her heart and eyes going crazy.

They'd just made the aisle when something hot slammed into her side, ripped through her guts and sprayed blood all over the floor. The next moment she stared up at the ceiling, her midsection full of lava, blood in her mouth. "Paul! Help!"

A few moments later, Paul's face loomed over hers. "Hang on, honey," he gasped. "Hang on. I'll get us out of this."

"You're hurt!" She coughed, then felt a warm and wet trickle down her cheek. "Don't—"

"Just shut up and let me drive, will you?"

Nora rocked her head up enough to see that Paul had taken off his shirt and tied it to his thigh with his belt. The blood all over his pants terrified her even more than her own wound. *Don't let him die, Allah, if you're out there. Let me die, not him…*

Paul pushed himself across the floor with his good leg until his waist was even with her shoulder. Then he grabbed her shirt collar and heaved, screaming in pain. She slid a foot or so. "I'm so glad. You never. Got fat. Like your mom. A little help?"

They dragged themselves away from the battle and the smoke a few inches at a time. Every move was true, blinding agony. After a few minutes that seemed like hours, Nora surprised herself by thinking, *where are you, Luis? Help us. We need you.*

Luis lay back gasping, his head spinning from its collision with the concrete. He probed the spot where the sledgehammer had hit him, finding torn Kevlar but no blood. After a minute, he managed to roll over and grab his pistol.

The door to the storage room stood open about fifteen feet away. The firefight was sputtering out inside the warehouse, though it still roared away outside. Some DEA guys chased the remaining Zetas into the shelves—sudden bursts of automatic fire marked when they met up—while the rest secured what was left of the American delegation.

Luis crawled on his elbows and knees over shards of loading door, dropping whenever a SWAT trooper looked his way. His wounded shoulder screeched with every move. At the storage-room door, he found Casillas draped over a mound of junk, chest torn open, his body drenched in blood. Dead already. Luis felt a surge of bloodthirsty disappointment that he hadn't been able to kill the asshole himself.

"Bel?" he called into the doorway. "You there?"

"Lucho?"

They crawled to each other to avoid the bullets pinging through the wall. What Luis saw of Bel shocked him—black eyes, bruises on every bit of exposed skin, blood splattered across her face and clothes, a bloody rag wrapped around her right hand. She dragged an AK along with her, its sling like a tail. Luis risked an upright lunge to get to her.

They crushed together on the floor, kissing and touching and crying. Luis couldn't take his hands off Bel for even a moment; he was so afraid she'd slip away or turn into a mirage. "It's okay," he whispered, "it's okay, we're safe, it's over, God I love you, I'm so sorry…"

After a couple minutes that went by in a flash, Bel pulled back enough so she could knuckle the tears out of her eyes. Then she slugged Luis' healthy shoulder. "You took long enough." She snuffled, then kissed him again.

Luis smiled. "I'll do better next time. What happened in TJ? How'd they get you?"

"They were waiting for me at the station. Ray's playing both sides, huh?"

"Yeah. I figured it out a minute too late." He hugged her again, ran his fingers through her hair, beamed as she told him what a big dummy he was and how she'd never let him out of her sight again.

Then she asked, "Where's Nora and Paul and the kids?"

He nodded toward the former window. "Out there. Last I saw, she and Paul were with the FBI guys. The boy's hiding and the girl's at a church downtown."

Bel pulled back and squinted into his eyes. "Shouldn't you go get them?"

"Out there? People are still shooting at each other. Nora'll be okay. She'll hunker down. I'm not leaving you alone."

Bel frowned. "You went through all this for them. You ripped up our lives for them. You'd better finish the job."

"But—"

"No 'but.' Make sure they're okay. They might need your help." Bel grabbed both his ears. "This is absolutely the last time you're *ever* doing this, so do it right. I'll wait."

Luis opened his mouth to argue but saw that dead-set stubborn look in Bel's eyes and didn't bother to say a word. Instead, he kissed her and cupped her face in both hands. "Stay here. I'll be right back." He nodded toward the AK. "Keep track of your little friend there. I love you." Then before he could change his mind, he scrambled to the door, stepped over what was left of Casillas, and charged into the thinning fogbank of smoke.

The first team had breached the warehouse by the time an LZ opened up for McGinley's chopper. The firefight was just on its downhill slide when he ducked through the blown-out loading door and squatted in the near corner, getting his bearings. Weapons noise bouncing off the metal walls, wounded bawling their heads off, damn white smoke everywhere. The situation plot on his tactical goggles showed a dozen green spots scattered all over the warehouse.

Damn shame there weren't red dots. One of them would be Alcala.

He switched his carbine to single-fire, then crabbed from one shot Mex to the next, comparing each face (or what was left of it) to the photo of Alcala off to the right on his display. He disarmed the wounded ones, zipped up their hands, and moved on. Bullets burned over his head and sparked off the concrete floor, but he paid them no mind.

Nine faces later, he was hard up against the nearest metal shelf stack, wheezing from all the smoke. That rat-faced bastard was still alive somewhere, probably back yonder in the warehouse where all the shooting was. McGinley needed to find him before some ICE or DEA troop shot the man down. If someone was going to kill the fucker, it was going to be McGinley—but not until they'd had a chat. That blond hair from the RV didn't have enough testable material for a DNA match. He needed Alcala alive.

Most of the noise was coming from the right-hand bank of shelves. McGinley scrambled down the central aisle, stopped at each row, squinted through the smoke and dust to see if anyone was there. He found another couple dead Zetas—not Alcala—and a couple live ones the DEA boys had corralled.

Ojeda's picture showed sixteen Mexes. McGinley had found thirteen so far. Did that sumbitch get away? A dose of anger made him move faster and ignore the crossfire more. If that piece of shit escaped, McGinley was going to have him some squad-leader ass for supper.

Halfway down the warehouse, he saw a Mex in a suit blur by the side wall going the other way, toward the breach. McGinley spun and sprinted down the center aisle. He made a big target but didn't give a shit.

He rounded the last shelves just in time to see the suit duck through the hole in the door. McGinley fired a couple rounds his way, then followed the Mex out into the dark. *Mucho* action out here: the gunship circling, a passel of Zeta *sicarios*, and firefights all around. He switched his goggles to night vision and lit out after the green suit dodging through the green cars.

This fucker was *fast*. He jinked through the rows of cars, slid over hoods, crawled under trucks. McGinley tried to end around as much as he could, letting the suit wear himself out trying to be cute. While he didn't fall any farther back, he didn't catch up none, either.

Then the suit broke into the open, trying to reach another line of cars. Just as he made it, two of them blew apart bad enough to blank out McGinley's goggles. The gunship hummed by over his head. McGinley shoved the goggles off his face and ran full-tilt toward the last place he saw the suit, cussing out the drone in case it'd fried the Mex.

The man staggered up on his hind legs about twenty yards off, took a few wobbly steps, then tried to trot away.

No you don't, asshole. McGinley stopped, wiped his eyes clear, switched his carbine to full auto. He fired a burst into the man's legs. The suit screamed loud enough to hear over the fires and explosions and gunfights all around them.

McGinley tossed the man's pistol into the weeds, chased it with his backup weapon, then zipped his hands together. He stuck a knee in Alcala's chest to keep him from squirming around, then bore down a tad more to get his attention. "Cordero Alcala? I've been looking for your ass. Glad to meet you."

Alcala's face was all twisted up from the pain and from McGinley's knee crushing all the air out of him. "Who are you?" he croaked. "What do you want?"

Not bad English for a Zeta. "Me and you, we're gonna have us a nice long talk right soon, maybe in the hospital after they cut them legs of yours off." That got Alcala wiggling around some more. "Right now, I got two questions. First. Were you in a convoy that got all shot to shit on Fed Highway Two three days back? Big ol' green Olympia? Remember that?"

Alcala stared at him. "Why? What do you want?"

McGinley got a solid grip on his carbine, then drove the stock into one of the holes in Alcala's legs. The Mex howled like a coyote. Then McGinley drew his tactical knife from his calf sheath and stuck the tip into Alcala's nose, sharp edge outward. "I'm asking the damn questions, son. Were you in that convoy?"

"*Si.* Yes."

"Y'all had whores in them RVs, right?" Alcala nodded fast. "Any American ones? Maybe a little blond Texas girl? You remember her?"

Alcala gave him a look that said *are you crazy?* McGinley answered that question by pounding another of the Mex's leg wounds with his carbine.

After he stopped yelling and carrying on, Alcala yelped, "Yes, a *rubia!* Yes. But a *Mexicana*, not a *gringa*."

"You sure?" McGinley pushed the knife a skosh farther in. Blood dribbled down the man's cheek. "How many American whores you got?"

Alcala coughed, likely from the blood pooling in his sinuses. Self-waterboarding. "I don't know. I don't run the whores."

"Ain't what I heard." McGinley flicked the knife through the side of Alcala's nostril. He wiped the blood on the man's nice suit jacket while Alcala screamed out the pain. When he was done, McGinley stuck the knife up the other nostril. "Let's try that again. Y'all got an American whore called Carla Jean from San Antonio. Snatched her in Matamoros. You seen her lately?"

The Mex tried to back his head away from the blade but ended up with his chin pointing at the sky. The other nostril blew blood bubbles. "I don't know," he panted. His eyes looked ready to pop out. "Don't know names. One of my men. He runs them. He knows. Not me. Not things like that. Almost nine hundred in the region. I know that. I don't know names."

McGinley considered whacking another of Alcala's new holes but didn't. Nine hundred whores, minus the twenty kicked loose at the mine. That sounded mighty close to being the truth. He glared into Alcala's eyes. "What's this boy's name, and where's he work out of?"

For a moment, McGinley thought he saw Alcala's spine grow back. He twisted the knife so it didn't fit so good in the man's nostril and pushed. Alcala let out a wolf howl and tried to slither away, but that just made the blade cut deeper and poured more blood into his sinuses.

"Dominguez! Ivan Dominguez. He's mobile, like me. His base is Nogales. He has a list. He knows."

Another name. Another link in the chain. Not what he'd hoped to get, but better than nothing. McGinley felt tired all of a sudden. He wiped his knife on Alcala's shirt, climbed off the man, and watched the firefights wink out one-by-one around him. Then he kicked Alcala in the ribs, just because. "That'll do for now, hoss. Me and you ain't done yet. Not by a long shot."

He turned and jogged toward the warehouse. He still had to find Khaled. Then he had to decide what to do with her.

Nora raised her head from whatever Paul had rigged up for her pillow. Everything between her ribs and her hips was a solid mass of pain, but numbness crept in everywhere else. Even lifting her head a few inches threw her brain into a whirl. The long, red smear trailing out into the central corridor fascinated her. *That used to be in me. What a mess.*

The backs of Paul's fingers stroked her cheek. "Hold on. We'll get you to a hospital. You'll be okay."

She wished Paul was right, but wishing was all she could do. "No, I won't," she whispered. Talking took effort and concentration. He'd spent a lot of time and energy trying to plug the holes in her sides with no success. She'd finally told him to stop. It wouldn't help anyway; she'd just bleed inside.

"Don't say that." Paul sat beside her, his leg splayed at an awkward angle in front of him. The bullet must've broken his thigh bone, yet he'd managed to drag her this far out of the battle that sputtered on around them. He clutched at her carbine, laid across his lap, and she had no doubt that even though he'd never fired one in his life, he'd try to use it to defend her. Pain fogged his eyes. His beautiful brown eyes. They were so scared, so sad.

She'd come all this way, gotten this close, and some random bullet got her. Each breath was a struggle. She could barely focus her eyes or her mind on anything. How much longer did she have? "Paul? Darling? Hold my hand. Please." He rubbed away a tear, then fumbled for her hand. She felt the pressure but not much else. "You need to go… without me."

"No, honey, no. They'll make you better, they'll—"

"No. They can't. It's okay. I love you."

"Don't you give up. I won't let you. Don't leave me!" Paul leaned over her, tried to look brave, but his pain defeated him.

"Sorry." If her heart wasn't already broken, it would've started cracking open now. She was going to leave Paul and the kids. She didn't want to, but that choice wasn't hers to make anymore. She let her head fall back on the makeshift pillow. It snapped—bubble wrap. She wanted to laugh but didn't have the strength. "Find Luis. He has my pendant. Take the kids. Get away."

"You're gonna be there with me—" His head snapped up, facing the other end of the aisle. She watched him pick up the carbine with trembling hands. "Stop! Who's there?"

"Stand down, Paul." A familiar voice. Luis.

She heard running feet, then Luis was kneeling to her left, checking her wounds. He was dirty and scratched and had blood on his face, but just seeing him gave Nora a little lift. Paul would be okay now. The kids would be okay. Luis would make them safe. He'd promised.

Luis swiveled and gripped her shoulder. He murmured in her ear, "I'm so sorry."

"Not your fault," she whispered. "Bel?"

"She's okay."

His face, Paul's face, and the ceiling spun around her. "Peter?"

"Safe. He's hiding. Want me to get him?"

An instant mind-fight: *yes, let me see my son. No, it's too much for him.* "I don't want him… don't… he can't see this." She tried to touch his hand but didn't have the strength. "Get them out. Paul, the kids. To England. He knows… knows the story. Give him my pendant. You promised."

"I know. I will."

"Thanks." Nora rolled her head toward Paul. Everything was so dark. "Darling?"

"Honey?" He took her hand. She could barely feel it.

"I'm sorry." All she could see was Paul's face and the tears streaming down his cheeks. *Don't cry, darling. I can't bear it.*

"Paul," Luis rasped, "if you've got anything to say, say it now."

Paul gazed through the swirling black fog into her eyes. "I… I love you… so much."

Nora tried to speak but couldn't find her lips. Her last conscious thought before her long slide into absolute blackness was, *I know.*

75

McGinley found Ojeda jacked up against a big industrial shelf unit in the warehouse, zip-tied, with a DEA troop holding a carbine on him. "Son, I'll take this one."

That's when he noticed the bodies on the floor. One of his boys, a medic, strapped a folding splint on a civilian man's leg. McGinley didn't know the man—he looked the right color for a Mex—but he did know the dead woman next to him. He didn't like what she was, but she was a gutsy lady, he'd give her that. "Well, shit."

"Yeah." Ojeda stood rubbing the red stripes the plasticuffs had left on his wrists, looking like someone had taken away all his favorite toys. "Think you guys took long enough?" He sounded mad, and McGinley didn't blame him for it.

"Weren't my call. My chain in D.C. wouldn't make a decision. Then the DEA got the 'go' and all sudden like, we got tasked to support the drug dogs." When the medic charged away, McGinley pointed to the Mex man with the bum leg. "Who's he?"

"Paul Khaled," the man croaked. "Her husband."

Ojeda told McGinley, "He took one in the thigh. Busted his leg. He'll need a hospital."

"But not one in the States, right?"

"There's a couple big ones downtown here. They'll be fine. Cheaper, too."

And lots of practice with bullet wounds. "The little ones?"

"Safe. Peter's here, hiding. I need to get him. Hope's at the church."

Good. Whatever happened, the kids didn't deserve to have it happen to them. "Your wife?"

"She's here. I need to get her, too. Can you arrange for your guys to not shoot me?"

"I can do that." McGinley noticed an ICE troop leading a bedraggled woman down the aisle. "But I reckon I don't need to."

"What?"

His man stopped a couple paces away. "Sir?" The woman was a mess: her clothes all dirty, hands all bloody. But even though one eye was swollen shut and the other was bright red from the smoke and what-all-else, the open one had the same fire as the last time they'd met.

"Evening, Mrs. Ojeda."

"You again?"

Ojeda shoved past McGinley, scooped up his wife in his arms and actually picked her off the floor. McGinley waved away his man and retreated a few steps, giving them room to kiss and hug and all that. It'd been a long damn time since anyone had been that happy to see him; he didn't need to remind himself of it.

Once the reunion had settled down, he rejoined them where Khaled lay. The husband sat next to her, crying, holding her hand. McGinley had never realized she was such a little thing. She'd seemed plenty big enough when they met.

"She needs to be buried," Ojeda said. "Within twenty-four hours, in the clothes she was martyred in. Can you…?"

"How in the *hell* am I supposed to do that?" McGinley snapped. "I gotta take her body to prove I got her. I ain't burying her. Besides, don't she need to be in a rag cemetery or something?"

"No, just not a Christian one." Ojeda's voice sounded like someone had let all the air out of him. "Never mind." He waved toward the battlefield. "What's the count?"

"Out there? Don't know." Didn't much care, either. The ones the gunship got, they'd be counting legs and dividing by two anyway. "In here, ten or so Zeta KIAs, the rest wounded. You promised me Esquivel, and I ain't seen him yet. He get away?"

Ojeda pointed toward the front wall. A pair of DEA troops headed out the door carrying a man on a sagging black tarp.

McGinley noticed Mrs. Ojeda looked mighty pleased by this. "Well, thank you kindly for not killing him. We got Zambreño alive and Salgado and Casillas dead, which won't help my promotion chances none, though I can't say I'm sorry for it." He'd have some more words with Alcala on the way home, maybe find out more about this Dominguez asshole who had the list Carla Jean's name was on. "On the blue side, we got half a dozen KIAs and some State Department muckedy-muck who's madder'n a wet hen."

Ojeda nodded. "How's this work now, McGinley?"

He wasn't quite sure. Khaled's husband was a fugitive. So was Ojeda, for that matter, and probably the wife, too. But given everything, that was pretty chickenshit. He watched his men going about their business at the end of the warehouse, lining up bodies, slinging out the wounded. "Well… I reckon the birds are gonna be full of casualties. And the prisoners. And I reckon we gotta move out those D.C. peckerheads. I expect we just ain't got room for all y'all." He pointed toward Khaled's husband. The man looked plenty peeved. "I ain't entirely sure *he* was even here. Looks like a Mex civilian to me. Don't you think?"

"Could be." Ojeda had a grim little smile on. "Janitor, maybe."

"That's my thinking." McGinley squinted through the last of the smoke into Ojeda's eyes. "Tell me you're out of this game, *amigo*."

"I am."

He turned to the missus. "Ma'am, y'all keep him to that, y'hear?"

She snorted. "You better believe it."

"All right, then. I don't reckon we'll be meeting again."

Ojeda let his wife go and held out his hand. "Thanks."

McGinley considered the man and his hand. *Oh, what the hell.* He shook with Ojeda, nodded to the missus, then walked away.

76

The end of the paper-based newspaper and the broadcast news programme has posed new challenges for media companies... Internet-based news outlets have surpassed banks as the chief targets of both official and private hackers... Readers of publications such as The Guardian *and the* New York Times *take a perverse pride in the frequency with which those websites are offline due to attacks by aggrieved groups or governments...*
-- *"Business: All the News That's Fit to Hack,"*
Economist.com

MONDAY, 16 AUGUST

There came a time—between sunset and when the sky faded from purple to black—when the breeze off the Gulf slowed to a whisper, the lights in the windows matched the yellow fringe of sky behind the Belizean rainforest, and the day's heat left the shore behind on its way west.

This was when Luis liked to stand on the little beach a hundred yards from his sagging rented cottage and watch the water. It calmed him even if he didn't get in it, which he did before work. The morning swim; the evening pause. Habits—rituals—he'd established quickly and clung to even as the undertow of the strangeness of this place and their new life sometimes threatened to suck him under.

He could ride a bike to his work as maintenance manager at the resort hotel down the road. The GM, a U.S. Army vet from the Somalia campaign, had hired him on without a resume. Hard work, but good. Dirty physically, but clean otherwise.

"Hey, there." Bel's voice behind him. A few seconds later, she snaked an arm around his waist. "Lost or something?"

"Waiting for a pretty girl to come find me." They kissed. "How was your day?"

"Not bad." She dangled her gym shoes from her free hand and had already rolled up the cuffs of her scrub pants. She worked five miles up the coast at a small hospital in the "big city" of thirteen thousand. "We're getting more kids in for vaccinations before school starts, plus the usual stuff. Tourists are really dumb, you know that?"

"I've noticed. They're good at breaking things, too."

"Including arms." She gave him a squeeze. "Did you see the news?"

"Sure did." The *Guardian* website's home page: "U.S. FBI Files: White Militia Responsible for 10/19 Attack." A full dozen stories, images of the most damning documents, the promise of an entire site dedicated to the huge dump of data Nora and Paul had smuggled out of Washington. Links to the stories they'd run in June about the aborted relationship with the Zetas. Nora's picture: a snapshot with Paul. Luis had stalled out when he saw that, but for once didn't flash back to her dead on the warehouse floor. He wondered how Paul and the kids were doing in England and what their lives would be like from now on.

The story had already spread to MSNBC and the BBC, to CBC and AFP, to AP and Reuters and Xinhua. Not to Fox, of course. The New York *Times* site was down mysteriously, but the Washington *Post* and Los Angeles *Times* sites had managed summaries and links to the *Guardian* before they, too, went down. Twitter was going nuts. Google News listed 5,281 related stories after only twelve hours.

"She'd be proud," Bel said. "It kicks those bastards right in the nuts."

"Yeah. Now we get to see if it makes any difference."

"I have to hope."

Even after so little time, it was hard for Luis to feel any connection to what happened up there. The FBI seized the house, which still pissed him off even though they'd never have squeezed any money out of it. Mom and Dad were driving his sister Lourdes crazy in Denver. There really wasn't anything left to tie them to what used to be home.

Bel dropped her shoes and wrapped her arms around his waist

from the side. "Think we'll ever be able to go back?"

"Do you want to?"

She watched the tiny waves splash the sand, a rhythmic *swush*. Luis held her against his side. They owned almost nothing—a bed, a little table, a couple chairs, a beat-up armoire that fit their few clothes, some thrift-shop dishes. He'd borrowed his bicycle from the resort. But the people were nice, no one here was afraid, and there were these moments—between sunset and when the sky faded from purple to black—when he could hold Bel and know, deep in his soul, how lucky they were.

"Maybe someday," Bel finally said. "When it turns back into America." She kissed his cheek. "I'm in no hurry."

Stars began to fill the black sky over the Gulf. "Neither am I."

The Adventure Continues...

<u>DOHA 12: An International Thriller</u>

Jake Eldar's and Miriam Schaffer's names may kill them.

An assassination in Qatar thrusts twelve innocents into the crosshairs of a hit team bent on revenge. But two of them refuse to die quietly.

"*Doha 12* is an exciting and hard-to-put-down read of fiction, not to be overlooked." – *Midwest Book Review*

Buy DOHA 12 today at your favorite online bookselling site!

Like What You Read?

Share your experience with friends! **Leave a review** on your favorite online bookselling site, on a readers' social network (such as Goodreads) or promotion site (such as Bookbub), or just on your blog or Facebook wall. Someone told you about this book; please pass on the favor.

About the Author

Lance Charnes has been an Air Force intelligence officer, information technology manager, computer-game artist, set designer, *Jeopardy!* contestant, and is now an emergency management specialist. He's had training in architectural rendering, terrorist incident response, and maritime archaeology, but not all at the same time. Lance's Facebook author page features spies, archaeology, and art crime.

Official Website
https://www.wombatgroup.com
Sign up for Lance's newsletter! Be the first to find out about new books, special deals, and the occasional giveaway.

Facebook Author Page
https://www.facebook.com/Lance.Charnes.Author

Goodreads
https://www.goodreads.com/lcharnes

The DeWitt Agency Adventures

Carson used to have a life. Then a crooked superior in the Toronto Police Services framed her for corruption, her husband turned out to be a serial cheat, and her father didn't pay back the millions he borrowed from Gennady Rodievsky, a Russian *mafiya* godfather.

Now Carson (that's only one of her names) answers to two masters: the DeWitt Agency, which "fills needs" for not-always-honest people and organizations; and Rodievsky, the criminal she tried to take down as a detective.

Follow Carson as she shuttles around the world, dealing with friends and enemies, victims and tormentors, fighting to do the right thing in places where even the right thing may be wrong. Someday she may pay off her debts, work out her demons, and be free of a life that can kill her in an instant... but will there be anything left of her when she does?

Praise for The DeWitt Agency Adventures

"A breakneck tale where enemies and friends are often indistinguishable and the heroine's life is literally minute-to-minute. Highly recommended." – *DP Lyle, award-winning author of the Jake Longly and Cain/Harper thriller series*

"Charnes, a capable writer, crafts an exciting and alluring storyline...The author provides enough breakneck action and unexpected circumstances to keep readers entertained, while the Ukrainian backdrop is well conceived." – *The Booklife Prize*

To learn more, go to your favorite online bookselling site, or to https://www.wombatgroup.com/dewitt-adventures/.

The DeWitt Agency Files

Matt Friedrich has a very particular set of skills that he learned while working in a crooked L.A. art gallery, and other knowledge that he gained while hanging out in federal prison with Wall Street types who had bad lawyers. He's out on supervised release and working for $10 an hour at Starbucks to pay off over half a million in debts and restitution.

Matt's the DeWitt Agency's newest employee. The Agency "fills needs" for not-always-honest people and organizations. When a client has a need to fill that involves art in whatever form, Matt gets the project.

Follow Matt around the world, where he sees new places, meets new friends, avoids new enemies, and discovers (or pulls off) new scams. If he plays his cards right, he can make a lot of money, pay off his debts, and build a new life. All he has to do is not screw up...which is much harder than it sounds.

Praise for the DeWitt Agency Files

"*The Collection* is a breezy read in the way the very early Leslie Charteris' Saint novels were breezy: entertaining with an underlining of grit below the surface..." – *Criminal Element*

"Interlacing storylines give this series its charm... It's nice to have some modern *It Takes a Thief* escapism to slip away to in this world gone awry. Suffice it to say, I can't wait for The DeWitt Agency Files #3." – *Criminal Element*

"A brilliant heist story filled with fascinating art history reminiscent of Dan Brown or Steve Berry. Only better." – *Seeley James, author of the Sabel Security thriller series*

To learn more, go to your favorite online bookselling site, or to https://www.wombatgroup.com/dewitt-agency-files/.